MURDER
BY MAGIC

MURDER
BY MAGIC

LESLEY COOKMAN

Published by Accent Press Ltd – 2012

ISBN 9781908192042

Printed and bound by CPI Group (UK) Ltd, Croydon, CR0 4YY

Cover design by Sarah Ann Davies

Acknowledgements

I have several people to thank for their expertise during the construction of *Murder By Magic*. First, Justin Monahen, magician extraordinaire. Next, Doctor Joanna Cannon for her professional advice and finally, Suzanne Sutton and the Reverend Frances Wookey for their invaluable help on the procedures of the Church of England.

And once again, sorry to all British Police Forces for taking such liberties.

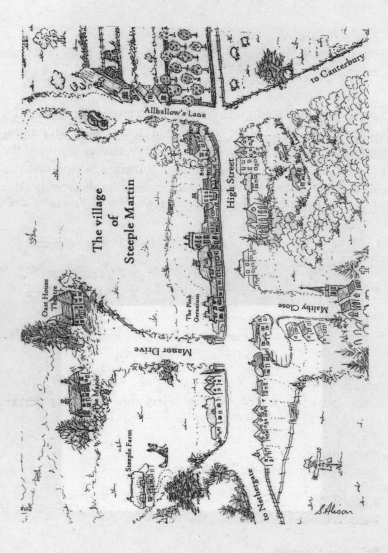

The village of
Steeple Martin

to Canterbury

Allhallow's Lane

High Street

Oast House
Theatre

The Pink
Geranium

Pub

Malby Close

Manor Drive

The Manor

Steeple Farm

to Nethergate

S.Alison

WHO'S WHO IN THE LIBBY SARJEANT SERIES

Libby Sarjeant
Former actor, sometime artist, resident of 17, Allhallow's Lane, Steeple Martin. Owner of Sidney the cat.

Fran Wolfe
Formerly Fran Castle. Also former actor, occasional psychic, resident of Coastguard Cottage, Nethergate. Owner of Balzac the cat.

Ben Wilde
Libby's significant other. Owner of The Manor Farm and the Oast House Theatre.

Guy Wolfe
Fran's husband, artist and owner of a shop and gallery in Harbour Street, Nethergate.

Peter Parker
Ben's cousin. Free-lance journalist, part owner of The Pink Geranium restaurant and life partner of Harry Price.

Harry Price
Chef and co-owner of The Pink Geranium and Peter Parker's life partner.

Hetty Wilde
Ben's mother. Lives at The Manor.

Greg Wilde
Hetty's husband and Ben's father.

DCI Ian Connell
Local policeman and friend. Former suitor of Fran's.

Adam Sarjeant
Libby's youngest son. Lives above The Pink Geranium, works with garden designer Mog, mainly at Creekmarsh.

Lewis Osbourne-Walker
TV gardener and handy-man who owns Creekmarsh.

Sophie Wolfe
Guy's daughter. Lives above the gallery.

Flo Carpenter
Hetty's oldest friend.

Lenny Fisher
Hetty's brother. Lives with Flo Carpenter.

Ali and Ahmed
Owners of the Eight-til-late in the village.

Jane Baker
Chief Reporter for the *Nethergate Mercury*. Mother to Imogen.

Terry Baker
Jane's husband and father of Imogen.

Joe, Nella and Owen
Of Cattlegreen Nurseries.

DCI Don Murray
Of Canterbury Police.

Amanda George
Novelist, known as Rosie.

Chapter One

The voices receded and the heavy iron-studded door swung shut. Silence fell, and the weak sun sent pastel-coloured lozenges of colour on to the stone floor before the altar. A few dead leaves rustled in the breeze from under the door, which also lifted the sparse grey hair of the woman in the brown coat, whose now sightless eyes stared at the prayer book still clutched in her claw-like hands. Someone looked out of the vestry, paused and silently withdrew. All was well.

'I wish you'd come and look into it,' said the querulous voice on the other end of the phone. 'I'm sure you could help poor Patti.'

'Poor Patti?' repeated Libby Sarjeant. 'Who's that?'

'I've just *told* you! The vicar!'

Libby sighed. 'Look, Alice, I'm not a private detective, you know.'

'But you've been involved in all those murders. And the police are stumped. Or else they really don't think there's anything fishy about it.'

'They could be right,' said Libby. 'After all, didn't you say this was an old lady? Couldn't she have had a heart attack or something?'

'Oh, they looked into all that.' The voice that was Alice sounded impatient. 'There was a whadyercallit – a post – post …'

'Autopsy. Post mortem. Yes, there would be in a case of sudden death.'

'There, you see,' said Alice in triumph. 'You know all about it. Why won't you come?'

'Because I'm not a detective, I've already said. And I don't

1

know any of the people, so I can't go round asking questions.'

'Oh, but I told Patti you would!' wailed Alice. 'What can I say now?'

Libby sighed again. 'Exactly what I've just told you.'

'What about your friend? The psychic one. Would she come?'

'Even less likely,' said Libby. 'Alice, I'm sorry, but the less I have to do with mysteries and possible murder the better I like it. And the police hate interference.'

'I don't see how they could hate interference in this, they've written it off.' Alice was now indignant. 'If I can't change your mind, I'll let you go, you're obviously busy.'

'Er – yes. Thank you.' Libby cleared her throat. 'How's Bob, by the way?'

'Fine. Getting under my feet as usual.'

'Ah. Right. Nice to hear from you Alice,' Libby lied, and switched off the phone feeling guilty.

'I can't just go butting into things which are none of my concern,' she complained when her significant other arrived home in time for a drink before dinner. He cocked an ironic eye at her. 'You know what I mean,' she said, grinning.

'Yes,' said Ben, 'I do. I also know that given the slightest excuse you'll be off after the scent.'

Libby shook her head firmly. 'Not this time.'

'Where does this Alice live?' asked Fran Wolfe the next day when she and Libby met for lunch at The Sloop Inn, yards from Fran's cottage overlooking the sea at Nethergate.

'Not that far from you, round the coast a bit. One of those funny little villages on a cliff top. Rather isolated.' Libby perused the menu. 'Did I like the sausages here?'

'How do I know?' Fran looked up in surprise. 'Don't change the subject. What's the name of the village?'

'St Aldeberge.' Libby looked a little guilty. 'I looked it up.'

'You surprise me. Why, in particular?'

'It's a funny name. Apparently it's the alternative – and presumably the original – name of Queen Bertha.'

'Who?'

'She was married to – er – Ethelbert, I think. There's a church in Canterbury that's all about her. Near the prison.'

'Right. So why else did you look it up?'

'Just to see if there was anything about the murder on the net.'

'But you said it probably wasn't a murder.' Fran was looking suspicious.

'It didn't hurt to have a look. And there was something. But although the police called it "unexplained" it doesn't seem to have been followed up.'

'And why does this Alice want you to look into it? Who is she, by the way?'

'A friend from years ago when I was still living the other side of Canterbury. She moved away too, to St Aldeberge, I suppose. But we've been in the local papers, haven't we? She tracked me down. Because there's a whole lot of suspicion and gossip been stirred up, mostly against the vicar, I think.'

'Poor man.' Fran grinned. 'Always a target.'

'No, this one's a lady vicaress. Patti. Or Poor Patti, as Alice referred to her.'

The waitress arrived to take their order. When she left, Fran looked thoughtful.

'Nothing to lose by going and having a look round,' she said.

'Really?' Libby narrowed her eyes at her friend.

'What did it say on the net?'

'This woman whose name I can't remember was found dead in a church after a big reunion service. As far as I can see, as I suggested to Alice, it was a heart attack, although she hadn't been under the doctor for her heart. So unless the police are keeping something to themselves, it doesn't bear any further investigation.'

'So why are the villagers up in arms?'

'Because there'd been a lot of ill-feeling, particularly between this lady and the vicar. I can imagine an old church hen not liking a new lady vicar, can't you?'

'Yes, but maybe she wasn't an old church hen. You're using

generalisations again.' Fran took a sip of her white wine. Libby scowled at her mineral water. She was driving.

'What are you doing this afternoon?' said Fran after they'd both been served.

'I thought I was spending it with you.' Libby took a bite of sausage. 'Lovely.'

'Why don't you drive us over to St Aldeberge and we can have a walk round the village? We could even call on your friend Alice.'

'So you don't think it was a simple heart attack.' Libby leant back in her seat and surveyed her friend.

'I don't know. But your friend Alice is concerned, and where there's concern, there's sure to be a cause.'

Libby sighed. 'I was trying to keep out of it, you know.'

'I know, but you're also bored.' Fran put her knife and fork neatly together.

'No, I'm not.'

'You are. You don't normally call me and suggest lunch for no reason.'

'I haven't seen you much lately.'

'We saw enough of one another in the summer,' said Fran, 'let's face it.'

'Seems ages ago, though,' said Libby.

'So let's go and have a look at St Aldeberge.' Fran watched Libby's expression with amusement, knowing she would give in.

'Oh, all right. Shall I ring Alice?' Libby said, with a resigned sigh.

'Do you want to? We might decide not to do anything about it, and then it would be difficult to back out.'

'But you said we could call on her.'

'We might.' Fran stood up. 'But let's go and have a look first.'

'You're hoping for a moment, that's what,' said Libby, following her out of the pub.

Fran grinned over her shoulder. 'It had occurred to me,' she said.

Fran's "moments" were occasional flashes of scenes or sensations which appeared in her mind like established facts. She had felt deaths and seen places and events, some of which had helped the local police force, in particular Chief Inspector Ian Connell, solve crimes. It was this that gave her the sobriquet Special Investigator, and which had alerted the media to some of the adventures in which she and Libby had become involved.

St Aldeberge sat in a small hollow about half a mile from the cliff top. Below the cliff was a natural harbour at high tide, to which rough steps had been cut in the chalk, allowing a few intrepid small boat owners access to their craft which at low tide would lie at drunken angles on the sand. Libby drove slowly through St Aldeberge and followed the road out of the village to its end, and stopped.

'Look,' she said, getting out of the car. 'Isn't that lovely.'

Fran looked down at the little natural harbour, high tide now, with the few boats bobbing gently at their moorings.

'Those steps don't look very safe,' she said.

'They don't, do they? And those rings set into the cliffs don't look very secure, either. One good storm and they'd be pulled out.'

'Perhaps they've been set into concrete or something,' said Fran. 'We can't see from up here.'

'No.' Libby turned and looked inland. 'I suppose now we go back to the village. Then what do we do?'

'Look at the church,' said Fran. 'And then we'll see.'

The church, dedicated unsurprisingly to Saint Aldeberge, stood on a triangular plot in the middle of the village, facing a wide street which divided either side of it. Feeling very exposed, Libby tried the big iron handle on the studded oak door. Almost to her surprise, it opened.

'I though churches were kept locked these days,' she whispered to Fran as they sidled in.

'Are they?' said Fran. 'I thought they were supposed to be kept open for everyone to come in when they wanted.'

'Used to be, but things get stolen these days.'

They stood and looked around. In front of them a stone font stood, its wooden lid surmounted rakishly by a little stone figure poking its tongue out.

'That looks like a gargoyle,' said Fran.

'Yes, but actually it's what's called a "grotesque",' said Libby. 'Gargoyles were water spouts.'

'I never knew that,' said Fran, giving the little monster an amiable stroke. 'Odd place to have it, though.'

Libby was looking through the inevitable stack of leaflets arranged either side of an honesty box. 'Look,' she said, 'they've got a community shop in the village. Open ten till two Mondays, Wednesdays and Fridays. That's enterprising.'

'Can I help you?' A voice echoed from the other end of the nave.

Libby and Fran peered into the darkness near the altar and saw a figure clad in an old-fashioned cross-over apron emerge from a side door.

'Er – no – we were just looking,' said Libby lamely.

'It's so unusual to find a church unlocked these days,' said Fran. Libby shot her an indignant look.

'I'm afraid ours is usually locked, too,' said the woman approaching up the aisle. 'It's only because I'm here doing the flowers.'

'Oh, I'm sorry,' said Libby. 'We'll get out of your way.'

'No, please stay and look round if you want to,' said the woman, tucking a wisp of greying fair hair into a kirby grip. 'I'll be here for a while. Was there anything you particularly wanted to see?'

'Actually,' said Libby on a note of inspiration, 'we wondered if there was anything about Saint Bertha, because this is her church, isn't it?'

'Only a window, over in the Lady Chapel,' said the woman, 'and we've got a little leaflet about her life, of course. Most people go to St Martin's in Canterbury.'

'May we see the window?' asked Fran.

'Yes, of course.' The woman turned back down the aisle and they followed her down to the first pew, where she pointed to the right. 'In there,' she said. 'Not very big, as Lady Chapels go, but at least we've got one.'

Libby and Fran went through glass doors into the little chapel. To their left, they looked up at Queen – or Saint – Bertha, piously gazing heavenwards.

'Don't all churches have Lady Chapels, then?' asked Fran in a whisper.

'No, although we've got one in Steeple Martin. It's usually big churches and cathedrals. I suppose this is quite a big church.' Libby looked round at the small electric piano and modern light oak pews. 'And this has been recently done up, too. Not much like the church itself.'

They left the chapel and Libby called out goodbye to their unseen guide, who popped her head out of what was presumably the vestry door.

'Pleasure,' she said, and withdrew.

Libby and Fran took a leaflet about the Saint and dropped some coins into the honesty box, feeling they'd justified their visit.

'Well,' said Libby, as they emerged into the watery daylight again, 'did you get anything in there?'

'Not a thing,' said Fran. 'Shall we call on your friend?'

'I thought you wanted to look round?'

'There isn't much to look round, is there? The shop isn't open and there isn't anything else here.'

'You're such a townie,' laughed Libby. 'Villages are like that!'

'Your village isn't,' said Fran.

'Steeple Martin is a big village with several shops. This is far more typical. Like Steeple Cross. Small villages have lost their shops and schools and often their pubs, too. It's criminal.'

'All right, I'm sorry. So will we ring Alice?'

'Oh, all right.' Libby fished her mobile out of her pocket and then, with a triumphant 'Ha!' put it back in her pocket.

'What?' said Fran.

'I haven't got the number!' said Libby. 'I never call her, so it isn't in my phone. In fact, I doubt if I've even got it written in an address book anywhere.'

'Right. What's her surname?'

'Gay,' said Libby, 'only she isn't, in either sense.'

Fran turned back towards the church door and went briskly inside. Libby stayed where she was.

'Number four Birch Lane, down on the left,' said Fran, emerging once more from the church. 'I asked the flower lady.'

'Enterprising,' murmured Libby, following her friend down the wide, empty street.

Number four Birch Lane turned out to be a substantial brick and flint cottage built in the shape of a letter L. Libby rang the bell, and was just about to suggest there was no one in and they might as well go home, when the door opened.

'Libby!' gasped Alice.

'I'm sorry we didn't ring, but I didn't have your number,' began Libby, but she was interrupted.

'Oh, that doesn't matter,' beamed Alice, holding the door wide. 'It's just perfect timing. You see the vicar's here already!'

Chapter Two

'Ah,' said Libby.

'Is this Fran?' asked Alice, giving Fran a warm smile.

'Yes, Fran Wolfe,' said Fran, holding out her hand. 'I'm so sorry to barge in like this.'

'Not at all, not at all.' Alice closed the door, pulled down her brown cardigan and gestured to a door on their left. 'I didn't think Libby was interested in helping, so it's a lovely surprise.'

'Well –' said Libby and Fran together, and looked at each other.

'It was my idea actually,' said Fran.

'It doesn't matter,' said Alice, with another tug on her cardigan. 'We just need some help.'

She gestured again to the door on their left, and, reluctantly, Libby led the way in.

Low-ceilinged and heavy with dark wood and floral chintz, the room achieved the same faded prettiness as its owner. Before the empty fireplace stood a dusty-looking arrangement of autumn leaves and a vicar.

'This is our vicar, Patti Pearson,' Alice announced proudly. 'Patti, this is my friend Libby Sarjeant and her friend Fran – er – Wolfe, did you say?'

Fran nodded and smiled. 'Hello.'

Libby held out her hand. 'Hello, Reverend,' she said.

Patti Pearson made a face. 'Please don't call me that! Patti will do fine.'

'Now, I'll go and put the kettle on again. Would you both like tea?' asked Alice.

'Thank you,' said Fran, and Alice left the room.

'I understand Alice thought you might be able to help us with

9

our bit of trouble in the village,' said Patti, sitting down in a chair by the fireplace, while Libby and Fran sat side by side on the sofa.

'She called me, yes,' said Libby, 'but I don't see what we can do. If the police don't think the lady was murdered, then there's nothing to look into.'

'So why are you here?'

'I thought I might –' Fran paused and looked briefly at Libby. 'I thought I might pick up something.'

'Ah.' Patti put her head on one side. 'You're the psychic.'

Fran looked uncomfortable. 'I'm not sure what I am,' she said, 'and I know that the church disapproves of – well, that sort of thing.'

Patti gave a wry little smile. 'In some cases,' she said, 'but you know we also have a Deliverance Minister for each diocese, so we admit the existence of "that sort of thing". In fact, it's one of my areas of interest. It's another of the things the congregation doesn't approve of.'

'Deliverance Minister?' said Fran.

'Exorcist,' said Libby. 'Isn't that it?'

'It is, although it's frequently more a case of psychologist.'

Alice came into the room precariously carrying three mugs.

'I hope you all take milk?' she said setting them down on a piecrust table and slopping a little. 'Shall I fetch the sugar?'

'No, that's fine, thank you,' said Libby, eyeing the greyish mixture warily. The other two shook their heads.

'So have you told them what's been happening?' Alice sat on another chair, smoothing an ancient-looking cotton skirt over her knees and giving another tug to the cardigan.

'I haven't had a chance yet,' said Patti. 'Fran tells me she's the psychic.'

'Ah, yes. But Libby said you wouldn't want to come?' Alice gave Libby a faintly accusing stare.

'I simply wondered if there was anything in the atmosphere.' Fran was looking even more uncomfortable. 'I understand the police are no longer interested, which usually means foul play is ruled out, but if I could pick anything up, it might bear a little further investigation.'

'So we went to the church,' said Libby.

'And did you?' Patti asked Fran. 'Pick anything up?'

'Nothing, I'm afraid.' Fran took a tentative sip of her tea and hastily put down the mug.

'But you haven't looked inside,' said Alice.

'Actually, we have,' said Libby. 'There was a lady there doing the flowers. We went to see the Lady Chapel.'

'Sheila Johnson,' said Alice and Patti together.

'Quite a large lady with a crossover apron,' said Libby. 'Very pleasant.'

'Very,' said Alice, darting a look at Patti. 'She's another of the flower ladies. Oh, I suppose you know that.'

'You say "another"?' said Libby.

'Yes. Joan Bidwell was a flower lady.'

'She was the one who died,' explained Patti. 'So Sheila Johnson has taken over the rota.'

'Although she seems to be doing most of it herself. The other women don't appear to be interested.' Alice sniffed disapproval.

'Don't you do flowers?' asked Libby, surprised. 'I thought you would have done.'

Alice coloured slightly. 'I'm hopeless with flowers. And I get hay fever.'

'Even at this time of year?' said Fran.

'There's still pollen in some of the shop-bought flowers,' defended Alice.

'Alice is invaluable on the PCC,' said Patti. 'And she sings in the choir.'

'Oh, yes, you always used to be in the chorus of our pantomimes, didn't you?' said Libby.

'Did you?' Patti sounded amused. 'I never knew that. We ought to try and set up a drama society here.'

Alice looked alarmed.

'Very time-consuming,' said Libby. 'We've got a community theatre and drama group in our village.'

'Oh yes. Your Oast Theatre,' said Alice. 'It's getting quite a reputation, isn't it?'

'Is it?'

'There was that first play you put on and the murder,' said Alice.

'But that was nothing to do with the theatre,' said Libby.

'And you've done some really good things since.' Alice turned to Patti. 'It's always in all the local papers and local radio. Libby's got something to do with it.'

'I'm a director,' said Libby. 'My partner's family own it and he redesigned the oast house as a theatre.'

'Oh, a board director,' said Alice. 'I thought you meant –'

'Yes, she does that, too,' put in Fran.

'Anyway, to get back to your problem,' said Libby, 'tell us exactly why you think there's something to be looked into in Mrs Biddle's death.'

'Bidwell,' corrected Alice. 'It's actually all to do with the vicar.'

Patti sighed and tucked dark bobbed hair behind an ear. Her round face shone with cleanliness and goodness – and no make-up. Libby was prepared to like her.

'For a start,' she said, 'Joan Bidwell didn't like me at all. She was of the generation that totally disapproved of the ordination of women.'

Libby shot Fran a triumphant look.

'It isn't always generational, though,' said Fran. 'I've met quite young people who don't agree with it.'

'But they tend to be people brought up in a Catholic or a religious household,' said Patti, 'not that I mean that Catholicism isn't religion. Most younger people today don't go to church and the world is increasingly secular and doesn't much care what sex the vicar is.'

'Except when they suddenly want to be married in church,' said Alice quite viciously. 'Or have their child baptised.'

'When they haven't been near a church in years.' Libby nodded wisely. 'I've always found that so hypocritical. I've even heard of people choosing the prettiest church in the area and ignoring their own parish church.'

'That happens all the time,' said Patti. 'I'm inured to it, now.

But to get back to Joan Bidwell, she disapproved of me and opposed many of the changes I've tried to bring in.'

'What changes?' said Libby.

'How did she die?' said Fran.

Patti looked from one to the other and laughed. 'You don't waste any time, do you?'

Libby looked surprised. 'But I thought that was what Alice wanted? For us to ask questions.'

'Well, yes,' said Alice. 'But I don't …'

'It's fine,' said Patti, clasping her hands round her knees. 'I'll tell them.' She put her head on one side in an attitude of thought. 'When I came here the congregation was small. It's a small village, of course, but hardly anyone came to church. It was run by the two churchwardens, the PCC and the flower ladies, some of whom were on the PCC. And they more or less made up the congregation.'

'Were you on the PCC?' Libby asked Alice, who nodded.

'So when I came,' Patti resumed, 'and suggested a few changes, some of these people were dead against them. I look after another church in the area, too, and they adopted the changes quite quickly, mainly because it's a much younger congregation and when I suggested a proper Sunday School and a crèche they were enthusiastic. Here, I had a fight on my hands for everything.' Patti looked down at her hands. 'Not just because the changes went against everything they were used to, but because I was a woman.'

'It's unbelievable that sort of prejudice still exists, isn't it?' said Fran.

Patti looked up. 'But it does.' She sighed. 'Anyway, I persevered, and people like Alice helped, until we had won over most of the people who were objecting. And then just the few, Joan Bidwell, Marion Longfellow and Maurice Blanchard and Gavin Brice, the churchwardens, were holding out. We now have a children's service once a month, the choir is more active and we can incorporate different elements into the services. So that was where we were when we held the reunion service.'

'Yes – what is a reunion service?' asked Libby.

'The miners,' said Alice.

'Miners?' Fran looked blank.

'Kent had productive coalfields,' said Patti. 'All closed by the end of the 1980s. It was an awful time. Anyway, we decided to hold a reunion service for all the survivors of the mines who live, or used to live, in or around the village. Representatives from all the mines attended, and the one remaining colliery band played for us. It was a great service.' She looked out of the window, a small smile on her face, remembering.

'And then we all adjourned to the village hall for a buffet,' said Alice. 'The pub provided some of the food and a small bar –'

'Which our ladies disapproved of, naturally,' put in Patti.

'And everything was going really well, until someone, I can't remember whom, realised Joan wasn't there.' Alice went pink. 'I'm afraid I dismissed it, rather. I thought she was just showing her disapproval by not attending.'

'But Sheila Johnson went to look for her.' Patti pulled a face. 'And there she was. Just sitting in her pew. Dead.'

'Of course, we all thought it was her heart, or a stroke, or something,' said Alice.

'And the post mortem didn't really turn anything up. Her heart just stopped. Her arteries were furred, but nothing else was found.'

'Nothing in her stomach?' asked Libby.

'No.' Patti coloured slightly. 'Of course, that was what the village was saying, that somehow I'd poisoned her with the host –'

'Host?' asked Fran.

'Communion wafers,' explained Libby. 'You don't know much about the church, do you, Fran?'

'Never been a church-goer,' said Fran. 'Neither was Mum.'

'So how did the congregation think you'd done that? Managed to poison one wafer out of dozens?' Libby returned to the vicar.

'Because it was reserved sacrament,' said Patti, looking agonised.

14

Fran opened her mouth and Libby frowned at her.

'That's for people who take communion sitting in their pew, isn't it? Or even at home?' she said.

Patti nodded. 'Yes. You see, Joan wasn't that well. She had diabetes and arthritis, and found it difficult to get to the altar rail, let alone kneel.'

'How did she do the flowers?' asked Fran.

'Oh, she'd come in her wheelchair,' said Alice, 'but she couldn't sit in her wheelchair in the aisle because it blocked access.'

'Health and safety,' said the vicar, looking gloomy.

'So she was helped to get to "her pew".' Alice made quotation marks with her fingers, and Libby winced.

'And no one noticed her wheelchair was left behind?' said Fran.

'It was always pushed right out of the way in the Narthex –'

'The lobby,' said Alice and Libby together.

'All right,' said Fran peaceably. 'I get it. The place where we found the leaflets and the honesty box?'

'That's right,' said Patti. 'Someone would normally go and get it for her after most of the congregation had gone.'

'So why didn't someone this time?' asked Libby.

'Because when Gavin Brice went to look for the wheelchair it wasn't there.'

Chapter Three

After a pause, Libby said, 'But didn't he check to see if Joan was still in her pew?'

Alice shook her head. 'He says he went for the wheelchair, saw it was gone and assumed she'd been taken out by someone else. He didn't look back.'

'And so she was,' said Libby. 'Taken out, I mean.'

'Libby!' admonished Fran. 'And Gavin Brice is …?'

'One of our churchwardens,' said Patti.

'And had he left the chair in its usual place?' asked Fran.

'No, that was the odd thing. He took it right outside because of all the extra people in the church. We'd filled the Narthex with chairs, you see.'

'Can I interrupt for a moment?' said Alice. 'Only Patti had actually come round to talk about the next children's service and I've got to pick up Nathaniel in a little while.'

'Oh.' Libby looked blank.

'Where do you have to pick him up from?' asked Fran.

'The village primary,' said Alice, beaming. 'Then I have him until Tracey gets home.'

'Is Tracey your daughter?' asked Fran, while Libby, who couldn't remember a thing about Alice's family, silently thanked her.

'Yes. We moved here after Bob retired. Tracey was still living with us then and when we came here she met Darren. Then they had Nathaniel.' Alice was still beaming. 'And now she's pregnant again. We're so pleased.'

Patti turned to Libby and Fran. 'Are there any more questions you'd like to ask?' she said. 'Because I'd be happy to talk to you. Anything to try and sort this mess out.'

'Would you like to come to one of us?' asked Fran. 'Off home ground, so to speak. Then you wouldn't get interrupted.'

'That would be great,' said Patti. 'Where do you live?'

'I'm in Nethergate, which is nearer you,' said Fran, 'and Libby's in Steeple Martin.'

Patti brightened. 'Steeple Martin? I have a friend there, Anne Douglas. Do you know her?'

'I don't think so.' Libby looked doubtful.

'I could combine a visit to her with a visit to you, perhaps,' said Patti. 'If I could time it right.'

'Does Anne work?' Fran correctly interpreted this remark.

'Yes, she's a librarian in Canterbury.'

'So if you came over late afternoon one day, perhaps, you could go and see your friend for supper?'

'That would be good.' Patti looked more cheerful than ever.

'Well,' said Libby standing up, 'you get hold of your friend and find out when she's free, then we can liaise.' She scribbled on a piece of paper. 'There's my number,' she said, handing it over. 'We'll look forward to hearing from you.'

Both Patti and Alice accompanied them to the front door.

'So you do think there's something to be looked into after all?' said Alice to Libby.

'Fran does,' said Libby. 'And I trust her.'

Patti smiled at them both. 'And so do I.'

'That went well,' said Libby, as they drove back to Nethergate through the grey afternoon.

'Yes, it did,' said Fran, her eyes on the equally grey sea. 'Nice woman.'

'Who, Alice?'

'No, Patti. Wish I knew why they become vicars.'

'Because they're Called,' said Libby. 'Just because you and I don't have that sort of faith –'

'It's all fairy stories, Lib.' Fran turned her gaze to the coast road ahead. 'You can't possibly think anything else.'

'It doesn't matter what I think,' said Libby uncomfortably, 'but what the vicars do. It's up to them, surely?'

'I've told you about my cousin, haven't I?' said Fran, in a settling-down sort of tone.

'Your cousin? I didn't know you had any cousins.'

'You do, perfectly well. Cousin Charles.'

'Oh, gosh! Of course. What's he got to do with anything?'

'You remember his side of the family came from Steeple Mount? Well, there was another cousin who became a vicar.'

'And?'

'He left the ministry when they decided to ordain women.'

'Well, good riddance!' said Libby. 'How ridiculous. Was he very ancient?'

'No, that was the trouble. He was about ten years younger than I am, and this, remember, would have been in 1994, so he would have been quite young.'

'I suppose it's like a lot of things,' said Libby, 'we think it's ridiculous now, but anything new has always been held in suspicion. I mean, we think it's terrible that people couldn't hold certain jobs if they were married, but thirty or forty years ago it was quite normal.'

'What was ridiculous,' Fran went on, 'was his absolute conviction that the Bible said it was wrong. I cannot believe that someone intelligent enough to go to university believes that farrago of lies.'

'Steady on!' said Libby, alarmed. 'Farrago of lies?'

'Look,' said Fran patiently. 'It's been almost incontrovertibly proven that most of the stories are either allegorical or written years and years after the event by people who weren't there. Can you honestly believe that what is supposedly God's law is actually true?'

'Um,' said Libby, and decided to leave well alone.

It was later that evening when Patti rang Libby to ask if it would be convenient for her to call round on the following afternoon.

'My friend Anne will be home early, so if I came about three I could go to her as soon as you've had enough of me,' she said.

'That'll be fine,' said Libby. 'I'll make sure Fran can be here.'

Fran arrived just before two thirty to plan their approach.

'I thought we would just ask her for her version of events,' said Libby, surprised. 'I didn't know we needed a plan.'

'Yes, but do we suspect her of doing the dirty deed?' Fran sat down in the armchair by the fireplace. 'And do we need to know her beliefs?'

'Look, Fran, we're not going into a theological discussion,' said Libby firmly. 'This is simply about Joan Bidwell's murder and the events surrounding it. Not about Patti's faith or calling. I'm still not sure what we're supposed to do about it even if we do think there's something in it, but we can at least stick to the brief.'

Fran looked stubborn but merely said, 'Could we have a fire? It's turned chilly.'

Libby looked at her suspiciously, and turfing Sidney off her lap, knelt down to riddle out the ashes.

'What do we know already?' mused Fran, leaning back in the chair. 'Joan was a flower lady set in her ways. She didn't like Patti as a vicar.'

'Didn't approve of her,' corrected Libby, laying kindling on top of a firelighter.

'All right, didn't approve. But I don't suppose she liked her, either. And what's this business about reserved sacrament?'

'I told you yesterday. People who are unable to get to the altar are taken the wafer and the wine to their pew by the vicar or a curate. If it's taken to them in their home someone else can do it – like a churchwarden.'

'So it was definitely Patti who went to her in her pew?'

'Looks like it.'

'And then there she was dead at the end of the service?'

'What I can't understand,' said Libby, sitting back on her heels and watching the flames take hold, 'is how it was so long before she was discovered. I mean, at the end of a normal service, the vicar would go to the door to say goodbye to the congregation, and when they'd all gone, go back through the church to the vestry. Why didn't Patti see Joan then?'

'That's something we'll have to ask. And was the wheelchair found?' Fran frowned down at Sidney, who'd relocated to her lap.

'It is all a bit odd,' said Libby. 'And why aren't the police involved?'

'We don't actually know they aren't,' said Fran.

'There should be an inquest, shouldn't there?' Libby racked her brains to remember the previous cases where inquests had been held.

'If the coroner has been informed about the death, which he obviously was in this case,' said Fran, 'and there is no obvious cause of death. I think that's how it works.'

'But what,' said Libby, getting to her feet, 'about when the cause of death *is* known? Like a dirty great bullet hole or something?'

'Well, obviously then, and they have to decide if it's murder or suicide or accident.'

'I'll go and put the kettle on,' said Libby.

Patti arrived just after three o'clock, wearing a fleece over jeans.

'It's very nice of you to take an interest in this,' she said, accepting a mug of tea and sitting on the sofa beside Libby.

'Oh, it's just us being nosy,' said Libby cheerfully.

'Not at all,' said Fran, noting the strained look on Patti's face. 'We can't do much, but if we get any sort of inkling of the truth, we do have a sympathetic policeman we can go to who will listen to us.'

'Local?' asked Patti.

'He's based in Canterbury, so I don't know if St Aldeberge comes under his jurisdiction, but he'd know the right person to tell.'

'So tell us the whole story of the service when Mrs Bidwell died,' said Libby, swivelling in her corner of the sofa to face Patti, who looked down thoughtfully into her mug.

'OK,' she said, looking up. 'Well, as I told you, it was a Miners' Reunion service. There were a lot of people there, including the colliery choir and two visiting ministers from other villages where there'd been mines.'

'Did you take the service together?' asked Fran.

'I led it, but they did readings and one of them, old Mr Roberts, gave the sermon. Then he and the other minister, David Rattleby, helped me at communion.'

'But you took it to Mrs Bidwell?'

'Well, no.' Patti looked uncomfortable. 'Actually it was Mr Roberts. She asked Gavin if he could arrange that.'

Libby and Fran exchanged glances.

'Why was that?' asked Libby. 'Or can I guess? She'd prefer a male vicar any day rather than her own female?'

Patti's smile was sad. 'Yes, that was it, I'm afraid. And she'd known Mr Roberts when he was still vicar at St Martha's.'

'St Martha's was in a colliery village?'

'Yes. The population's less than half what it was. They never appointed a new vicar, and now it's one of my churches.'

'So after Mr Roberts had taken the – er – communion to Mrs Bidwell, what happened? She took it, I gather?' said Fran.

'Quite normally, Gavin said.'

'Gavin? Was he with her?' Libby said.

'He assisted Mr Roberts, who isn't all that steady on his feet, so Gavin carried the chalice and then swapped it for the paten –' Patti paused and looked at Fran '– that's the plate which the wafers are carried on. And he said Joan took the bread and the wine perfectly normally. And had her eyes closed when he and Mr Roberts left her to come back to the altar.'

'And after that?' prompted Libby.

'The service continued until the end. After the blessing, the choir sang again and I went to the door to say goodbye, although most of them were going to the party anyway.'

'And when you went back to the vestry did you notice her still in her pew?' said Fran gently.

'I didn't go back to the vestry.' Patti looked surprised. 'I went in there after the blessing when the choir started singing and took off my surplice, so I had no need to go back into church. I went straight to the hall.'

'Right.' Libby frowned. 'So what happened after she was

21

found dead?'

'We got Doctor Harrison to come and look at her. Luckily, he was in the hall for the party and was her doctor.'

'And he wasn't satisfied that it was a natural death?' said Fran.

'Not exactly. He hadn't seen her for months. The medication she was on was keeping her stable, and she had regular blood tests to keep an eye on her diabetes, but that was it. And he said we had to notify the coroner under those circumstances.'

'And did you do that?' asked Libby.

'No, he did. He knew all the procedures. The coroner's officer came, and he arranged for her body to be taken away for the post mortem.'

'And did the police look into it?' said Fran.

'They came and talked to us, but they obviously weren't taking it seriously, and the post mortem didn't show anything up.'

'So they've released the body? Have you already had the funeral?'

'No, there's an inquest. And half the village are muttering about no smoke without fire.' Patti looked miserable.

'But you didn't go near her,' said Libby. 'Why do you think they're muttering about you?'

Patti sighed. 'Apparently I could have poisoned either the wine or the wafers because I didn't like her.'

'By magic?' Fran laughed. 'How could you poison just one wafer and hope Mrs Bidwell took it? Or poison the wine? Hadn't several people already had it?"

'Oh, I don't think anyone's really thought it through. But it's horribly unsettling, and I've even had one or two anonymous letters. And emails.'

'That's disgraceful!' Libby burst out. 'I hope you've told the police.'

Patti looked surprised. 'No, I haven't. Should I have done?'

'Of course. Did you get a name for any of the police who came to see you?'

'No.' Patti was now looking even more bewildered. 'It was

only two constables.'

'They must have given you a card?' said Fran.

Patti shook her head.

'Up to us, then,' said Libby. 'I hope you've kept the letters?'

'No. And I deleted the emails.'

'Bugger,' said Libby.

'Do you mind if we tell the police?' asked Fran, getting out her mobile. 'I'll do it unofficially, of course, but I really think, if there's going to be an inquest they should know.'

'If you think so,' said Patti, whose expression had gone from bewildered back to miserable.

Fran left a message on Chief Detective Inspector Connell's personal line, and put her phone away. 'If he phones back while you're here, all well and good,' she said. 'If not may I have your phone number to give him? You will talk to him, won't you?'

Patti nodded, and pulled a wallet out of her fleece. 'Here,' she said and gave Fran a business card.

'Right, now we've got that out of the way,' said Libby, 'who wants more tea?'

Fran and Patti both shook their heads.

'OK, then. So, Patti. Tell us a bit more about the relationships in the village. You told us there were people who were holding out against you. Was there anyone who would be malicious enough to start to spread rumours about you?'

'Oh, yes.' Patti sighed again. 'All of them.'

Chapter Four

'I thought there were only a couple?' said Fran.

'Joan, Marion and the churchwardens, yes, but to be honest there were more who didn't come right out with it. Although the congregation has increased a little, there are also a few who stopped coming, and a few who more or less sit at the back and mutter.' Patti shifted in her seat. 'I tried, I really did, but it just seems to be so ingrained in them that no woman should ever be allowed near the pulpit. A couple of the emails said I was a "silly little girl" who couldn't possibly have any opinions or know anything about God, the Church or the Bible.'

'That "silly little girl" approach seems to be everywhere,' said Fran. 'You've only got to look on the internet to see some of the appalling things said to female political or social commentators, and that's one of the most frequent. But it's not personal in those cases. Yours is.'

'That's what's so upsetting,' said Patti. 'I know it's rubbish, of course, and in general I'm probably better educated than any of these people, but it's infuriating that they think they know better than the Church itself, and really upsetting that someone dislikes me that much.'

'You did check who they came from?' said Libby.

'They were all from webmail addresses. No clues.'

'Set up just for the purpose and then deleted,' said Libby.

'Did you reply to any of them?' asked Fran suddenly.

'Yes, actually, I did,' said Patti, surprised, 'the first one.'

'And does your email programme keep your sent messages?'

'Yes.' Patti brightened. 'But what good would it do? There are no clues to who sent it, even if we do have the address.'

'But the police might be able to get hold of it. Or have an

expert who could.'

Patti shook her head. 'I doubt it. It's not as if it's a huge crime.'

'Well, we'll see,' said Fran. 'Is there anything else you can tell us?'

'I don't think so. Several of us have to appear at the inquest.'

'When is that?' asked Libby.

'Friday. In Canterbury.'

'So just as well we get hold of Ian before then,' said Libby to Fran.

'He might be nothing to do with it,' said Fran.

'But at least he'll know who is.' Libby turned to Patti. 'You've been very helpful, and I hope we can help you. It isn't fair that you're being victimised.'

'Thank you.' Patti gave a wan smile and stood up. 'And thank you for the tea. I'll get along to Anne's now, if that's all right?'

'Of course.' Libby stood up and led the way to the front door. Patti held out her hand.

'I really do appreciate this, you know.' She looked past Libby to Fran still seated with Sidney on her lap. 'Thank you for believing in me.'

'So,' said Libby, coming back into the room. 'What do we think about that?'

'I think it's more about persecuting the poor woman than anything else. This Mrs Bidwell's death has just given them an opportunity.' Fran stroked Sidney's head and gazed into the fireplace. 'And people say the youth of the country are a disgrace.'

'Embittered old people are the worst,' agreed Libby. 'Remember that woman Maud Burton we heard about last winter?' (*Murder Imperfect*)

'She wasn't that old, but it was the same church-hen sort of mentality, wasn't it? Only worse then, because it was in the 1950s.'

'Was it worse?' mused Libby. 'At least it was current thinking, then. Now it's only old anachronisms who think that a woman can't be a priest.'

'Or gay,' said Fran.

'Gay?' Libby raised her eyebrows.

'Oh, I think she is, don't you?' Fran peered into her empty mug, and Libby stood up.

'I'll make some more,' she said taking the mug. 'But what difference will it make if she is gay?'

'It's another weapon in their armoury, isn't it?' Fran put Sidney off her lap and followed Libby into the kitchen.

'That a woman can't be gay? Or a priest can't be gay?'

'Both,' said Fran, 'but particularly a gay woman priest. Hellfire and damnation, I should think. And even though the priesthood has accepted some gay priests, aren't they supposed to remain celibate?'

'Don't ask me!' Libby poured boiling water into a pot. 'And do you think that Patti isn't? Celibate?'

'I've no idea. But I wonder how close she is to this Anne she's gone off to see?'

'Fran! This almost sounds like prurience.' Libby fetched the milk.

Fran sighed and sat down at the kitchen table. 'It isn't. I'm just thinking about all the reasons the village could have to hate her. And a non-celibate gay woman priest is just about as many reasons you could get.'

'You're right.' Libby sat down opposite and poured milk into mugs. 'So do you tell Ian all this? Patti's not likely to, is she?'

Fran looked uncomfortable. 'I can't really, it's only guesswork.'

'But it does make sense.' Libby poured the tea. 'Except – how did that old biddy know?'

'If she did. I can't see an old biddy sending anonymous emails and hiding the ISP, can you?'

'OK – how did anyone know?'

'Oh, lord, I don't know. Let's hope Ian can pass it all on to the relevant authority and get it stopped. Patti's life must be a living hell at the moment.'

Libby thought for a moment. 'There's another thing. She said she had an interest in exorcism.'

'And the village didn't like it. I wonder why?'

'Perhaps they think of it as – oh, I don't know – the devil's work?'

'But it's against the devil, surely? Isn't that just what it exists for? To cast out the devil?'

'Perhaps her interest goes further than that, perhaps she's interested in finding out about the – er – alternative religions.'

Fran looked doubtful. 'Maybe. Perhaps we should have asked her.'

Fran left after another half an hour and Libby turned her attention to supper while thinking over Patti's case. It didn't say much for the good people of St Aldeberge that they were persecuting their vicar on the basis of some unfounded gossip – whether about her sexuality, gender or the natural death of a parishioner.

It was much later, while she and Ben were enjoying a glass of wine in front of the television news that the landline rang. Libby heaved herself out of the sofa to answer it.

'Ian just rang,' said Fran.

'And? Was he mad?'

'No, he was grateful.'

'Grateful? Are you sure he wasn't mad?'

'Apparently, the anonymous letters are going to the police, too.'

'Oh, how ridiculous,' laughed Libby. 'They'll trace them in a minute!'

'They won't. They're hand-written in ball-point pen on cheap computer printer paper and there are no fingerprints anywhere. And the envelopes are self-seal, so no tell-tale saliva DNA. Same with the stamps, of course.'

'So what does Ian say?'

'Strangely enough, everything we've been saying. We were behind, as usual.' Fran sighed.

'No we weren't,' said Libby. 'We've only just come into the case. So what do they say, these letters? That Patti killed Mrs Thing?'

'Yes, and they give the reason that she's a non-celibate gay female priest, which is against everything the bible teaches, apparently, and should be against the law.'

'I'm not going to say a word,' said Libby. 'Any other reason?'

'Only that Mrs Bidwell found out about it and was going to tell the Bishop.'

'I wonder if that's true.'

'So Ian was very pleased that Patti had been receiving emails as well as letters and is going to try and trace the ISP at least. They're very good at that sort of thing.'

'Not very nice being pleased that someone's being threatened,' said Libby.

'Pleased because it gives them something to work on. Also he was interested that the village seems to have turned against Patti, and wondered how that started. It couldn't have been Mrs Bidwell spreading rumours after she was dead.'

'That's a thought. Because most of the village had been won round, she and Alice said, didn't they? Except – who was it?'

'The churchwardens and another woman,' said Fran. 'One of the flower ladies, probably. Didn't they say the lady we met had taken over most of the flower arranging? That looks as though the others aren't co-operating.'

'So it looks like one of them is spreading the rumour just to try and get rid of Patti,' said Libby slowly.

'Unless Mrs Bidwell really was murdered,' said Fran. 'Then it would be the murderer spreading the rumours.'

'Mind you, Patti did say she thought there was still underground resentment of her, didn't she?' said Libby. 'Anyway, the police are going to look into the letters at least. And do we know if they think it was murder?'

'Ian wouldn't say much, but obviously if someone's accusing someone else of murder they have to take it seriously. They haven't released the body yet, anyway.'

'We'd better warn Patti she'll have the police knocking on her door,' said Libby.

'I tried her landline number just now and it went straight to voicemail, so I expect she's still at her friend's house.'

'And may stay overnight,' said Libby. 'We don't have her mobile number?'

'No. I left a message anyway, so whenever she gets in she'll find it.' Fran sighed. 'Right, I'm off to bed. I'll let you know if I hear anything.'

Libby recounted the conversation to Ben while refilling their wine glasses.

'So whether there was a murder or not, the police will have to look into the anonymous letters. I seem to remember it being a hazy area of the law,' she concluded.

'To do with slander?' asked Ben.

'No, that's oral defamation, libel's the written one. Yes, I suppose it might be that. Didn't we look into it before?'

'You might have done, my love. I didn't,' said Ben, and settled himself more comfortably on the sofa.

Out of interest, or just plain nosiness, Libby fetched the area telephone directory to see if Anne Douglas was listed in Steeple Martin, but there was no A Douglas listed at all. There were several Douglases, one in Lendle Lane, one round the corner in New Barton Lane and even one in Maltby Close, but Libby decided she could hardly go round knocking on doors or ringing telephone numbers on the off-chance. She sighed. She'd just have to wait.

It was the next morning when Patti rang.

'I'm sorry, I didn't have Fran's number to ring her back and someone else had left a message after her call, so I couldn't do the 1471 thing,' she said.

'That's all right,' said Libby, wiping her hands on a tea towel. 'What's happened?'

'How – oh, of course. You mean have the police called? Yes, they have. Or rather, a Chief Inspector Connell called last night. His was the message that prevented me from calling Fran.'

'Have you called him back? What did he say?'

'Not yet. I've only just got in.'

'Right,' said Libby, just preventing herself from saying "You stayed overnight, then?"

'I couldn't drive after drinking half a bottle of wine, could I? Don't want to get into even more trouble.' Patti answered the unspoken question.

'You're not in trouble. Ian's going to try and find out who's doing it.'

'Ian?'

'Our detective friend. The one who called you.' Libby decided not to say anything about the letters the police had received. 'So tell him everything. All about your initial reception in the village right up to now. Including Alice asking me and Fran. And all the emails. The lot.'

'All right.' Patti sounded doubtful.

'I mean it, Patti. We could only tell him a little because it's hearsay, so you must tell him the lot. With all the names.'

Libby heard Patti sigh. 'OK. I'll ring him now. I suppose he'll want to see me?'

'I expect so. Easier if you go to the police station rather than have them come to you, though. You don't want to give the gossips any more fodder.'

Libby put the tea towel back in the kitchen, thought for a moment and then rang Fran.

'I wonder if we'll hear any more?' said Fran.

'I suppose she might ring to tell us what Ian said, but there's no reason for anyone to tell us anything else.'

'You could ring your friend Alice to ask her how things are going,' suggested Fran.

'I will if we don't hear anything after a day or so,' said Libby. 'Now I'm going shopping and then on to Steeple Farm to get it ready for tenants.'

'You've let it? I thought it was only going to be for holiday lets.'

'It's a short-term let, just until Christmas. I don't know anything about them, they came out of the blue saying they'd been recommended.'

Libby wrapped herself in her old cape, despite Ben having bought her a brand new winter coat, thrust her feet into flowery Wellington boots and collected her basket. She did now own a couple of handbags, but when you needed to carry slippers and shopping, the trusty basket was best.

She visited Bob at the butcher's shop, Nella at the farm shop and the eight-til-late, where Ali was anxious to show her a picture of his new niece, only a day old.

'So that's where your brother is,' said Libby, handing the picture back. 'She's gorgeous.'

'Ahmed is very proud,' said Ali, standing the picture on a shelf above the till. 'He will bring her to the shop in a few days.'

No mention of Ahmed's poor wife, Libby thought, as she trailed off up the high street towards Steeple Lane, shifting her basket to the other hand. Stupid not to have done the shopping on the way home.

Steeple Farm stood halfway up Steeple Lane, its thatch eyebrows covering little slits of windows that Libby always found forbidding. Inside, however, Ben's team of builders, with help from Libby's son Adam's occasional boss, television celebrity builder Lewis Osbourne-Walker, had done a perfect restoration job, and Libby had to admit it was beautiful.

Ben had taken on the restoration project for his cousins Peter and James, whose mother Millicent still officially owned it. Since she had been in a luxury residential home for several years, it was unlikely she would come back to it, and Peter had suggested Ben and Libby might like to live there. However, after much shilly-shallying, Libby had decided she preferred her small redbrick cottage in Allhallow's Lane, and Ben had resignedly agreed.

Now, she looked round at all the polished wood and charming furniture selected by Lewis and Harry, cousin Peter's partner, who ran The Pink Geranium in the village, and admitted that it was really rather nice. If only she could get over those shivery eyebrows …

She whizzed through with dusters and vacuum cleaner and became aware that something was vibrating against her hip. She switched off the vacuum cleaner and switched on her mobile.

'Ian just called,' said Fran. 'There's been another death.'

Chapter Five

'Who?' said Libby, sitting down rather suddenly on the arm of a sofa.

'I think it's one of the other flower arrangers.'

'Not that nice woman we met the other day?'

'I don't think so. I think it's the other one who was in the anti-Patti league.' Fran sounded weary. 'And he wants to talk to us – or more particularly, me.'

'Oh? Why?'

'You'll never believe it, but there's a rumour going round that it's –' she paused, '– it's Black Magic.'

'Oh, lord. And you're the local witch, I suppose.'

Fran laughed, a little shakily. 'You could say so. After all, we had all that business with the Black Mass and then the nastiness with the Morris Dancers – it was all folk magic stuff and Satanism. I think Ian thinks we're experts.'

'But why you?'

'Because I see things, don't I?' Fran was exasperated now. 'Anyway, he's coming here to see me, so if you want to come too, you'd better get here within the next half hour.'

'Can't do that. I'm cleaning at Steeple Farm for the tenant, I told you. I'll come over as soon as I can.'

But in fact, when Libby did arrive at Coastguard Cottage forty-five minutes later, Ian still hadn't arrived.

'So why Black Magic?' asked Libby, while she watched Fran making tea in the kitchen.

'I don't know. I expect Ian will tell us.' Fran handed over a mug. 'Listen – that's him now.'

Detective Chief Inspector Connell hadn't changed much in the last few years. His thick dark hair was a little greyer at the temples, but his eyebrows were just as heavy over dark brown eyes. What had changed were deeper lines etched on his forehead and around his eyes.

'Here we are again,' he said, as he sank into one of Fran's deep armchairs. 'And I'm the one asking for help again.'

Libby looked smug and Fran frowned.

'What exactly is the problem?' she asked.

'Shall I start at the beginning – as I saw it?' Both women nodded. 'Right. The first we knew about it was when the local GP notified us, as is always the case in an unexplained death. The coroner's officer attended and the lady was taken to the morgue. A couple of officers were sent to ask preliminary questions, but it looked as if it was a perfectly natural death. The post mortem eventually confirmed it – as far as we knew. The deceased had diabetes and a general degeneration of some of her organs, but she was in her late eighties.' Ian took a sip of tea. 'Then we started getting the letters, as I told you, and we had no way of tracing the sender. When you told me the vicar had actually received emails, we were delighted, because an ISP is easier to track. That's obviously why the perpetrator didn't send any emails to the force.

'There was also a suggestion, apart from the gay priest angle, that Miss Pearson was using the –' Ian frowned. 'Dark Arts, I suppose you'd say.'

'Oh, blimey,' said Libby. 'Do you suppose that's been going round the village, too?'

'I think so. Then we got the call about this other death.'

'Who is it?' asked Libby.

'Marion Longfellow. A flower lady, I'm told.'

'And where was she? Who found her?' said Fran.

'She was at her home, and one of the churchwardens – a Gavin Brice – found her because he'd gone to pick her up to take her to church.'

'And what about this Black Magic suggestion?' said Libby. 'What's happened?'

'I think you've seen it before.'

'Tyne Hall and down in Cornwall,' said Libby. 'So what is

33

it? Black feathers? Blood?'

'The whole thing, I'm afraid.' Ian stared into the empty fireplace. 'Beheaded.'

'Ah. A black cockerel.' Libby felt sick.

'And the inverted cross. The lot. And the body was laid out.' Libby swallowed. 'Hands folded?'

Ian nodded.

'So this one's definitely murder?' said Fran.

'Yes, although we aren't sure of the method.'

'Could be the same as Joan Bidwell's,' suggested Libby.

'It's almost as though it's been set up just to confirm that the vicar killed Joan Bidwell by Black Magic,' said Ian crossly. 'And as the vicar has a perfectly good alibi for the last twenty-four hours, it's backfired somewhat.'

'So what do you want us for?' asked Fran, after a moment.

'Who do you know in the village apart from the vicar?'

'Only my friend Alice who introduced us to Patti the day before yesterday,' said Libby.

'Oh.' Ian's face showed his disappointment.

'We could ask around,' said Libby hopefully. 'You know how good we are at that. And Patti really wanted our help.'

'She'll need all the help she can get now,' said Ian. 'Not that she's in any danger from us, but I should think the parishioners and the bishop will be making her life hell.'

'That's what I said,' agreed Libby.

'And Fran, I know you've been to the church –' Ian hesitated.

'You want me to look at the place this other woman died.' Fran's face and voice were expressionless.

'I'm sorry.' Ian was contrite.

'Don't be. Will you take me?' She looked at Libby. 'Us?'

'I'll take you both,' said Ian.

'Now?' Libby looked at her watch.

'Are you in a hurry?'

'I've got to get back to let a new tenant into Steeple Farm at four.'

'I'll get you back here by half past three,' said Ian. 'Well

34

before.'

To Libby's surprise, Ian didn't drive them into the village of St Aldeberge, but further along the coast road, before crossing a bridge and turning down a lane. They stopped before a large cottage which overlooked the inlet, where blue and white police tape fluttered in the sea breeze.

The door stood open, a police officer in a high-vis jacket standing outside and glimpses of white-overalled SOC officers to be seen inside.

'I can't go inside,' said Fran firmly, stopping at the gate. 'I'd need to be suited up.'

Ian looked startled. 'Yes, you would. I've got the suits for both of us in the boot.'

Fran shook her head. 'No. I don't need to.'

Libby touched her friend's arm. 'Fran? What have you seen?'

'Nothing.' Fran's eyes were fixed on the window to the right of the door. 'That's where she was found, wasn't she?'

'Yes.' Ian was frowning now. 'What is it Fran?'

'Where did the other victim live?'

'Eh?' Libby's and Ian's eyebrows rose simultaneously.

'Where did she live?'

'Actually, over there.' Ian turned and pointed.

Libby followed his pointing arm along the edge of the inlet to where a lone bungalow stood halfway down the cliff.

'That's a bit isolated for an elderly lady,' she said.

'It is,' agreed Ian, 'and quite difficult to get to, especially as Mrs Bidwell used a wheelchair.'

'How did she manage that?' asked Fran, now looking down the lane towards the bungalow.

'She had a ramp built, zig-zagging slightly to reduce the slope. She even had railings put up.'

'I wonder why she didn't move?' murmured Libby.

'I don't know. Perhaps your friend will,' said Ian testily. 'We're actually here about Mrs Longfellow.'

'She died because Mrs Bidwell died,' said Fran, looking back at the cottage. 'I'm certain of that. It was the only reason for her death.'

'And the feathers? The Black Magic stuff?' asked Ian.

Fran shook her head. 'I don't know. All that I can see is that she had to die because Joan Bidwell had.'

'Revenge?' suggested Libby.

'I have no idea,' said Fran, 'but I doubt it.'

'You don't want to go inside, then?' said Ian.

'I don't need to.' Fran shuddered. 'So much blood.'

Libby kept her quotation from Macbeth to herself, although the thought prompted her next remark.

'Witchcraft,' she said. 'The three witches.'

'There are only two,' said Ian sharply.

'And both infernal gossips and nuisances,' said Libby. 'Modern day equivalents of the medieval witch.'

'Do we know that?' asked Ian.

'Oh, yes,' said Fran. Libby looked at her sharply.

'All right.' Ian sighed heavily. 'Come on, back to the car and I'll take you home.'

'I'm sorry if you don't think I was much help,' said Fran, once she was settled in the front seat of Ian's car. 'But what came into my mind was quite clear. And the detail can surely be left to your officers?'

'I suppose so,' said Ian. 'Thank you for doing it.' He was reversing down the lane. Once he was back on the main coast road, he flicked Fran a look and said, 'You mentioned blood. What did you see?'

'Blood, of course,' said Fran, surprised. 'Mainly cockerel blood, I think. And as to knowing that she died because Mrs Bidwell did, I can't tell you. It was just there, you know, like a fact.'

Ian sighed. 'I know.'

After he dropped them at Coastguard Cottage, Libby took out her own car keys.

'I'd better get off,' she said. 'See to the new tenants.'

'Hasn't Ben told you anything about them?' asked Fran.

'I'm not sure he knows. It was arranged through an agency. I'll let you know what they're like.'

The autumn evening was drawing in as Libby drove back up

Steeple Lane, past the dewpond, to Steeple Farm. Inside she switched on lights and laid a fire in the large sitting room fireplace. She was just dusting off her hands as the doorbell rang.

'Hello, Libby!' said a bright voice, and Libby found herself staring into Rosie George's blue eyes.

Chapter Six

'Rosie?' Libby gaped at the older woman. 'What are you doing here?'

'I'm your new tenant,' said Rosie, stepping through the door. 'I've brought Talbot – you don't mind do you?'

'But ...' Libby followed Rosie into the hall. 'Why didn't you talk to me about renting the Farm? And why do you want to?'

Rosie put down the cat basket she was carrying and bent to undo the straps. Talbot, the large black and white cat, emerged, sat down and stuck a leg in the air.

'I'm having the kitchen and bathroom re-modelled,' Rosie turned to the mirror on the wall and patted at her fly-away hair, 'and I decided I couldn't stay there. As to why I didn't talk to you, well, that's obvious, isn't it? You would have felt compelled to let me have it for a low rent, or worse, for nothing. I heard you'd let some people stay here last year for nothing. So I booked through the agency.'

'Well, I'm delighted, of course.' Libby leant forward to kiss her friend's cheek. 'Where's your luggage?'

'Outside in the car. No – don't bother now. Just show me round.' Rosie twirled round, smiling delightedly. 'I knew I'd love it. I pinched a leaflet when we were here for the writers' weekend.'

'Er – what about Andrew?' Libby asked tentatively, following Rosie into the sitting room.

'Professor Wylie and I are no longer an item.' Rosie turned to face Libby. 'In fact –' she stopped, looking confused.

'In fact, what?' prompted Libby.

'Oh, nothing. Maybe I'll talk to you about it another time.' Rosie turned back to the fireplace. 'That's terrific. Shall we light it?'

By the time Libby had lit the fire, made a cup of tea, and shown Rosie all the amenities of Steeple Farm it was quite dark.

'I must get back home,' said Libby. 'I haven't sorted out dinner yet.'

'Oh – let me take you to dinner! Is that lovely young man still running his restaurant?'

'The Pink Geranium? Yes, of course.'

'Why don't you give him a ring and see if he can fit us in tonight? And Ben, of course.'

'Of course,' agreed Libby with a wry grin. 'I'd better ring him first, though.'

She relayed the surprise information to Ben and conveyed Rosie's invitation.

'Ben says he'd be delighted,' said Libby, pressing The Pink Geranium's number on speed dial.

She booked a table for three at eight o'clock, and having made sure Rosie remembered the way to the restaurant, left Steeple Farm to go home and change.

Rosie was better known as the novelist Amanda George, whom Fran had met while taking a creative writing course. The two women had given her some help with a mystery in her past, and she had joined them as a guest lecturer on the writers' weekend held at The Manor in the summer. She and Andrew Wylie had appeared to become very close after he had helped a good deal with research, but Libby had always put Rosie down as somewhat flighty and flirtatious, despite being in her sixties, so she wasn't altogether surprised at Rosie's announcement.

The Pink Geranium wasn't unduly crowded for a Thursday evening. When Libby and Ben arrived slightly before eight o'clock, Harry's right-hand woman Donna showed them to the sofa in the window to wait for their table and for Rosie. Libby ordered red wine.

Rosie arrived in a flurry of scarves and smiles ten minutes late.

'Sorry,' she said, 'I had to unpack before I could find anything to wear, and it took me longer to walk here than I thought.'

'You walked?' said Ben. 'On your own?'

'Well, yes! How else would I get here? I didn't want to drive down – not if I want a glass or two of wine.'

Libby sighed. 'We'll walk back with you.'

'Oh, you don't have to,' said Rosie, accepting a glass. 'I'm sure a woman on her own is perfectly safe in Steeple Martin.'

'Not necessarily,' said Libby. 'Anyway, Ben's always had a rooted objection to unescorted females at night.'

'How sweet.' Rosie beamed at him and Ben scowled. 'He's going to get even more annoyed with me then.'

Ben and Libby looked at each other. 'Oh?' said Libby.

'I've joined an online dating site.' Rosie, looking delighted, waited for their reaction.

'That's all right, isn't it?' said Libby.

'You want to be careful,' said Ben.

'See? I told you,' said Rosie to Libby. 'That's always the reaction.'

'What do you expect her to do?' Libby asked Ben. 'Run off with a toyboy half her age who'll steal all her money?'

Ben looked as though he wouldn't put it past her, but shook his head.

'Look, Ben, I'm being perfectly honest on there, I'm ignoring anyone under 60 who contacts me, and if I decide to meet someone, I'll do it in a public place. I'm a novelist, for goodness' sake. I do know something about people.'

'Has anyone contacted you yet?' asked Libby.

'Not yet. I might have to change my profile picture and description. You could help me if you like?'

'That's what you were going to tell me earlier, isn't it?' said Libby. 'Is that why you've come here, so I'm on tap?'

A faint colour appeared on Rosie's cheekbones, belying her cool reply. 'Of course not. I'm here because I picked up your leaflet when we had the writers' weekend, I told you.'

'Well, I don't mind helping,' said Libby. 'I've always thought the people who went in for online dating were a bit sad, but if you're doing it they can't be. But what happened to poor

Andrew?'

'Nothing. We just found we didn't suit.' Rosie picked up the menu. 'So – is there anything new I should try?'

They didn't return to the subject of online dating until the end of the meal.

'Will you come up and have a look at my profile on the dating site?' Rosie asked, after handing her credit card over to Donna.

'I'll give you a ring,' said Libby. 'I'm not quite sure of my movements at the moment.'

'Oh?' Rosie raised her eyebrows, but got no reply.

'Thank you for the meal, Rosie,' said Ben, standing up and pulling out her chair.

'It was a pleasure. You must come up and have a meal at Steeple Farm while I'm here, too.'

'Lovely.' Libby smiled and peered round the door to the kitchen. 'Bye, Hal.'

Harry Price wiped his hands on a tea-towel and hurried out of the kitchen.

'Sorry I couldn't get out to join you for a drink,' he said. 'Hello, Rosie. Nice to see you again.'

'And you,' said Rosie. 'I shall be a regular visitor for the next few weeks.'

'Oh?' Harry looked at Ben and Libby for an explanation.

'Rosie's renting Steeple Farm,' said Ben.

'Oh,' said Harry again.

'Yes, well, we'll be off,' said Libby, reluctant to discuss Rosie's romantic exploits in front of Harry, Donna and two tables full of interested diners. 'We're seeing Rosie home.'

'As if I couldn't walk on my own,' said Rosie with a slight laugh.

'Better safe than sorry,' said Harry. 'Go on, you old trout. I'll give you a ring tomorrow.'

'For the gossip,' said Libby to Ben in an undertone, as they followed Rosie from the restaurant.

As they walked, Libby entertained Rosie with the sad tale of Amy Taylor, who had drowned herself in the dewpond on the other side of Steeple Lane from Steeple Farm. (*Murder Imperfect*.)

'That's not a very nice story for someone who's going to be looking at it every day for the next few weeks,' said Ben.

'Oh, no, it's romantic,' said Rosie. 'I shall have to get the whole story from you Libby. It could make a good book idea.'

'There are people still alive who might be affected by it, though,' said Libby hastily. 'I found that out some years ago.'

They left Rosie making a fuss of Talbot, and linking arms, walked slowly back down the hill.

'It looks quite pretty from up here, doesn't it?' said Libby, stopping to look out over Steeple Martin.

'Like a picture postcard village,' said Ben. 'Lucky, aren't we?'

'Do you really think Rosie's having her kitchen and bathroom done up? Or is that an excuse?' asked Libby, as they resumed their slow progress.

'A very expensive excuse,' said Ben. 'No, I think she is, she got quite animated talking about spa baths, after all. But I think she's happier being away from home while she's doing her computer dating thing. Which makes me wonder if she really has broken up with Andrew.'

'Oh! You mean he could be in and out at home and might see what she's doing? She's planning to two-time him?'

Ben laughed. 'Yes, the jade! You do use such dated language sometimes.'

'And that was a terrible pun,' said Libby, digging him in the ribs, 'even if you didn't mean it.'

The following morning Libby rang Fran to tell her about Rosie. Fran was surprised at her arriving at Steeple Farm, but not at her attempt at online dating.

'We knew she was a flirt, didn't we, we've seen her in action. And I never thought Andrew was quite right for her. A bit too finicky.'

'Yes, he's very neat, isn't he. And she *so* isn't.' Libby smoothed down her rather rumpled sweater. 'So shall I go up and help her set herself up, or is there anything to do with the St Aldeberge murders I need to be looking into?'

'Not that I know of,' said Fran. 'I can't get the cockerel feathers out of my head, though.'

'Remember Ian said it was almost as if this one had been set up to make us think the same about Mrs Bidwell?' said Libby thoughtfully.

'Yes?'

'Well, that's very odd, isn't it, if Mrs Bidwell's death had been set up to make it look like a natural death?'

'You're right. That is odd,' said Fran in surprise. 'Why didn't I think of that?'

'Either it was really a natural death and someone's trying to capitalise on it, or it was murder, and the murderer thinks the police have realised it.'

'I expect they have now,' said Fran. 'I'll have to think about what exactly Ian said yesterday.'

'And find out what he said to Poor Patti,' said Libby. 'Dare I ring her?'

'I'd leave her alone if I were you,' said Fran. 'She'll have enough to deal with at the moment.'

But half an hour later, Patti was on the phone.

'Have you heard?' she said, her voice rising to a squeak. 'I can't believe it! And the villagers are already saying it's voodoo or something.'

'It was made to look like that,' said Libby. 'But at least they can't think this one's anything to do with you – you weren't there.'

'Hmm, yes,' said Patti thoughtfully. 'Actually they probably wouldn't have known I wasn't there. I've just fitted one of those timer switches to turn the lights on and off, to deter burglars. So anyone passing on Wednesday evening might have thought I was having my day off at home. Anne goes off to visit her aunt sometimes so I'm not always away on Wednesdays.'

'I see,' said Libby.

'They practically crossed themselves in the shop this morning,' said Patti, her voice returning to patent gloom. 'I always support them, because I think it's such a good idea for the community, and I even help in there sometimes. But today it was as though I was a pariah.'

'Tell the bishop,' said Libby. 'You shouldn't be in this position.'

'If I do that it's like wimping out.'

'No, it isn't. And your parishioners need a bloody good talking to. He might come down and harangue them himself next Sunday.'

'He can't do that, he's busy,' said Patti, 'but actually, that's quite a good idea – to get someone else in to preach and tell them how awful they're being. Do I sound terribly self-pitying?'

'Not at all,' said Libby, 'but tell me, what have you heard about this other murder?'

'Other murder? So you do think Mrs Bidwell was murdered?'

'It certainly looks like it,' said Libby, 'although the facts haven't changed, but I think the police are going to have another look at it.'

'Thank goodness.' Patti was silent for a moment. 'You obviously know a bit about yesterday's murder?'

'Yes.' Libby chewed her lip. 'Actually Ian – Chief Inspector Connell – took Fran and I out to the scene yesterday.'

'He *what*?'

'He wanted to see if Fran could pick anything up. We didn't go in.'

'Did she? Pick anything up?'

Libby thought about what she should say and decided to be uncharacteristically circumspect.

'Not really. She said there was a lot of blood, but we knew that already.'

'And feathers,' said Patti slowly. 'And she didn't pick up on that?'

Libby sighed. 'If you mean witchcraft, of course, but she and DCI Connell, and I, for that matter, think it's a set-up.'

'Really,' said Patti. 'Well, the village doesn't. The village thinks I'm a witch.'

Chapter Seven

Oh, here we go, thought Libby. 'What makes you say that?' she asked aloud.

'I had another delightful anonymous phone call.' Patti sounded tired. 'Apparently "everybody" now knows I'm a witch and I've been holding Black Masses in the church.'

'Tell Ian straight away,' said Libby. 'Or one of his team.'

'Would it be all right if I told him at the inquest?' asked Patti after a pause.

'Oh, the inquest! No, try and get hold of him before then. When is it?'

'Eleven thirty this morning. I was just leaving.'

'Tell you what, I'll try and get hold of him. You get going,' said Libby. 'But he must know before he goes into the inquest.'

'Why?' Patti was obviously puzzled.

'It may affect it, that's what. Go on, get going.'

Libby tried the police station switchboard. Ian's extension was answered almost immediately.

'DCI Connell's phone, Maiden speaking,' said a voice Libby recognised.

'Hello, Sergeant Maiden,' she said. 'It's Libby Sarjeant. I've got some information about the St Aldeberge murders.'

'Hello, Mrs Sarjeant, nice to hear from you. Would that be the inquest that's about to happen?'

'Yes. I'm reporting it because one of the witnesses told me and she's actually on her way there.'

'OK, then, fire away,' said DS Maiden. 'I'll get it to him straight away. Although I think he's going to ask for an adjournment anyway.'

Satisfied she'd done all she could, Libby switched off the

phone and trailed back into the kitchen to wash the breakfast things. She'd hardly managed to plunge her hands into hot water when the phone rang again. By the time she'd dried her hands and got halfway across the living room the answerphone had cut in.

'It's Rosie here, Libby. I wondered if you'd be free to pop up here and have a look at my dating profile. I think I'm going to use it for a situation in a book, so it's a legitimate piece of research. Give me a ring.'

Libby sighed and went back to the kitchen. Just like Rosie to expect everyone to drop everything to rush to her aid, but the answerphone had given her the perfect excuse to ignore the invitation and do what she wanted, which today was to concentrate on the two murders in St Aldeberge.

'The Flower Lady murders', she murmured out loud. 'Bet that's what the press will call them.'

No one, she remembered, as she propped plates against mugs on the draining board, had asked about the wheelchair. Didn't Patti – or Alice, she'd forgotten which – say it was missing, which was why the churchwarden thought Mrs Bidwell had been taken out of the church? Ian hadn't even mentioned it. Surely that should have been enough to alert suspicion?

Well, it had, but only in the minds of Patti's congregation, apparently. And Ian was right, it appeared that the second murder had been constructed to confirm that suspicion. Except that it had backfired.

Right. She wandered back into the sitting room and curled up on the sofa with the laptop. Undetectable poisons, that's what she wanted. Because Mrs Bidwell had no obvious cause of death. Libby frowned. But every pathologist knew all the signs to look for; almost invisible puncture marks under the nails or in the hairline or minute petechiae, so nothing would have been overlooked, and, as far as anyone knew, undetectable poisons were a myth. 'A little known poison of South American origin,' she murmured to herself. 'Beloved of Golden Age mystery writers. But not forensic pathologists.'

So what else? Rohypnol, the date rape drug? But that was

detectable, surely. Libby entered it into the search engine. Yes, it was detectable in urine within seventy two hours. And surely, the post mortem was done within seventy-two hours? So that was out. She trotted aimlessly around the internet for another twenty minutes, then shut the laptop with a sigh, wondering how Patti and Ian were getting on at the inquest.

Which, of course, she reflected, going into the kitchen to make more tea, was an indication of doubt about the cause of death. Inquests were only called by the coroner if there was still doubt after the post mortem.

With her mug, Libby strolled out into the wintry garden. Dead hollyhock stalks drooped over the pathways, and a clump of Michaelmas daisies rusted quietly in a corner. In all, it was depressing. Sidney, intrigued as to why she had ventured into the garden, followed, pouncing on stray leaves and generally trying to pretend he was a real cat. When the phone rang inside the house he got tangled up with her feet and allowed the answerphone its chance again.

'You didn't ring back,' said Rosie's voice plaintively. 'I have to go out now, but perhaps you could come up later?'

'Oh, for goodness' sake,' said Libby out loud. 'Did I say I'd help you?'

Sidney, now convinced that she'd tricked him into making a fool of himself, gave her a "what-else-have-you-got-to-do?" look, and jumped onto the sofa. Libby gave an exasperated snort, swallowed the rest of her tea and collected a duster and spray cleaner ready for a determined assault on the week's accumulated dust.

It wasn't until after a lunch of yesterday's soup that Patti called.

'They adjourned it.' Her voice sounded tired.

'Thought they would. Did you talk to Ian?'

'Your policeman? Yes, before we went in. He seems very nice.' Libby heard a yawn. 'Sorry. I'm not sleeping well.'

'I'm not surprised. What did Ian say you should do?'

'He didn't, really. An expert's coming round to look at the computer and see if they can work out who sent the emails, and he's suggested that we make them public.'

'Public? How?'

'He said he'd call someone on the local news programme. He said we could put a spin on it. I don't know what he means.'

'I do.' Libby grinned to herself. 'He's going to try and shame someone into giving something away.'

'How?' Patti sounded bewildered.

'I'd watch the Kent and Coast news this evening and see if he's managed it,' suggested Libby.

When Patti rang off, Libby found Campbell McLean's number in her phone.

'I wondered if I'd hear from you,' he said, before she could announce herself. 'I've been speaking to your pal Ian Connell.'

'Ah.'

'So you got him involved in this case?'

'No, he – or the police, anyway – were already involved. Fran and I were simply trying to help poor Patti.'

'Poor Patti? Oh – the vicar? Yes, I gathered it was something of the sort.'

'So are you going to do something?'

'I'm forbidden to actually talk to the vicar, apparently, merely to report that in the wake of the murder yesterday she's been receiving some very unpleasant threats and accusations. I haven't quite worked it out, yet. But I've cleared it to go and do a piece to camera outside the church – or some other location in the village.'

'At the top of the lane where both victims lived, I would have thought,' said Libby.

'Both? Did you say both?' Campbell's voice sharpened.

Bother, thought Libby. 'Forget I said that,' she said aloud.

'Now, Libby –'

'No, really, forget it, Campbell.' Libby cut him off. 'I don't suppose Ian's given you too much information anyway, has he?'

'No, but he's agreed to be interviewed tomorrow for a longer piece. Will he tell me then?'

'Possibly, I don't know. Anyway, do your best for Patti, won't you? She's having a hell of a time.'

Fran called about ten minutes afterwards.

'I've just had Campbell McLean on. What's going on?'

Libby sighed. 'Patti called to tell me the inquest was adjourned and that Ian was going to get on to local media. So I phoned Campbell, and he said Ian had already called him. I wouldn't tell him anything else. What was he trying to get out of you?'

'Oh, dear.' Fran echoed Libby's sigh. 'He asked me what I knew about the murders, because he'd been talking to Ian. I said not much. He said, "Oh, so there has been more than one, then." I gave it away.'

'I expect Ian will tell him when they meet tomorrow. Campbell's doing a piece from the village on the news tonight.'

'He told me. So tell me about Patti and the inquest.'

Libby related her conversations from that morning with Patti and Sergeant Maiden. 'I guessed Ian would be asking for an adjournment in view of the second murder. I expect the full panoply of the law will descend on the village now. Next we'll have Jane calling one of us.'

Jane Baker was assistant editor of the *Nethergate Mercury*, who lived with her husband Terry and baby daughter Imogen not far from Fran and Guy.

'Well, if she does, I shall keep quiet,' said Fran. 'Let me know if you hear anything else.'

'I will, but I expect we'll be kept out of it now. No one will be able to be nasty to the vicar if it's all made public, so our job here is done.'

'I'm not so sure,' mused Fran. 'They might be even nastier to her now. See her as the cause of all the trouble.'

'Really?' Libby thought for a moment. 'I suppose you could be right. Oh, well, I'm sure we'll hear about it eventually.'

Ben was home in time to pour Libby a glass of wine before sitting down to watch Campbell MacLean doing his stuff outside the church in St Aldeberge, which looked appropriately eerie in the late autumn dusk. He spoke earnestly into the camera about the problems the vicar was having with murder on her patch, but made no mention of the death in the church. There was a subtle reference to the Black Magic aspect of yesterday's murder, insinuating that this was a direct insult to the vicar and intended to be so.

'Well, that wasn't so bad,' said Libby. 'Let's hope Fran wasn't right about making it all worse.'

But Fran was right.

Chapter Eight

'It's absolutely disgusting!' Alice was shrieking down the phone. 'Blood – blood – and – oh, my God!'

'Alice, calm down!' Libby shouted, having tried normal-toned interruptions for the last two minutes and got nowhere. 'Whose blood? Where? What's happened?'

Alice took a shaky breath. 'I told you. At the vicarage.'

'Patti?' Libby's insides performed that operation usually described as stomach sinking.

'No – you're not listening! At the vicarage. On the doorstep.'

'Ah. Was it a cockerel?'

'I don't know,' wailed Alice. 'It had feathers and its – its –' she stopped with a gasp.

'I can imagine,' said Libby grimly. Somebody had access to a lot of chickens, she thought. 'Did Patti find it?

'I did,' whispered Alice. 'I went to see if she was all right first thing this morning. Did you see that piece on the local news yesterday?'

'Yes,' said Libby. 'I thought it might stop people having a go at Patti.'

'Well, it didn't. And nobody knows what's going on. And it all seems to be since you turned up.'

'What?' gasped Libby. 'But you asked me to!'

'You said you wouldn't come.'

'Oh, for goodness' sake, Alice. You're being stupid. And by the way, the police hadn't shelved the matter, you know. They were still looking into it.'

'Why didn't they tell us, then?' Alice was obviously affronted.

'Why should they? It was nothing to do with you.'

'So why did they tell you?'

'Because –' Libby searched for the right answer, 'because we gave the police some information.'

'What information?' Alice's voice was rising again.

'I'm afraid I can't disclose that, obviously,' said Libby, feeling cornered.

'Well, I just wished I'd never mentioned it, that's all.'

'Alice, why did you call me this morning? If you wish you'd never mentioned it in the first place.'

'I –' Alice stopped. Libby heard her clear her throat. 'I don't know. I thought you ought to be told. Patti says you know all about the other murder.'

'Yes. Thank you for telling me about this, too, Alice. Is Patti all right? Has she told the police?'

'Yes, while I was there. I stayed until someone arrived.'

'Who was it, do you know?'

'It was bobby in a police car – what do you think?'

'No plain clothes?'

'No! But I think he was just there to sort of – guard it. He said someone else was coming. So I came home. And then I phoned you.'

'Thank you, Alice. I'm so sorry this has upset you, but it really isn't my fault, you know.'

'I know.' Alice sounded tired now. 'I was just –'

'In shock,' supplied Libby. 'And so would I be. Make a cup of tea and sit down. And let me know if there's anything I can do.'

Fran, it transpired, was looking after the shop. Her husband Guy was an artist who ran a shop-cum-gallery a few yards away from their cottage on Harbour Street in Nethergate. His daughter Sophie now lived in the flat above where he had lived before his marriage to Fran.

'He's gone off on some buying trip,' said Fran, 'and with business so bad at the moment it would be mad to shut the shop even with so few tourists.' She sighed. 'In fact I'm not sure how long we can afford to keep open anyway.'

'Bad as that, eh?'

'Fraid so. Anyway, what did you call about?'

Libby told her.

'Do you know,' said Fran eventually, 'this gets odder and odder.'

'You're not kidding!'

'No – not in the obvious way. Look at the facts. Mrs Biddle – '

'Bidwell.'

'Bidwell – gets murdered in the church. It looks like a concealed murder made to look like a natural death.'

'Except for the wheelchair.'

'Yes – I wonder why that hasn't come up? Anyway, the next thing is the start of the rumours about poor Patti and her anonymous letters. This obviously brings up the thought that perhaps it was murder after all. So then we get the flower lady's murder which, with its references to Black Magic is an attempt to point at Patti. That backfires, and then we get the cockerel on Patti's front step. Making it look as though there is a Black Magic community – or coven – and they've set their sights on the poor woman.'

'It does seem as though someone's playing it by ear, doesn't it. And panicking, maybe?'

'On the one hand suggesting that Patti has something to do with Black Magic or covens or Satanism, and on the other suggesting that she is their target. But I would guess that none of it's real. As you say, panicking.'

'So what we need to do is find out why Mrs Bidwell had to die. Because if she was murdered, there was a reason for it. The other things follow on from there.' Libby pulled at her lip and stared out of the window at the soggy November day.

'We?' said Fran.

'Well, yes. We can't leave it now. And we can at least go and poke about in the village. Once Alice has calmed down she'll help. And Patti would like us around, I'm sure.'

'I don't know.' Fran was doubtful. 'We might have to make do with it as an intellectual exercise.'

'Look,' said Libby firmly. 'I know I said in the beginning we shouldn't get involved, but we are now, especially since we told Ian about Patti. And every time we dither about we end up in the middle of it eventually, whatever we say.'

'But we haven't even got the excuse we had last time, when it actually happened on your premises.'

'No, but we haven't had that excuse in the past either. The point is that people locally know we've been involved in the past and ask us to help. Whether we can or not – well. We can always try. And we do pick up the odd bits that the police don't. Especially if you have the odd moment.' Libby paused. 'Like you did at that woman's cottage on Thursday.'

'It was only a picture,' said Fran.

'But it meant you'd tuned into it.'

'Maybe not,' said Fran. 'After all, we already knew the woman had been found dead. It could have been my imagination.'

'I doubt it,' said Libby. 'Anyway, when will you be free?'

'It's Saturday, Lib. And Guy and Sophie are both away. I can't just leave the shop. If you're so keen, why don't you go over to St Aldeberge on your own?'

'I might later, if Ben is going to be up on the estate. He's going to go and check on Rosie and the cottages.'

'Oh, yes, Rosie. How's she getting on?'

'Driving me mad,' said Libby. 'She keeps phoning and asking me to go up and help her with this bloody dating site. I'm avoiding her.'

'I'm still not sure about her reasons for renting Steeple Farm,' said Fran. 'Oh, listen, I've got a customer. I'll try and sell one of your paintings.'

Libby switched off the phone and sighed. Outside, Romeo the Renault stood gently rusting on the little curved green opposite Number 17 Allhallow's Lane. The almost bare hedge above it dripped disconsolately. She turned away and rang Ben.

'What's up?'

'Where are you? You sound as if you're outside.'

'Walking across to the Hoppers' Huts. Why?'

'I just wanted to know if you're coming home this

54

afternoon?'

'I can do. I was going to do a bit in the office –'

'No, it's all right. Something else has happened at St Aldeberge, and I thought I'd pop over and see if Patti's OK. I won't be long.'

She heard Ben sigh. 'All right. But don't forget we're out tonight.'

'Oh, Lewis's party. I'd forgotten. Are we sharing a taxi with Pete and Harry?'

'With Pete, yes. Harry's driving over after he's closed the caff.'

'Poor soul won't be able to have a drink,' said Libby.

'I think they're staying overnight. We were invited, too.'

It was Libby's turn to sigh. 'I know. But I'd prefer to come home, and I'll pay for the taxi. What about Ad?'

'What about him? He's your son. Don't you know if he's going?'

'Not exactly. And I forgot all about it when I was talking to Fran just now. They're coming, aren't they?'

'Look, Lib, it's not my party! I expect Lewis has invited all the usual suspects. So off you go to St Aldeberge and try and be back in time to get yourself ready.'

Before she called Patti, to see if it was all right for her to visit, Libby called Adam.

'Yes, of course we're going,' he said. 'Sharing a taxi with Fran and Guy.'

Libby felt a twinge of jealousy. Adam and Fran's stepdaughter Sophie had been seeing one another for a couple of years now, and although she occasionally stayed over at the flat above The Pink Geranium, Adam was more frequently to be found at the flat over the gallery. Therefore, he spent more time with Fran and Guy than with Libby.

'OK,' she said. 'We'll see you there. Is it dinner? Or nibbles?'

'Dinner, of course,' said Adam. 'He's got that woman who does the TV catering in again. He loves her food.'

Libby agreed appreciatively. Lewis had filmed an entire

series at his estate, Creekmarsh, showing the development of the house and garden and Libby had been lucky enough to sample the crew's food.

She then called Patti.

'I thought I might come over if you need support.'

'You've heard, then?' Patti sounded shaky.

'Alice called.'

'Oh, God. She was hysterical.'

'Yes, she was on the phone. Look I won't come if you don't want me to –'

'No, please! Come over. I need to talk to someone.'

'OK. I'll be there in half an hour,' said Libby. 'Can I bring anything?'

'Oh – yes, if you wouldn't mind. I can't get out at the moment.'

Patti gave her a list and Libby drove down to the eight-til-late to fill it, before driving off to St Aldeberge.

Chapter Nine

The village was busier than it had been last time Libby was here, only four days ago, she realised. There were people in the street, people outside the church. It wasn't until she arrived that Libby realised she didn't know where Patti lived. Making a snap decision and an emergency stop which frightened Romeo into a stall, she turned into Birch Lane and parked outside Alice's house.

'What do you want?' Alice appeared with a tissue clutched in one hand, the other hand pulling at a cardigan the twin of the first, and red eyes.

'Patti asked me to come over,' said Libby, 'and I realised I don't know where she lives.' She stepped forward and took Alice's arm. 'Why don't you come in and let me make you some tea? Where's Bob?'

'At the allotment.' Alice seemed to sag, and let Libby guide her into the kitchen, where she sat down at the kitchen table and waved listlessly at the kettle.

'Have you called him?' Libby was opening cupboards looking for tea.

'No. He hasn't got his mobile with him. He never has.'

'Well, you take it easy,' said Libby, finding teabags and mug. 'You've had a shock as I said before.' She poured water into the mug. 'I'll call in on my way home, shall I? Or will you be all right? What about your daughter?'

'Oh, no, she's got enough on her plate,' said Alice. 'I wouldn't want to bother her. No, I shall be fine, don't worry.' She managed a wan smile. 'It was kind of you to call and make me this.'

'No problem,' said Libby. 'If you could just tell me where

Patti –?'

'Oh, yes. Take the left-hand fork past the church and the vicarage is next door. Far too big for one, of course.'

The vicarage, a sturdy, double-fronted Victorian edifice, had a gravel sweep where Libby was able to park. To her surprise, part of the doorway had police tape across it, and a small plastic tent had been erected over the step. A window to her right opened and Patti stuck her head out.

'Can you come round the side, Libby? They don't want anyone to use the front door until forensics have finished.'

Libby found the side gate into the large untidy garden which backed on to the church, and where Patti stood at the kitchen door.

'Forensics?' she asked, as she followed Patti into her study. 'But I gather it was a cockerel. What other forensics are they going to find?'

'It wasn't a cockerel,' said Patti. 'They don't think it was a bird at all. Just a lot of entrails and feathers, but apparently from different animals.'

'Oh.' Libby frowned. 'Alice thought … She does seem terribly shocked, doesn't she?'

'Yes. Odd. I mean, it was unpleasant, but …' Patti stopped and shook her head. 'Her reaction seems out of proportion.'

Libby nodded. 'I know. She was screaming at me down the phone – said it was all my fault. And just now – I had to sit her down and make her tea. She's in an awful state.'

'How could it be your fault?'

'I think because we talked to you and after that the second murder was discovered. She seemed to think that was cause and effect. Although she did apologise when she calmed down a bit. I wonder what she's frightened of?'

'Fear. Of course, that's what it is.' Patti looked out of the window where a small white van had just pulled up. 'More forensic people I suppose.' She opened the window and leaned out. 'Do you need anything?' she called as two figures emerged.

'No thanks,' called a female voice. 'We'll just carry on, and after that you can use your front door.'

'They've already had half a dozen people scouring the garden and drive,' said Patti, closing the window. 'I don't know what they thought they'd find.'

'I'm surprised Alice was the first one to find the – um – remains. Hadn't anyone else noticed them?'

'The postman doesn't come until mid-day at least, and I don't suppose anyone walking past could see what was on the doorstep, it's too far from the road.'

'Pity we don't have milkmen any more,' said Libby. 'Then you could say what sort of time it was left.'

'There is a milk van which delivers here, but I don't use it. I don't use that much milk being on my own.'

'What time does it come round? Does it pass here?'

'I think about seven, but I don't know where it delivers. Anyway, the driver would hardly be looking at anyone's doorstep where he didn't deliver, would he?'

'No, but I just thought if he was particularly early he might have seen someone lurking about.'

'The police were going to ask all the neighbours if they saw or heard anything, but, to be honest, if I didn't hear anything, actually living here, how would anyone else have done?'

'I wonder,' mused Libby, 'if that's why Alice is scared?'

'What do you mean?' Patti looked puzzled.

'I wonder if she knows someone was wandering about in the night?'

'Like who? Her husband? Poor old Bob, he wouldn't say boo to a goose.'

'That's true, of what I remember. Her daughter?'

'Tracey? Good lord, no. And her husband Darren – I can't see him tiptoeing round the village at night. More likely singing or fighting.'

Libby pulled a face. 'Oh, dear, poor Alice.'

'Oh, Darren's all right.' Patti sighed. 'He just gets a bit carried away on Friday and Saturday nights in the pub.'

'So there could have been people around late last night?'

'But not after twelve. The landlord's strict about his closing time.' Patti smiled. 'Just as well, as the pub's only over the road!'

'Is it? Where?'

'Just on the right as you go past the church from here. It's set back a bit from the road, but it's the classic old village set-up, pub and church virtually opposite each other.'

'So someone coming out of the pub might have noticed someone lurking around your place?' Libby persisted.

'Only if they came this way on their way home, and considering what state most of them are in when they leave I doubt they'd notice anything.'

'Oh, well. I expect the police will have asked all those sorts of questions anyway,' said Libby. She smiled at Patti. 'At least you sound better than you did on the phone.'

'Yes, I think talking about it helps. What I don't understand is the reasoning behind this.'

'Ah, well.' Libby reported her conversation with Fran. 'So you see, it almost seems as if someone's panicking and trying to divert suspicion.'

'Whoever's spreading the rumours, you mean?' said Patti.

'Maybe, but look, in the first place Mrs Bidwell's murder – we're all sure it *was* murder now, aren't we? – was concealed and made to look like a natural death. Then the rumours started about you, so perhaps the murderer, realising that Mrs Bidwell was going to be looked into, so to speak, decided to take advantage of the situation and point the finger at you.'

'What – and just to do that he murdered poor Marion Longfellow? That's appalling!' Patti looked horrified.

'No, there must be a reason to kill her,' said Libby, 'and Fran was convinced the two deaths are linked. The Black Magic setting was to confuse and point towards you because of the rumours.'

'So why the – thing – on my doorstep today?'

'God knows,' said Libby. 'Oh, sorry.'

'That's all right,' said Patti with a grin. 'I expect He does.'

Libby laughed. 'Well, I wish he'd let you in on the secret, then! Actually, it occurred to me driving over here, is there any history of Black Magic or witchcraft connected with the village?'

Patti looked interested. 'I don't know. It's the sort of thing I should know, isn't it? Hang on, I'll see if I can find –' She stood up and went to the crammed bookshelves that lined two of the walls. 'Here,' she said, coming back to her desk with a large old-looking book. 'This belonged to my predecessor. It's a history of the village written in the thirties.'

'Will it have an index?' asked Libby, shifting her chair a bit nearer. 'Otherwise we don't know what to look for.'

'No, but it does have chapter titles,' said Patti, turning the yellowed pages. 'Here – forty-four of them.' She ran her finger down the list. 'Folk-lore of the village and surroundings. Could that be it?'

Together, they scanned the contents of the folk-lore chapter but discovered no more than a few May Day and midsummer rituals.

'What about this?' said Libby, turning back to the contents list and pointing. 'Listen: "Cunning Mary and the Willoughby Oak". That sounds like it. Didn't they call witches "cunning-women"? Or the "cunning craft"?'

Patti found the chapter and they began to read.

'That's it!' said Libby triumphantly. 'We've found it! Now, where's the Willoughby Oak?'

'I've never heard of it,' said Patti, looking bewildered. 'And anyway, although it says she was a witch and hung from the oak, it doesn't say anything else happened there.'

'No, but I bet it did. Maybe still does. Poor woman was only a wise woman, after all. Just because some stupid farmers accused her of causing a murrain.'

'I've always wondered what a "murrain" was,' said Patti, pulling her laptop towards her. 'Oh, just a general term for disease in cattle and sheep.'

'But look,' said Libby, 'it does say it became synonymous with witchcraft. Anyway, that's not the point. Put Cunning Mary and the Willoughby Oak in.'

Patti dutifully did so, and to their gratification up came several sites, mostly those devoted to witchcraft and the paranormal. As Patti's book had said, Cunning Mary lived in the late sixteenth century and had the reputation of a "wise woman". As with most such women, she was regarded with fear and distrust by many, and eventually, in sixteen twelve, the same year the Pendle Witches were tried, a mob forced her out of her tiny cottage and took her to the Willoughby Oak, where they summarily hanged her.

But two of the websites went further than the book. According to them, every year on the anniversary of Mary's murder, for that, said Libby, is what it was, strange goings-on were reported from the oak. There were various theories about this. Some said it was Mary's ghost coming back to cast vengeful spells on her killers. Others, reporting strange lights in the tree, that other wise women, or witches, were using the force-field created by Mary to further their own spells. However, the most up-to-date report stated quite unequivocally that there were meetings of a Black Magic coven beneath the tree on the anniversary of Mary's death every year.

'And look when her death is,' said Patti.

'All Hallow's Eve,' they said together.

'Samhain,' said Libby. 'We found out about it before, when we got involved with Morris dancers.'

'Their most important festival,' said Patti. 'We had to learn quite a lot about it in college.'

'Really? Is that when you got interested in Deliverance?' Libby was interested. 'I've often wondered what you learn.'

'Yes, I got very interested in Deliverance and the areas of spirituality that seemed to clash with the doctrines of the church. I suppose that's why the rumours began that I was a witch. I should have known about poor Cunning Mary.'

'Did you do a degree in theology?'

'Yes, although I did a Sociology degree first. I thought it would help.'

'And has it?'

'I'm really not sure. The application of the two disciplines is fairly contradictory sometimes.' Patti sighed and looked out of the window again. 'They're going, look.' She waved as one of the forensics team put up a thumb and climbed into the van.

'I suppose I ought to be, too. I've got a party to go to tonight.' Libby stood up. 'I don't think I've helped at all.'

'Oh, you have.' Patti stood up.

'Have I?' Libby looked dubious.

'Now I'm going to pop over and see Alice. I mean, she came here this morning with the same idea – to see if I was all right.'

'Shall I give you a lift over there?' Libby fished out her keys as Patti opened the front door.

'No, it's only a step. I'll walk.' Patti looked down at the scrubbed doorstep. 'I hope I get over not wanting to step on it.'

Libby jumped up and down on it. 'There. Now all you'll think of is a middle-aged woman making a fool of herself.' She gave Patti a kiss on the cheek. 'Take care of yourself.'

'I will. And let me know if you hear anything else.'

'Ditto,' said Libby, climbing into the car.

Chapter Ten

'Do we know what sort of party this is?' asked Peter, as he folded his tall body in beside Libby in the back of the taxi.

'I know it's being catered,' said Libby, 'so I don't suppose it's a small intimate one.'

'Hmm. I don't fancy staying overnight if there are going to be a lot of media types swanning around. I wonder if Hal would mind driving home?'

'Poor Harry,' said Ben, turning round from the front seat. 'You'll condemn him to a drinkless evening.'

'But you aren't staying, neither are Fran and Guy, so we wouldn't know anyone,' complained Peter. 'We don't know your Lewis very well, after all.'

'He isn't "our" Lewis,' laughed Libby.

'You know him better than the rest of us,' said Peter, and lapsed into a morose silence.

Creekmarsh was lit up like the proverbial Christmas Tree. Since Lewis had opened it up as a wedding and conference centre, although he was very choosy about whom he permitted to use it, it had allowed him to indulge a passion for theatrics, and any amount of lights and lasers were hung in trees and mounted on roofs and were playing against the walls. Several cars including Guy's stood on the drive, which was lit with flares, Libby noticed.

Inside, Lewis's mother Edie was, as usual, in her best black and sequins, and her assistant Charlene was again in her French maid's outfit. Lewis was ushering a group of people into the refurbished grand hall, and turned to welcome them.

'Great, this, isn't it?' he said waving a hand at the brocade hangings and heavy, dark furniture. 'Look at that fire!'

Sure enough, in the huge manorial fireplace a log fire of immense proportions blazed. No one was standing remotely near it.

'Great,' the party of three murmured as a tray of champagne glasses appeared under their noses.

'Right,' said Lewis. 'Come and meet people.'

It was some time before Libby could manoeuvre herself next to Fran and tell her what she'd learnt that day in St Aldeberge.

'It's definitely all a bit odd,' she finished. 'And we must find out about Cunning Mary and the Willoughby Oak.'

'The Willoughby Oak?'

A masculine voice behind them made them both jump.

'Sorry.' A tall fair man ducked his head with a smile. 'I couldn't help overhearing.'

'That's all right,' said Libby, warily.

'Oh, it's all right,' he said sticking out a hand. 'Tim Bolton, Lewis's producer.'

'Oh.' Libby smiled her relief and took the hand. 'I'm Libby Sarjeant – with a j – and this is Fran Wolfe.'

Interest sparked in Tim Bolton's eyes. 'Ah – the psychic investigators!'

'No, no,' Libby hastily corrected. 'I'm distinctly un-psychic.'

'But –'

'It's me,' said Fran, a little wearily. 'I'm supposed to be psychic.'

'I thought Lewis said –'

'We helped a bit when they discovered those bones in his garden,' said Libby. 'That's all.'

'I heard slightly differently,' said Tim Bolton. 'In fact, I asked Lewis if he thought we could do a programme about you.'

'What?' Fran let out a horrified shriek, loud enough that several people, including her husband and step-daughter started towards her.

'No, no, it's fine,' soothed the embarrassed Bolton. 'He said nothing on earth would induce you to allow that, so I didn't pursue it.' He took a deep breath and changed the subject. 'But I heard you mention the Willoughby Oak. It's near here, isn't it?'

'Do you know about it, then?' asked Libby, waving away concerned relatives with an imperious hand. 'I only heard about it today.'

'Oh.' Tim Bolton looked disappointed. 'It came up in my research into a programme about the four hundredth anniversary of the Pendle Witch Trial.'

'Yes, another witch was hanged from it in the same year,' said Libby, 'but I don't know where it is.' Out of the corner of her eye she noticed a strange expression on Fran's face and hurried on. 'If you find out, perhaps you'd tell Lewis and he could tell me?'

'Of course,' said the amiable but shrewd Bolton, 'but you have to tell me why you want to know first.'

'Oh – just interest,' said Libby. 'A friend and I were looking something up on the internet and it came up in one of those side paths you always find your self wandering ...' She floundered to a stop.

'Right. If I find out where it is I'll let you know.' He gave her a quizzical look and turned to Fran, whose eye, conveniently, was caught by her step-daughter.

'Sorry,' she said, 'my daughter ...' and with a vague smile pushed her way through the throng.

'I upset her, didn't I?' Tim Bolton ruefully followed Fran's progress through the crowd.

'Don't worry,' said Libby, glad that the subject of the oak tree had been abandoned. 'Fran's very sensitive about her abilities. She doesn't quite believe in them herself.'

'I can understand that.' Tim Bolton was still watching Fran as she talked to Sophie and Guy. Adam stood close by with Peter and Ben. 'Of course, four hundred years ago she'd have been called a witch.'

Libby's breath caught in her throat and she felt as if she'd received a blow in her solar plexus.

'Sorry.' Tim Bolton returned his attention to her. 'It's all this research into witches I've been doing for the programme.'

'Oh, you and your witches.' Lewis appeared beside them waving new champagne glasses. 'Come on, Lib, we're nearly ready to eat. You'd better go and find that woman of yours, Tim.'

'Was he bothering you?' Lewis asked quietly, as he shepherded Libby towards her family. 'I saw Fran take off.'

'Not really. He said he'd suggested doing a programme about Fran to you.'

'He did. About both of you, but concentrating on Fran's – y'know – psychic stuff. I said no.'

'Yes, he said.' Libby gave Lewis's arm a squeeze. 'Thank you.'

'He can't help it. He used to be an investigative journo until he went into production. He part-owns our company now. Why did he start talking to you?'

Libby told him about the Willoughby Oak.

'If he finds anything out, I'll let you know,' said Lewis, 'and I won't ask any questions.' He gave her a wink and delivered her into the arms of her friends.

The food, as always was exceptional.

'I suppose if we ate like this all the time we wouldn't appreciate it,' said Libby to Ben.

'I'd watch what you answer there,' said Peter.

'And better not repeat it to Harry,' agreed Ben with a grin.

'Oh, you know what I mean,' said Libby. 'Anyway, Harry doesn't do beef. He's a veggie.'

'He has kept your favourite *pollo verde* on the menu, though. And the odd bit of fish.' Peter scraped the last of his Beef Wellington off his plate and sighed. 'That was great, though.'

'So tell us about this Willoughby Oak,' said Guy, leaning forward. 'Fran hasn't told me anything.'

'She doesn't know much. I haven't had the chance to tell her,' said Libby, pushing her plate away.

'I know where it is, though,' said Fran.

'Thought you'd had a little moment.' Libby nodded. 'While I was talking to that Bolton person.'

'Yes,' said Fran. 'But I don't know the rest.'

So Libby related the day's events.

'Bloody hell, Ma,' said Adam. 'You do get yourself into

some messes.'

'They both do,' said Sophie gloomily. 'It can be quite embarrassing.'

'Sophie!' Guy looked shocked.

Fran and Libby laughed.

'Parents are supposed to embarrass their children, even step-parents,' said Fran. 'It's in the rule-book.'

'What I'm not absolutely sure about,' said Peter, 'is why you want to find this oak?'

'Because of the Black Magic coven that meets there,' said Fran.

Everyone looked at her.

'Well, they do,' she muttered, burying her face in her wineglass.

'OK,' said Libby slowly, 'so they do. Do we know if any of them have connections to the village or Patti?'

'How do I know?' said Fran. 'I don't get a printed list. I simply know there's a coven and they meet there.'

'There you are, then,' said Libby with a weak smile. 'That's why we want to know.'

It was much later when Libby and Fran had a chance to talk again. Harry had arrived and, to Libby's surprise, had agreed to drive home rather than stay the night, so while they waited for him to enjoy the supper Lewis had saved for him, they settled down in a corner away from everyone else.

'Is there a connection, do you think?' asked Libby.

'If there is, it's an oblique one. As we said earlier, it looks as though someone's setting a stage. It isn't real.' Fran tapped her fingers on the arm of her chair, looking thoughtful.

'So someone, perhaps, who knows about the coven and wants to point the finger at them?'

'Perhaps. Although the second murder was meant to imply Patti had something to do with Black Magic.'

'Which was promptly discounted when they found out she wasn't around, so they've thought up this latest nonsense. This is what we thought anyway, though, isn't it? I haven't gone very far in progressing the theory.' Libby sighed.

'I think we have,' said Fran. 'There would have been no point in using a Black Magic cover if the murderer didn't know there was a coven operating in the area. Which argues that he or she must either be a member of it –'

'Which isn't likely, because he or she got things a bit wrong,' interrupted Libby.

'Or,' continued Fran, 'at least knows quite a lot about it. Perhaps been threatened himself?'

'That's possible. But we still don't know why Mrs Bidwell was killed in the first place.'

'Or why Mrs Longfellow was in the second. Although her murder was definitely a result of Mrs Bidwell's. I'm certain of that.'

'So we need to find someone who had a reason to murder Mrs Bidwell and who's a member of, or knows a lot about, a Black Magic coven,' said Libby. 'Not much then.'

'You remember all that business with the coven up at Tyne Hall chapel,' said Fran. 'The members of that coven were simply using it as an excuse for bad behaviour, weren't they?'

'Orgies with blackmail,' said Libby. 'Perhaps that's what all Black Magic covens do.'

'That's what I was thinking. Could this person – the murderer – have been blackmailed by Mrs Bidwell?'

'From what we've heard I can't see Mrs Bidwell knowing anything about Black Magic covens!' said Libby.

'No ... But when did Patti get the first anonymous letters talking about Black Magic?'

'Or was it just rumour?' Libby frowned. 'Oh, goodness, this is complicated.'

'And we should be leaving it to the police,' sighed Fran. 'What are we like?'

Libby was saying goodbye to Edie when Tim Bolton appeared at her side.

'I shall remember about the Willoughby Oak,' he said. 'I think there's a story there.'

Libby swallowed hard. 'I hope you find it,' she said, turning back to Edie. 'See you soon, Edie. Come over one day to see

Hetty.'

'Oh, bugger,' she said to Ben, Peter and Harry as they drove away from Creekmarsh.

'What now?' sighed Ben.

'That Bolton person. He thinks there's a programme in the Willoughby Oak.'

'What's the Willoughby Oak?' asked Harry.

'Don't ask!' said Ben.

'I'll tell you later,' said Peter.

'And who is he, exactly?' Ben turned to look at his inamorata, who was huddled inside her coat and looking cross. She explained.

'And it would matter why?' Peter turned from the front seat to ask.

'If there is a coven meeting there,' began Libby.

'Oh, not the bloody witches again!' said Harry. 'Remember that awful woman with the moustache who was into witchcraft?'

'Yes, sadly,' said Libby. 'And yes, it is the bloody witches again – or someone wants us to think so.'

'Someone wants *you* to think so?' repeated Ben.

'All right, someone wants the *police* to think so.'

'Did Fran tell you where she thinks the Oak is?'

'No, I shall have to ask her tomorrow. And Ben –' Libby hesitated.

'What?'

'I'm going to go to church tomorrow. To support Patti.'

'That's a bit hypocritical, isn't it?'

'I don't see why. I'm not a confirmed atheist like Fran. It was after last Sunday that Alice called me for help, so, on the basis that, if the village really is making life difficult for Patti, it might well be worse tomorrow, I thought I'd go over. I'll be back in time for lunch.'

'Do you know what time the service is?'

'Bother, no I don't. I'll have to call Alice first thing.'

'Would you like me to come with you?'

Libby turned to him in surprise. 'Would you? I never thought to ask. You don't like getting involved in my stuff.'

'No, I know, but I do feel some sympathy for this poor woman.' He patted her hand. 'I'll come, and then I can make sure we're back well in time for lunch at The Manor.'

Libby gave him a grateful smile, and settled back to peer out at the darkened countryside.

Chapter Eleven

Alice was out when Libby called her in the morning.

'Early service,' said her husband Bob. 'God knows why she has to go more than once on a Sunday.'

'I expect He does,' said Libby. 'And I expect it's to support Patti. Do you know what time the next service is?'

'Eleven,' said Bob. 'Why? Are you going?'

'I thought I might,' said Libby. 'Ben's coming, too.'

'Who's Ben?'

'My other half. Of course, I forgot, you wouldn't know him.'

'I only remember your husband. Derek, wasn't it? Good bloke, I thought.'

You would, thought Libby. 'Until he went off with a younger woman,' she said aloud.

'Yeah, well ...'

'Anyway, I expect we'll see you at eleven, then,' she said brightly.

'Oh, I don't go,' said Bob. 'Load of rubbish, if you ask me.'

'What does one wear to church these days?' asked Ben peering into his half of the wardrobe. 'It's not suits any more, is it?'

'I should think it's anything you like,' said Libby. 'I can get away with anything under my coat, so it doesn't matter.'

Under immense pressure, Libby had finally given up her ancient blue cape and taken to wearing the new coat Ben had bought her. The cape did, however, hang on a hook by the back door to do duty in the garden if required.

'Churches are cold, aren't they? I shall go for the traditional country gentleman look. Then I can wear a jumper over the shirt.' Ben removed some items from the wardrobe.

'Oh, not a sheepskin coat and a cap?' Libby dragged a cardigan on.

'I couldn't grow a handlebar moustache in time,' grinned Ben.

Not much to Libby's surprise, there was a steady stream of people entering the church as they approached. Inside, Alice was handing out hymn books and service sheets.

'Thank you for coming,' she whispered. 'Bob said you'd phoned. There's a lot of people here.'

'Nosy, or support?' asked Libby.

'Nosy.' Alice sniffed. 'But Patti's got a surprise for them.'

The service was a straightforward Communion, and Patti, thought Libby, conducted it as if she had no worries in the world. However, when she came to the lectern, which had been used for the gospel readings, to deliver the sermon, she lifted her head a little higher and delivered her surprise.

'Let he who is without sin cast the first stone.' Her voice was strong and her eyes swept the congregation with a fierce intensity. 'I didn't cast any stones, but someone has. This is an unusual step, but has the sanction of the Bishop. I invite Detective Chief Inspector Connell to speak to you.'

A collective gasp followed by a murmur like approaching thunder ran round the church. Libby and Ben looked at each other with raised eyebrows as Ian Connell appeared from the vestry.

'Ladies and gentlemen,' he began, 'as Miss Pearson has said, this is a very unusual step, but I have, myself, been to see your bishop and he agrees that as the tragic events recently relate closely to the church, it is perfectly appropriate.' He looked over the congregation as if waiting for someone to disagree with him, and sure enough there was a subdued muttering from the back.

'I can assure you all that both the police and your bishop have every confidence in Miss Pearson, and we are all horrified at the wicked attempts to involve her in the crimes that have been committed.' He paused again. 'To that end, we would like to invite every member of this congregation to speak to the police, particularly if they have anything relevant to this enquiry

73

to tell us. I hope Miss Pearson can continue to count on the support of you all in the future. Thank you.' Ian gave a quick nod and disappeared into the vestry, leaving behind him a stunned silence.

'Perhaps "start" to support would have been more truthful,' Libby muttered as they stood for the next hymn.

The service continued quite normally after that. Libby kept an eye out for renegade parishioners who might leg it, but no one did. In fact, at the end of the service, when Patti stood by the door to bid the congregation goodbye, everyone wanted to speak to her, and from what Libby could see, perfectly pleasantly. By the time Ben and Libby reached her, a smug Alice by her side, Patti was looking weary.

'Well done,' said Libby, giving her a kiss on the cheek. 'That was brave. This is Ben.'

Ben and Patti shook hands.

'It could have gone horribly wrong. They all could have got up and left, despite the Bishop. It was you who gave me the idea.'

'I did? Oh, good.' Libby looked round. 'Where did Ian get to?'

'He and a sergeant are just down there,' Patti pointed. 'Being a visible presence in case anyone really does decide to talk to them.' She shook her head. 'I doubt it, though.'

'Did he really go and see the Bishop?' Ben asked.

'He called him. I spoke to the Bishop first, and believe it or not, it was his idea to involve the police. He's very annoyed about people who profess to be Christians behaving badly and presuming to know more about the practices and teachings of the Church than the professionals.'

'I agree with him,' said Libby. 'It's presumptuous in the extreme.'

'It was really kind of you to come this morning,' said Patti. 'Did you think there might not be anyone here?'

'Partly, or that there'd be a baying mob.'

'Told you, they're all nosy,' said Alice. 'And I hope they're ashamed of themselves.'

Ian, with a brightly smiling Sergeant Maiden, greeted them with a degree of reserve.

'I suppose anyone can go to a church service,' he said, after shaking hands with Ben.

'But not anybody can preach,' said Libby, with an innocent smile.

Ian sighed. 'It was all cleared –'

'By the Bishop. I know,' said Libby. 'Any more news?'

'Not so far.' Ian eyed her suspiciously. 'What have you got?'

'Nothing. Seriously. Just speculation about witches, Black Magic and the Willoughby Oak.'

'The what?'

Libby explained. 'We thought it might be someone who knew that witches used the Oak for meetings and decided to pin the blame on them.'

'By using the feathers and other symbols?'

'Yes. What other symbols?'

'The body of Mrs Longfellow was enclosed in a pentagram for one thing.'

'That'll do it.'

'It had, of course, occurred to us as well,' said Ian, 'but we didn't know about the Oak. We'll look into it. Don't want any more of those blasted play-actors around here.'

'I don't think they are acting, Ian, or not in their own eyes, anyway.'

'Nonsense.' Ian's faint Scots accent became more pronounced. 'It's all made-up rubbish to cover up sexual bad behaviour.'

'Fran said that,' said Libby.

'Always said she was a sensible woman,' Ian said with a small smile.

'Anyway, you don't believe it's anything to do with Black Magic?'

'Of course not. Any more than it's anything to do with the vicar. So we need someone else with a motive for killing Joan Bidwell and Marion Longfellow.'

'Fran says Mrs Longfellow was killed as a direct result of the death of Mrs Bidwell,' said Libby.

'Yes, she did, but why exactly? Revenge? I can't believe that.'

'Well, there must be a reason. That is, if you're certain now that Mrs B was murdered.'

'She was.' Ian nodded. 'A very clever forensic pathologist has come up with the method.'

'And what was it?' Libby asked.

'Can't tell you just yet, but we have to look at that, too, as a pointer to our murderer. And it's probably the same for Marion Longfellow.' Ian grinned at Libby's obvious frustration. 'I'll give you a clue. It's Sux.'

'It sucks?' echoed Libby in bewilderment.

'No – just sux,' said Ian. 'It's a perfect clue.'

'But what sucks?' asked Libby, as she and Ben drove away from St Aldeberge. 'Just sucks? Sounds vaguely rude.'

'He's obviously giving you something else to worry away at to keep you out of his hair,' said Ben. 'And he didn't say *something* sucks, he said just "sucks". I'd get to some serious web searches, if I were you.'

'I shall,' said Libby firmly, 'and so will Fran.'

They drove straight to the Manor, where Hetty had cooked a huge roast dinner and invited her brother Lenny, best friend Flo, and Peter and Harry. Harry's spasmodic Sunday opening routine was currently in abeyance, but would start up again nearer to Christmas, and he was quite happy to come and eat all the vegetables Hetty provided with the roast beef. They sat round the long scrubbed kitchen table and discussed the recession, the prices in the eight-til-late and the up and coming pantomime.

'Aren't you having anything to do with it this year?' asked Hetty.

'Who? Me or Libby?' asked Peter.

'Both. One of yer always poking yer oar in somewhere.'

'Actually, I've designed the set and I'm helping to build it,' said Ben.

'We helped to cast it,' said Libby, 'but I'm sitting back and taking it easy this year.'

'Unless you have to take over a role again,' said Peter.

'I'm keeping an eye on the Queen,' laughed Libby. 'I'm daring her to fall over or catch flu.'

'So what you doing then, gal?' asked Flo. 'Another murder?' Libby choked.

'That'll be one o' them undetecting poisons, then,' said Flo, when Ben had explained.

'There aren't any left,' said Libby.

'Bet there are,' said Flo. 'What about that feller who was killed with an umberella?'

'But they detected that poison,' said Libby, 'and even the Russian who was in hospital. They found out what was wrong with him in the end.'

'That could be what "sucks" means,' said Ben, with an air of discovery.

'Sucks?' repeated the entire table.

'Something Ian said to us – said it was a clue.'

'A real clue!' said Harry. 'I'd watch it – you'll be turning into detectives.'

'Don't be sarky, Hal,' said Libby. 'I'm going to Google it the minute I get home. Bother.' She fished in her bag for her warbling mobile and switched it off.

'Not important?' asked Peter. 'You looked a little pissed off, if you don't mind me saying.'

'Rosie again,' sighed Libby. 'I suppose I shall have to ring her back eventually.'

Both having had several glasses of Hetty's excellent claret, Ben and Libby left Ben's car at The Manor and strolled home.

'I suppose I'd better ring Rosie,' Libby said as they negotiated their way round Sidney into the sitting room.

'You do that and I'll light the fire,' said Ben. 'And I'll even put the kettle on.'

'Rosie. It's Libby.'

'Libby! Where have you been? I've been ringing and ringing.'

'I know, and I'm sorry, but I've been rather busy. Only just got in, actually.'

'Oh?' Rosie sounded disappointed. 'I was hoping you could come up here and give me a hand.'

'A hand? With what?' Libby tried not to sound exasperated.

'This dating website. I told you.'

'How could I possibly help? You have to put your own details on there. I can't do anything.'

'You could check over some of the men I've been looking at.'

'I don't think I could. Just don't agree to meet any of them.'

'No. So you won't come up? I've got some cake and a nice bottle of red.'

'Rosie. I've just told you, I've this minute walked through the door and Ben's making me a cup of tea. I've been very busy and I'm knackered.'

'Oh. I suppose I'll have to wait until tomorrow,' said Rosie, sounding very hard done by.

'Come down to supper tomorrow night,' said Libby suddenly, 'and you can show me on my computer. It'll have to be earlyish, as I've got a panto rehearsal at a quarter to eight.'

'Oh, all right, thank you.' Rosie didn't sound that grateful. 'What time shall I come?'

'About five thirty? Then we can look at your website before supper.'

'You haven't got a rehearsal tomorrow night,' said Ben, bringing two mugs of tea through as Libby switched off the phone.

'I know, but otherwise we'd be stuck with her for the whole evening, and I can't take that much of Rosie.'

'I'd noticed,' said Ben. 'I'm surprised she hasn't.'

Monday morning dawned wet. Libby decided to concoct something to cook in the slow cooker so that she had no preparation to do when Rosie turned up, so, forsaking the village shops in favour of a ride in the car, she drove out to the nearest supermarket and tried not to feel guilty about depriving the locals of her custom.

By the time Rosie arrived at half past five, a savoury smell was wafting through number 17, Ben had once more lit the fire and made tea, and Libby had the laptop open on the table in the window.

'So let's have a look at this website,' said Libby, pushing the laptop towards Rosie.

'Here.' She turned the screen so Libby could see it properly. 'These are my "matches". I've been in touch with some of them.'

Libby scrolled down through the mini pictures and self-descriptions.

'They're all so old, Rosie.'

'So am I, dear. But some of them sound interesting. Look.' She clicked on a picture and the whole profile came up. 'There. He sounds all right, doesn't he?'

'He sounds as boring as hell,' said Libby. 'And not terribly bright. Aren't there any men doing exciting things? Or who aren't intellectually challenged?'

Rosie sighed. 'Actually, that's exactly what I've been thinking. I expect this is the wrong site for me.'

'I thought it was for research, not for you?' said Libby, raising an eyebrow.

'It is,' said Rosie, but a faint colour appeared in her cheeks. 'But I've got to do it properly. I could have signed up with a picture of someone young, and made up the details, but that wouldn't have fitted the book.'

'Hmm,' said Libby, and clicked through to another profile. 'This one's even worse.'

'I know.' Rosie sighed again. 'You see, I really did need you to check it with me. I was almost going to arrange to meet this one.' She clicked on to another profile. 'Here.'

Libby frowned. 'I'm sure I've seen that face,' she said. 'Where does he come from?'

'Just says Kent. I suppose you could have seen him around if he lives in this part of Kent.'

Libby was still frowning. 'I've seen him recently. Don't meet him until I've remembered, will you?'

'I won't meet him at all,' said Rosie, and closed the laptop. 'You've made me see sense. Now, tell me what you've been so

79

busy doing?'

Relieved, Libby gave her an edited version of the recent events in St Aldeberge.

'And yesterday, Ian Connell gave Ben and me a hint about the murder method, only we can't find it. Fran can't either.'

'What did he say?'

'It sucks.'

'That's it?'

'Well, he then said – *just* sucks.'

'Sucks.' Rosie frowned. 'It rings a bell. I did some research a year or so back … Have you checked the spelling?'

'How else could you spell sucks?'

'I'm almost positive –' Rosie paused. 'Have you tried S U X?'

Libby, looking faintly astonished, opened the laptop again and typed S U X into the search engine.

'An airport? Sexual racism?'

'Let me look.' Rosie pulled the screen towards her. 'There, look. I knew I knew it: succinylcholine, also known as suxamethonium chloride or just "sux".' She pushed it back to Libby with a triumphant grin. 'I have my uses.'

Chapter Twelve

Astonished, Libby read the description. Ben came to read it over her shoulder.

'It explains everything,' said Libby, 'but that means it must have been either that other old vicar or the churchwarden.'

'Why?' said Ben and Rosie together.

'Because Mrs Bidwell was killed in her pew, and they were the only people who went near her.'

'We don't know that,' said Ben. 'Anyone could have gone up to her afterwards. Was anyone else in her pew? Or did people stop to say goodbye to her?'

'Oh, I don't know. I suppose they must have done. But you'd have to be very close to inject someone, wouldn't you?'

'Let me see.' Rosie pulled the laptop back towards her. 'It can be injected intravenously when it works almost immediately, or intramuscularly when it takes a bit longer. But even then, she wouldn't have been able to call out. And how did they detect it? Doesn't it say it disappears after twenty-four hours?'

'It occurs naturally in the body, and breaks down ...' Libby frowned at the screen, then up at Ben. 'So how do they know this is what she died of? By the time the post mortem was done it would have gone.'

'Ian did say something about a very clever forensic pathologist,' said Ben. 'Obviously there was a reason for them to decide she didn't die a natural death. And now, if you've finished your tea, I suggest we eat, or you'll be late, Libby.'

Rosie didn't see him wink.

They discussed the drug throughout dinner, Rosie becoming more and more animated.

'She'll be using it in her next book,' said Ben, as they closed the door thankfully behind her.

'Probably.' Libby went to collect plates. 'I'm going to pop up to the theatre in a bit, or I'll feel bad.'

'To justify your lie to Rosie?' Ben grinned. 'I'm going anyway. I've got something to do in the workshop. And the hirers aren't always as careful with our stuff as I would like.'

The Oast House Theatre, converted by Ben and run by him, Peter and Libby, with help from other members of the family occasionally, and Harry when he could get away, was hired out to other companies occasionally, and had recently seen a run of five nights of comedy. It had been very successful, but trying for the beleaguered technical staff of the theatre. Visiting comedy acts and their managers were sometimes careless of any existing sets or lighting and sound rigs. Damage was frequently done, sighed over and repaired or replaced. Subsequently, hiring charges had gone up and hirings themselves had gone down.

Libby and Ben found Peter in the lobby bar checking stock, the pantomime director looking harassed and talking earnestly in a corner with a young woman who looked supremely uninterested, Bob and Baz, the perennial funny men, working on a piece of business on stage, and the rest of the cast including the rehearsal pianist, sitting around looking bored.

Libby sat in the back row of the auditorium and Ben went backstage to the workshop.

'I don't think it's going well, dearest,' said Peter's voice in her ear. 'All is not well in the ranks.'

'I thought this director had experience,' Libby murmured back.

'He has, but not with a company like this.'

The Oast House theatre was not run as a normal amateur theatre company, but a trust. Libby, Ben, Peter and his brother James were all on the board, and their productions were a mix of amateur and professional. Libby herself was an ex-professional actor, and professional musicians, choreographers and directors were frequently brought in. The dancers for the panto chorus these days, after a series of elephantine mistakes, were usually retired pro-dancers, young women who had left the business for motherhood or marriage – sometimes even both.

'Did we look into him?' asked Libby, watching as the director made his way to the front of the auditorium and clapped his hands for attention.

'Oh, yes, but I've now discovered that this company he was supposed to be director of in Surrey is a tiny little church society with a grand name. It's a toss-up between him leaving and us firing him.'

'Oh, we can't fire him,' said Libby. 'Poor bloke. Perhaps we could give him a production assistant?'

'He's got one. Young Kylie.'

'Oh, good God,' spluttered Libby. Kylie being one of the youngest, most enthusiastic, and clumsiest of the youth theatre members.

'What were we saying at Het's yesterday?' said Peter, plopping down in the seat next to her and swinging his legs over the seat in front. 'Nothing to do with us this year?'

'What are you saying?' Libby shot him a nervous look.

'That at least one of us might have to intervene.'

'Look, I've already taken over once recently. When the cow fell on the fairy. People will say I'm a jinx.'

'They'll say more than that if this farce is allowed to continue,' muttered Peter, watching the director trying to keep control of his cast, while chorus members stood around in boneless attitudes of boredom.

'Bloody hell,' said Libby after ten minutes, 'he couldn't direct himself out of a paper bag.'

Another ten minutes. 'Who chose the songs?'

'He did, with the help of his wife.'

'Who's playing the Queen. Haven't seen her yet. What's she like?'

'You saw her when she auditioned. And you said yesterday you'd been keeping an eye on her.'

'Yes, but I assumed she was a bit shy, what with being in a new place. And I was being metaphoric.'

'Here she comes now.' Peter gave her a sharp nudge, as a woman entered cautiously from upstage, hesitated, looked round and said: 'Do I go down here, dear?'

Libby buried her face in her hands, before recovering herself and following Peter back into the lobby, where he went straight to the bar and poured her a stiff whisky.

'So what do we do?' he asked, after pouring himself a gin and tonic. 'This can't be allowed to go on. We've got a reputation to keep up.'

'Why haven't you told me before?' said Libby, sitting down at one of the little white wrought iron tables.

'I thought it would get better. I was going to give it to the end of the week and invite you down, but you pre-empted me.'

'Why hasn't Ben told me?'

'He hasn't seen it, really. He potters in during the day, mostly, and they're only just about to start construction, so he hasn't kept up with it. He has wondered why he hasn't had a production meeting since it was cast.'

'No, he said that. Has the director approved his designs?'

'I don't know. Come on, let's go round the back and ask him.'

They crept through the auditorium and the pass door and round the back of the stage into the workshop, where they found Ben standing in the wingspace looking on with horror. He turned towards them.

'This is terrible!' he whispered. 'Why didn't you tell me, Pete?'

'That's what Libby just said. We're holding an impromptu council of war. Come back to the bar.'

'We can't let it go on,' said Ben. 'My family own this place, and we're all directors. All the work we've put in to make it as near pro standard as possible – this would send it straight down the pan.'

'I don't honestly think he wants to go on,' said Peter, 'but he doesn't know how to get out of it.'

'I don't suppose the cast are that bad,' said Libby. 'After all, we know Bob and Baz are OK, and Tom, and even young Amy's fine, although she's so young. It's just they aren't being directed. And don't look at me like that,' she added as both Peter and Ben sent meaningful looks her way.

'Well, who else can take over?' asked Peter reasonably.

'You could,' said Libby. 'Even Ben could.'

'Thanks for the faint praise,' said Ben.

'You know what I mean. Unless any of our straight play directors would take it on?'

'So we are agreed, then?' said Peter. 'He has to go?'

'Unless we can find some way of helping him, yes,' said Libby.

'Definitely,' said Ben. 'But give it until the end of the week. You never know, he might suddenly perk up.'

'Come on, then,' said Peter. 'I said I'd meet Harry in the pub. Might as well make the most of it before he starts opening on Sundays and Mondays for Christmas.'

They found Harry draped over the counter talking to Jim the barman, who was idly polishing glasses.

'Well, well,' said Harry. 'The theatrical contingent. What'll you have, darlings?'

Seated round a table by the fire, Harry handed round drinks and sighed.

'Oh, go on. What's happened now?' he said. 'You all look like you've lost a pound and found a penny.'

They explained their concerns between them and Harry put his chin in his hands and listened.

'Sack the bugger and his wife, you direct, Pete, and you take over Queenie, ducks.' He picked up his glass. 'Problem solved.'

'That's all very well,' said Peter, 'but we do have lives to lead.'

'You do it every other year,' said Harry. 'What's different?'

Peter and Libby looked at one another.

'Nothing, I suppose. But how are we going to sack him?' asked Libby. 'I feel awful about it. After all, we gave him the job.'

'Think about it. Sleep on it,' said Harry.

'But I really don't want to take over direction,' said Libby. 'I suppose I wouldn't mind taking over as Queen, unless there's someone else who would like to do it.'

They ran through the names of people who had auditioned for the part of the Queen, but found no one else who could take it on. Two of them had been cast in other productions and the other two were not up to the part.

'What this will do to our investigation ...' Libby stared into the log fire.

'Libby, it isn't your investigation, it's the police's investigation. Ian's, in fact.' Ben patted her hand. 'Fran can always keep an eye on it for you.'

'Fran!' Libby looked up excitedly. 'She could do the Queen!'

The three men looked doubtful.

'I can't see our Guy liking that. She hasn't done it since before they married, has she?' said Peter.

'She played the Baroness to our Ben's Baron,' said Harry. 'The year of the unpleasantness at Anderson Place.'

'Don't talk about our wedding like that,' said Peter.

Harry snorted with laughter. 'You know what I mean.'

'She wasn't entirely hooked up with Guy at that time,' said Ben. 'He might not take to the idea.'

'Oh, come on, dearie,' said Harry, leaning across to pat Libby's cheek. 'You know you'd love to play the Queen.'

'I did deliberately stay away this year,' said Libby.

'Only because you thought people would say you hogged the best parts. And you've taken over before, once in that same production Fran was in, and again when the cow fell on the fairy,' said Ben.

'You're a fraud, you old trout,' said Harry. 'You love it really.'

'If,' said Libby darkly, 'it comes to it, I shall do it. But next year, I want to be the witch.'

'I'd be careful about saying that just at the moment, petal,' said Peter. 'You'll have the dark forces gathering around us as we speak.'

'Yes, tell us the latest goss,' said Harry. 'We haven't heard for ages. Oooh –' he pretended to think. 'Not since, let me see, yesterday lunchtime.'

'No need to be sarky,' said Libby, as Ben got up to fetch

more drinks. By the time he came back, she'd filled the other two in on the evening's surprising revelations by Rosie.

'I'm still not sure about that woman,' said Harry.

'Neither am I,' said Peter. 'She seems incredibly self-centred.'

'Perhaps it's being a writer?' suggested Libby. 'You know, being on your own all day. You've only got yourself to think about.'

'There are writers who have families, dearie,' said Harry. 'They aren't all self-centred. No, it's just her. She's an oddity.'

'She's a bloody nuisance,' said Libby, 'but she was useful today. At least we think she was. If we can find out from Ian if it is this succo-stuff that's the murder weapon. And if it is, how on earth did they track it down?'

Chapter Thirteen

Libby called Fran in the morning to tell her about the previous evening's discoveries, and no sooner had she switched off the phone, than it rang again.

'I'm afraid it has come to pass, petal,' said Peter. 'I knew he didn't want to carry on.'

'Oh.' Libby sank down on the step below Sidney on the stairs. 'Our director. He's quit?'

'Appeared on the doorstep half an hour ago. Apparently his wife is missing the family and friends they've left behind in Surrey.'

'Bloody hell, it isn't Australia! It's an hour up the M20,' said Libby.

'This is an excuse, Lib. Let him have the dignity of that. He had the grace to apologise for leaving us in the lurch, and actually said he thought we'd better off without them.'

'Oh, bless him. I feel bad, now.' Libby stared down at her feet. 'Are they actually moving back?'

'Apparently so. They'd only let out their house, so they'll go and stay with their son until the tenants move out. He said his wife couldn't bear to miss Christmas in their old home.'

'I wonder why they moved here in the first place?' said Libby.

'A desire for rural retirement. Lots of people do it and regret it. It's a bit different here from suburban Surrey.'

'It is.' Libby sighed. 'So, am I Queenie or directrix?'

'How archaically learned, darling. Queenie, I suppose, as I can't play her.'

'Oh, you could, you could,' giggled Libby.

'No, dear, Hal could. But still, it'll have to be you, and I'll direct. I'd better have a meeting.' Peter sighed heavily. 'Is Ben up at The Manor? Could you both come to me tonight?'

Assured that they could, Peter rang off and Libby called Fran back.

'It's annoying,' she said. 'But we can't let the rest of them down. And there's actually plenty of time. You wouldn't like to do it, I suppose?'

'No, my acting days are over,' said Fran. 'Besides, last time I did it, I was still living over The Pink Geranium. It'd be a bit of a nuisance driving from here every night.'

'I know.' Libby sighed. 'No help for it, I suppose. Anyway, did you look up that succo stuff?'

'Yes, and it looks incredibly hard to detect unless a post mortem's done very quickly. Ian's forensic pathologist must have been very clever indeed. I thought tox screen results took weeks to come back though.'

'That's perhaps why they've only just confirmed it was murder. We must find out.'

'Why must we? You're going to have enough on your plate without this.' Fran laughed. 'I shall enjoy seeing you up there again. And how's Pete taking to directing once more?'

'I think he's going to rather enjoy it. It was a shocking mess, you know.'

'Well, before you get immersed in being a Queen – what is it again? Sleeping Beauty?'

'Yes. I sleep for one whole scene then I'm awake again.'

'Well, before you do that, do you want to go and have a look at the Willoughby Oak?'

'You've found it?'

'I told you I knew where it was. Do you want to come?'

'Today?'

'Yes, if you've got time. I thought we might go this afternoon.'

'I'll be over after lunch,' said Libby, and switched off the phone.

Under a gloomy sky, Libby parked on Harbour Street at just after two o'clock. She joined Fran in her little Smart car and they set off towards St Aldeberge. Fran turned inland, however, just before the village,, crossed a small bridge, and soon turned on to a rutted lane that led upwards to an empty field, where a huge old tree stood creaking in the sudden wind.

'It's impressive,' said Libby, after they had stared at it for several minutes. 'Where exactly are we?'

'On the outskirts of the Dunton Estate. That's over the rise in that direction.' Fran waved a hand to her right. 'It belongs to them, but it's fairly obviously used for something by others, even though it's dead.'

'How do you know that?'

'Look.' Fran got out of the car and approached the tree. Libby followed. 'Here.'

Faint marks were scratched into the trunk of the tree, and there were scraps of fabric clinging to its lower branches.

'And here.' Libby pointed to the ground, where there were several marks, including darker staining, making Libby shiver.

'And tyre tracks,' murmured Fran.

'Could be the police?' wondered Libby doubtfully. 'We told Ian about this place.'

'It could be Tim Bolton,' said Fran. 'Looking for his story.'

'Oh, lord, and now us. It's a positive Piccadilly Circus,' said Libby. 'I suppose it's more likely to be Tim Bolton. The police would do a bit more in depth research before bothering to come out here.' She looked round at the empty field and shivered. 'It's quite spooky, isn't it? You wouldn't think it would be, being so open.'

Fran was staring at the ground. Libby watched her for a few minutes.

'OK – what have you seen?'

Fran looked up. 'I'm not sure. It was dark. And I get the feeling this is nothing to do with our murders, but to do with the village.'

'Which backs up our theory that whoever's behind them is simply using Black Magic or witchcraft as a cover.'

'Maybe.' Fran looked round the field. 'But whoever is using this tree has been here recently.'

'Have they? Shall we go then, before they come back?' said Libby nervously.

Fran looked amused. 'They're hardly likely to come mid-afternoon when it's still light.'

'I suppose so. Still, I do have to get back. I need to cook before we go to Pete's for this meeting tonight.'

'All right.' Fran looked up at the tree, reached out and pulled off a piece of fabric that fluttered from a twig just above her head. 'I'll see if I can get anything off this.'

'Should you tell Ian you've done that?' said Libby dubiously.

'I don't see why.' Fran stuffed the scrap into her pocket. 'Come on then. Will you have time for a cup of tea before you go?'

Libby decided she could afford another half an hour when they arrived back at Coastguard Cottage, and settled down in front of the fireplace with Balzac the cat on her lap.

'I think,' said Fran coming in from the kitchen with two mugs in her hands, 'that this fragment is part of one of those blasted cloaks they all wear.'

Libby shuddered. The cloaks worn by others who had been members of a Black Magic coven some years ago had distinctly unpleasant memories. 'But not sinister in itself?'

'No, just caught on that twig while its wearer pranced about, presumably naked underneath.'

'Yuck.' Libby made a face and sipped her tea. 'I reckon they are all just a cover for bad sexual behaviour.'

'All covens?'

'And Satanists. Or are they the same?'

Fran sat down in the chair opposite looking thoughtful. 'According to their own literature, there is only one kind of magic and people use it for either good or evil, and if evil, they are obviously linked with the Devil. But Satanists are a bit different. Satanism itself was a term only really coined in the last century; before that it was simply Devil worship and not necessarily anything to do with magic, although magic was supposed to be employed at some level. It's all terribly complicated. I was looking it up on the internet.'

'I gathered.' Libby grinned at her friend.

'There's one particular sect who say they are a "small religious group that is unrelated to any other faith, and whose members feel free to satisfy their urges responsibly, exhibit kindness to their friends, and attack their enemies". Actual Devil worship is nastier. And collectively it's all known as "The Left-Hand Path".'

'And some of them use the nastier aspects to – er – satisfy their urges.'

'Not always responsibly, either.'

'So we still don't know anything about our murderer.' Libby absentmindedly rested her mug on Balzac's head. He didn't seem to mind. 'He knows about the coven, or whoever they are, but it's not actually connected to the murder.'

'It doesn't seem to be.' Fran frowned. 'Perhaps Ian will find out more.'

'Or Tim Bolton will. Although he doesn't know its connection to the murders – or not.' Libby smiled grimly. 'And I'd like to see how far he gets now Ian knows, anyway.'

Later, throwing together a quick spaghetti bolognese, she found out.

'Tim Bolton's cross with you,' said Lewis, obviously in a car.

'You're not talking while you're driving, are you?' said Libby.

'Course not. I'm not an idiot. No – our Tim's been warned off by the coppers. Your copper mate Ian, in fact.'

'Really? How?'

'Found out where it was, didn't he, and when he got there your Ian's there with a couple of uniforms and a lot of crime scene tape.'

Must have been after we went there this afternoon, thought Libby. 'So why is he blaming me?' she asked aloud.

'He reckons you were looking into it, and seeing as how you're in with the coppers, it must have been you what put them up to it.'

'Yes, well, it probably was,' said Libby, a trifle

92

uncomfortably, 'but it had nothing to do with your Tim Bolton. He just said he came across it while he was researching something else.'

'I know, love. But you know what these media types are like. Go mad for a story.'

'I know.' Libby sighed. 'Tell him I'm sorry – although I don't quite know what for.'

'I won't tell him anything of the sort.' Lewis laughed. 'Do him good. But don't be surprised if he finds out where you live and comes bothering you. He can be a right nuisance, the bugger.'

'I had a feeling he could.' Libby sighed gustily. 'OK, forewarned is forearmed, Lewis, thanks. Where's Adam, do you know?'

'Working for your mate for a few days. I'm off up to London doing some filming. I'll give you a call when I get back.'

Libby repeated all this to Ben as they ate their meal. 'He can't do anything to me,' said Libby, 'but if he does decide I know something about what is obviously a police case, he could become very persistent.'

'All you've got to do is tell him you'll report him to the police for harassment,' said Ben.

'But he's almost a – well, not a friend, exactly, but we met him socially.'

'You did. I didn't. I wouldn't worry about it, if I were you. Now eat up, or we'll be late for Pete's meeting.'

Peter and Harry's cottage lay just beyond The Pink Geranium and the Manor drive, on the High Street. Libby waved at Adam through the window of The Pink Geranium as they passed.

Settled in her favourite sagging, cretonne-covered chair, with Peter, Ben, the stage manager, Frank, Bob and Baz and the dame, Tom, arranged around the sitting room, Libby put the whole question of St Aldeberge and the Willoughby Oak out of her mind. This was much more her world, she told herself, and prepared to enjoy it.

Chapter Fourteen

The joy of email and social networking sites, Libby thought the following morning, as she informed the entire cast and crew of the pantomime of the changes agreed upon last night. The plan hammered out for the transformation of the production was a little radical, especially as the musical director and choreographer had not been informed of the changes in the music. There was, in fact, plenty of time to implement changes, but this was not, she reminded herself, professional theatre, where panto would get two weeks rehearsal for the principals if lucky. The MD and choreographer were paid "honoraria", but everyone else was a volunteer, although they were lucky to have several professional or ex-professional actors and technicians, who liked to keep their hand in, on whose talents they could call.

The trickiest thing, she decided, was going to be the new gauze which a) cost money b) needed to be painted – a tricky job – and c) had to be hung from one of the lighting barrels, none of which appeared to be free as far as the lighting designer's plan showed. Oh, well, she thought with a sigh, as she shut the laptop, it wasn't her concern, it was Peter's, as he was now in overall charge of the production as well as director. Young Kylie had been kindly informed that Peter didn't work with a PA, and despatched back to the chorus.

When the landline rang, she was surprised to hear Fran's voice at the other end.

'That Bolton person managed to get hold of me,' she said, sounding angry.

'Who?' Libby's brain did the difficult switch from panto to real life. 'Oh! Lewis thought he might come after me.'

'Oh, he did, did he? Why didn't you let me know?'

'What would I have said? Tim Bolton's angry with me because Ian Connell warned him away from the Willoughby Oak?'

'Yes. I would have known what he was going on about. The bastard tried to trick me into telling him the whole story.'

'Oh, Fran! He didn't? You didn't?'

'No, of course not.' Fran was now sounding irritated. 'I don't know why Lewis has anything to do with him.'

'He's got money in the production company,' said Libby. 'How did he get hold of you?'

'He Googled me!' Fran was now amazed.

'We've been told before we come up in search engines,' said Libby. 'I've just never tried it.'

'Apparently, a mention of our wedding came up in a link, and of course he saw Guy's name, which is still quite well known in the art world, found out where the shop was and bingo. He rang the shop, asked for me, and Sophie, bless her, handed him over.'

'I wish our investigations were that simple.'

Fran made a noise that sounded like "hmph".

'Did you get anything out of him about what Ian was doing at The Oak?'

'No. He took the line that of course I knew about the police's interest in the tree and so did he, so what did I think about the whole case.'

'Cheeky.'

'Precisely. Luckily, by that time, not knowing Ian had gone out there, I had the wit to ask what case he was talking about. And that set him floundering. He was a little bit disingenuous.'

'I suppose he's only doing his job,' sighed Libby. 'But annoying. We shall have to watch out for him. Did you get anything else from the piece of cloak?'

'No, but after Bolton rang me, I left a message for Ian. I expect he'll call back at some time today. I'll let you know.'

'OK, but I think we should be concentrating on finding out why Mrs Bidwell died. We seem to have forgotten that.'

'I don't think "we" should, Lib. We did what we could to

help Patti, who now seems to be off the villagers' hook –'

'How do you know that?' interrupted Libby.

'I – I –' Fran stopped. 'I don't actually. Well, I do, but I don't know how.'

'We'll take it as read, then,' said Libby. 'And surely we've got to try and find out what happened? We can't leave it here.'

'We'd just be being nosy for nosy's sake,' said Fran. 'If anyone asks us to do something, that's different. Meanwhile, I think we should get down to real life. We're doing a Christmas-themed display for the shop, and you're rehearsing panto. How did last night's meeting go?'

When Libby rang off, she sat chewing her finger for a moment, thinking. Fran was, of course, quite right. There was no reason for them to look into the St Aldeberge's murders now that the police had them in hand and Patti had been cleared of involvement. And Libby now had lines to learn and her duties as Peter's unofficial deputy which would keep her busy enough. But Libby's fuse of curiosity had been lit, and once lit was terribly hard to put out.

She wandered into the kitchen, made herself a cup of coffee for a change and punched Patti's number into the phone.

'Just wanted to see how you were,' she said.

'That's kind, Libby. And thank you so much for coming over on Sunday. I can't tell you what a difference Ian's sermon made. All of a sudden people were speaking to me again, and not only that, asking me to help with things. It's been a great few days. Except for Joan Bidwell's son.'

'Why, what did he do?'

'He turned up wanting me to do the funeral. He doesn't live here, he moved away years ago, when he married, I think he said.'

'Sensible,' said Libby.

'Yes, well, he wants his mum to have a church service here, as she loved the place. I said we couldn't do that until the police released the body and he went off on one.'

'He must have already been told that by the police if he was her next of kin.'

'Apparently his sister was down as next of kin, but as she'd had nothing to do with Mrs Bidwell for about forty years, she wasn't bothered, and when this Dennis Bidwell asked her about it, she said he could do what he liked, only didn't tell him about the police having the body.'

'What a mess. No wonder he was upset.'

'Yes,' said Patti, 'but after all, he hadn't spoken to his mother in years, either.'

'From what you've told me, I don't blame him.'

'Probably feels guilty,' said Patti with a sigh. 'They often do.'

'Shame he didn't know her better,' said Libby. 'It might have helped find a motive for her murder. Or has anything turned up in that regard?'

'Not as far as I know,' said Patti. 'Hasn't your nice Ian said anything?'

'I haven't spoken to him, but he's under no obligation to tell Fran or me anything. Rather the opposite, usually.'

'But he asks for your help, doesn't he? And look how you've helped in this case.'

'I know, but once he's in charge, unless he thinks we can actively help, he'd rather we kept out of it. We get under his feet a bit.'

Patti laughed. 'Well, I'm glad you do. It's helped me enormously.'

'Oh, we didn't do much,' mumbled Libby.

'I disagree. Look, I'm coming to see my friend Anne again today as it's my day off again –'

'Blimey! A whole week since you last came!'

'Yes, so I thought, would you like to come to dinner with us? We're going to that nice restaurant in your High Street.'

'The Pink Geranium? My friend Harry owns it. Actually, I couldn't tonight, I've got a panto rehearsal – perhaps we could see you for a drink in the pub after you've eaten?'

'Yes, lovely. Panto, eh? We'll have to get you down to give us some advice if I do manage to set up a drama group.'

'Alice didn't look thrilled with that idea,' said Libby, with a laugh.

'Oh, she'll join in. She usually does,' said Patti. 'What time will you get to the pub?'

'We finish rehearsals at ten, so about ten past if I can get away. See you then.'

By the time Libby pushed open the glass doors of the theatre at a quarter to eight that evening, it was already warm. Peter greeted her from the top of the spiral staircase that led to the sound and light box.

'Looking forward to it, petal?' he said.

'Of course, as long as the cast aren't too upset about the changes.' Libby unwound her scarf. 'Ben in the auditorium?'

'No, he's already in the workshop with some of his team showing them the amended designs. Go on, in you go.'

The cast and crew were, gratifyingly, only too pleased about the changes, and though Libby asked if anyone would like to be considered for the part of the Queen, no one volunteered. New notes were given, the musical director resignedly accepted all the music changes, and the choreographer sighed.

'Much as usual, then,' grinned Libby, as she went to join the cast for the first scene, where the wicked witch Carabosse curses the baby Aurora in revenge for being refused an invitation to the christening. 'So far so good.'

'So, how do you think it went?' asked Ben two hours later as they walked back down the Manor drive.

'Very well, considering. Pete's made it a lot easier. He must have worked his socks off today. Good job he didn't have to go into town.'

'Oh, the beauties of broadband,' said Ben. 'He can work at home as much as he wants, these days.'

Libby spotted Patti and her friend straight away as they entered the pub.

'Hi,' she said, going over to the corner where they sat near the fire. 'This is Ben, Patti.'

Patti stood to shake hands. 'We met on Sunday, didn't we?'

'Oh, yes, of course you did, sorry.'

'This is my friend Anne, who lives just round the corner from you in New Barton Lane.'

'Really? When I was trying to hold of Patti I looked in the directory and couldn't see any A Douglases.'

'The phone's still in my mother's name.' Anne Douglas held out a small hand and Libby realised she was in a wheelchair. Her small, elfin features beamed out from beneath a feathered mousy fringe.

'I'm Ben.' Ben leaned over to shake hands and she turned her beam on him.

'Lovely to meet you. I've seen you both around of course, and I come to your theatre.'

'Do you? Oh, lovely. We've just been at a panto rehearsal.' Libby looked round at Patti. 'Sorry – what would you like to drink? Ben?'

'No, I'm getting them,' said Patti. 'This is to say thank you for propping me up over the last week.'

When Patti went off to the bar with Ben in tow to help carry, Libby sat down next to Anne. 'I can't say I've seen you around,' she said.

'I tend to drive everywhere, so you wouldn't, unless you saw me in your audience,' said Anne. 'Then I'm usually quite conspicuous.'

Libby laughed. 'I suppose you are, but I've still not seen you. Patti says you're a librarian in Canterbury.'

'Yes. We met when we were at uni.'

'Before she became a priest?'

'Yes. We were both doing Sociology.' Anne looked down at her lap. 'She's a very good person, you know. She was devastated about all the –' she paused and looked up. 'Well, you know.'

'I know. Having a death in your church is bad enough, without all the subsequent nastiness. Still, at least the villagers seem to be back on her side now.'

'Oh, yes, there's huge support. But that doesn't mean they've found out about the letters and emails, or the murders, does it?' Anne frowned. 'It's so unsettling for her.'

'Well, good that she can come here to you once a week for

some respite,' said Libby. 'If she does come once a week, of course.'

'Ever since she came to St Aldeberge. We were both delighted that she should be so near. I've lived here all my life, and when my mother died it was easier for me to stay here because the house had already been adapted.'

'Do you go to church here?' Libby asked, as Patti and Ben returned with the drinks.

Patti laughed. 'I've never been able to convince her to give God a try.'

Anne grinned. 'No, never been a God-botherer.'

'Which is one of the reasons she couldn't understand how deep some of the feelings within the church and its congregations go,' said Patti.

'I don't think Mrs Bidwell's murder was church-related, though,' said Libby. 'I think someone started the hate mails as a cover. Then there was the attempt to implicate you, to send suspicion well away from the real murderer and the real murder.'

'But what was it?' asked Anne. '*Who* was it?'

'That's what's such a puzzle,' said Libby. 'The police have cleared away some of the mud, but the central problem's still there.' She turned to Patti. 'I meant to say, how are the parishioners reacting to the murders now? They're reacting better to you, but they must now be worried about a murderer being at large.'

'Do you know,' said Patti, in tones of wonder, 'I don't think that's occurred to them! Yet they should be worried, shouldn't they?'

'Considering that two of their flower ladies have been done to death in suspicious circumstances, yes they should,' said Libby.

'Do you think,' said Ben, putting his pint back on the table, 'it is someone within the church community?'

Patti looked startled. 'Yes, I suppose I'd assumed it was.'

'But it might not be. The day Mrs – the first victim – was found, Libby tells me there were a lot of strangers in the church.'

'Yes.' Patti looked at Anne, then Libby and back at Ben. 'I never thought of that.'

'Did she appear to know any of them?'

'I couldn't say.' Patti rubbed her forehead. 'I was aware of her in her pew, but not that anyone spoke to her. Except when she took communion, of course. But the church was packed.'

'I expect the police have asked who was sitting in her pew with her?' said Libby.

'They asked me, but I couldn't tell them. I suppose they've asked everyone they can, but perhaps …' Patti looked worried.

'Perhaps people don't want to tell them?' suggested Ben. 'That would be a normal reaction, wouldn't it?'

'Perhaps Ian should have added that to his sermon on Sunday,' said Libby. 'But Ben's quite right. It might not have anything to with the church, Just someone – again – trying to cover up. We really need to know what that motive was.'

Chapter Fifteen

'That was really clever of you,' said Libby, as she and Ben strolled home. 'Everyone's been assuming it was someone within the congregation, but of course it needn't be at all. I really want to know what was going on in Mrs Bidwell's life.'

'Not a lot. She was a flower lady and in a wheelchair,' said Ben.

Libby dug him in the ribs. 'I'm glad you didn't say that in front of Anne back there,' she said. 'She doesn't seem to have a problem, and she's living alone and working.'

'But she's not in her eighties,' said Ben.

'True. But there must be something Mrs B knew, or saw, or perhaps possessed, that made someone kill her.'

'And Fran saying the other one was killed as a result of her death means she knew it or saw it, too.'

'Or saw who killed Mrs Bidwell.' Libby stopped outside number 17 while Ben got out his key.

'And how will you find that out?' asked Ben, as Libby tripped down the step and fell over Sidney.

'I don't know. I know Fran says we should stop, and I know we should, but I really want to know what happened. I can't ask Ian any more, there's no reason for me or Fran to be involved.'

'What about this son and the funeral?' Ben switched on lights and held up the whisky bottle. Libby nodded.

'What about the son?' she said. 'He doesn't know anything. He hasn't seen her for donkey's years.'

'Shame you don't have a reason to get inside the community somehow,' said Ben, handing over a whisky.

'No, I –' Libby stopped, her eyes brightening. 'But I do!'

'You do?' Ben looked amused.

'Drama! Patti's said twice she'd like to get something going over there. She even said she'd have to get me down there.'

'There you are, then. Two things, though – remember you've now got a panto to deal with here, and remember what happened last time you got involved with someone else's production.'

Libby called Patti as soon as she decently could the next day, giving her time to get back home from Steeple Martin.

'Listen,' she said. 'You know you said you'd like to get something going in St Aldeberge? Like panto?'

'Ye-es,' said Patti cautiously.

'Well, I was thinking, it's too late for panto this year, but how about a Nativity Pageant?'

There was such a long silence at the other end that Libby decided she must have mortally offended her new friend.

'Actually – I think it's a brilliant idea,' said Patti eventually. 'Almost no rehearsing and no lines to learn.'

'Do the children do a Nativity play?'

'In school they do.'

'Could you borrow them to be extra angels or sheep or something?'

'I expect so. Do you mean we have a grown-up Mary and Joseph?'

'Yes, and,' said Libby, struck by a brilliant idea, 'it could be Alice's daughter and her partner!'

'When would we do it?'

'That's up to you. Could it be a candlelight service?'

'Like the nine lessons and carols?'

'I don't know,' said Libby. 'Is it?'

'Yes, although we don't have one here. Christmas Eve would be the best time, wouldn't it?'

'If you say so.'

'I'll put it to the PCC – not formally, but I'll phone them all. Oh, this is so exciting! You will help us, though, won't you?'

'Of course,' said Libby, relieved, and feeling slightly guilty that this was the only reason she'd suggested it. Although, she said to herself after Patti had rung off, she was only doing it for the good of the village, the church and Patti.

'I thought it would be a good idea,' she said to Fran later on the phone. 'We could maybe find out more about Mrs Bidwell and the other woman.'

'Oh, Libby,' said Fran with a sigh. 'I said we've got nothing else to do with it. We did what Alice asked us in the first place. That's an end to it.'

'OK, if you're not interested I shall go on my own,' said Libby. 'I bet you'll want to know if I find anything out.'

'Let's not fight about it, Lib. And I can't imagine Ben will be that pleased about you getting even more involved.'

'As a matter of fact,' said Libby, with a certain air of smugness, 'it was his idea.'

'I don't believe it.'

'It was. Ask him. We went for a drink with Patti and her friend Anne after rehearsal last night. Oh, and her friend Anne's in a wheelchair. Nice woman.'

'Oh.' Fran sounded taken aback. 'Well, I suppose …'

'See? I said you'd be interested.'

'Look,' said Fran hastily, 'I don't necessarily want to be involved, but I'll help if I can.'

'That's a bit of an oxymoron!' laughed Libby.

'You know what I mean. When are you going down there?'

'I don't know, Patti's going to speak to the PCC first.'

'PCC?'

'Parochial Church Council,' said Libby. 'Not to be confused with the Parish Council, which is secular. More or less.'

'I shall never get the hang of the church,' said Fran with a sigh.

Ben arrived at lunchtime with a message from Hetty.

'She's asked Rosie for supper and wants us to go, too.'

'For protection?'

'Possibly! I must admit I was surprised. I didn't notice them getting on together particularly well in the summer.'

'No, neither did I. Of course, Rosie was often in the kitchen with us rather than the other guests. Maybe they saw more of each other than we thought?'

Ben and Libby had hosted a Writers' Weekend with Rosie as a tutor during the summer. Unfortunately, a body had turned up and rather spoilt it all. (*Murder at the Manor*)

'I expect she's just feeling she ought to, as Rosie isn't the ordinary sort of faceless tenant. Anyway, I said we'd go.'

'I wonder if Rosie's given up on the dating site since Monday,' said Libby later, as they trudged together up the Manor drive. Ahead lights shone out of the theatre where the musical director and choreographer were rehearsing the chorus in the new words and music for the pantomime.

'You haven't heard from her since then, so maybe she has,' said Ben, pushing open the heavy oak door to the Manor. But from the sound of the voices coming from the kitchen, Rosie hadn't.

'And there's this one man,' she was saying, 'who seems ideal. Such a gentleman.'

Hetty grunted, and Ben led the way into the kitchen.

'Still at it, then, Rosie?' said Libby, going forward to give Hetty a kiss.

Rosie, pink in the face, gave a little laugh. 'Well,' she said, 'you know. Research.'

'You said on Monday you were going to stop.' Ben was pouring a noble claret into glasses for himself and Libby.

'Looking for myself, yes.' Rosie cleared her throat.

'Well, on your own head be it,' said Libby. 'How are you, Hetty?'

Hetty had, as usual provided a sumptuous meal, but left most of the talking to her three guests, which made Libby certain that she had indeed felt an obligation to invite Rosie, as tenant of a family property, but needed Ben and herself as back-up.

'Can't see,' she said eventually, when the talk turned again to the dating site, 'what you want with another man at your age.'

Rosie opened her mouth and shut it again.

'Mum!' reproved Ben. 'Rosie said, she's only using it academically.'

'Didn't sound like it.' Hetty rose and began gathering plates. 'I'd be careful, gal, if I were you.'

'What do you know about these sites, Hetty?' Libby asked, amused.

'I watch the telly, don't I, and read the papers. Great place for them stalkers, dating sites. Young blokes looking for old women to get at their money.'

'Old –?' gasped Rosie.

'Older, then,' conceded Hetty. 'See it all the time.'

'Well, there's a plot for you, Rosie,' said Libby, smacking Ben on the hand to stop him laughing.

'I'm working on something quite different,' said Rosie, whose colour was still heightened.

'Is it your usual genre?' asked Libby, trying to get the conversation back from the brink of disaster.

'A family-relationship novel, yes,' said Rosie, calming down a little. 'Tell me, did you find any more out about your murder method?'

'On the internet, yes,' said Libby, 'although the police are thoughtlessly not telling us anything, so we've no confirmation. But Fran and I are off the case now we've done what we were asked to, so I doubt if we'll hear any more about it.' She avoided Ben's surprised stare.

'Oh, you'll have more time then,' Rosie began.

'Sadly, she won't,' said Ben, 'she and our friend Peter have just had to step in to rescue the pantomime.'

'Didn't tell me,' said Hetty, serving bread and butter pudding.

'Didn't think you'd be interested, Mum,' said Ben, accepting his plate.

'Theatre's next door, ain't it? Course I'm interested. Who's doing the costumes?'

Ben and Libby exchanged surprised looks.

'The usual team, I think,' said Libby. 'I don't know how far they've got.'

'I'll do yours, if you like,' said Hetty. 'If you're gonna be in it.'

'Oh, Hetty!' Libby felt her face go pink with pleasure. 'Yes, I am – I'm the Queen!'

Rosie, looking slightly put out, picked at her bread and butter pudding. Ben took pity on her.

'Actually, Rosie, that's given me an idea.'

Rosie looked up.

'Hetty's theory about stalkers on dating sites. I wonder if that was what was behind our first murder?'

'Mrs Bidwell on a dating site?' said Libby. 'I wouldn't have thought so! She was in her eighties, and I doubt if she had a computer. She sounded such a died-in-the-wool traditionalist.'

'Yes,' said Rosie, 'but Ben's right.' Her interest piqued, she leant forward. 'It wouldn't have to be a dating site, it could simply be someone visiting her, making a fuss of her. Hetty's right, too, you hear of it all the time. The carers who persuade old people to leave them their money, the fake solicitors – there are so many!'

Libby, surprised, looked round the table to see Hetty and Ben nodding. 'You're right,' she said. 'It could be exactly that. I wonder if the police have thought of it?'

'I expect they have,' said Ben. 'There's no flies on Ian. They'll be looking at the will to see if there've been any changes recently, and who benefits.'

'Not her son and daughter, then?'

'If they haven't seen her for thirty years, probably not.'

'Hmm.' Libby tapped her spoon against her plate and stared at her wineglass. 'What would you do with it in a story, Rosie?'

Rosie picked up her own glass. 'I'd have to think about that. It would have to be the least likely person on the surface, of course.'

'Which would probably be Patti herself,' said Libby, 'and we know it isn't her. Oh, well, we'll see what the pageant turns up.'

The minute she said it, she could have kicked herself.

'What pageant?' said Rosie.

With a sigh, Libby explained.

'You've got time to do that, then,' said Rosie.

'Rosie,' said Ben, with a rather tired smile, 'this is to help a community get back together, not to help a writer with a plot.'

Hetty caught Libby's eye and gave her a grim smile. Rosie

pushed her plate away, and Libby put a hand on her wrist.

'Rosie, I do have other things in my life, you know. I'm sorry if you feel I'm neglecting you, but I didn't ask you to come, did I?'

This time, Rosie looked as if she was going to cry, and Libby hastily topped up her wineglass.

'Come on, cheer up,' she said, 'you've been a great help to us already.'

'On a case you're not even on any more,' said Rosie.

'But on which we might be able to offer help,' persisted Libby.

'Hmm.' Rosie sipped at her wine and didn't look at anyone. Hetty stood up.

'Coffee?' she asked.

Predictably, Rosie refused coffee and Ben's offer to walk her home, thanking Hetty for inviting her before trudging off down the Manor drive managing to look like a refugee being turned from the door.

'That went well,' said Ben, leading his mother and Libby into the cosy sitting room. 'I should think she might go home, soon.'

'Not if her kitchen's not finished,' said Libby, 'but I meant what I said. The suggestion of a stalker – or rather – of someone trying to do her out of her savings – is a good one, and we wouldn't have thought of it without her.'

'We wouldn't have thought of it without my mum,' said Ben, and gave her a hug.

Chapter Sixteen

When Patti called the following morning to say everyone she'd spoken to was in favour of a version of the Nativity story live in the church, Libby was delighted. There was a panto rehearsal that night, but she agreed to go over and have a brief meeting with some of the people involved that afternoon. She called Fran to tell her the news, but didn't invite her to the meeting. She had a feeling that Fran, with her atheistic tendencies and complete non-understanding of the Church, would be a hindrance in this particular instance.

Ben, too, was delighted, and even offered to cook their evening meal. Not that this was an unusual occurrence, Ben was very hands-on as a house-sharer, which had come as a great surprise to Libby, whose former husband had been a died-in-the-wool chauvinist.

She drove over to the St Aldeberge vicarage in the drippy greyness of a November afternoon. Patti was coaxing life into a fire in a shabby, comfortable room at the back of the house, and five other people, one of whom was Alice, sat round watching her.

'Sheila Johnson I believe you've met,' said Patti, waving a hand at the large lady whom Libby had last seen in the church, 'Kaye Cook, who also helps with the flowers,' she indicated a small woman with mousy hair and a pursed mouth, 'and Gavin Brice and Maurice Blanchard who are our churchwardens. Alice you know.'

Gavin Brice was a pleasant-looking middle-aged man with a round pink face and an air of permanent cheeriness, who didn't look as though he had ever disapproved of Patti. Maurice Blanchard, on the other hand, was tall and lugubrious, his long cheeks creased with vertical lines. He eyed Libby with vague suspicion as she smiled brightly round at the company, and Patti began her opening remarks.

'So all we have to do is come down the aisle in procession,' said Libby, when Patti had finished, 'and take up various positions as the story is read out. Luke, would you say, Patti?'

'With the Magi from Matthew tacked on,' agreed Patti. 'Everybody happy with that?'

'What about the Annunciation?' asked Maurice. 'That's in Luke.'

'We could start with that, and then when we get to Luke Two the progression can begin,' said Patti. 'What do you think, Libby?'

And so the arrangements went on until Libby suggested they might ask for volunteers to take the various parts.

'Your Tracey would be ideal for Mary,' she said to Alice. 'Would she do it?'

'She wouldn't have to ride on a donkey, would she?' asked Alice doubtfully.

'I don't suppose we'd find a willing donkey,' laughed Libby. 'No. Would her partner do Joseph?'

'No.' Alice shook her head firmly. 'Specially if it's Christmas Eve. Darren goes to the pub on Christmas Eve.'

'How old was Joseph?' asked Gavin.

'Older than Mary, but under forty as far as we can tell,' said Patti, eyeing Gavin nervously.

'Oh, not me, love!' Gavin's laugh was as cheerful as his face. 'I meant my own Joseph. He's much of an age with young Tracey, isn't he?'

'Yes, he's a definite possibility,' said Patti looking relieved. 'Now, shepherds and Kings.'

'Why don't you,' said Libby, 'put a notice up in your community shop asking for volunteers?'

'That's an idea.' Sheila Johnson nodded. 'Pity we don't open again until Monday.'

'Yes, but you've got Sunday in between. Patti can make an announcement then. Bit different from last Sunday's, but cheerier.' Libby beamed at them all.

So it was decided and Patti and Alice went into the kitchen to make tea.

'So you're the detective lady?' said Sheila Johnson. 'I saw you when you were looking for Alice, didn't I? With the other lady.'

'You did, but I'm not a detective,' said Libby.

'And why are you helping with this whatever-it-is, pageant?' asked Maurice.

'Because I'm an ex-professional actor, I still act in and direct community theatre and Patti asked me,' said Libby, stung by his attitude.

'I think it's great,' said Gavin. 'I've said for years we should have a drama group here. I have to go over to Felling if I want to do anything.'

'Oh, you act, do you?' Libby turned to him.

'A bit.' Gavin put on the modest air Libby associated with the amateur who thought he was a good deal better than he was. 'I'd do more, but Felling's a long way off to pop over in the evenings.'

'I don't think I know it,' said Libby.

'It's a couple of miles further inland, at the end of our little inlet,' said Kaye, speaking for the first time in a surprisingly deep voice. 'The police keep an eye on it.'

Everyone looked at her.

'Do they?' said Libby and Sheila together.

'They think illegal immigrants are coming ashore there,' said Kaye.

'In Felling?' Maurice almost sneered. 'Where would they go when they got there? You can barely get out of the town as it is.'

'Why can't you?' asked Libby. Four voices answered her.

'One road in –'

'Through the Sand Gate –'

'Ring road –'

'One way system –'

Libby laughed, as Patti and Alice came back into the room with a tray of mugs.

111

'What was that about?' asked Alice. Libby told her, and it was Alice's turn to laugh.

'Felling is a very old town, possibly even Roman, but certainly developed in Saxon times, and became very important in medieval times. Now, it's simply very small, with very narrow streets and the only way in or out is through the Sand Gate. Anyone trying to slip out unnoticed would be hard put to it.'

'In that case, why are the police watching it?' asked Kaye reasonably. 'They must have some kind of information.'

'Perhaps it's not illegal immigrants?' suggested Gavin. 'Perhaps it's drugs. You could smuggle those through in an ordinary car.'

'Coming ashore at Felling Quay?' said Maurice, still sneering. 'You can't get anything bigger than a rowing boat up the creek between us and Felling. It's unnavigable.'

Gavin shrugged. 'I don't know then. It's not important, anyway, is it?'

'Not in the least,' said Patti, handing out mugs. 'Anyone want a biscuit? I haven't any cake, I'm afraid.'

When the other four had gone and Patti, Alice and Libby sat alone around the fire, Libby had a suggestion to make.

'I quite understand that you might feel you should do it,' she said, 'but Kaye's got such a beautiful voice, I wondered if she might do the reading?'

Patti smiled. 'I was going to suggest it myself. She often does the readings in church for that reason.'

'And what's up with Maurice? He spent the whole meeting looking like Eeyore.'

'That's just his way.' Alice sighed. 'He lives alone and likes to make sure everyone knows he's an old misogynist.'

'Only he isn't really.' Patti giggled. 'He's got a lady friend that no one knows about.'

'Really?' Alice looked astonished.

'Yes, really, but don't ask me any more, because I won't say. He's also kindness itself, and by far the largest donor to the collection.'

'He'd actually make a good king – Melchior, probably. "Myrrh is mine, its bitter perfume, breathes a life of gathering doom",' said Libby.

'That's Balthazar, and it's gloom, not doom,' corrected Patti, 'although it comes to the same thing, and I see what you mean. Are we going to do that, by the way? Intersperse with hymns?'

'Gosh, yes! I'd forgotten that. All nice traditional ones. That one, and While Shepherds Watched ...'

'O Little Town of Bethlehem?' suggested Alice.

'And *not* Little Donkey,' said Patti.

'Well, of course not, that's not traditional,' said Libby.

'You'd be amazed at the people who think it is,' said Patti gloomily.

'So, Gavin. He'd make a cheerful innkeeper? Or shepherd?'

'Oh, innkeeper,' said Alice. 'He's always happy-looking, and the innkeeper did give them a place to sleep, after all.'

'Is he always that happy?' asked Libby. 'And why did he disapprove of you? He doesn't seem to now.'

'I don't really know,' said Patti. 'I think he keeps his real self under wraps, like Maurice, although I don't know why I think that. His son Joe's a nice boy and they seem to get on fine, so I don't think there's anything nasty going on. Perhaps a bit of tragedy. I suppose it was mainly because I'm a woman that they both disapproved. I know Maurice at least has very high church leanings.'

'His wife left,' said Alice. 'Perhaps that's it.'

'Oh, dear. When ?' asked Libby.

'Oh, years ago now. Before we came to the village. It's always been just him and Joe.'

'What about Sheila and Kaye?'

'What about them?' said Patti.

'Are they married? Have they been here long? How did they get on with Joan Bidwell and Marion Longfellow?'

'Is that what this is all about?' asked Patti shrewdly. 'An undercover investigation into the murders?'

'No!' said Libby, feeling a little heat creeping into her cheeks.

'Well, if it is, I think it's a very good idea,' said Patti, laughing. 'The police don't seem to be doing anything.'

'I expect they are, only they don't have to keep everyone up to speed,' said Libby. 'Fran and I, having served our purpose, are no longer in the loop. Once we'd put him on to the Willoughby Oak, that was it.'

'Did you?' said Patti.

'What's that?' asked Alice.

'It's place near here where they hold Black Magic rites,' said Libby, 'Yes, we told Ian and he went to look just after Fran and I did, and warned off that Tim Bolton I told you about.'

'So you've seen it?' said Patti.

'Who's Tim Bolton?' asked Alice.

Libby patiently explained the whole saga of the Willoughby Oak, Cunning Mary, the witch trials, and finally the involvement of Tim Bolton and Lewis's production company.

'And has that helped the investigation into the murders?' Alice was frowning.

'It has a bit, because of the insinuation that Black Magic was involved first in Joan Bidwell's death, and subsequently Marion Longfellow's. But we – the police, I mean – don't think it's actually someone involved in Black Magic, simply using it as a cover.'

'It was my interest in all the alternative religions and deliverance that did it,' said Patti with a sigh. 'That's why all the mutterings started. I wonder if it was the murderer or someone else?'

'We thought,' said Libby slowly, 'that the murder was committed as it was in order to look like a natural death, so perhaps whoever started the Black Magic rumour wasn't the murderer, but just a nasty busybody, and then the murderer latched on to it.'

'Oh.' Alice didn't look convinced.

'Anyway, I must get going. Panto rehearsal tonight, and we're still trying to knock the damn thing into shape. Trouble is, with volunteers, you can't sack them.'

'No, you can't,' said Patti with feeling. 'Oh, not you Alice.'

'Will you let me know when you've assembled a cast?' asked Libby, standing up and reaching for her coat.

'Oh, yes, I'd like you to come and cast a professional eye on it, perhaps direct it a bit?'

'Yes, I will, but bear in mind I shall be rehearsing in the evenings.'

'Not every evening, surely?' said Alice.

'No, but I don't necessarily want to spend my evenings coming to other rehearsals,' said Libby.

'And so you shouldn't,' said Patti. 'It's very kind of you to help, Libby. We just need someone to point us in the right direction.'

'And that,' Libby told Ben later, 'was how it was left. Honestly, Alice is as bad as Rosie thinking everyone should do what she wants.'

'Perhaps that's what normally happens,' said Ben.

'Not if I know it. Alice's husband Bob does just as he likes, and I think their Tracey's the same. And I should think she lets her grandson push her around, too.'

'Rosie, on the other hand,' said Ben, dishing up a prawn stir-fry, 'is used to people doing her bidding, even poor old Andrew Wylie. Must come of being a semi-celebrity.'

'Anyway, I can't see how I can be of much help as they'll be rehearsing in the evenings and so will I.' Libby forked up rice. 'This is nice.'

'We could go down on an evening we're not rehearsing,' said Ben.

'We?' Libby turned to stare at him. 'Why are you so interested?'

He shrugged. 'I don't know. I suppose it rubs off, this detection business. Besides, I feel sorry for Patti.'

When Ben and Libby arrived at the theatre, Peter had the cast and crew gathered at the front of the auditorium discussing the rehearsal schedule. He waved them to seats.

'Now,' he was saying, 'I know that formerly you had all been asked to be present at every rehearsal, which doesn't seem to be necessary.'

There was a murmuring and shaking of heads.

'So we're going to work out who we need in what scenes and set rehearsals accordingly. The chorus can rehearse separately until we need to coalesce.'

'What's that?' could be heard muttered through the rows of seats.

'Until we have to come together,' grinned Peter. 'I was saving your blushes.'

A splutter of laughter grew into a roar, and Peter held up a hand for silence.

'So let's organise ourselves so that we know what we're doing. This is what I've worked out so far. Tell me if I've got anything wrong.'

'No one would dare,' whispered Libby, getting out her rehearsal sheet and a pencil. 'At least we'll get some time off to go to St Aldeberge.'

Chapter Seventeen

Much to Libby's surprise, Patti called on Sunday afternoon to say the parts were all cast.

'We put a notice in the window of the community shop even though we were closed, and one on the church notice board, and even before the service this morning we had so much interest we'd been able to cast it. In fact we're having our first meeting tonight. I don't suppose you could come?'

'Regretfully not,' said Libby. 'Both Ben and I consumed vast quantities of his mother's very good red wine at lunch, so we wouldn't be safe to drive. What a pity.'

'Have you any other nights off this week that you could pop down? I don't want to put you under any pressure.'

'As it happens, Tuesday's free.' Libby decided to keep quiet about Friday also being free. She wanted the occasional night off.

'I'll try and get them to come on Tuesday, then,' said Patti. 'I'll let you know as soon as I can.'

On Tuesday, after a productive rehearsal on Monday, Ben drove them both to St Aldeberge. The church was surprisingly brightly lit, and Patti was serving coffee in the Narthex.

'Hello again,' said Kaye Cook. 'You see we got going straight away!'

'Yes, it's great,' said Libby, surveying the thirty or so people of all ages milling about. 'What are the children going to do?'

'Mini shepherds and angels.' Sheila Johnson came up behind them carrying two mugs.

'Thank you,' said Libby, taking one. 'This is Ben. Ben, this is Kaye and this is Sheila. Are you both taking part?'

'Kaye's doing the reading,' said Sheila.

'Which apparently you suggested?' Kaye smiled at Libby.

'I did, yes. You have a lovely voice. What about you, Sheila?'

'No, I'm just going to help with the organising. And I'll be doing the flowers, of course. Kaye will help with that.'

'Are you both on the flower rota, then?' asked Ben.

'The only two left,' said Sheila with a sigh.

'Oh, I see.' Ben nodded and looked at Libby.

'I actually asked Patti how Joan Bidwell managed the flowers in her wheelchair?' said Libby, although she couldn't remember if she *had* asked Patti.

Kaye shrugged. 'She had to ask for things to be lifted down for her, but otherwise she was fine. We've a ramp into the Narthex, and it's level all the way to the Chancel steps, and into the vestry and the Lady Chapel.'

'Have you ever heard what became of the wheelchair after she died?' asked Libby, all innocence.

'No.' Sheila frowned and looked at Kaye. 'Wasn't it there?'

'No, it was gone, that's why no one went back to look for her,' said Kaye. 'Gavin looked for it after we found her, but it was gone.'

'Oh, yes. Things were a bit confused, weren't they? Now,' she turned back to Libby and Ben. 'Will you excuse me? I'm in charge of the children this evening. Patti will be free in a moment.'

'So who else is in the pageant?' Libby asked Kaye, as Sheila bustled off to round up the children, some of whom were in Cub and Brownie uniforms and had no doubt been dragooned into taking part.

'Gavin's the innkeeper, Maurice is Balthazar, both just as you suggested. Tracey didn't want to be Mary – didn't think it would be dignified, apparently.'

Libby laughed. 'Could that be translated as couldn't be bothered?'

'She's also terribly tired,' said Kaye, pulling a face. 'You'd think no one else had ever been pregnant, except herself of course. Alice is looking after little Nathaniel more and more these days.'

'And will no doubt have to have him when Tracey comes home with the new baby,' said Libby. 'Honestly, some of them don't know they're born, do they? I never had my mother to rely on when I had mine.'

'Me neither,' said Kaye, 'and I've made sure that my daughter doesn't rely on me.'

'Oh, have you grandchildren? I didn't think you were old enough,' said Libby.

'Not yet.' Kaye's face lit up with a grin. 'I'm just preparing the ground.'

'How did you get on with Joan Bidwell, if you don't mind me asking?' said Libby after a pause while they watched Patti speaking to the children. Ben had wandered away to look at stone plaques in the walls.

There was a pause before Kaye answered.

'Not very well,' she said eventually. 'She was opinionated and bitter. She hated having a female vicar, complained loudly about new forms of service, hated having the children in services – you name it, she disapproved of it. I was practically a scarlet woman, being divorced.'

'It's astonishing that there are people like that still around,' said Libby. 'Was there anybody she did like?'

'I don't think she actually *liked* anyone,' said Kaye, 'but she tolerated Sheila. Mainly because she was a stay-at-home wife and mother, and Joan viewed her business as a "little hobby".'

'Sheila's business?'

'She paints and sells individual greetings cards. I say individual, she will do them to order, but they're mainly prints.'

'Really? I shall have to talk to her. I paint a bit myself.'

Kaye looked dubious. 'Oh. Right.'

Libby laughed. 'No, I do. I paint little sea views for a gallery in Nethergate. Some of those are turned into cards, too.'

Kaye's face cleared. 'Ah! For Guy Wolfe's gallery?'

'Yes.' Libby was pleased. 'He's married to my friend Fran. I introduced them, in fact.'

'Is that the psychic lady?'

'That's right.'

'Can't she find out what happened to Joan and Marion?' Kaye suddenly shivered. 'Only it's a bit scary, being one of only two flower ladies left, after two of us have been murdered.'

'I wish she could,' said Libby, 'but she can't do these things to order, and we have no official standing in the investigation.'

'But Alice and Patti asked you to help, didn't they?'

'Yes, they did, and we helped as much as we could, although I'm not sure that we didn't do more damage. I keep feeling that if we hadn't interfered Marion Longfellow might still be alive.'

Kaye looked shocked. 'You weren't interfering. You'd been asked. And you didn't actually do anything, did you? Besides ...'

'Besides?' prompted Libby, after a moment.

Kaye looked at her quickly. 'Oh, nothing. It was just something Marion said.'

Libby's interest quickened. 'What was that? When?'

'It was when Sheila told us about you coming over to see Alice and Patti.'

'How did she know that was what we were doing?'

'Alice told her. She was picking up Nathaniel from school, and Sheila was picking up her grandson. So Sheila told us when we met that evening to discuss Christmas decorations.'

'And what did Marion say?'

'Nothing much. Just that it was about time somebody looked into it, and she'd tried to talk to someone.'

'She had? Who?'

Kaye looked surprised. 'I don't know. I thought she probably meant she'd tried to talk to the police, but they hadn't been around much. It just made me think she knew something. Or thought she did.'

'And if it wasn't the police she talked to, then it could have been the murderer,' said Libby grimly.

'Oh, God!' Kaye put her hand to her mouth.

'What's up?' Patti appeared before them. Libby told her.

'Will you tell the police?' said Kaye.

'Either I or Patti will,' said Libby. 'That's really very helpful,

Kaye. Although,' she said in a low voice to Patti as they walked towards the Chancel, 'it would have been a lot better if she or Sheila had something about this earlier. And Ian will have a fit.'

After that, she and Patti tried to assert some sort of order on their cast of characters. Mary and Joseph, a pair of flighty teenagers whose parents were both shepherds, did nothing but giggle. The shepherds were stolid and grim, the kings gloomy, and the child angels and shepherds fidgeted. Gavin, as the innkeeper, overacted in mime and made Mary and Joseph giggle even harder.

Eventually, the procession up the aisle was sorted out, the entrances of the shepherds and kings settled, (one lot from the vestry, the others from the Lady Chapel,) and the disposition of the angels (the choir stalls) established. Patti wiped her brow and asked why Libby ever got involved in theatre direction.

'I was going to suggest a children-only rehearsal some time this week during the day,' said Libby. 'I could do that. I don't suppose they all go to the same school, do they?'

'Sadly not, but we could probably get them together by four thirty in the church hall one day,' said Patti, turning to Kaye. 'Kaye, what do you think?'

'Good idea. Shall we suggest it now?'

The idea was adopted with a sense of relief by the adults, and the following day, Wednesday, was decided on as being the only day when no after-school activities were taking place.

'Come to me first,' said Patti, 'and I'll take you over. Can you be there, Sheila?'

'Of course,' said Sheila, now holding the hand of a small person in a cub uniform. 'I shall be bringing Jack anyway.' Jack beamed up at her.

'I'll see you tomorrow, then,' said Libby. 'And I'll make sure Ian gets the message,' she added to Kaye and Patti, while Sheila looked puzzled.

'But they'll tell her now,' she said to Ben as they drove away from the church. 'And I don't know whether to send Ian a text on his personal number now, or wait and call him in the morning.'

'Send him a text now,' said Ben. 'He's got the opportunity to ignore it and come back to you tomorrow or call you back.'

The phone rang almost immediately Libby had sent the text.

'What is it now?' Ian sounded tired.

'Just something I thought you ought to hear,' said Libby. 'You didn't have to ring me back straight away.'

'I'm aware of the fact that occasionally you offer me a little gem.'

'Sarky,' said Libby, and told him what she'd heard.

'And that's all?' Ian sounded puzzled.

'It sounds as if Marion Longfellow either knew or saw something to do with Joan Bidwell's murder, doesn't it?'

'I wonder who she tried to talk to. I'll check the original reports, see if there's anything there.' He became brisk. 'Thanks, Lib. I'll come back to you.'

'I bet she tried to talk to the murderer, not the police,' said Ben, as Libby switched the phone off.

'I don't suppose we'll ever know,' said Libby with a sigh.

Chapter Eighteen

Although she wasn't due in St Aldeberge until four thirty, Libby decided to go down in time to see the community shop while it was open, and accordingly arrived at a quarter to two.

'Just realised,' she said to Patti, who was behind the counter, 'it's your day off, isn't it? And now we've eaten into it.'

'We won't be very long,' said Patti. 'I'll drive over afterwards. Are you rehearsing your panto again tonight?'

'Yes. Will you and Anne be having a drink?'

'We will.' Patti gave her a conspiratorial grin. 'See you there. Now, did you come to have a look at us, or to buy something?'

'To have a look, really,' confessed Libby, 'but I must say, those home-made cakes look wonderful.'

'Oh, they are. All made by members of the WI.'

Libby bought a cake and went outside to wait for Patti, who soon appeared with the other person who'd been helping in the shop.

'This is Dora Walters, Libby.'

'Nice to meet you,' said the woman, holding out a hand.

'And you,' said Libby, shaking it and reflecting that all the women in this village looked as if they still lived in the fifties.

'You're here to help with the Nativity, aren't you?' said Dora, folding her hands over her handbag.

'That's right.' Libby looked at Patti to see if she wanted to add anything. 'Just at the beginning. I don't suppose I'll need to come back.'

'Libby's in panto over at Steeple Martin,' explained Patti. 'She's a bit busy to help us regularly.'

'Oh, I always go to that panto,' said Dora, with a "there now" sort of hand gesture. 'Thought I knew your face, but I didn't put it on the stage, somehow! You were the Fairy Queen the other year, weren't you?'

'Yes, I was. Glad you enjoy them.'

'Oh, we do.' Dora drew a little closer, confidingly. 'Do you know, we even go without any children!'

Libby laughed. 'A lot of our regulars don't bring children. I shouldn't worry.'

'Would you like to come and have a cuppa? Vicar?' Dora turned to Patti, who glanced at Libby and caught an imperceptible nod.

'Yes, we'd love to, wouldn't we, Libby? We didn't stop for one in the shop.'

'Good.' Dora beamed on them both. 'Come along then. Just round here.'

Dora's cottage was in the middle of a terrace, not unlike Libby's own, although the plethora of china ornaments and lacy mats were distinctly unlike. Dora bade them sit down and hurried out to the kitchen.

'Why did you want to come?' whispered Patti.

'Village gossip,' Libby whispered back. 'Useful. And I told Ian what Kaye said, by the way.'

Dora bustled back in.

'Won't be long,' she said. 'So, how do you come to be helping our vicar?'

'We have mutual friends,' said Libby, 'and we thought it would be a good idea. Besides, the village needs cheering up after those awful murders, doesn't it?'

Dora sniffed. 'Don't know what it's coming to,' she said, although Libby wasn't sure what "it" was. 'Murders in the church, no less. Not that I go much meself. Chapel, I was, but there isn't a chapel to go to round here.'

'You're not from the village, then?' said Libby.

'North Kent, I am,' said Dora. 'Excuse me, I'd better see if the kettle's boiled.'

'I assumed she was one of your flock,' said Libby.

'Because of the shop? Oh, no, it's nothing to do with the church. I just help out because I want to,' said Patti.

'And it's a good way of keeping your finger on the pulse.'

'There is that,' said Patti, with a rather shamefaced grin.

'That's why I –' Libby stopped as Dora came back with a tray of tea.

'There,' she said. 'Do you take sugar?'

When they were settled with their tea, Libby returned to the previous conversation.

'So what sort of chapel did you go to in North Kent?'

'Nonconformist. Quite strict, it was. Can't say I was sorry not to go no more.'

'Funny, isn't it,' said Patti. 'All the Nonconformist movements were set up because they didn't agree with the Act of Uniformity, and all the regulations surrounding worship, yet they've become even stricter than the church.'

'I don't know about that,' said Dora. 'I just went to Chapel because me mum and dad did. Married there, and all.'

'And when did you come here?'

'My Fred was a miner, so we come down here.' She shrugged. 'All gone now, o' course.'

'Didn't you go to the Miners' Reunion service in the church?' asked Patti.

'No, vicar, but I went to the party after. Although that went a bit flat, didn't it?'

'Yes, poor Mrs Bidwell,' said Libby.

Dora snorted. 'She was a difficult old besom, that one. Always complaining about the stuff we had in the shop. Said it was too expensive.'

'That's true,' said Patti. 'And if I happened to be there, she would never be served by me.'

'Oh, dear,' said Libby. 'But I suppose you get all sorts in the shop, not just the church congregation. Some of the others must be difficult.'

'It's mainly the old folks,' said Dora, 'who can't get to the big supermarkets. Some of the young mums come to buy fresh veg, but most o'them say it's too dear. That Gavin Brice, he do take some of them up to Felling or into Nethergate in his minibus.'

'That's nice of him,' said Libby, thinking that, apart from his overacting, she rather liked Gavin Brice.

'You'll never believe it, but Maurice takes a regular group in his car. And drives some of them to hospital,' said Patti. 'He used to take Mrs Bidwell.'

'That longfaced strip o'bacon?' said Dora in disbelief. 'Well, I never!'

'Good old Maurice,' said Libby. 'So you know all the people who go to church even though you don't go yourself, Dora?'

'Can't help it in a village this size,' said Dora. 'The things I could tell you.' She sent a quick glance to Patti. 'But there, I won't.'

Bugger, thought Libby.

'Actually, Dora,' said Patti, 'I'm sorry to rush away, but I've got to open the village hall for the –' there was the smallest pause, 'flower ladies. They're starting the decorations for the church. Don't worry, Libby, you finish your tea and I'll come back and collect you.'

Libby thought this was a very obvious ploy, but Dora didn't seem to notice and after she'd seen Patti out, she came back to her chair and leant forward confidentially.

'As I was saying, there's things go on here that the vicar wouldn't know about.' She shook her head. 'Some o'them young people, the things they get up to of a night. Drinking out in the street – and worse.'

Libby forbore to say that the youth of St Aldeberge were hardly in the minority in this respect.

'And there's more than one couple not abiding by their marriage vows.' Dora nodded wisely. 'That Marion Longfellow, for a start.'

'Mrs Longfellow?' Libby was surprised. 'But I didn't think she had a husband. Wasn't she a widow?'

'Oh, *she* were, yes,' said Dora, looking saintly.

'Oh,' said Libby at a loss. Could she ask who?

'And him younger than her, too. Although not much, and she wasn't bad-looking, I'll give her that.' Dora lifted the teapot. 'More tea?'

'Yes, please,' said Libby. 'So do you think this man, whoever he is, could have been Marion's killer?'

Dora looked surprised. 'I though she was killed by same one as old Bidwell?'

'We don't know. I mean the police don't know. You must have heard what people think in the village, though?'

'As to that,' said Dora, going pink, 'there was a lot of talk about the vicar at first. Course, I never held with it. Good to me, she's always been.'

'Yes, I know about that,' said Libby. 'But that stopped after Mrs Longfellow died, didn't it?'

'Course it did. Weren't even here, were she? *I* know Wednesdays she sometimes goes off after she does her stint at the shop and often comes back Thursday mornings, but looks like some folk didn't.'

'So you think it was someone who didn't know the vicar very well? Or didn't know her routine?'

'She didn't always come back on Thursdays, mind,' said Dora, determined to be fair. 'Sometimes she came back Wednesday nights. I see her, see. I see her headlights as she turns onto her drive. Can't help it.'

'But you think most people don't know?'

Dora shrugged. 'Don't know. Maybe just me because I work with her at the shop.'

'What about Mrs Longfellow? Do you think most people in the village knew she was having an affair?'

'Now, I didn't say that, did I?' Dora looked uncomfortable.

'You implied that she was having an affair with a married man,' said Libby. 'Was it just guesswork?'

'People talk,' said Dora obscurely.

'So some of the village thought she was and talked about it?'

'That's about it.' Dora drew herself up and tried to go back to looking saintly. 'And I won't say any more to blacken her memory.'

At this moment Patti reappeared in the doorway and Libby reluctantly stood up.

'Thank you so much for the tea, Dora. I hope I see you

again.'

'Did you get any more out of her?' Patti asked as they walked back towards the vicarage.

'Not a lot, but she implied that Marion Longfellow was having an affair with a married man. When I pressed her on it she rather backtracked and said it was just gossip.'

Patti made a face. 'I ought to be shocked, but actually, I wouldn't be surprised.'

Libby was shocked. 'But she was a flower lady!'

'They are normal people.' Patti laughed at the expression on Libby's face. 'But funnily enough, Marion was the one who was most competitive about the flowers, at least when Joan Bidwell was alive, even though they pretended to be the greatest of friends.'

'I thought Joan Bidwell didn't like anyone?'

'She didn't, but Marion used to bring her to church and she had to be grateful. She used to go into Felling with Gavin sometimes.'

Libby frowned. 'Then why was Gavin picking Marion up the morning he found her dead if she normally drove herself?'

'Apparently she got nervous about coming to church, so Gavin started driving out to pick her up. Completely out of his way, of course. I told you Sheila Johnson seemed to be doing most of the flowers, didn't I? That was because Marion was nervous. And Kaye works.'

'I expect it was also because of the feeling being stirred up against you,' said Libby.

Patti sighed. 'Of course. Are you going to wait here with me until the children arrive, or have you got somewhere else to go?'

'No, I confess I was being nosy about the shop, and hoping to pick up some gossip. That's the only reason I came over early.'

'Well, you did pick up some gossip, even if it's not very useful.' Patti opened the vicarage door and ushered her visitor inside.

'Oh, I don't know.' Libby took off her coat. 'She was also complaining about the young people's behaviour, and it did occur to me that if you have a regular group of youngsters who

128

hang around the village at night they might have seen something the night Marion died.'

'If they saw anything in the village it would simply be someone driving through. You couldn't tell where they were going.'

'But,' said Libby, frowning again, 'if someone was driving in from the coast? Or towards it? There's only the one road.'

'With a lot of houses along it,' said Patti, leading the way into the kitchen. 'No, that wouldn't work. Have you had enough of Dora's tea, or would you like more?'

'I don't think I could,' said Libby with a grin, 'but we could have a piece of my new cake.'

Settled at Patti's kitchen table, Libby returned to the subject of Marion Longfellow.

'I suppose if we could find out who the man was we might have a viable suspect, but as Dora said, we thought the same person killed both women, so why would Marion's lover kill Joan Bidwell?'

'To keep her quiet?' suggested Patti, picking crumbs off the plate.

'And then killed Marion because she found out? That's a possibility.

'Why didn't you ask Dora who it was?'

'I don't think she'd have told me. She got a bit evasive, as I said. So who could it have been, do *you* think?'

'It could be someone from outside the village,' said Patti.

'No, because if it was, Dora wouldn't have known anything about him.'

'Oh, yes. Well,' said Patti, looking miserable, 'I don't really know. This isn't my area.'

'I'll help,' said Libby. 'Start with the people she knew at church. Gavin, obviously, but it can't be him because he's not married. Maurice? Oh, no. You said he was a widower with a secret girlfriend.'

Patti looked at her severely. 'Who is a very respectable widow. They keep things to themselves and I'm not saying anything more about them.'

'Who else, then?'

Patti listed a few men who were regular churchgoers, including the occasional organist.

'But there must be a lot of other people in the village she knew. I got the feeling she had a good social life, and that didn't centre on the church.'

'So we need to ask other people who might have been her friends,' said Libby. 'Apart from Joan Bidwell, who were the women she was friendly with at the church?'

'I don't know. She was vaguely pleasant to everyone. I don't know much about her, except that she didn't like me.'

'Don't look so miserable,' said Libby. 'You don't have to know the ins and outs of every parishioner.'

'But I ought to be able to help if they've got problems.'

'You could hardly help this one, though,' said Libby. 'Her problem is that she's dead.'

Chapter Nineteen

The children's rehearsal went well, and, at the end of it, when mothers and grandmothers arrived to collect their charges, Libby buttonholed Sheila Johnson.

'Any idea if Marion Longfellow was having a relationship with anybody? Only I've picked up a rumour.'

Sheila's lips tightened. 'If she wasn't, it wasn't for want of trying. She'd thrown her hat at practically everyone over fifty in the surrounding area.'

Another Rosie, thought Libby. And then – she gasped.

'What is it?' said Sheila.

'I was just wondering – do you happen to know if she used internet dating sites?'

Sheila looked bewildered. 'No idea! I don't even know if she had a computer.'

'Right, thanks. But you don't know about a current relationship, anyway?'

Sheila shook her head, and Libby went on to Alice, whose small grandson Nathaniel was performing, even if his parents weren't. She asked the same question. She got the same answer.

'Why hasn't anyone mentioned this before?' said Libby, exasperated. 'It's surely relevant to the investigation.'

'It's gossip,' said Alice, her nose lifting slightly.

'In a murder investigation, Alice, gossip is relevant,' said Libby. 'You wouldn't believe the trouble that's caused by people deciding for themselves what's relevant and what isn't.'

'Well, I'm sorry, but I don't like to pass on that sort of thing,' said Alice, her face reddening.

'So you don't know if there was anyone in the picture at the moment? The rumour I heard was that it was a married man.'

'What rumour? Where did you hear that?' Alice looked startled.

'Do you honestly think I'd tell you? And do you know if she had a computer?'

'No, I know nothing about the woman except that she was on the flower rota at church.' Alice practically dragged Nathaniel away as Patti came up behind Libby.

'Not getting anywhere?' she murmured.

'Not so's you'd notice,' said Libby, with a sigh. 'But I can't understand why this side of her character wasn't immediately pounced on. That would be normal. You would have thought everyone would have been muttering "Serves her right" and "Always said she'd come to a bad end" or the equivalent.'

'Perhaps they were all too busy talking about me?' suggested Patti with a smile.

'True. Well, I shall mention it to Ian and try and find out if she had a computer, and if she had, if she was on any internet dating sites.'

'Oh, she had a computer,' said Patti. 'I asked her once where she'd bought a very nice sweater and she said it was from an online site. Apparently she did most of her shopping online – and I certainly remember the supermarket delivery van going down to her cottage when I was visiting Mrs Bidwell.'

'So you visited Mrs B? How did she take that?"

'Not very well, but as I used to take her the occasional bit of shopping, she had to put up with it. And she would never have me take the reserved sacrament to her.'

'No, she wouldn't in church either, would she? How did she manage in ordinary communion services?'

'She had to put up with it then.' Patti grinned and took a bunch of keys from a pocket. 'Come on, let's lock up, then we can both get back to Steeple Martin.'

'Aren't there other things you'd like to do on Wednesday?' asked Libby, as she watched Patti lock up.

'Yes, but I'd like to do them with Anne,' said Patti. 'And what with her job and her situation, that's difficult. We always arrange our holidays together, though. We're both culture vultures, so we go off to Italy and Greece and do the sites – as much as we can with the wheelchair.'

'But that must be difficult,' said Libby. 'I mean, you can't go up to the Parthenon in a wheelchair, can you?'

'No, but you'd be surprised at the amount of places that now have disabled access.'

'Well, I'm glad about that,' said Libby, getting out her car keys. 'See you later in the pub, yes?'

'Yes,' said Patti, suddenly coming forward and giving Libby a kiss on the cheek. 'I'm awfully glad I've met you. Thank you for being so understanding.'

'Ian called while you were out,' said Ben, meeting her at the door of number 17 thirty minutes later. 'I told him where you were and said you'd have your mobile, but he said it didn't matter.'

'That was in response to last night's call, I suppose. That was all he said?'

'Yes. Come on, if we don't eat now we'll be late for rehearsal.'

'You won't, but I will,' said Libby. 'Gosh – pillar to post. I'm too old for this.'

Peter's tightening up of the script, the music and the acting was already beginning to pay off, and at nine thirty he pronounced himself satisfied and dismissed the cast.

'Going to the pub?' he asked Libby. 'Hal said he'd be able to get away early.'

'Yes, I'm meeting my new vicar friend. I told you she had a friend here, didn't I?'

'Did you? I expect you did. Will she mind us being there, too?'

'Course not. I expect half the cast will be, too.'

When Ben, Peter and Libby walked into the pub ten minutes later, it was to find Ian Connell sitting at a table with Patti and Anne. Libby came to an abrupt halt in surprise, and Peter cannoned into her.

Ian stood up with a grin, kissed Libby and shook hands with

Peter and Ben, offering to buy drinks. Peter went with him to the bar, and Ben pulled up more chairs.

'I gather that this is a social occasion rather than an official one,' said Anne. 'We were very surprised to see him.'

'I thought he'd come to find me,' said Patti, with a shudder. 'But he said no, he was waiting for you.'

Ian and Peter arrived with drinks.

'So why did you want to see us?' asked Libby, eyeing Ian warily.

'I'm not always on duty,' said Ian. 'I was driving this way, and as Ben had told me you were rehearsing tonight I thought I'd look in on the off chance.'

'So, no talk of the case, then?' said Peter. 'Pity.'

'Not unless there's something Libby wants me to know.' Ian looked her with a small smile. 'Or something she wants to ask me.'

Libby looked round the table rather shamefaced. 'Actually,' she said, 'there is.'

'Shall I go first, then?' asked Ian, his smile broadening. Libby nodded and Ian turned to the rest of the table. 'Libby told me that, according to one of the women at Patti's church, the second murder victim had tried to speak to someone after the first had been killed, and I said I would try to find out from the original reports who she had spoken to.'

'And did you?' asked Peter.

'No. She had been questioned, along with everyone else. But she said nothing that could be construed as information to the officers.'

'So we conclude that she intended to speak to someone else, who was probably the murderer,' said Libby.

'Possibly, but it's purely conjecture, unless anyone else comes forward with information.'

'We heard a bit of gossip today, didn't we, Patti?' Libby looked over at the vicar, who was looking uncomfortable again. 'It's all right, I'll tell it. I know you don't want to.'

'OK, Lib,' sighed Ian. 'What is it?'

'The rumour is that Marion Longfellow was having an affair

with a married man.'

Peter whistled. 'I thought she was quite old?'

Libby bristled. 'No older than me, as far as I know.'

'Sorry.' Peter grinned at Ben, who rolled his eyes.

Ian was frowning. 'So why did no one tell me that at the time?'

'Apparently,' Patti took up the tale, 'None of the people at the church knew, although none of them seemed surprised. It was a rumour in the village rather than the church.'

'Not the same thing, then?' said Ian with a half smile.

'Not at all, I'm afraid.' Patti shook her head. 'We are an increasingly secular society, and only a small minority of the village residents come to church.'

'So how did you find out?' said Ian, turning to Libby.

'Talking to one of the women who serves in the community shop.'

'I should have thought about it before,' said Patti. 'It just didn't occur to me.'

'Did you talk to any of the rest of the villagers?' Libby asked Ian.

'We talked to most of the people who had been at that particular service, which I gather was an exceptional one with a lot of outsiders?' Ian looked at Patti. 'I wasn't involved at that stage.'

'Yes, there were a lot of people from outside the area – ex-miners and their families.'

'But it would have to be someone who got near enough to inject her, wouldn't it?' asked Libby.

The others looked at her in surprise.

'Oh, sorry, we haven't actually talked about that, have we? Were we right in guessing suxamethonium chloride, Ian?'

'Yes.' Ian raised his eyebrows. 'Clever of you.'

'Rosie put us on to it, actually,' admitted Libby. 'But it's difficult to get hold of and you'd need a lot to inject intramuscularly.'

'OK – now you've lost me completely,' said Anne. 'Can we go from the beginning?'

'I shouldn't,' said Ian, 'but in this company I don't think it'll compromise anything.' He looked at Patti. 'Except for you, vicar. I'll have to swear you to silence.'

Patti looked shocked. 'Of course.'

'Suxamethonium chloride is used in operations for getting the patient to relax all muscles, most particularly in the case of intubations. It inhibits all conscious and unconscious reactions within seconds if injected intravenously, slightly longer if intramuscularly. They can't breathe or call for help. Unfortunately, it occurs naturally in the body, so is often not picked up. It's also, Libby,' he smiled at her, 'used in equine medicine occasionally.'

'Oh.' Libby pulled a face. 'Are we on the lookout for more vets, then?'

'We could be. What we need to find is somebody who stood or sat close enough to Mrs Bidwell to inject her. We did find the injection mark, although it was first dismissed as an insulin injection.'

'And somebody who has access to that drug. What was it again?' asked Anne.

'Known as "sux",' said Ian. 'I'm pretty sure it's available through the illegal drugs trade, so we might have to set up an investigation along those lines, too. We've got people looking into it, but no luck so far.'

'And then whoever did it killed Mrs Longfellow?' said Libby. 'And did she see them do it? If she had, wouldn't she have said straight away?'

'She could have tried her hand at a spot of blackmail,' said Ben.

'Not that sort,' said Patti. 'She appeared very comfortably off.'

'Perhaps that's how she appeared comfortably off?' suggested Peter.

'Doubt it,' said Patti. 'Besides, you'll have looked at her finances, won't you, Chief Inspector?'

'Please call me Ian off duty, and yes, that's being investigated, too, as are Mrs Bidwell's.'

136

'So,' said Libby frowning, 'could it be that Mrs Bidwell was threatening to blackmail Mrs Longfellow, or her boyfriend, and was killed because of that? And Mrs Longfellow naturally suspected the boyfriend and accused him?'

'It's a theory,' said Ian with a shrug, 'but we need more evidence. Who was it who told you about the affair?'

'It was Dora Walters who helps in the community shop,' said Patti, 'but she'll be furious if she thinks we set you on to her.'

'She did backtrack quickly when I tried to pin her down,' said Libby. 'Said it was just general gossip. As we said earlier, none of the church ladies could confirm it, although they all thought it was likely. In fact ...' her voice trailed away and she stared at the table.

'In fact what?' said Ben.

'Nothing.' Libby looked up, her face pink. 'I'll tell Ian on his own.'

'To save my blushes?' said Patti. 'No need. I think I know what you were going to say. Sheila Johnson suspected her husband of being the married man. Right?'

Chapter Twenty

'I did wonder,' said Libby. 'I just –'

'Didn't want to indulge in gossip in front of me,' Patti finished for her. 'I know, but I'm beginning to realise that gossip may well be integral to police investigations.'

'It's sad, but true,' said Ian. 'And it's what holds up hundreds of cases, when people don't tell the police this sort of thing "because it's only gossip".'

'I said that,' said Libby smugly.

'It's also,' continued Ian, 'why, against every better judgement, I find myself involving Libby and Fran. They're good at uncovering gossip and Fran's occasional moments can be illuminating.'

'But she hasn't had any this time, except to be convinced Mrs Longfellow's death was a direct result of Mrs Bidwell's,' said Libby.

'Well, we're a little further on now, thanks to you,' said Ian. 'But don't show off about it.'

Everyone laughed.

'And what about Tim Bolton?' Libby asked Ian, after the conversation had turned general and Patti and Anne were asking questions about the theatre.

'I had to make a snap decision,' said Ian. 'I think it's probably a red herring, but we have to make sure, so I turned it into a crime scene straight away. I have a feeling it isn't, but there's no doubt some odd goings-on have been happening there.'

'Really? Have you got evidence?'

'Some, and it's distasteful, so don't ask,' said Ian.

'No blood or evidence of sacrifice, then?'

Ian sighed. 'No, Libby. And don't you or Fran go delving into witchcraft or Black Magic again.'

'We never mean to,' said Libby. 'You've got to agree there.'

'You never mean to do anything,' said Ian. 'But yes, today's information could be useful. We know next to nothing about the village, and the only crime that's been committed there in the last few years has been of the drunk on a Friday night variety. Oh, and a Red Cross collection box pinched from the pub counter.'

'I expect our Dora will have a theory about that, too. She strikes one that way. The trick will be to get her talking and not pin her down too much. As I said before she backed off when I did that.'

'She'll not be pleased with you for letting the cat out of the bag,' Patti dropped in to the conversation.

'On the other hand, it might make her feel important,' said Libby. 'But I don't know what you're going to do about Sheila Johnson's husband. You probably can't go smack up to her and say "Was your husband having it off with Marion Longfellow?" can you?'

'Delicately put, as always,' said Ian. 'No, we can't. What we might have to do is ask for DNA samples from every man in the village.'

'From – ? Don't tell me she was –'

'Raped, no. But there will be some trace evidence at the scene, you know that. I do hate having to do it, and the boss will hate having to sanction the expense. I suppose I shall just have to send in a team tomorrow and start turning things upside down.'

'Won't you go yourself?' asked Patti.

'Not for a house to house, but to question certain people, like your Dora – what was her name?'

'Walters,' said Patti. 'You'd better come to me first and I'll give you names and addresses of all the people I know who knew them both. Although most of those will have been questioned after the miners' service.'

'When we didn't know what we were looking at,' said Ian,

'so it's time we went in again anyway.'

'Oh, I know what I was going to ask,' said Libby suddenly, nodding thanks to Ben who put a fresh drink in front of her. 'You've taken Mrs Longfellow's computer, I suppose?'

'Yes.' Ian looked surprised. 'Why?'

'Well apart from any emails from illicit boyfriends, might she have been a member of an online dating agency?'

'I've no idea. What makes you ask?'

'I realised she was an older woman who was obviously still looking for lurve, just like our Rosie.'

'Ah, yes. Your Rosie.' Ian smiled sourly.

'Well, you hear all sorts of stories about dodgy people on those sites, don't you?'

'Good heavens.' Ian shook his head admiringly. 'What an imagination.'

'I think it's great,' said Patti. 'She's made me look at all sorts of things differently.'

'Have I?' said Libby in surprise.

'I'll look into it,' said Ian. 'And I'll see you tomorrow,' he said to Patti. 'I'm off now.' He gave Libby a kiss on the cheek and shook hands with the others, and with Harry, whom he passed in the doorway.

'Oh, there, I missed the lovely Ian,' said Harry, flinging himself down in Ian's chair. 'You were in the caff earlier, weren't you?' He smiled over at Patti and Anne. 'You didn't tell me you knew this old tart.'

Patti looked shocked, but Anne laughed.

'They wanted to get fed, not have you regale them with unsavoury tales of my past,' said Libby.

'You've been in quite regularly, haven't you?' said Harry, ignoring her.

'Yes, at least once a month,' said Anne.

'Do you live here?'

'Anne does, but Patti's from St Aldeberge,' put in Libby.

'Gawd'elpus, the lady vicar!' said Harry.

Patti burst out laughing. 'I take it you know our story, then?' she said.

'The old trout's told us about the ghastly murder in the church,' said Harry. 'She always has to ask our advice.'

Peter appeared with a drink for Harry.

'Don't take any notice of him,' he said. 'Nobody else does.'

'So, have you been putting the lovely Ian right?' Harry asked Libby, ignoring his beloved completely.

'Yes. Now say "thank you, Peter, darling, for my nice drink".'

Harry looked across at Peter, now re-seated, and exchanged a grin with him. 'I shall thank him nicely later,' he said with a wink.

'I'm sorry for talking about it with Harry and Peter,' said Libby, 'but I usually do. They don't tend to get names, though.'

'That's all right,' said Patti. 'It's quite like being famous. After all, it's in the public domain, now, isn't it?'

'I haven't been following. Is it?'

'Yes, it was on Kent and Coast TV the night after Marion Longfellow's murder, and in the *Nethergate Mercury* at the weekend,' said Patti.

'Jane didn't tell me,' said Libby.

'Perhaps it wasn't Jane working on the story,' said Harry. 'I don't suppose she tells you about everything that gets reported in the paper.'

'I shall call her tomorrow. And Campbell McLean hasn't got back to me. I think I let slip there'd been more than one murder at the time. He said he was forbidden to talk to you.'

'Do you know him? He seemed quite pleasant,' said Patti. 'He didn't interview me, but I did speak to him to show him where to stand and so on. He didn't mention the second murder to me, but he knew about it.'

'I'm surprised you haven't been inundated with media, then,' said Libby. 'Murder in the church is bad enough.'

'It's your Ian and the Bishop. They've managed to muzzle the media between them. I don't know how.' Patti shook her head.

'It won't last,' said Libby. 'If it's been in a local paper or on local TV a stringer will pick it up and the big boys will get it.'

'Not if a Section D notice is slapped on them, surely?' said Harry.

'Do they still have those?' asked Libby doubtfully. 'After all the media leaks over the last year or so?'

'They wouldn't get taken to court if they didn't,' said Harry.

'But our murder isn't sensitive material, or a terrorist threat, so they wouldn't slap a D Notice on it, would they?' said Patti.

'No, but maybe it's simply a request because it's the church? Perhaps the media are just playing nicely for once?' Libby looked from one to the other.

'Can you see that?' Harry laughed. 'No, it'll all be out there for the world to pick over soon enough, betcha.'

Events were soon to prove him right, Libby found when she popped out to the eight-til-late the following morning.

'Terrible, this witchcraft murder at St Aldeberge, isn't it?' said Ali as he handed her the change.

'What?' Libby gaped. 'Where?'

'Here.' Ahmed opened a red top in front of her. 'We thought you would know.'

'I do,' said Libby, gazing at the creatively photographed Willoughby Oak and the inset of St Aldeberge church. 'Is it in any of the others?'

'Ah!' said Ahmed. 'One of your cases, then is it?' He and his brother began riffling through copies of red tops and broadsheets alike, and finally pushed three across to her. Gloomily, she bought them and knocked on the door of The Pink Geranium. Harry, with one look at her face, let her in.

'You were right,' said Libby, sitting at the big pine table in the right-hand window. 'Look.'

Together they read the three pieces, none of which contained much actual information, mainly speculation, and eventually Libby came across the source of the pieces, Tim Bolton, actually quoted in one of them.

'He was cross with me because I wouldn't tell him anything, and I put Ian onto him, too, to prevent him contaminating the Willoughby Oak site.' Libby sighed.

'Was there anything there?'

'Apparently, but Ian didn't think it was necessarily to do with the murders. Now, how did Tim Bolton manage to slide under the radar?'

'Because he's concentrating on the Oak and the witchcraft angle. Even though the murder in the church is mentioned in the copy, it's not a headline. No one noticed.'

'Or did, and didn't care,' said Libby with a sigh. 'Oh, poor Patti. She'll be besieged now.'

'Ian won't be too pleased, either,' said Harry. 'Want a coffee?'

The light was flashing on the answerphone when Libby got home. The first call was from Patti, the second from Fran, the third, unsurprisingly, from Campbell McLean and the fourth from Jane Baker at the *Mercury*.

'I can't believe you didn't tell me, Libby,' said Jane, sounding hurt.

'The police and the vicar were trying to keep it quiet,' said Libby.

'But we had it in the paper last weekend. Why didn't you tell me it was one of yours?'

'Low profile, Jane. You ought to know that. I've had Campbell McLean on, too.'

'Well, you would. If you do know anything that's printable, will you tell me?'

'Of course, we always do,' said Libby, 'but at the moment there's nothing to tell. And it's ages since the first murder anyway. This blasted piece Tim Bolton's put out has just revived interest.'

'Who is he, anyway?' asked Jane.

'A partner in Lewis Osbourne-Walker's production company. Used to be Lewis's producer. We met him at a party at Lewis's. He was interested in the Willoughby Oak for a programme on witches.'

'Oh, of course it's the 400th anniversary of the Pendle Witch Trials coming up, isn't it?'

Libby was always surprised at the amount of general knowledge Jane had at her fingertips.

'Anyway,' she said, 'there's nothing more to tell you at the moment, and we're not investigating anyway. Just providing the odd bit of gossip for Ian to help him along.'

'All right. As long as you let me know first if anything happens,' said Jane.

After asking after Jane's husband Terry and daughter Imogen, Libby listened to the message from Campbell McLean, to which she didn't bother to reply, then called Fran, who was angry.

'That bloody man,' she said. 'He could ruin everything.'

'Tim Bolton? Why? How do you mean?'

'There are going to be people all over the Willoughby Oak now.'

'But Ian's got it tagged as a crime scene,' said Libby. 'They can't get near it.'

'A piece of blue-and-white tape fluttering in the breeze won't stop the sightseers. And there's no one on duty out there.'

'It's not an actual crime scene, though, Fran. Ian couldn't afford to keep someone out there all this time.'

'But it is a crime scene,' insisted Fran. 'Maybe not a murder, but I'm pretty sure that's where the drugs come from.'

Chapter Twenty-one

Libby was silent from sheer surprise.

'Drugs? What drugs? The only drug in this case so far is the suxamethonium chloride,' she said when she found her voice.

'No, the drugs that are being run up the river to Felling.'

Libby was silent again for a long moment.

'How do you know about that?' she said eventually.

'Well, aren't they?'

'I heard gossip,' said Libby unwillingly. 'Someone said the police were watching the Felling harbour side. Or dock side – no. Quay. That's it. But apparently the river's too narrow and shallow to bring anything up to Felling. Anyway, I heard it was illegal immigrants, not drugs.'

'I don't know about that, but drugs are coming into Felling and being distributed at the Oak. Under cover of one of those awful Satanist meetings.'

'That was a pretty big moment,' said Libby. 'When did it come to you?'

'When I read the piece in the paper. You know how it is, it was just there in my mind as a fact, like I know that Guy's in the shop at the moment and Sophie's out with Adam.'

'Have you told Ian?'

'No. How will he take it? You've spoken to him, haven't you?'

Libby told her about yesterday's visit to St Aldeberge and Ian appearing in the pub last night.

'And Harry was saying he bet it didn't stay under wraps for long, and this morning, there it was in the papers. I'd better call Patti and see how she's getting on.'

'Swamped with bloody reporters, I should think. Listen.'

Fran sounded brisk. 'If she's got any sense she'll have taken the phone off the hook, so I'll drive over there and try and get in to see her. I'm nearer than you are.'

'OK. Call me when you can.'

Drugs? Illegal immigrants? Libby shook her head. It was all getting far too complicated. It was time to try and get life back into perspective. Which probably meant learning lines.

It was while dozing in front of the fire later in the afternoon with her script open on her lap that the phone rang.

'It's me,' said Fran. 'We were right. Ghastly reporters and cameramen, including Campbell. I fobbed him off, and luckily the police were there to keep most of them off the vicarage doorstep.'

'Which was the aspect they seemed most interested in?'

'Oh, the witchcraft, naturally. I hate to think what the gutter press are going to cook up.'

'And nothing about illegal immigrants or drugs?'

'That aspect hasn't come under consideration yet, has it?' said Fran. 'That's merely speculation on someone's part and my bloody mind.'

'I think,' said Libby, 'that Ian may have people looking into the drugs connection because of the sux. Someone must have got hold of it illegally – it's not available outside operating theatres, is it?'

'I expect he has. We must remember we're not privy to an entire investigation. We only ever know the bottom-line human part, and not always that, either.'

'But in this case, at least we've supplied him with helpful gossip.'

'I hope it doesn't upset the applecart, though,' said Fran. 'Patti was worried about her flock being upset. Oh, by the way, she said was there any possibility you could go over before church on Sunday for a quick run-through? She doesn't want to bother you during the week again, and if she can just keep up the momentum until the service with a weekly rehearsal that should be enough, she says.'

'I suppose so,' said Libby, 'although I'd really rather my

Sundays were sacrosanct.'

'Tell you what,' said Fran, 'you and Ben come here for supper tomorrow, stay the night and pop into St Aldeberge on the way home.'

'It's not exactly on the way home, though, is it?'

'Oh, Libby! How ungrateful! We're nearer than you are. And I'll see if Jane's mum will babysit so they can come, too.'

Jane Baker's mother had a self-contained garden flat in Jane and Terry's Peel House. Since moving in, from being a cantankerous and rather unlikeable women, jealous of Jane's good fortune in inheriting Peel House from her godmother, she had become distinctly softer, and, luckily, doted on her granddaughter.

'Well, it would be nice,' said Libby. 'I'll ask Ben.'

'Tell him, don't ask. It'll get you away from panto, too.'

It was easy, then, to tell Patti she could only spare a little while on her way home on Sunday morning. 'But of course I want to help.'

'Oh, sorry, Libby,' sighed Patti. 'I tend to forget that other people's Sundays aren't work like mine.'

'No, it's fine this week because we'll make a detour to you on our way home, but if we could organise some other time after that. Although it's difficult with most people working through the days and me having rehearsals in the evening.'

'Several of them don't work and could always brief those that do,' said Patti hopefully.

'In that case, at the risk of you losing your Wednesday afternoons, we could do it then, possibly?'

'We'll check Sunday morning, shall we? We can always rehearse the hymns and carols at normal choir practice.'

So it was arranged that Libby and Ben would present themselves at the church at ten fifteen on Sunday morning. Ben, amiable as ever, didn't mind and was pleased to have the invitation to supper at Coastguard Cottage.

'I think,' said Libby, as she got out of the car on Saturday evening and went to lean on the railings above the beach, 'that if I ever lived anywhere but Steeple Martin, it would have to be by the sea.' Ben joined her to look towards the sea rippling with creamy splashes and a soft susurration onto the sand.

'But you won't leave your cottage,' he said, and Libby felt a twinge in her stomach.

'We can't leave the village, anyway,' she said, turning the conversation away from the difficult subject of Steeple Farm, where it was obviously headed, 'because of your mum. Not to mention Uncle Lenny and Flo.'

'Mum, yes, she's my responsibility, but the others aren't,' said Ben. 'Come on, let's go in. It's not that warm.'

Jane and Terry had managed to persuade Jane's mother to babysit, and were already ensconced on the sofa in front of the fire, which crackled with huge logs, being a much deeper and wider fireplace than Libby's small Victorian one.

'Not that she needed much persuasion,' said Jane. 'She's perfectly happy to sit in front of our TV rather than her own. So, tell us all about the St Aldeberge murders.'

Fran and Libby exchanged an uncomfortable look.

'There's no more we can tell you than you've already seen,' said Libby. 'Patti was besieged yesterday, thanks to this bloody Tim Bolton. Fran went down to help.'

'Yes, and to be perfectly honest, Jane, there really is no more to it than the murder of two flower ladies from the church. We think the first one was spite of some kind – she wasn't a particularly nice woman – and the second murder was because the victim knew something about it. That's what Ian thinks, as far as we know.' Fran offered glasses of fizz to Ben and Libby. 'Just to start off with,' she said. 'We go on to the cheap stuff later!'

With common consent the subject of the St Aldeberge murders was dropped and Jane asked after the panto. She herself had been briefly a member of the Oast House company, just after Libby and Fran had first met her and she had few friends in the area. Now, she was established in her job, was able to work part of the week at home, had an adoring husband, a reasonably compliant mother and a gorgeous baby daughter.

'I haven't been to Steeple Martin for ages,' she said. 'I still remember that lovely birthday party you held for your mum at the theatre, Ben.'

'When your sister sang for us, Terry,' said Ben. 'It was a good do, wasn't it?'

They all fell silent, remembering the aftermath of the party when Terry had been attacked.

To everyone's relief, Jane started telling them about all the local events she and her team had been covering recently, including the sillier ones.

'And then there's the Literary Musical festival over the Golden Hind pub. Priceless. According to the organiser: "Esoteric music with erudite criticism." Sadly I fear no Quo!'

'Sounds like something Hinge and Bracket would send up,' laughed Libby.

'Who?' Terry frowned.

'Difficult to explain,' said Ben, also laughing.

'Two men,' explained Guy, who was a fan, 'who dressed and performed as genteel ladies of a certain age with a background in light opera and operetta.'

'I still don't know what you mean,' said Terry. 'I'm too young. Aren't I?' He grinned at his wife.

'So am I, darling, but I know who they are. I bet your sister does, too. We'll have to dig something out on the internet and show you.'

'So what else is going on in Nethergate and beyond that's capturing your attention?' asked Guy. 'I must apologise for not keeping up these days.'

'I don't suppose you really want to read about missing dogs and presentations to the playgroup, do you?' said Jane. 'Although there is some suggestion of an undercover police operation with Revenue and Customs going on somewhere in the vicinity. We've had no confirmation, but you know how rumour spreads.'

'Drugs?' asked Libby, desperately trying not to look at Fran.

'Could be, or illegals.' Jane shrugged. 'You ought to know how much of a problem that is.'

'Don't we just,' said Libby. 'Poor buggers.'

No one asked if she was referring to the police or the immigrants.

'Think it's the same operation as the police keeping an eye on Felling?' Libby asked Fran when she helped carry plates into the kitchen.

'It's the same area, but one lot could be an investigation into drugs, the other into illegals. Nothing to do with us, except as far as the Willoughby Oak connection,' said Fran, taking a perfect lemon meringue tart out of the Aga. Libby had to agree.

'Coincidence, though,' she said next morning, just before she and Ben left for St Aldeberge.

'I expect there are covert operations going on all the time,' said Fran. 'After all, Kent's a county with a large coastline and the biggest entry port from Europe. Revenue and Customs have a huge job here.'

'That's true. Oh, well, we'd better go. See if Ian's had any more luck amongst the faithful.'

When they arrived at the church, Patti looked harassed. 'I'm sorry, Libby, but could you just take the kids through their bit?'

'Just the kids?' Libby looked round at the crowd huddled together in a corner of the Narthex. 'Not them?'

'They're all a bit upset, and all of them aren't here.'

'What's upset them?'

Patti sighed. 'The police. Ian's had a team here interviewing all the men and taking DNA samples.'

'Ah. Who isn't here?'

'Sheila and Alice, of all people. The men are all here.'

'Get them all together. It'll take their minds off it.'

Looking anguished, Patti went over to the group. Libby watched as she talked earnestly to them, waving her hands for emphasis. Ben arrived, having been looking round the graveyard for interesting tombstones.

'What's going on?' he asked. Libby told him. Just then, Patti came back with relief on her face.

'It's OK, they've decided to get on with it.'

'Good. Let's start them off.' Libby clapped her hands and led the way into the nave.

The short rehearsal went as well as could be expected with a crowd of under-rehearsed and inexperienced adults and children. Libby told them she'd be over at four thirty again on Wednesday, if as many people as possible could make it and beat a hasty retreat. However, as she and Ben prepared to leave the church, Kaye and Patti caught up with them.

'We're worried about Sheila and Alice,' said Patti.

'Neither of their husbands are regulars at church, but they were both seen by the police,' said Kaye. 'And now Sheila and Alice haven't shown up. Do you think that's significant?'

'I don't know,' said Libby. 'I suppose I could pop in to Alice's house on my way home.'

'No,' said Ben. 'We're in a hurry, remember. Anyway, that might be insensitive. Better to give her a ring.'

'If you want to know what the problem is,' said a voice behind them, 'we can tell you.'

Chapter Twenty-two

All four turned and found themselves facing Gavin Brice and Maurice Blanchard.

'Gossip,' said Maurice, his disapproving expression growing even more pronounced.

'It's hardly gossip.' Gavin's cheerful face was sombre. 'The police have taken DNA samples from all the men. They already had mine, because I found – er –'

'Marion Longfellow, yes,' said Libby.

'The trouble is, a few men refused.' Maurice snapped the words.

'Ah.' Libby looked at Patti and Kaye. 'I think I see.'

'What?' The two other women looked bewildered.

'Any man refusing would be immediately suspected of having something to hide,' said Libby.

Patti's mouth dropped open and Kaye gasped.

'I don't know Sheila's husband but I do know Bob,' said Libby. 'I'd find it difficult to believe he had the energy to play around. Or murder someone.'

Maurice made a sound like "pshaw" and stumped off into the church.

Gavin's face fell. 'I don't think anyone can imagine me doing it, either.'

'I'd be grateful, then,' said Libby. 'And I don't suppose you know much about witchcraft, either.'

It was Gavin's turn to look bewildered. 'Eh?'

'The – um – accoutrements – you know – round the – er –'

'Body,' Gavin said. 'Oh, yes. Is it witchcraft? I thought Devil Worship or something. Dennis Wheatley sort of thing.'

'I think it comes to the same thing in this case,' said Libby.

'Who's Dennis Wheatley?' asked Patti.

'A writer famous in his day for writing occult novels,' said Ben. '*The Devil Rides Out* and *To The Devil a Daughter* were the most well known, I think.'

'Well it's all most unpleasant, whatever it is,' said Gavin, shaking himself like a wet dog. 'And it doesn't belong in a church, or with anyone connected with a church.'

And he, too, turned and stumped off towards the church.

'I think he was quite sad not to be considered as a bit of a roué,' said Kaye, watching him go.

'Then he's an idiot,' said Patti. 'Come on, Kaye. Time to minister to the faithful.' She turned to Libby and Ben. 'Thanks again for coming. I'm sorry to have involved you in this.'

'Pleased to help,' said Libby, patting the vicar's arm, while Ben made an indeterminate sound of vague assent.

'So what do we think of that?' said Libby, as Ben drove out of the village.

'I don't think anything of it, frankly.' Ben looked over his shoulder and took a right-hand turn.

'This isn't the way home,' said Libby, surprised.

'It's a short cut,' said Ben. 'You've not looked at a map since you first went to St Aldeberge from Nethergate. This joins up with our main road just after the Steeple Mount turning.' He sent a quick, triumphant grin. 'It's just a bit narrower.'

Luckily, they didn't meet anything coming the other way, or Libby felt certain they'd have had to back up for miles, but it certainly was quicker.

'I'll go this way in daylight,' she said, as they emerged on to the main road, 'but I don't think I'd risk it after dark.'

Peter joined them for Sunday lunch at Hetty's, but Harry was stuck at The Pink Geranium.

'Closing Sunday evenings,' said Peter, sipping a frosty glass of sémillon. 'And has decided he's not going to open Mondays any more, either, even at Christmas.'

'Can't have Sunday dinner on Sunday evenings,' said Hetty, plonking a large rib of beef before Ben and handing him a carving knife.

'No, Het, I know,' said Peter. 'He doesn't mind, and he doesn't eat the meat, anyway.'

'Hmm.' Hetty sniffed as she placed blue-and-white dishes of enormous antiquity on the table, filled with an array of perfectly cooked vegetables.

'I wish I could do roasts like this,' sighed Libby.

'Can't do your fancy stuff,' said Hetty, 'so we're quits.'

Libby gave her almost-mother-in-law a fond smile.

'So,' said Peter, helping himself to roast potatoes, 'what are you going to do with all these rooms you've got here now?'

'Difficult,' said Ben, topping up Libby's glass. 'We've been put off by what happened here in the summer.'

'I know you have,' said Peter, 'but it's months, now.'

The Manor had been renovated and its guest bedrooms revamped with en suite bathroom "pods" before the ill-fated writers' weekend. The hop pickers' huts had also been renovated and were let out on a self-catering basis, as was Steeple Farm, but so far the Manor's rooms had stood empty.

'At least Mum has it to herself,' said Ben.

'Didn't mind having people here,' said Hetty. 'Different.'

'What you could have,' said Peter, 'is a mini festival.'

'What sort of festival?' asked Libby.

'Literary. Well, not literary exactly, but a book festival, mainly for readers. See if you could get some well-known writers along.'

'We couldn't afford it,' said Libby. 'You couldn't expect famous people to come out here for nothing.'

'No, but you could sell tickets and put them in the theatre. They could stay in the Manor.'

'Meanwhile, we've still got the panto to occupy us,' said Libby, 'and my Queen isn't coming along as I'd like.'

The talk fell to pantomime and other local topics, including the application of a supermarket giant to put a small store in a disused pub at the end of the village, which was generally agreed to be ruinous for the other shops.

'After all,' said Libby, 'we've got Nella and Joe's farm shop and the eight-til-late. They would be put out of business.'

'That's something for Ben to get on to his council pals about, then,' said Peter.

Later that evening, curled up on the sofa with the laptop, Libby was idly searching local news sites when she came across an item about a dawn raid on a drug smuggling ring. It had no relation to the St Aldeberge murders, but it made her think.

'You know,' she said to Ben, who was pretending to watch a natural history documentary, 'if Fran's right and there's a drugs connection to our murders, and she's sure there is, with landings at Felling and distribution at the Willoughby Oak, then they would be coming in at the St Aldeberge inlet.'

His eyes opened. 'Hmm,' he said.

'And Mrs Bidwell's and Mrs Longfellow's cottages overlook it.'

'And aren't themselves overlooked.'

They looked at each other and grinned. 'That's it!' they said together.

'Hold hard,' said Ben, 'if we've thought of it, you can be sure Ian has. If there really is a surveillance operation up at Felling, then the inlet is the only place drugs can be coming in.'

'So why isn't there a surveillance operation at the inlet?' said Libby with a frown.

'That's a point,' said Ben also frowning. 'We've gone wrong somewhere.'

'Not necessarily. Maybe the Felling operation isn't actually concerned with the river? After all it's so narrow and shallow I don't know how any boat could get up to the Quay anyway. Maybe it's coming in somewhere else.' She clicked on a map of the area and an enlarged map of Felling appeared on the screen.

'Yacht basin,' said Ben. 'There must be another river if they've got yachts there.' He widened the view of the screen. 'Yes, here, see. Right out the other way. It flows into the yacht basin and out into the creek down to the inlet.'

'That's it!' said Libby excitedly. 'Of course! It's loaded at the Quay to go up river. So it hasn't come in by boat at all.'

'Or, if it has,' said Ben, 'it's been landed somewhere else and brought up by road.' He sighed. 'Thank goodness this isn't our problem.'

'It might not be, but if it helps find out who killed Mrs Bidwell and Mrs Longfellow ...'

'There's still not anything you can do about it,' said Ben, patting her shoulder. 'Now, what do you say to a little nightcap?'

'I'd say make it a large one and you're on,' said Libby.

Libby phoned Fran on the Monday morning.

'Fancy a recce?' she said. 'I want to put a theory to the test.'

'What theory?' asked Fran warily.

'About drug smuggling and Felling. And no, it isn't dangerous, and as far as I know we won't be trespassing.'

'That sounds as though it could be dangerous and we probably will be trespassing.'

'No, promise,' said Libby. 'Can you meet me in Felling?'

'Yes, it is going to be dangerous,' sighed Fran. 'Where in Felling?'

'Is there a car park near the Quay?'

'I don't know! I've never been there. I'll find the nearest one and then meet you on the Quay. When are we going?'

'Today? This afternoon?'

Fran sighed again. 'Two o clock, then.'

'Great.' Libby beamed at the phone. 'See you later.'

Libby drove into Felling under the great stone gatehouse and straight on to the ring road she'd been told about at the meeting in the vicarage. It would be difficult to get out without being seen, she realised. The ring road was almost like a castle wall, enclosing the whole small town. She went over a bridge and saw a tourist information finger post pointing to the Quay, with the large blue and white "P" next to it, meaning she would be able to park.

Fran was already there, leaning on the stone wall above the moorings.

'That's the tiny little river to the St Aldeberge inlet,' she said pointing to where a narrow stream ran out of the basin. 'And that's the other way, straight inland.'

From the other end of the basin, a much broader river went

under the bridge Libby had crossed.

'Ben and I discussed this last night,' she said, 'and no one can be smuggling anything in from the inlet. There just isn't room. So why are the police watching the Quay?'

'Because something's coming in from the other direction?' said Fran.

'No, we thought of that and it doesn't make sense, because there's nowhere else for them to go.'

'So why are we here?'

'To try and find out if there *is* another way out. You see, I suddenly realised something. Joan Bidwell's and Marion Longfellow's cottages both overlook the inlet, so something could have been landed there and they could have seen it. But if whatever it was couldn't get up to Felling, it must have gone somewhere else.'

Fran's eyes narrowed. 'So why are we here?'

'I mean, it must have gone some other way to Felling.'

'Or nothing was landed there at all. If there's no way up-river from there, the murders and the police operation here probably have nothing to do with each other.'

'I'm just sure they have,' said Libby. 'I want to have a look round the area. Look there's a public footpath sign over there.'

With Fran reluctantly following, Libby struck off down the footpath, which led them over a small footbridge and on to marshy, reedy ground at the other side of the yacht basin.

'You know,' Fran called, as she picked her way over the soggy ground, 'the one thing we've done nothing about is to find out who could have killed Mrs Bidwell in the church.'

'Oh, I expect the police are on to that,' Libby called back and came to a stop. In front of them, the river ran sluggishly between reedy banks, tussocky grass stretching out on both sides. A stile set into a low hedge led onto another footpath winding away from the river.

'Not easy to get anything up or down river this way, either,' said Fran, after they had stood surveying the scene in silence for a long moment.

'No.' Libby swivelled and looked down the other footpath,

which led away into a stand of trees.

Fran narrowed her eyes. 'However …' she said slowly.

Libby waited. 'What?' she said, finally.

'Over there. Behind those trees. That's the Dunton Estate.'

Chapter Twenty-three

'The Willoughby Oak!' breathed Libby.

'Of course, it's just a coincidence.' Fran looked at her doubtfully.

'No such thing as coincidence,' said Libby. 'Shall we go and see where it goes exactly?'

'No, we might be seen.'

'But it's a public footpath!'

'I still don't think it's a good idea. Some of the Dunton Estate's still private – this might lead straight up to a large wire fence.'

'OK, but it's a shame.' Libby turned and surveyed the scene, including back the way they had come, to the yacht basin, the Quay and old town beyond. 'It wasn't a waste of time coming here after all.'

'No, but I expect if you'd looked at a map properly you could have seen it.'

'Only an ordnance survey map, not a normal one,' said Libby. 'Come on, let's go back and see if there's a museum or anything.'

The museum was housed in a small Georgian building facing the town square, which also contained the tourist information office. There was a good deal of smuggling memorabilia and maps of when the marshy ground beyond the Quay had actually been sea. The Dunton Estate, they discovered, bordered the sea wall in those days.

'Would that have been when the witches were about?' asked Libby in a low voice.

'Probably.' Fran turned to the door into the tourist office.

'Excuse me,' she said to the bored-looking woman behind

the counter. 'We were wondering if you had anything about the Willoughby Oak?'

The woman reached into a folder and pulled out a leaflet.

'Funny,' she said, 'you're the third people to ask about it in a week. Pity we haven't got more.'

'Right,' said Libby, not knowing whether to pursue this or not, but Fran decided for her.

'And there's nothing in the museum?' she said.

'There's a blown-up photograph and drawing, the same as in the leaflet, with a plaque underneath, but, again, it's the same as the leaflet.'

'Thank you,' said Fran, and withdrew into the museum.

'Tim Bolton?' said Libby, as they shuffled round the walls looking for the Willoughby Oak.

'Expect so. I wonder who the third person was? Wouldn't have been the police.'

'A week,' mused Libby. 'So it wouldn't have been someone looking for info to use in Marion Longfellow's death.'

'No, but could be someone trying to find out more about it. The details did get out.'

'Hmm.' Libby came to a stop in front of the two blown-up pictures. One was a photograph obviously taken some time in the recent past, the other a drawing dating from the early nineteenth century. 'Well, I suppose we've come to a dead stop.'

'We can't always be lucky,' said Fran. 'Come on, we might as well go. Did you pick up those smuggling leaflets?'

They retired to a small café on the square, cunningly known as the "Tea-Square", which, as Fran said, probably meant nothing to most people.

'So, what were you saying earlier about Mrs Bidwell's murder?' asked Libby, when they were sipping fragrantly steaming Assam from bone china cups.

'Seeing that you show no signs of letting up on this case, I wondered why we haven't heard more about how she was killed.' Fran stirred her tea thoughtfully. 'I mean, that was the most mysterious event of all, wasn't it?'

'You mean that no one could see how she had been killed?'

'Yes, although that's been solved now, it was this drug – what's it called?'

'Succo – something. Sux for short.'

'And it's a muscle inhibitor?'

'It's used particularly for intubation, so the doctors can slide –'

'Yes, all right,' said Fran hurriedly. 'What exactly would happen?'

'The body becomes paralysed. Can't breathe or call out, or anything. There wouldn't be any thrashing about, or anything to call attention to the fact. And no smell of bitter almonds like prussic acid in the old detective stories.'

'So she would have just remained where she was and died. And injected where?'

'That's the thing. Intravenously would be too difficult, so it would have to be intramuscular, just jabbed through the clothes. She was a diabetic, so small puncture wounds went unnoticed at first. And that, being intramuscular, would have taken more of the drug, apparently.'

'So who has access to it? Oh, yes, you said. Vets, again.'

Libby made a face. 'But there aren't any in this case.'

'And who was near enough to administer it?'

'The old vicar and Gavin Brice when they gave her communion,' said Libby, 'but they cancel each other out. The old vicar didn't know her, and he would have seen Gavin Brice doing something odd. And as far as I know, she took communion perfectly normally.'

'And we don't know who was sitting near her in church,' said Fran.

'Some people might have been going back to their seats from the altar rail, but it was a special service, don't forget, and packed.'

'With a lot of people from outside the village, so there's almost no chance of tracing them.'

'They did get names from the party afterwards, but I don't suppose that was everybody,' said Libby. 'Neither do I suppose that anyone remembers now where they were sitting. They all know where she was because she always sat in the same place, but because there were a lot of visitors I expect even the regular churchgoers didn't get to sit in their normal places.'

'So we'd never get anywhere trying to find out who was near enough or had access to the sux stuff,' said Fran. 'I don't envy the police.'

'No wonder Ian's actually listened to us. He must be clutching at straws. So, what other avenues are there?'

'The situation with the men? The two men whose wives didn't turn up yesterday?'

'Sheila Johnson's husband and Alice's Bob,' said Libby. 'I suppose their DNA has turned up. Amazing how quickly they can get results these days. It used to be weeks.'

'Turned up at Marion Longfellow's house, you mean. But that would suggest they had been there, not that they killed her.'

'Yes, but it's significant that they had been there. Neither Alice nor Sheila said they knew her well, so why did their other halves visit her?'

'I wish I'd seen her,' said Fran. 'I imagined her as nearly as old as Mrs Bidwell for some reason, but obviously she wasn't.'

'But I thought you saw –' began Libby.

'I saw the scene, not her face,' said Fran.

'Right. I do feel sort of responsible for those poor men. If I hadn't told Ian about what Mrs Dora had said.'

'Poor men nothing. If they'd been having affairs with Mrs Longfellow they deserve what's coming to them.'

'That's a bit harsh,' said Libby.

Fran cast her a militant look. 'When your ex left you for another woman, didn't you think he deserved a battering?'

'I threw him out, actually,' said Libby, 'so I suppose yes, I did.'

'Because you found out. He didn't volunteer the information?'

'No, I found him out.' An unpleasant internal tremor told Libby that she still hadn't got over that particular betrayal.

'So, unless those two men have reasonable explanations, they're going to be for it from their wives.' Fran tapped her saucer with her spoon to make her point.

'They probably aren't the only two in the village,' said Libby. 'We only know the church-related people. And Mrs Dora didn't say it was anything to do with the church.'

'I wonder if the police have interviewed her now?' mused Fran. 'I expect she told them who she meant.'

'And I don't suppose Ian will tell us,' said Libby with a sigh. 'On to the next point, then, because if Mrs L was killed by a lover –'

'Or an angry wife,' suggested Fran.

'Oh, yes! Hadn't thought of that. So will they take the DNA of the wives of any men who had been in Mrs L's house?'

'Might do, I suppose, and they'll check alibis, won't they?'

'Of course. But that still means her murder had nothing to do with Mrs B's, and you were sure it did.'

'I was probably wrong,' said Fran.

'But you don't think you were?'

'You know how it is. I think I have a fact, but who knows? I can only really be certain of things I can see and hear now, this minute. Although I can remember my wedding as a fact, it's quite possible that I've forgotten parts of it, or think it happened one way when in fact it didn't. That's what the police always say, isn't it? When they interview witnesses to crimes, each one remembers it differently yet swears it's fact.' Fran stared out of the window across to the museum. 'So I might be entirely wrong.'

'Oh,' said Libby, worried.

'It doesn't make a lot of difference what I believe, anyway,' said Fran. 'It's what the police believe.'

'Right.' Libby looked at her doubtfully, while Fran continued to stare out of the window. 'So we add jealous wives as possible suspects. But not for Mrs B's murder. And I can't believe we've got two separate murderers.'

'No.' Fran turned to grin at her. 'That's why I'm still sure they're connected. And I still don't see why the witchcraft element was brought in.'

Libby frowned. 'No, because it wasn't until after Mrs L's

death that the rumour began about Patti, was it? Or was it? And that could just be someone latching on to facts of the murder.'

'I wonder if the suggestion had been made before either of the murders,' said Fran. 'If Mrs B had been trying to blacken Patti's name, for instance?'

'And someone picked up on that when it began to look as if the police were going to look into Mrs B's death? But surely, no one would have killed Mrs L just to blacken Patti's name? That's ridiculous.'

'I wouldn't have thought so.' Fran pushed back her chair. 'Come on, I must get back.'

'The other thing that's bothering me,' she said as they walked back across the square to the car park, 'is where on earth is that bloody wheelchair?'

Chapter Twenty-four

'Who can I ask about the wheelchair?' Libby said to Ben later that day.

'No one as far as I can see.' Ben poured wine into the glasses on the table.

'No. Can't ask Ian. I suppose someone in the village would know if it's been found.'

'Ask your gossipy friend Dora. Wouldn't she know?'

Libby put plates on the table. 'Only if it's very general knowledge. I should think people are fairly careful about what they say in front of her. Gavin might know, as he was the one who usually pushed her.'

'Ask Patti.' Ben sat down and lifted his glass. 'She can ask around for you.'

The pantomime rehearsal went as well as could be expected. This year there was no panto horse or cow, due to several injuries having resulted from their antics in past productions, and the ensemble was beginning to look much better. Libby's Queen was even earning laughs from the cast.

'Keep it up, dearie,' said Peter, as they walked to the pub. 'It's getting slicker. I'm doing a couple more re-writes, but only to cut out extraneous stuff. Won't affect you.'

'Good,' said Libby, and pushed open the pub door. 'Good lord, Rosie!'

Rosie, sitting alone looking uncomfortable at a table away from the bar, looked up. 'Hello.'

'What are you doing here?' Libby went over to the table while Peter and Ben went to the bar.

'I was bored. I thought you might be in here so I came down.'

'We've been rehearsing,' said Libby. 'Pity you were bored. When can you go back to your house?'

'I suppose I could go now,' said Rosie, looking down into her glass. 'It hasn't been as much help as I thought being away.'

'If that's a dig at me not being around to help you, I'm ignoring it,' said Libby. 'Now, do you want to join us and the theatre crowd?'

'If you don't mind,' said Rosie meekly.

'Come on then.' Libby led the way to where Peter, Ben and other cast and crew members were already drinking.

'I've just thought,' said Libby, accepting her half of lager from Ben, 'Your cottage isn't far from St Aldeberge or Felling, is it, Rosie?'

'No.' Rosie looked surprised. 'St Aldeberge's where your murders are, isn't it?'

'Where they happened, yes. But Felling's come to our notice, too. What do you know about the river that comes up from the St Aldeberge inlet?'

'It's hardly a river,' said Rosie. 'I don't think you can even get a rowboat up it. Once at Felling it goes off through the marshes on its way inland.'

'Yes, Fran and I saw that today,' said Libby. 'And that the grounds of the Dunton Estate are bounded by the marshes.'

'Isn't that where …?' Ben raised his eyebrows.

'The Willoughby Oak is, yes.'

Peter sighed and moved to a just vacated table. 'Come on, there's bits of this story I've missed. Fill us in.'

Libby brought them all up to date with a quick précis of events.

'So you've got guilty husbands, revengeful wives, drug smugglers and practising witches in the mix now, have you?' said Peter, amused.

'I think I'd start with the first murder,' said Rosie, looking thoughtful.

'Well, yes, you would,' said Libby.

'Don't be sarcastic. I'm just thinking about it as I would a book plan. Start with some kind of change. A murder is a change, isn't it? But there's a reason for that murder. The rumours about your vicar friend started after that.'

'There were murmurings before,' said Libby, 'although not as malicious.'

'But the malicious ones and anonymous letters started after the first murder,' said Rosie, 'and that would appear to be in order to lay the blame on the vicar. Then the second murder happens with all the trappings of witchcraft surrounding it. I could almost believe that was simply to point the finger at the vicar.'

'And all the subsequent rumours about her are just red herrings?' Ben looked interested.

'Maybe. So the most important point is who had reason to murder the first woman?"

'Well, yes, obviously,' said Libby, 'but we can't think of any. She's estranged from her children, she lived right out on the little lane to the headland, just below the second victim, actually. No other neighbours.'

'That's suggestive, then, isn't it?' said Rosie. 'If they both lived in the same isolated place they could both have witnessed something illegal.'

'But we've established that the inlet isn't big enough to get up to Felling –'

'Why does it have to go to Felling?' interrupted Peter.

Taken aback, Libby stared at him. 'I suppose it doesn't.' She shook her head. 'That's us amateurs putting two and two together and coming up with seven hundred and fifty. We heard the police were mounting an operation at Felling, the rumour was that it was about either drugs or illegals, and Fran is convinced someone's been dealing drugs at the Willoughby Oak under cover of Black Magic meetings.'

'I think I can see where that tortuous reasoning comes from,' laughed Peter.

'It all made sense when we thought of it,' said Libby.

'They still could have seen something illegal at the inlet,' said Rosie. 'After all, it would be a good place to run in a small boat under cover of darkness and unload something.'

'That's why I said why Felling,' said Peter. 'Much more likely to land whatever it is and get away over land rather than take a boat up river to Felling where it would be much more noticeable – except of course, that they couldn't anyway.'

'So the Felling operation's nothing to do with our murders, then.' Libby sighed. 'I guessed as much. Or Fran did.' She took a sip of lager. 'But what about the Oak and the drugs?'

'I'm sure that's a different case altogether. How did you get on to the Oak in the first place? How did it come up?' asked Rosie.

'We looked up witchcraft connections with St Aldeberge. Patti had it in an old book about the village. That was after the cockerel or whatever-it-was was left on her doorstep.'

'Oh.' Rosie looked a bit sick. 'You didn't tell us that bit.'

'Somebody was trying to force a Black Magic connection if you ask me,' said Peter. 'I bet it doesn't come into it at all.'

'I expect you're right.' Libby sighed again. 'And I don't suppose there's a drug connection either.'

'And,' said Ben, patting her hand, 'I expect Ian's all over it anyway.'

'Did you ever find out if the second woman had been on a dating site, by the way?' asked Rosie.

'The police had her computer for analysis, so I don't know, although I did mention it to Ian' said Libby. 'It's so frustrating not to know!'

'I wonder if I could find her on the site I've been on?'

'Could you do that? How? And wouldn't they have taken her details off by now?'

'If the police get in touch with them, yes, but they might not have. I could put in the search engine "Woman, between – " what was she? Age-wise?'

'I don't know, but I'll guess at sixty, Maybe younger, fifty-five.'

'OK – "Woman, between fifty-five and sixty, five-mile radius of Nethergate." Then, if she's there, she'll come up.'

'She might have lied about her age or where she lives,' said Ben. 'Everyone does that, don't they?'

Rosie shrugged. 'It's worth a try.' She looked at Libby. 'Do you want me to?'

'Yes, please,' said Libby, feeling guilty that she hadn't spared more time for Rosie in the last two weeks. 'I'll pop up tomorrow morning, shall I?'

'Do you realise that it's three weeks since I had that first call from Alice?' said Libby, as she and Ben walked home. 'Seems incredible that the police have made no progress. Especially since the second murder.'

'I expect they have,' said Ben, 'just that you don't know about it. After all, they found out what had killed the first woman, didn't they? Up until then, it looked like magic. And they've spread their search. All the DNA matches they'll be trying to take ...'

'I know, I know,' sighed Libby. 'And I feel we put Ian on the wrong track with the Willoughby Oak, too. He won't be too pleased with us.'

'You gave him the village gossip. That was worthwhile.'

'Except that it's caused rifts in two marriages.' Libby stared miserably at the ground. 'Perhaps we should stop meddling.'

'You aren't meddling.' Ben put his arm round her shoulder. 'Alice and Patti asked you in and you've been trying to help. See what happens when you go over on Wednesday.'

But the following morning, on the way up to Steeple Farm to see Rosie, Libby's mind once again returned to the wheelchair.

'Someone must have seen who moved it,' she said aloud. 'It was gone by the time everyone left the church, so they were all still there when it was moved.'

She turned into Steeple Farm's gravel forecourt and knocked at the door. Rosie answered immediately, an excited grin on her face.

'Look what I've found!' she said, practically dragging Libby into the sitting room, where she had her computer set up on a table by the fire. Talbot, stretched out in an armchair, barely twitched a whisker.

Libby found she was looking at the profile page of a blonde woman of around fifty, although the age stated was fifty-six.

'See? Actually says "near Nethergate". And read the description.'

'Hobbies – indoor sports. Is that a euphemism? And – golly! Flower arranging. And she says she's interested and involved in village life.'

'Could that be her?' Rosie was almost hopping with excitement.

'It could,' said Libby, 'but I'm surprised that if it is, the police haven't found her account on her own computer and got it off the site.'

'Perhaps she used a different computer? If she never accessed the site from her own ...'

'But they're web-based sites. Emails would go straight to your own computer.'

'Not if you had a different email address associated with – well, say a smart-phone. A different email programme that you only accessed from there?'

'But if she had a smart-phone or a tablet the police would have found them, too.' Libby shook her head. 'Unless they were stolen. Anyway, I'm not sure any more if this is relevant to her death.'

'What about if she had seen something odd and because she didn't really know someone well on this site, she confided in him? You know how it's occasionally easier to tell a stranger?'

'Possible.' Libby looked up at Rosie. 'Do you think I ought to tell Ian? It might not be her.'

'But if it is, he needs to know,' said Rosie. 'I think you should tell him.'

'All right.' Libby heaved a sigh. 'I'll tell Fran first, then pluck up courage.'

'Good.' Rosie patted her shoulder. 'Now, how about coffee?'

Libby called Fran from her mobile while standing looking over the dewpond half an hour later.

'I thought I'd send him a text with the screen name of the woman and the site, then he could look into it himself.'

'I suppose that's better than taking up his time with a phone call,' said Fran. 'Do you think it's her?'

'It could be. The dating site would have her real details, wouldn't they, if she's a paid-up member? The police would be able to check.'

'What was the screen name? I could go and do a free search, couldn't I? Or do they insist on you signing up first?'

'No idea,' said Libby. 'I'll go home and try it, too.'

She sent the text to Ian, sniffed appreciatively at the sharp November air and set off down the hill. Peter came out of his cottage as she passed and swept her up to join him for coffee in The Pink Geranium.

'So, did you have a look at the dating murder victim?' They sat at the big pine table in the left-hand window, where Harry had spread a collection of daily papers.

'We found one we think might be her,' said Libby, 'and I've sent a text to Ian. But all I feel we've done is talk about it over and over again and not done anything. I wish I could do something else.'

Harry set down a cafetière between them.

'You go doing anything else and you'll get into trouble,' he said. 'Remember what's happened in the past.'

'There's not going to be much of a risk to me when I don't know anything,' said Libby. 'And I can't see any of the people I've met so far being a murderer, either.'

'Just you be careful,' said Harry, and went back to the kitchen.

'He's right, you know,' said Peter. 'And look.' He pushed one of the tabloids over to her.

Libby, horrified, saw a picture of St Aldeberge church, either taken at night or skilfully doctored, heading an opinion piece on Black Magic and the established church. It even mentioned Patti and both victims by name.

'Oh, bugger,' she said. 'They aren't going to let this go, are they?'

'No, and you'd better make sure your phone isn't hacked by journalists, especially now you've sent Ian those details.'

'Oh, no.' Libby covered her face with her hands. 'But that's all been stopped now, surely?'

Peter shrugged. 'I'm in the business, remember. It was much more widespread than the general public have been led to believe. Phones and emails were routinely hacked, and I can't see how it can be properly policed.'

'How depressing.' Libby pushed the plunger down. 'But they wouldn't get on to me, would they?'

'Suppose they hacked Patti? Then they'd see how much you were involved.'

'Oh, don't! You're really worrying me, now. But surely, with all the media interest in this sort of thing they wouldn't risk it yet?'

Peter poured coffee into Harry's large cream mugs. 'Let's hope so.' He pushed a mug towards her. 'Now drink up and think of a nice project to occupy you this afternoon, like helping me block the rest of act two. It isn't quite working.'

In fact, an afternoon walking through all the moves in act two of Sleeping Beauty helped keep Libby's mind off the problems of St Aldeberge. Ben turned up half way through, however, to construct a couple of pieces of scenery and told Libby there was a message for her on the home answerphone. She went to find her mobile, left in her coat pocket in the dressing room, and discovered a reply from Ian.

'Will check, he says,' she told Peter and Ben. 'Oh, well, can't expect him to tell me any more.'

But when she and Ben reached home later in the afternoon, Ian had left an expanded message.

"We think this is Marion Longfellow and have asked the site to provide her details. We will check all the contacts she made, and we're cross checking with her bank. Please don't say anything about this to anyone else, Libby, and ask your friend Rosie not to. And thank her, I suppose."

'Well, I'll tell her,' said Libby, deleting the message, 'but I have a strange feeling that she'll see this as a challenge.'

'And do what?' Ben called from the kitchen where he was filling the kettle.

'Set herself up as a target?' said Libby.

'She won't know who's been talking to the Longfellow

woman, so how can she set herself up?'

'I don't know,' said Libby darkly. 'But she will. You see if she doesn't.'

Chapter Twenty-five

'Told you so,' said Libby, reading an email later that evening.

'What?' Ben kept his eyes on the television screen.

'Rosie's had a reply from someone on her dating site.'

'Well? That's not unusual, is it?'

'No, but she changed her profile details, apparently, to say that she lives near St Aldeberge.'

'Is that all?'

'Look.' Libby pushed the laptop towards him. 'This is the message he's sent: "A dear friend of mine lived in St Aldeberge. You look as lovely as she was." Spooky, eh?'

'I don't see what's spooky about it,' said Ben. 'Why is it?'

'Well it sounds as if he's talking about Marion Longfellow, doesn't it?'

'Oh, Lib, that's ridiculous! How on earth do you make that out? It could be anybody. Even the other woman.'

'I know, but there must be something in it, surely?' Libby took the laptop back. 'Anyway, Rosie's replied. She says she'll let me know.'

'I just hope she won't do anything stupid,' said Ben, returning to the television.

'And I said I knew she would,' said Libby. 'And I was right.'

The following morning, Libby sent Rosie a text to say she was on her way to see her and set off with a basket of goodies like Red Riding Hood.

Rosie had the coffee percolating by the time she got there, and her computer open at the dating site.

'See? This is him,' she said, pointing at the little profile picture of a grey-haired man looking slightly off camera.

'That's the one I said I thought I'd seen before,' said Libby, peering at the screen. 'But I don't think I have, after all. Yet he looks so familiar. Weren't you going to meet him?'

'I was thinking about it.' Rosie poured coffee. 'But after I came to you for supper I decided against it. But then I changed my profile just to see if I could flush out anything, and he got in contact again.'

'Is the woman we think is Marion still there?'

'I haven't checked.' Rosie typed in some details and they watched as a list of women appeared on screen. 'No, she isn't. Can you remember what her screen name was?'

'Marigold, wasn't it?'

Rosie typed in Marigold and came up with several profiles of Marigolds with various numbers, but none of them were the profile they had seen the day before.

'So, it looks as if it was Marion Longfellow and the police have had the profile taken down. In which case they'll be looking at all her contacts through the site.' Libby looked up at Rosie. 'Ian said you weren't to say anything about this to anyone at all, by the way.'

A delicate pink tinged Rosie's cheekbones. 'Well, of course …'

'You've told someone already haven't you? Oh, Rosie.' Libby sighed. 'Who was it?'

'Andrew, actually.'

'I thought you and he were no longer an item?'

'I was a little hasty,' said Rosie, concentrating on the screen. 'He's offered to let me stay in the flat with him until the work's finished in my house.'

'Rosie, tell me the truth,' said Libby sternly. 'Did you actually come here to try and find a new man on this site, and keep it out of Andrew's way?'

The pink in Rosie's cheeks grew deeper. 'There was a bit of that, I suppose. But I really am having the house done.'

'And Andrew would have said come and stay with me, but you wanted to find someone else to flirt with. Honestly, you're the end. Remember how you flirted with that bloke up at Cherry Ashton? And how that turned out?'

'That wasn't because I flirted with him,' said Rosie with some heat.

'Anyway,' said Libby, 'I think you ought to go and stay with Andrew and not carry this thing on any more. What did you reply to this chap?'

Now Rosie's colour was practically the same as the dining room carpet.

'Come on – what?' Libby grabbed the keyboard and clicked on the "sent messages" column. And swore. She turned to Rosie, aghast.

'You actually asked if it was your "friend" Marion? You *idiot*!' She stood up, pulling her phone from her pocket.

'Ian, I know you'll be cross, but she didn't tell me what she was doing. Rosie's been trying to flush out contacts of Marion Longfellow on the dating site.' She clicked the phone shut. 'And now, don't be surprised if an irate policeman comes knocking on your door.'

'He won't know where to find me.' Rosie looked smug.

'Of course he does. He knows you're here, and if you're gone, which I strongly suggest, he'll go straight to Andrew.'

Rosie's face fell as her colour faded. 'What shall I do?' she asked.

'For a start don't reply to this – what's his name – Bruno51. Phone Andrew and get packing.'

'I'll have to clean up –'

'No, we'll take care of that,' said Libby. 'Go on, call Andrew and I'll help you pack and load the car.'

While Libby was collecting various items from the kitchen, Ian called. Predictably, he was angry with Libby.

'How could I help it?' she asked reasonably. 'I didn't suggest she went on the dating site in the first place, nor did I suggest this latest wheeze. It was while I was telling her that you'd imposed silence that this came out.'

Ian sighed. 'All right, so what happened?'

'I gather you found Longfellow on the site and had it pulled? So did you have a look at her messages?'

'Of course.'

'And was there anything from a Bruno51?'

There was a short silence, then Ian blew out a long breath. 'OK – I give in. What little gem have you picked up now?'

Libby told him.

'I'm afraid your Rosie is going to have to hand over her computer,' said Ian. 'I hope she's got a back-up. And tell her not to bother trying to delete anything – we always find it.'

'So who is Bruno51?' asked Libby. 'Can't you track him through his bank account? They pay by credit card, don't they?'

'If this man is really Longfellow's murderer, do you think he'd leave that sort of paper trail? No, there'll be a bank account in a false name. There always is.'

'So how do you catch him?'

'We'll have to do some checking up first before we try that, then we'll think out a strategy.'

'A honeytrap!' said Libby

'Libby, you've been watching too much television. Now go away and tell Rosie someone will be along to collect her computer.'

'She's off to Andrew Wylie's actually, so hadn't you better go there?'

'We'll ring her to let her know we're on our way and she can tell us where she is. Go on, now Libby, and I'm sorry I was cross. Actually, it could be a blessing in disguise.'

'That's what I thought,' said Libby. 'All right, all right, I'm off.' She went.

'My computer?' wailed Rosie.' How can I work?'

'Put everything onto a memory stick and use Andrew's while you're there. Or go and get your office computer. And when you've got it, don't try and open the dating site or any emails from them. They'll leave a trail.'

Non-comprehension pervaded Rosie's face. Libby sighed irritably. 'Just get on with packing. And get out that memory stick.'

By the time everything including Talbot was packed into Rosie's car, she had calmed down.

'I'm going to pay a cleaning company to come and go over

the house,' she said, leaning out of the driver's window. 'I'm sorry it had to come to this, Libby. But I might have been some help to the police, don't you think?'

'We use a company called MaidsinaRow.com,' said Libby, 'and yes, I think that last piece of information about Bruno has been useful. I only hope they find out who he is quickly.'

'I could always arrange to meet him –' began Rosie, a thoughtful look on her face.

'*No*! You mustn't Rosie. Let the police look after it now. They have far more resources than we have.'

'Oh, OK. But let me know what happens, won't you?'

'If I can,' said Libby. 'Good luck.'

She watched Rosie drive off and turned slowly back into Steeple Farm to check all the doors and windows were locked. A very good job, she thought, as she went round the first floor, that she had decided to come and look at Rosie's computer this morning, or goodness knows what would have happened. Rosie might have arranged to meet this Bruno and that could have been a disaster. He would have found out that she didn't know Marion Longfellow, if that really was to whom he was referring, and that he was suspected of murdering her. Libby shuddered.

Ben, she knew, was in the estate office at the Manor, so she went straight up to see him and tell him she'd been right about Rosie and the dating site.

'Come into the kitchen,' he said when she'd finished. 'Hetty will rustle up some lunch.'

Hetty had, in fact, got home-made soup simmering on the Aga, and dished up large bowls while listening to Libby's story.

'Nice woman, but flighty,' was her pronouncement. 'Coulda got herself into a bit of danger, there.'

'So she could,' said Ben, 'and it's what I'm always worried about with this one.' He gave Libby a fond prod in the arm.

'I don't think I'd do anything that silly,' said Libby. 'It could have been lethal.'

'Do you think that's what the police will do, though?' Ben tore a chunk off a warm cottage loaf. 'Use a stand-in for Rosie?'

'A honeytrap. That's what I said to Ian, but he wouldn't say.

He says they've got to do research first.'

'Very odd how it's all linked up,' said Ben, shaking his head. 'I mean, Rosie's nothing to do with St Aldeberge, yet she just turns up at the right time and provides a link to a killer.'

'We don't know he's a killer yet,' said Libby, 'but yes, it is odd. If it was in a book, you'd never believe it.'

'You said you rekkernised him,' said Hetty.

'He looked familiar, but I think he must just look like someone I know. I compared him with all the men I've met in St Aldeberge and it isn't any of them. I wonder if it's the younger man our Dora meant when she said Marion Longfellow was having an affair?'

They had to explain about Dora to Hetty, and then, after Libby had offered to wash up and was refused, she said she was going home to tell Fran all about it.

'You'd better get a move on, then,' said Ben. 'It's Wednesday.'

'Wednesday? What –? Oh, lord – the rehearsal,' said Libby, gathering coat and basket and making a run for the door. 'Thanks, Ben.'

Hetty shook her head. 'Daft as a brush, that one,' she said.

Ben gave his mother a hug. 'But you love her for it.'

Libby had time for a rushed call to Fran putting her in the picture, before having a quick wash and brush-up and driving out to St Aldeberge.

The nights were drawing in fast now, and it was already twilight when she arrived at the church and made her way to the hall. Patti was already there with both churchwardens, and, to her surprise, Alice and Sheila Johnson. She said a cheery hello to them in general and drew Patti aside.

'What's happened about the husbands? Are they in the clear?'

'I don't know.' Patti looked unhappy. 'But both the women turned up to a meeting here yesterday and not a word was said. I don't like to ask.'

'OK.' Libby thought for a moment. 'But I've got a little progress in the case to report, so I might as well do that to all of you.'

Sheila and Alice sent their small charges off to play with the other children while they waited for the remaining cast to appear.

'Just thought you'd like to know there's been some progress in the case,' said Libby casually, senses sharp for reaction, which was instant.

'What?' Sheila's voice was sharp. 'Is it to do with those DNA tests?'

'No, it isn't,' said Libby happily. 'Nothing to do with them at all.'

There was an instant release of tension, even from the two men.

'All I can say,' she went on, 'is that the police have a line of enquiry they're following about Mrs Longfellow's murder and they seem quite certain they're on the right track.'

'But what about Joan – Mrs Bidwell?' asked Gavin, with a wrinkled brow. 'I thought it would have been the same murderer. Isn't it?'

'I don't know,' said Libby. 'All I know is, they seem pretty certain they're on Mrs Longfellow's murderer's trail.'

Chapter Twenty-six

'And you're sure it's nothing to do with the DNA test?' said Alice after a pause.

'They've got on to this particular line of enquiry from a completely different angle,' said Libby, aware that several other members and parents of cast were now listening.

'How do you know?' asked one woman clutching a small girl's hand.

'I was told so by the police,' said Libby, wishing this wasn't always a question that was asked.

'She's that woman who was with the police the other Sunday,' another woman murmured.

'Oh, the one who's always in the paper?' The first woman subjected Libby to a searching glare.

Patti began to herd her flock into the appropriate places, and Alice, Sheila and Gavin joined them. Maurice, however, hung back.

'You sure it wasn't anything to do with that DNA?' he muttered.

'This particular lead isn't,' said Libby, fixing him with an inquisitive eye.

'Ah. Only my DNA would be in the cottage.' He nodded slowly. 'And I think a lot of men from around here would have been there.'

'Oh?' Libby's mind raced.

'She was a terror for getting people to do her a favour. Perfectly able-bodied, but a nuisance.'

'And you did her a favour?'

'Several.' Maurice put on a winsome expression. 'Oh, Mr Blanchard, the lock on my back gate's sticking so badly, and I can't seem to get anybody to fix it …' He reverted to his normal sneering expression. 'Then she'd try and get you to stop on and have a drink. Pshaw!'

Libby tried not to laugh. 'And you think she did it to everybody?'

Maurice nodded. 'That's why some of the idiots round here got the wind up. Half the time the Longfellow woman would have asked their wives to send them round, so I don't know what they've got to be worried about.'

'Maybe some of them gave in to her?'

Maurice's expression turned even darker. 'Silly buggers, then,' he said and stomped off, leaving Libby with further food for thought.

After the rehearsal, she buttonholed Alice before she hurried off to deliver Nathaniel to his parents.

'Alice, did Bob refuse to have his DNA taken because he thought it would be found in Marion Longfellow's house?'

Alice turned white, then red and gasped. 'How did you know?'

'Something Maurice said.'

Alice looked furious. 'What's he said, the old bugger?'

'All he said was that half the men in the area would have left DNA in the house because she was always asking people to help her. He said she even asked the wives to ask their husbands.'

The relief was obvious as Alice's shoulders slumped and she loosed her grip on Nathaniel's hand.

'I told him,' she said. 'I said there were loads of others, but he wouldn't have it. He was sure if they found his DNA there he'd be arrested.'

'Him and half the men in the village,' said Libby. 'I expect those that gave their DNA freely would have explained that to the police. Why didn't he?'

'I don't know. And I think Sheila's husband must have felt the same.'

'Have you and Sheila talked about it?'

Alice shook her head. 'No. I haven't said anything to anybody.'

'I think you should,' said Libby. 'And I think you should tell Bob he's an idiot.'

'I will,' said Alice, squaring the slumped shoulders. 'And I'll tell Sheila to do the same.'

'I think I might have helped,' Libby said quietly to Patti as she left the church hall. 'Let me know if there are any developments.'

'I will.'

'And could you ask around and see if anyone can remember anything about the wheelchair? It seems to have been completely overlooked.'

Patti looked surprised. 'Of course. And I won't ask what the new police lead is, although I'm dying to.'

Libby grinned. 'It was something on her computer, that's all. And no, not porn!'

Patti laughed. 'That wouldn't surprise me, either.'

There was a phone message from Rosie when Libby got home in time to eat a quick meal before her second rehearsal of the day.

'Your Ian sent a very nice young man to collect my laptop, and Andrew took me to collect my office computer, so I'm up and running again. The house is almost ready, but covered in dust. I shall report tomorrow.'

'Report what?' Libby said to Ben. 'I hope she's not gone back on that dating site again.'

'It would be just like her to set herself up as bait,' agreed Ben. 'You'd better tell Ian.'

'I can't keep bothering him. With any luck they've already shut the bloke's account down, then she won't be able to get in touch with him.'

'I wouldn't put anything past Rosie,' said Ben. 'Pass the mustard.'

After two hours of rehearsing being asleep in a castle, Libby was ready for a drink, and, as usual now, found Patti and Anne already in the pub.

'I hope your friend Harry won't be upset, but we didn't eat in The Pink Geranium tonight,' said Anne. 'I cooked for us at home.'

'Course he won't be upset,' said Libby, sitting down at their table, while Ben went to buy drinks. 'At least Ian isn't in here tonight.'

'I thought he was a friend of yours?' Patti said.

'He is, more or less, but we did actually meet him as a policeman in one of the earlier cases we got involved with. And then he got interested in Fran, and somehow we became friends. He asks us – or Fran, actually – if he thinks there's an aspect she can help with, and sometimes we get him involved with cases. Like this one, although he already was involved, we just didn't know it.'

'So what other cases have you been involved in?' asked Anne. 'I know I've seen occasional references in the local paper – there was something up at Anderson Place, wasn't there?'

Libby nodded, and by the time Ben and Peter arrived was deep in the details of the Anderson Place mystery.

'I have particular reason to remember that,' Peter broke in. 'It was immediately before Hal and I had our civil partnership there.'

'Oh, you did it properly?' Patti turned to him.

Peter inclined his head. 'We did. I have family, although Hal hasn't, and I didn't want any property going anywhere but to Hal. Civil partnership gets certain rights, not least to call yourself next of kin in the event of a hospital stay.'

'See.' Anne nudged Patti, who turned very pink. Libby smiled sympathetically.

'Not something you can do, or even talk about, is it?' she said.

Patti looked at her with a certain relief, and the pink faded. 'I guessed you'd realise,' she said.

'No, it wasn't me. It was Fran. It wouldn't have occurred to me.'

Patti nodded. 'We don't even let Anne come to visit me at St Aldeberge,' she said.

'In fact,' said Anne firmly, 'I'm trying to persuade her that a

184

church which doesn't allow certain forms of love isn't a church worth bothering with.'

'But I don't see it that way,' said Patti. 'I'm really sorry, but I knew my vocation long before I met you.' She patted Anne's hand. 'I suppose I'm betraying you *and* the church.'

Peter leant forward and put a hand over both theirs. 'I can't say I don't agree with Anne, because I do, but I'm really sorry about the situation you're in.' He leant back. 'Harry and I are lucky. We are accepted as completely normal among our friends and relations, no one thinks twice about it. We have come across some quite vicious homophobia in our time, though.' He looked at Libby with a half smile. 'And that's yet another case.'

'And one I'm not going into now,' said Libby firmly. 'We are now all going to cheer up – and look, here comes Harry to help us.'

But Harry looked gloomy as he swung his long legs across a chair.

'What's up?' asked Libby.

'Donna's only gone and got herself pregnant.' He looked up at Peter. 'I'm gutted.'

Libby and Ben burst out laughing.

'That's much like your reaction when she said she was getting married,' said Libby.

'Yeah, well,' said Harry sulkily. 'I said this would happen, didn't I?'

'It was fairly inevitable,' grinned Peter. 'I'll go and get you a drink.'

Libby and Ben explained to Patti and Anne that Donna had been Harry's right-hand woman since he'd opened the restaurant, how she'd met and subsequently married a young house surgeon from Canterbury.

'Oh, he's gone up in the world now,' said Harry, accepting his drink from Peter. 'He's a registrar now.'

'I expect that's why they've decided to have a family,' said Ben. 'More money and better hours.'

'Do registrars have better hours?' asked Libby doubtfully. 'I thought only the top bods got away with nine to five.'

'Well, congratulations to Donna,' said Peter. 'I shall come and give her a hug tomorrow.'

Harry sighed. 'I know, but who's going to look after the accounts for me? And sort out the bookings? And she knows all the regulars ...'

'Someone else will have to learn, Harry,' said Libby. 'I should try and get somebody before Donna leaves so she can train them up.'

'And perhaps she could do some of the accounts and bookings from home?' suggested Ben. 'She could probably do with the money.'

Harry brightened. 'That's an idea. I'll suggest it tomorrow.'

'And don't pressure her,' warned Libby, 'or she'll get stubborn.'

The following day Libby invited Fran to lunch for a catch-up and case conference.

'Soup and bread and cheese,' said Libby. 'Is that OK?'

'Lovely,' said Fran, sniffing appreciatively. 'Leek and potato?'

'My speciality,' said Libby. 'Will you risk a glass of wine?'

They sat before the fire in the sitting room and Libby went through all the recent Rosie-related events and finished up with confirmation of Fran's feelings about Patti and Anne's relationship.

'Poor dears,' she said. 'Patti's obviously very torn and Anne doesn't share her beliefs.'

'That I can understand,' said Fran, frowning. 'I've told you–'

'Yes, you have,' said Libby hastily, 'but it doesn't help them. Anyway, back to the murders.'

'You said someone told you something at the church yesterday.'

'Oh, yes.' Libby repeated the conversations she'd had with Maurice and Alice. 'So it's not as suspicious as it looked.'

'I wonder how many of those she lured over her threshold succumbed?' said Fran.

'Do you think any of them would have?'

'You know men,' said Fran. 'And she was attractive from her

photo on the dating site, you said?'

'Well, yes, in a mature sort of way, but by all accounts she was a bit snooty, and the men in the village aren't exactly pin-ups. Very ordinary elderly and middle-aged men, as far as I've seen.'

'You've also got the evidence of the lady from the shop. A younger man, she said. Yet she didn't mention a stream of lusty lads in and out of the cottage.'

'No, but she was relying on hearsay and gossip, I gather. I just haven't tracked any of that down yet. I wonder if Ian has?'

'Pity you can't ask him.'

'I can't though,' said Libby. 'Ben thought I ought to warn him about Rosie, but I couldn't.'

'About Rosie? Why?'

'Oh, she said she'd report today and she'd collected her office computer to use at Andrew's.'

'Why would you need to tell Ian that?'

'Because he'd already told me to warn Rosie off, which I'd done, and she still suggested she set up a meeting with this Bruno51. I told her not to, obviously, and hopefully the police have pulled his details from the site, but, as Ben said, you wouldn't put anything past Rosie.'

'So do you think she might still manage it?' Fran looked worried.

'I don't know what to think. But the stupid woman actually asked the man if he knew "her friend Marion from St Aldeberge". Can you believe it? He's probably tracking her down as we speak.'

'If the police can't track him down, he won't have much luck with Rosie, surely?'

'No, if she wasn't standing up waving a flag over her head and shouting "Here I am!" As it is, she's a sitting duck.' Libby sighed. 'Do you think I ought to tell Ian?'

'I don't know. I think he might get a bit shirty about being interrupted for something as trivial as that.'

Libby stood up. 'It wouldn't be trivial if something happened to her,' she said gloomily.

Chapter Twenty-seven

After lunch Libby suggested visiting Hetty at the Manor, as she and Fran hadn't seen each other for several weeks. Harry waved from inside the restaurant as they passed, and Flo Carpenter waved from across the street where she was buying greengrocery from the Cattlegreen Nursery's farm shop.

'This is such a friendly village,' said Fran, as they turned into the Manor drive. 'I hardly know anyone in Nethergate.'

'Oh, you do!' Libby looked at her in surprise. 'Jane and Terry, for a start, then there's George and Bert and Mavis –'

'I don't exactly socialise with two seasonal boat owners and an equally seasonal café owner.'

'No, I suppose not. Perhaps it's because you don't belong to anything over there. We've got the theatre, here.'

'But you knew people before you had the theatre. All the shopkeepers talk to you. The only one I know is Lizzie in the ice cream shop, and she isn't open in the winter, either.'

'Hmm.' Libby sneaked another look at her friend out of the corner of her eyes. 'You're not – er – not thinking of –'

'No, of course not!' Fran turned to her laughing. 'After all the hard work I put in finding Coastguard Cottage?'

'So you are happy there?'

'Blissfully,' said Fran. 'I was simply commenting on how friendly everyone is here. And how all your friends happily include anyone new who is introduced.'

'Like you, you mean?'

'Yes, me, and Rosie, to an extent, and Patti and her friend.'

'I think everyone would be quite happy without Rosie,' said Libby with feeling.

Hetty was delighted to see Fran and, settling down for a chat in the kitchen, directed Libby to the estate office where Ben was wrestling with a tenant farmer's paperwork.

'I still haven't heard from Rosie.'

Ben looked up from his desk. 'Were you expecting to?'

'Yes, you knew. She said she'd report today. That was what was worrying me.'

'Oh, yes. Well, if you haven't heard, she's probably decided to leave it alone, wouldn't you say?'

Libby sighed. 'That's the sensible way to look at it, yes.'

'And Rosie's anything but sensible,' said Ben. 'I know.'

'I'll ring her. May I use the landline?' Libby perched on the edge of Ben's desk. He handed her the phone.

'No reply from her mobile. Goes straight to voicemail. Have we got Andrew's number?'

'You've got it in your phone,' said Ben.

'He's not there either,' said Libby after a moment.

'I gathered that from your message,' said Ben. 'Don't you think that might have alarmed him?'

'I only said I was trying to find Rosie and did he know where she was. It could have been about anything. She could have left something behind at Steeple Farm, for instance.'

'I seem to remember Andrew getting quite het up about anything Rosie-related in the past,' said Ben. 'I hope he doesn't turn up here raving.'

'I'm sure he won't,' said Libby, pressing another number on her phone. 'I'll try her home number in case she's just gone to check on the builders. You never know.'

But there was no reply there, either, and Libby went gloomily back to the kitchen to collect Fran.

'I feel I ought to go looking for her,' she said, on the way back down the drive. 'Where do you think she might have gone?'

'Look, Libby, she's an adult. She also has all sorts of things she has to do connected with her work. Perhaps today's a day she teaches a creative writing course.'

'I thought she'd stopped those? You don't go any more.'

'She stopped doing them at the Nethergate Institute, but she

189

might take some somewhere else. Then, she might have to go and meet her agent, or editor. Or be off on a research trip.'

'That's what I'm afraid of,' said Libby, as they turned the corner into the High Street. 'She's thinking of this whole thing as research and forgetting it's real. She was so excited at flushing out this bloke on the dating site.'

'If she went to look for him, where would she go?' asked Fran.

'She wouldn't. She would have had to arrange to meet him. He would have suggested the place, but I really can't think she'd be that stupid.'

'Then why are you worried?'

Libby sighed. 'I can't think *anyone* would be that stupid, but Rosie isn't just anyone.'

'What do you want to do?'

'I want to phone Ian, but I can see that he'd dismiss it.'

'Send him a text again. Then he can choose whether to respond or not.'

Libby stopped outside the eight-til-late and pulled out her phone.

'He'll be sick of me by now,' she said putting her phone back in her pocket. 'Come on, we've got time for a cup of tea before you go home.'

To both their surprise, Libby's phone buzzed in her pocket before they reached number 17.

'Tell me what's happened,' said Ian brusquely.

'We-ell,' Libby faltered, handing her door key to Fran, 'it isn't my fault. Just as she went yesterday she said she'd report today, and she hasn't. There's no reply from her landline, mobile or Andrew Wylie's landline. And it sounded to me yesterday as if she was thinking of setting up a meeting with this Bruno51. I told her not to, of course.'

'Of course,' said Ian dryly. 'As it happens, we found a message from her to him on the dating site yesterday, but nothing since. We left both their profiles up in order not to frighten him off.'

'But you're monitoring them?'

'Of course.'

'What about their emails?'

'Email addresses are not encouraged – in fact a bot picks them up if they appear and the message isn't sent.'

'So they couldn't have been in email contact?'

'Of course they could,' said Ian. 'There are other ways of doing that. A coded message will get through the dating site system.'

'And of course,' said Libby, almost to herself, 'Rosie is quite a famous author.'

'She wasn't there under her pen name, though,' said Ian.

'No, but she used her publicity picture. And said she wrote books. He could have found her through her website.'

'Well, if they did get in touch, I don't know where or when they would have met, if meet they did,' said Ian. 'I haven't got the time to waste on the stupid woman now, we're still trying to track Bruno51. He's registered as being near Canterbury, which doesn't help much. The experts are on it now.'

'I could go and look for Rosie?' suggested Libby.

'Where? She could be anywhere. No,' said Ian, 'leave it alone and get on with your panto.'

'I bet if she went anywhere to meet him,' said Libby, switching off the phone and going kettle-wards, 'it would be the inlet. Both those houses are empty now, there'd be nobody to see.'

'Rosie doesn't know where the inlet is,' said Fran.

'She knows St Aldeberge and Felling, and she only lives five minutes away, so I'm pretty sure she'd know the inlet.'

'Too late to go looking today,' said Fran. 'It'll be dark soon and you've got a rehearsal tonight, haven't you?'

'Yes.' Libby poured water into the brown teapot. 'I suppose we'll just have to leave it to Ian to find this Bruno person.'

'The community shop in St Aldeberge's open tomorrow, isn't it?' said Fran. 'Why don't we go and quiz this Dora person again?'

'She might not be on duty on Fridays,' said Libby, 'but it's an idea. We might pick up other gossip in the shop. And we could go and visit Dora.'

'She might not say any more, and what excuse would you have for going to visit her? She might be cross with you for setting the police on to her.'

'I know!' said Libby with inspiration. 'I'll take her a couple of panto tickets. She said she always went.'

The following morning, Libby called Patti to give her advance warning of the day's fishing trip.

'The panto tickets are a good idea,' said the vicar. 'And you could suggest that I take her if she hasn't got transport. I don't know who she normally goes with.'

'She said "we" didn't she?' said Libby. 'Anyway, we thought we'd have a look round and see if we can pick anything up. Do you know if Alice said anything to Bob after I spoke to her?'

'I think she did, and I heard her telling Sheila Johnson, too. Sheila looked relieved.'

But it wasn't Sheila who marched forward to shake Libby's hand as she and Fran entered the community shop later that morning. It was Sheila's husband.

The tall blond giant smiled down at Libby as he pumped her hand vigorously.

'Ken Johnson. Can't tell you how relieved I was,' he said. 'Old Bob, too. She was a blight, that woman.'

Libby stepped back onto Fran's toe. 'Pleasure, I'm sure,' she said, a trifle breathlessly.

'Always wheedling to get something done for nothing.' Ken Johnson's open face set in a grim frown. 'And for a lot more.'

'Ah, yes.' Libby cleared her throat. 'Could I have a word outside, Mr Johnson?'

'Just there were quite a few people in the shop,' she explained after he'd followed her outside.

'That doesn't matter,' he said, smiling again. 'Everyone knew what she was like.'

'Then why,' said Libby, exasperated, 'did nobody seem to know anything about her when the police asked?'

He shrugged. 'No one wanted to get involved. We're a small community, and after the police took those DNA samples everyone was afraid they'd be arrested.'

'But you and Bob refused?'

He coloured slightly. 'We thought …'

'Yes, I know what you thought, but when you realised that all the others had given samples, surely you saw that you wouldn't be alone?' Libby watched as the colour in his face deepened.

'Should have done.' He looked away and cleared his throat. 'Anyway, Bob and me went along yesterday and gave our samples.'

'That's good then.' Libby looked quickly at Fran who was frowning. 'So what did she have you doing? Mending fences? Putting up shelves?'

Ken Johnson's colour was receding. 'Oh, getting stuff out of her loft, fixing the lock on the bathroom door, you know the sort of thing.' He looked back at Libby and smiled again. 'Anyway, thanks again for putting us right about it all. And I'm glad the police have found the murderer.'

Libby started. 'They have? Where did you hear that?'

His face fell. 'But I thought you told Sheila …'

'No, all I said was that the police were following another lead,' said Libby. 'And as far as I know, they haven't tracked him down yet.'

'Right.' Ken Johnson looked at his feet. 'Well, I hope they find him. Those women didn't deserve to die, no matter how annoying they were.'

'So you think it was the same person who killed them both?' said Fran, suddenly coming into the conversation.

'Wasn't it?' Ken looked from one to the other, bewildered.

Fran shrugged. 'We don't know. Neither do the police.'

'It was nice to meet you, Ken,' said Libby hastily, holding out a hand. 'Glad we put your mind at rest.'

'Er – yes.' Ken's answering smile was somewhat lukewarm this time, and he went off studying the ground in front of him as if in deep thought.

'Have we found the person Dora was referring to, I wonder?' Libby looked at Fran, head on one side.

'I think he was at least having a fling with our Marion, don't you?' Fran watched the departing back.

'He went to fix the bathroom lock and fell backwards into the bedroom?'

'Something like that. But if he's the murderer ...'

'You don't know?'

Fran shook her head.

'How old would you say he is?' asked Libby.

'Early fifties? He looked younger than his wife, as I remember.'

'And therefore younger than Marion Longfellow.' Libby nodded. 'And it was interesting that he was so happy about going to give his DNA sample when he thought the murderer had been caught, yet when he realised he was wrong he got worried again.'

'And so he should. It all depends where his DNA was found, doesn't it? Suppose it's on sheets?'

'I would have thought our Mrs Longfellow was too fastidious not to change the sheets between guests,' said Libby. 'Are we going back in the shop?'

'Yes, I want to see what their vegetables are like,' said Fran, and led the way.

There were two people behind the counter today, one a woman Libby had seen at the rehearsals and the other an older man she'd not seen before. Neither seemed interested in her or in Ken Johnson's ebullient greeting, but the woman smilingly packed up leeks and cauliflower for Fran.

'You didn't say anything,' said Fran once they were back outside.

'I couldn't really. I hoped having seen Ken Johnson's little act they'd follow it up, but as they didn't ... well. Shall we go and see Dora?'

Dora Walters seemed unsurprised but delighted to see them. After introducing Fran, Libby hurried in with her explanation of the visit.

'Panto? Oh, that'd be nice, dear. And vicar says she'll take me? Can my daughter come?'

'Of course,' said Libby. 'You and the vicar decide which night you want to come and then the vicar can let me know.'

'Lovely,' beamed Dora. 'I'll go and put the kettle on.'

'So that'll be four free tickets, then,' said Libby. 'I can't make Patti and Anne pay if Dora's going free.'

'So have they caught the murderer, then?' Dora came back into the room and perched on the edge of a chair. 'Someone was saying in the shop …'

'No, not yet. We met Ken Johnson in the shop just now, and he seemed to think the murderer had been caught, too.' Libby waited hopefully for Dora's answer.

'Him.' Dora sniffed. 'He was one of them.'

'One of..?' Libby prompted.

'Her men. The Longfellow woman. He was always round there.'

'Is that who you meant when you spoke about a younger man last week?'

'Eh?' Dora looked confused. 'Oh – kettle.' She got up and went back to the kitchen.

'That's made it worse than ever,' said Fran. 'Now what?'

Dora reappeared with the tea tray and offered cake.

'Course, there's been a bit of talk in the village since you was here last,' she said handing round cups. 'All them men she had up there.'

'Yes, we heard, but she used to try and get people to do odd jobs for nothing, didn't she?' said Libby.

'That's what they *say*,' said Dora, with another sniff.

'When I was last here you said there was one particular man –' Libby tried again.

'Only gossip. Told you,' said Dora hurriedly.

Libby and Fran looked at each other.

'Of course, it all is,' said Fran, smoothly, 'all the talk about the men who went there. She often asked their wives to send them, so I don't think there was always an ulterior motive.'

'I wouldn't know,' said Dora. 'I just hear what they say in the shop. But I reckon there was something going on. I used to – ' she broke off and her eyes glazed over.

'Used to what?' Libby said softly.

Dora shook her head slightly. 'I – er – used to see her sometimes.'

'In the village?'

'Course. She lives here. Well, almost.' Dora sat up straight and picked up her cup. It was clear that whatever she'd been going to say she'd thought better of it.

'Did the police come to see you?' asked Libby, switching tack.

Dora beamed. 'Oh, yes. Very nice young man with a young woman. Asked me all sorts of questions about the village.'

'I expect you know more than most,' said Fran.

'Even if you did only come here after you were married,' added Libby.

'There's not many has been here as long as I have. Some of the really old ones, like that Mrs Bidwell, but not many. I could tell you some tales.'

But you won't, Libby thought. 'That's why the police came to you,' she said aloud.

'Yes,' agreed Dora with a satisfied smile. 'Although I did think you must've told them to come to me?' She cocked an enquiring eyebrow at Libby.

'You seemed to know more about the village than anyone else,' said Libby, crossing her fingers.

'Well, I wouldn't say that ...'

'Did you ever go out to Mrs Bidwell's or Mrs Longfellow's houses?' asked Fran.

'Me? No never.' Dora shook her head, her lips pursed. 'Don't like it down near the coast. They have landslides, you know.'

'So I believe,' said Fran. 'I live on the coast myself.'

'Do you, dear? Where's that?'

Fran and Dora settled into a cosy chat about Nethergate, which Dora loved, apparently, having taken the children there when they were young for ice cream and sand-castles. Libby let her attention wander. It was clear that Dora knew, or thought she knew something, but was afraid to say anything. So far, the fishing trip hadn't landed a catch.

Chapter Twenty-eight

'Well, that didn't get us anywhere,' said Libby, as they left Dora's house.

'In a way it did,' said Fran. 'She definitely thinks she knows something about someone who she isn't going to name. And that looks like fear to me. She's quite happy to talk about general gossip.'

'And what about Ken Johnson? Do you think she really knows if he was having an affair?'

'As much as we do, I'd say,' said Fran. 'What shall we do now?'

'Let's go and look at the inlet,' said Libby.

Fran drove them to where the road petered out. They looked across to Joan Bidwell's bungalow and Marion Longfellow's cottage standing in isolation. The remnants of the police tape fluttered outside the cottage. A dark cloud was boiling up out over the English Channel, and the sea could be heard slapping hard into the inlet. Libby went cautiously to the edge of the cliff.

'Look, you can hardly see the river,' she said.

Fran followed even more cautiously. 'You certainly couldn't get a boat up there.'

'So we've confirmed that nothing is being brought up to Felling and unloaded there. The police operation isn't connected with anything here.' Libby stepped away and began to walk to the end of the footpath, where she looked down at the inlet itself. 'I don't see how anything could be landed here anyway. It's too rough, and there's no way up the cliff.' She squinted to left and right and could see no obvious landing sites.

'But the Border Agency or whoever they are say that this whole coast is a prime area for smuggling,' said Fran. 'And they don't have the resources to catch all of them.'

'Well, I can't see how they could land so much as a parcel down there,' said Libby. 'So perhaps we got this all wrong.'

'But both women overlooked this area.' Fran was frowning.

'We could,' said Libby slowly, 'stake it out. What do you think?'

'Wha-at?' Fran turned in alarm. 'Oh, come on, Libby! Every time we've decided to act like idiots we've got into trouble. You're sounding as silly as Rosie.'

'I bet that's what she's done.' Libby looked across at the two houses on the other cliff top.

'What, staked this place out? I thought you said she'd been taken by the murderer from the dating site?'

'Yes, but perhaps she suggested going to Marion's house? Meeting there?'

'Oh, that really is far-fetched,' said Fran, turning round and trudging back to the car. 'However, on the basis that she might, for some arcane reason, have gone investigating, we might as well as drive round to the other side and have a look. Come on.'

They drove back to the little bridge and down the lane they had taken with Ian three weeks before.

'I don't fancy going all the way down that slope to the bungalow,' said Libby. 'You'd be very exposed.'

'Let's have a look round here, then,' said Fran.

The cottage was surrounded by a low stone wall, giving unrestricted views of all sides. Fran pushed the gate open and set off round the left-hand side, peering into windows as she went.

'Dead flowers in a vase,' reported Libby, as she came round the other side of the house. 'On the kitchen windowsill. The curtains are closed in that front room window.'

'Good.' Fran made a face. 'Nothing else to show, and nothing to hear. We might as well go.'

'No one would hide here,' said Libby, as they went back to Fran's car. 'It's too open. The bungalow is more difficult to get to and is slightly more protected.'

'You said it was more exposed,' said Fran.

'Yes, on the path down to it, but look.' Libby pointed. 'It's protected at the back by the side of the cliff, and there are walls round it. Proper ones.'

'I see what you mean.' Fran turned a full circle looking at both sides of the cliff top and back inland. 'It reminds me of a Rupert Bear landscape here.'

'So it does,' said Libby, and climbed into the passenger seat.

'Do you want to go anywhere else?' asked Fran, as they drove back to the village. 'Do you want to see Pattie? Alice?'

'No, thanks,' said Libby, who was sitting frowningly hunched up against the door. Fran shot her a quick look. 'What's up?'

'Nothing. Just what you said about Rupert Bear.' Libby sat up straight. 'Let's go home.'

Back in Steeple Martin, Libby began an internet search for Rupert Bear and at the same time phoned her daughter Belinda.

'Have you still got any of your old Rupert Bear annuals?'

Belinda laughed. 'Blimey, Mother! No, I haven't. You're more likely to have kept them than me. Why?'

'I was reminded of something in one of the stories,' said Libby. 'About smugglers.'

'I don't remember anything about smugglers, but then, I wasn't as devoted as you were to Rupert.'

After a brief exchange of news, Libby rang off. The sheer numbers of references to Rupert Bear on the internet was defeating her, and she gave up. Perhaps, if she just thought very hard, she might remember the story she was thinking of, and why it was relevant.

What happened in Rupert stories? There was usually some sort of quest, and it was often taking place on the common, with piles of boulders in evidence. So where would smugglers come in? And why had she thought of it?

'Did you have Rupert Bear annuals when you were little?' she asked Ben when he came in.

'Sometimes, why?'

'I vaguely remember a story about smugglers, and when Fran and I were over at St Aldeberge today she mentioned Rupert and the story popped into my head. I can't think what it means.'

Ben raised his eyebrows. 'I would have thought it was obvious,' he said. 'Everyone's wondered all the way through if this case had anything to do with smuggling, so you thought of a Rupert story with smugglers.'

'Yes, but why is it particularly relevant?'

'OK,' said Ben, sitting down at the kitchen table. 'Think it through. The area. Where were you exactly?'

'Down by the inlet where the two women lived.'

'OK, so fairly isolated and the inlet. Could that have rung a bell?'

'A beach, a cave?' Libby stopped chopping vegetables. 'That's it. It was a cove. An inaccessible cove.'

'There you are then. So is the inlet.'

'But there's no beach. Nowhere to land anything.' Libby returned to the vegetables.

'Was there a way out of the cove? Could that be it?'

Libby thought for a moment. 'That could be it. A tunnel, perhaps, that came out somewhere else?'

'There, you've got it. And now have a glass of wine and forget it. It's our night off.'

Twice during the evening Libby called Rosie's number, and when she finally got through to Andrew, she found him surprisingly calm.

'I've spoken to your Inspector Ian,' he said. 'I told him she went off on Wednesday evening not long after she'd come here. She was mysterious, but said I wasn't to worry, and I've had a couple of texts since to say she's fine.'

'She hasn't replied to me once,' said Libby, not sure if she should be pleased or worried about this news.

'She told me particularly not to say anything to you or Fran as you'd worry. I'm sure she's all right, Libby. She always manages to be, doesn't she?'

'Only if she's rescued by someone else,' muttered Libby.

'There is that.' Andrew sounded amused. 'I'm getting used to her now, and I admit she can be a bit – what do they say these days? Flaky? But –' he paused. 'To be honest, I enjoy the excitement. My life was very boring before I met her. Well, before I met you and Fran, in fact.'

'Have you got *any* idea where she's gone?'

'None,' said Andrew, cheerfully. 'I'm sorry, Libby.'

'The trouble is, of course,' Libby said to Ben when she'd rung off, 'that texts don't prove anything. Somebody else could be sending them.'

'I do understand you're worried,' said Ben, in a rather exasperated tone, 'but Andrew's told Ian and Ian will be on the case if there's anything to worry about.'

'But Ian hadn't told me.'

'Libby, you are *not* in the police force,' said Ben. 'Now, stop worrying.'

Saturday dawned as grey as the rest of the week had. Ben was off to London to meet his son, who had come down from somewhere near Manchester. Libby was vague about their exact relationship, only knowing it hadn't been easy. Ben spoke very little of his early life, although Libby knew he had worked in theatres when he was a student, which had given him the interest he still had.

Making up her mind, she called Harry at the restaurant and booked a table for herself for eight o'clock that evening, which Harry corrected to nine.

'Christmas is coming, ducks,' he said. 'Full up before then.'

Then, collecting Ben's old anorak and her Wellington boots, she set off to drive at a leisurely pace towards Heronsbourne and The Red Lion, a pub she and Fran knew well.

'Hello, George!' she said to the large man polishing the bar as she went in.

'Well, if it isn't Libby Sarjeant!' George put down his cloth and held out his hand. 'Not got that Fran with you today?'

'No, she's doing family things and helping in Guy's shop. Can I have one of your lovely coffees?'

'So what brings you out here, then?' said George, above the noise of the coffee machine. 'Not another murder, is it?'

'Well, actually,' began Libby.

'Course it is. It'll be they old women over at St Aldeberge, won't it?' George turned and winked at her.

'You know about it, then?'

'Course. In the local paper and on the news. And one of them women was a customer in here.'

'Really?' Libby hoisted herself onto a bar stool. 'Mrs Longfellow?'

'Not sure of the name, but recognised her picture in the paper. Used to come in here with a bloke.'

'Did she now? What was he like?'

'Quite nice-looking. Bit younger than her. Always wore a long overcoat. They never talked much. Always sat in a corner, over there,' he pointed, 'and sometimes had something to eat. Is that a clue?' he looked hopeful.

'Do you know, George, I think it might be,' said Libby. 'I don't suppose you've told the police, have you?'

'Didn't think they'd be interested. She coulda been in most pubs round here, couldn't she? They wouldn't want to know all of 'em.'

'I suppose not. I might drop a hint, though, if you don't mind.'

'You go ahead. You been asked to look into it?'

'Yes, by the vicar. She was having trouble over there.'

'I know she was, bless her.' George shook his head. 'Our St Martha's is one of hers, too.'

'Oh, really?' Libby was surprised. 'I know she said she had another church, but I didn't realise it was here. Did you hear about the Miners' Reunion service?'

'Hear about it? I was there!' said George, delivering his second surprise of the morning.

'Oh, George, you're a marvel!' said Libby. 'Can I buy you a drink?'

'Bit early for me, Libby.' He pulled a stool up behind the bar and sat on it. 'Go ahead, what do you want to ask me?'

'How do you know I want to ask you anything?' grinned Libby.

'Course you do.' He grinned back and patted her hand. 'Been asking questions since I first met you however-many years ago.'

'OK, then. You were at the church and the party afterwards?'

'I was. Went over with the missus. Old Father Roberts used to be our vicar here and he helped with the service.'

'Yes, in fact he took communion to the first victim.'

'The old woman who was found in the church? Cor, that didn't half cause a row.'

'A row?' said Libby.

'A fuss. Woman goes out and comes back in all of a fluster and calls for a doctor. Then a bunch of them goes out, then the doctor comes back and asks us all to stay put. Well, we was anyway, the party not having long got going, but course, everyone's talking about it, and asking what's happened. And then these two coppers come and asked us all if we'd seen anything suspicious or knew this old woman. And us who'd gone over from here were told we could go. Funny business.'

'Certainly was. And had you seen anything?'

'I wouldn't know if I had, would I now? There were people coming and going all the time, especially when it was communion. You know what it's like then.'

Libby thought for a moment while she sipped her coffee.

'Were there many people in wheelchairs there?' she asked suddenly.

'Wheelchairs? I don't know, except for the one outside the church.'

'You saw it?' Libby was almost holding her breath.

'I just saw this bloke putting it in the boot of a car. As we were going in.'

Chapter Twenty-nine

Libby stared, open mouthed.

'What's the matter?' asked George nervously. 'Wasn't I supposed to see that?'

'I don't suppose you were,' said Libby. 'That's the first time anyone's admitted to seeing that wheelchair after the beginning of the service. Can you describe the bloke?'

'Didn't actually see him properly.' George wrinkled his forehead. 'Only got his back view, and only for a second, you know?'

'It wasn't the man who came in here with Mrs Longfellow?'

George shook his head. 'Couldn't see.'

'So who is he?'

George opened his eyes wide in surprise. 'I don't know, do I? They always paid cash in here, and I never heard his name – or hers, come to that.'

Libby sighed. 'It's so frustrating. Do you mind if I tell the police you saw the wheelchair, George?'

'Course not. Tell 'em about her coming in here, too. Might help.'

Libby slid off her stool. 'Thanks, George. By the way, from here, how would you get to Felling?'

'There's a turning to St Aldeberge off the main road, and a turning to Felling off that,' said George. 'Or you can go down to Nethergate on the main road –'

'Yes, I know that way,' said Libby. 'I'll try the back way.'

'What do you want in Felling?' asked George. 'There isn't much there.'

'No, I know, Fran and I went there the other day. But I want to have a look at the Dunton Estate.'

George looked doubtful. 'Don't think you'll get there from Felling. You have to go St Aldeberge and on from there.'

'But doesn't it back on to the marshes at Felling?'

'Yes, but there isn't a road. Best go the other way.'

Luckily, Libby remembered the way Fran had taken her to the Willoughby Oak and found her way fairly easily. She passed the tree and went on until she came to tall, open, rusted gates and stopped the car.

It was very quiet. The drive that ran away from the gates was overgrown and rutted, but, oddly, showed signs of recent use. Libby got out and peered at it. Yes, there were definitely fresh tyre tracks. She looked around. The track had come to a halt by the gates, and dense woodland obscured her view that way.

'That,' she said aloud to herself, 'must be the woodland that borders the Felling marshes.'

Ahead of her was the drive, curving away towards more woodland and the top of a substantial house. Away to the right, open fields with no sign of life. Behind, back down the lane, the Willoughby Oak, poor Cunning Mary's gibbet. Above, a parliament of rooks suddenly broke free of the naked trees, and rose in the air, cawing and clattering.

'Judging the souls of the dead,' thought Libby, shivering and remembering a fragment of local folk-lore.

She locked Romeo the Renault and bade him be good, and set off to find a path through the trees, which seemed a better bet than striding purposefully up the drive under the eyes of who knew what.

Not that she was entirely sure what she was trying to do. In her muddled brain there was now a connection between the Willoughby Oak, the Dunton Estate, smuggling and the murders of Joan Bidwell and Marion Longfellow, although she wasn't sure how she'd managed to string them all together. And the smuggling seemed to have a link to Felling, despite the fact that nothing could get up the river to it, so coming at it from the other direction seemed like a good idea. Suppose, she reasoned, as she trudged through black, forest-floor mud and disintegrating leaves, something was being landed near St Aldeberge, and somehow brought overland here, and through the woods to the Felling Marshes.

That would mean being exposed a lot of the time and seemed a rather reckless method of transporting goods or people. She sighed, and tried to peer ahead through the tangle of trees and other – prickly – vegetation. She thought she could see the glimmer of water, but not quite how to get to it. Picking her way carefully along between the larger gaps in the trees, she suddenly found herself in front of a wide track.

To her right it wound away and behind, to her left, it ended at the wire fence she and Fran had seen on Monday from the marshes, so that was proof that there was a way from the Dunton Estate to the Felling marshes. She smiled triumphantly, then euphoria faded. What did that prove? Nothing. She was weaving silk out of cobwebs again.

Just to prove that she was by the marshes, she trudged down the track to the wire fencing, which was high and strong, and stood looking over at the quayside. Yes, she was where she thought she'd be. And behind her, somewhere, was the Willoughby Oak, and Fran was sure there was a drug connection there, if only they could figure it out. She turned and made her way back.

When she reached the Willoughby Oak again, she once more stopped the car and got out. A fragment of blue police tape still fluttered here, too, along with fewer fragments of other material than had been here when she and Fran had last visited, nearly three weeks ago. She walked up to it and, after a moment, stepped round it.

On the other side, free from the shadow it seemed to cast even when there was no sun, the ground was open. She could see ahead the roof of the house, nearer and clearer now, and away to the right a long expanse of open grassland, dotted with humps of grass and broken stone. This obviously wasn't part of the formal gardens of the Dunton Estate.

'I wonder?' she muttered to herself, as she took a step forward. Would this actually go right down to the St Aldeberge inlet, this open field? Would it, in fact, become a chalk cliff top?

Deciding it was too open to risk walking down it to find out, she returned to the car and thought about it. Even if it did lead to the top of the St Aldeberge cliffs, Marion Longfellow's cottage and Joan Bidwell's bungalow would be in the way, and it was so exposed, anyone, or anything, moving across the landscape would be seen. She shook her head, put the car in gear and bumped back down the track to the road, where she turned thankfully back towards Steeple Martin.

'You know I was thinking about Rupert Bear yesterday,' she said later to Fran on the phone, 'well, I've figured it out.'

'Were you?'

'Yes, you mentioned him. Anyway, I remembered a story about Rupert and smugglers where there's a little cave entrance just above the water line which leads to a tunnel that comes out on the cliff above.'

'And you think there's something like that at the inlet?'

'It would explain how things got in from the sea.'

'But, Libby, we don't know that they have! This is pure speculation.' Fran sounded amused. 'Where did you go today?'

'Why did you think I'd been anywhere?' asked Libby.

'Because I know you, and I know Ben's away.'

Libby related her morning's trip. 'It just all links up, somehow,' she said, 'but I'm not sure why.'

'No news of Rosie?'

'No, but as neither Andrew nor Ian appear to be worried, Ben tells me I mustn't be, either. I'm going off to the caff tonight to be reckless and indulgent all on my own and I suppose I'd better forget all about inlets and smugglers and murdered flower ladies.'

However, when Libby arrived at The Pink Geranium just before nine o'clock that night, she found Peter sitting on the sofa in the window waiting for her, a bottle of red wine open on the low table in front of him.

'What's this? A panto council of war?' she asked giving her coat to a glowing Donna.

'No, you ungrateful old trout. Company, and a chance for you to expound your most recent theories about your murders.'

'How did you know I might want to do that?'

'Because you always do.' Peter handed her a glass of wine. 'Off you go, and I shall burst each bubble as I see fit.'

'What, right from the beginning? But you know most of it.'

'Pretend I don't.'

'Oh, all right.' Libby sipped her wine and spent a moment putting her thoughts – and the events – in order.

'Well, it all started with the murder of Joan Bidwell,' she began.

When she finished, Donna appeared to take their order.

'So which bubbles will you burst?' said Libby when Donna had departed kitchenwards.

'I think that everything one learns afterwards casts each event in a new light,' said Peter. 'For instance, the motive for the first murder. If, as it looked like, it was done in order to look like a natural death, why then, was Marion –'

'Longfellow,' said Libby.

'Yes, her, why was she killed with such flamboyance and surrounded with all the Black Magic paraphernalia?'

'We know that! To point at Patti.'

'I don't believe that. I think it was genuinely to point at a Black Magic involvement.'

'But why? When Fran and I tracked down the Willoughby Oak it appeared to have some connection with drugs, that was all, so why should someone want to draw attention to it?'

'But no one knew that at the time, did they? Perhaps the Black Magic angle was a red herring?'

'A red herring in which aspect? Drugs or murder?'

'Both.' Peter picked up the bottle and his glass and led the way to the table Donna had ready for them. 'If the coven, or whatever it was, had been set up to draw attention away from drug smuggling, it might be useful to draw attention away from the real murderer, too.'

'Hmm.' Libby looked doubtful. 'So then, why Marion Longfellow?'

'Either she saw whatever the first victim saw, or she was in on it.'

'Wow! And she was killed to shut her up? Perhaps she tried blackmail!' Libby's eyes grew wide with excitement. 'That fits with her solitariness, except for all her men, of course.'

'And she wasn't exactly solitary there, was she, according to gossip?'

'I wonder,' said Libby slowly, 'if all this gossip about men didn't turn out to be another red herring. After all, most of them seem to have been there to do errands, and there's only one Fran and I think was actually – er – doing it. Apart from the man in the long coat that George described, that must be the one Mrs Dora meant.'

'Another smokescreen? So she and the man in the long coat were in whatever-it-was together.'

'It's just a question of what was it?'

'And the man on the dating site, of course. He's got to fit in.' Peter poured more wine.

'I almost wish something else would happen so we could actually see where things were going,' said Libby with a sigh. 'But I know I shouldn't really wish that.'

'You most definitely shouldn't,' said Peter. 'Especially with Rosie in the equation.'

'I do hope she isn't really in trouble,' said Libby as Donna placed their Taco starter on the table. 'I sort of feel responsible for her.'

'Shut up and eat,' said Peter.

Harry joined them as soon as he could leave the kitchen, and after coffee, suggested that he and Peter should accompany Libby home.

'Oh, don't be daft,' she said. 'It's only round the corner.'

'And you know how Ben feels about you going home on your own. Any woman, actually. Even that Rosie,' said Harry, finishing off his glass of wine. 'Come on. Get yer coat, you've pulled.'

Per lifted his aristocratic nose. 'So common, dear.'

Harry grinned. 'But you love me for it.'

They sauntered down the high street, Libby between them

with an arm through each of theirs. The didn't see or smell the smoke until they turned the corner into Allhallow's Lane.

Chapter Thirty

Harry broke into a run with Peter not far behind.

'It's my house!' gasped Libby, feeling the blood draining from her head.

Peter turned back and grabbed her as she stumbled. 'No, petal, it's behind your house. Come on. Hal's calling 999.'

But someone else had obviously already called the Fire Brigade, because they had hardly reached the front door of number 17 when they heard the sirens. Libby fumbled with the lock and Harry and Peter between them pushed her inside.

The conservatory was white hot and there was already a crack in the glass at the back. Libby opened the door into the garden as they heard someone at the front of the house. Peter went to direct the fire fighters round to the back of the property and Libby and Hal stepped into the garden to see the blazing hedge that bordered the woods. The fire had already consumed the flower bed at the back and was creeping down the dividing fences. Libby looked up to see the horrified face of her right-hand neighbour staring down from an upstairs window as a fire engine crashed through the wood, and within minutes hoses were being trained on the blaze and Harry and Libby were soaking wet.

They went inside and found Peter making tea.

'Get a towel, petal,' he said, 'then come back and drink this. The officers will want to speak to you.'

'Where's Sidney?' whispered Libby, who had just discovered that her legs wouldn't allow her to go and get a towel. Hal got up and went instead.

'I don't know,' said Peter, putting a mug in front of her. 'But it wasn't as if the house was on fire with him trapped inside it, was it? He'll have shot off out of it.'

'Here,' said Harry returning with towels, a dressing gown and a protesting cat. 'Under your bed. Said he didn't want to come out and didn't much like fires unless they were in your fireplace.'

Libby grabbed Sidney with shaking hands and found that she might be going to cry.

'Shock,' said Harry kindly, patting her on the shoulder. 'Now, drink that tea and get that dressing gown on.'

Without shame, through spending time in many mixed-gender dressing rooms, Libby stripped off her jumper and trousers and wrapped the dressing gown round her, while Harry swathed himself in her best blue towels. They all sat round the kitchen table watching through the conservatory as the fire was brought under control and the garden reduced to a soggy mess.

'They saved the cherry tree,' said Libby, as she watched beige-suited men picking through the wet undergrowth.

There was a knock on the open front door.

'In here,' called Peter.

The fire officer was apologetic about the mess in her garden.

'If it hadn't been for you I might not have *had* a garden, or a house, come to that,' said Libby, feeling slightly less shaky.

'I gather you were out tonight?' said the officer.

'Yes,' they all three said together.

After eliciting the information that there was nothing kept at the bottom of the garden that could have caused a fire, the officer left, saying that a police officer would shortly be calling.

'Arson, then?' said Harry.

'Looks like it,' said Peter. They both looked at Libby.

'I didn't do it!'

'No, but it does look a bit sus, doesn't it?' Harry poked a finger at her. 'Here's you, up to the neck in a murder investigation and all of a sudden someone tries to make a bonfire out of you.'

'But actually, they didn't,' said Libby reasonably. 'They set the back hedge alight. And because it's November and wet, the woods didn't go up, and it didn't spread as quickly as it might have. There was every chance that it would be put out before too much damage was done.'

'She's right, you know,' said Peter. 'So, what? A warning, you think?'

'Bloody right,' said Harry. 'Good job we came back with you.'

'Oh yes!' Libby grabbed both their hands. 'What would I do without you two? Thank you so much.'

'We didn't actually do much except act as moral support,' said Peter, patting her hand with his free one. 'However, now we've had the tea for the shock, I suggest you dig out your strongest spirits to revive us before the Spanish Inquisition.'

'Which is just about to start,' said a familiar voice. 'Did you know the front door was open?' And Ian strolled into the kitchen.

Libby gaped, while Peter, with a wry smile, stood up and went to fetch the whisky.

'They called me when the report came in,' said Ian, sitting on the remaining chair. 'The address rang a bell, apparently.' He leant forward to look critically at Libby. 'Are you all right?'

'Yes, fine now. I was a bit shaky but ... Ian, is this arson?'

'Of course it is,' said Ian, shaking his head as Peter waved the whisky bottle at him. 'So someone has decided you've been making too much noise over at St Aldeberge. Which means that, however accidental, somehow you've hit on part of the truth.'

Libby looked at Peter and Harry, then back at Ian.

'Which part?' she said, and wondered why they all laughed.

'Tell me what you've been doing since we last spoke,' said Ian.

'I'd rather know what you've been doing.'

Ian shook his head. 'Just give me a recap on your more outrageous exploits in the past few days and I'll see if I can satisfy your curiosity.'

'Better than nothing, I suppose,' said Libby, and proceeded to give him a précis of the last couple of days, concluding with the fact that she was still worried about Rosie and about her Rupert Bear theory.

'As far as Rosie's concerned, I don't think you've got anything to worry about. I think she *did* go off to do some sleuthing on her own, but I'm pretty sure she's all right. Yes,' he held up his hand, 'I know texts can be sent from anyone, but she's actually spoken to Andrew today, and apart from sounding rather mysterious, seems to be quite happy. Excited, even.'

'So what about my smugglers?'

Ian smiled. 'We are, in fact, pretty convinced there is a smuggling element concerned with all this and we're involved in at least two undercover operations, so I'm certainly not going to tell you anything about them!'

'And the second victim being involved with whatever was going on?' asked Peter.

'I can't say anything about that, either, I'm afraid,' said Ian, 'but what I will say, Libby, is that you must, repeat must, stop investigating. The police and customs operations are undercover so far, but you have been extremely visible, so whoever our murderer is, you're the one he – or they – see as a threat. So keep out of sight.'

'But what about the St Aldeberge Nativity?'

'I'm sure now you've set it up they could manage on their own,' said Ian. 'Now, we shall want statements from all of you, but I'll send someone round tomorrow.'

'We'll be at the Manor for lunch,' said Peter, 'at least Libby and I will. Harry will be at the restaurant.'

'Where's Ben?' asked Ian. Libby told him. Ian nodded. 'He's not going to be too pleased, is he?'

Libby's stomach sank. 'No,' she said. 'He's not.'

After Ian left, Peter topped up the whisky in their glasses.

'Do you want to come back and stay with us tonight?' he asked.

'No, I'll be fine. Whoever it is isn't likely to come back is he?' Libby looked over her shoulder towards the garden, where two fire fighters were still picking through the mess.

'Anyway, she wouldn't leave the walking stomach,' said Harry, peering under the table where Sidney was sulking.

'He'd be all right overnight, but I'll stay here anyway,

215

thanks, Pete.' Libby smiled gratefully. 'You ought to be going home now. It's getting very late.'

With Harry and Peter gone, Libby called out to the remaining firemen that she was going to bed if it was all right with them and locked all the doors and windows. But of course, when she finally got into bed, allowing a surprised Sidney to accompany her, she couldn't sleep.

The thought she couldn't shake off was that somebody had been watching her closely over the last three weeks. Which meant someone who knew right from the start that Patti had asked her in to investigate Joan Bidwell's death. Which pointed inexorably at Alice and Bob, but it couldn't be Alice. She was the one who had suggested Patti call her in. Bob? Who had shied away from the DNA test? It was possible, she supposed, and Bob would have been able to find her address, which presumably Alice had kept, as she had kept the phone number. But there didn't seem to be any reason for him to kill Joan Bidwell. He couldn't be involved in anything more complicated than a darts match, he was too indolent.

So who else? Neither Fran nor Libby had met anyone else in the village until Libby and Ben had gone to church, and then Libby's meeting with the Nativity committee. By that time both murders had been committed and everyone knew they were under investigation. There had also been the nasty business of the cockerel, or whatever it was, on Patti's doorstep.

So perhaps it was after this that the murderer began to get suspicious of Libby. After the visit to the Willoughby Oak, perhaps? That would have been a give away. Or maybe the first visit to the shop and Dora Walters. Dora was a gossip, and although she still hadn't confirmed who Marion Longfellow's serious lover was, it was a safe bet that he would know about Libby. But *who* was he? And was he Bruno51 from the dating site? And was he even the murderer?

At this point Libby found herself floating in a boat with Fran and Patti over a flat, grassy field. Patti was saying that of course this was how the murderer got away and Fran was complaining about her most recent grandchild climbing through holes … and she woke up with a start.

Without her noticing the night had passed and she'd slept. But the dream stayed vividly in her mind, and then it made sense.

'You see,' she said to Fran excitedly on the phone while she waited for the kettle to boil, 'I remembered the Rupert Bear story was about a coastguard seeing bad men around the cliff top and they suddenly vanished. And Rupert and his friends find a tunnel down to the foot of the cliff hidden in a clump of bracken. And that's what it must be. I already nearly had it, but the dream clarified it. And I expect it comes out somewhere near the Willoughby Oak. And after the fire –'

'Fire? What fire?'

'Oh.' To her surprise, Libby realised she hadn't told Fran about the fire first. She glanced out of the window to the sorry, soggy mess that was her garden, the cherry tree standing skeletal in the middle. 'Well, I had a fire last night.'

Putting boiling water into the teapot, she listened to Fran's horrified outpourings.

'It's all right, Fran, it was only the back hedge and part of the dividing fence. The garden's ruined, but nothing else was harmed except for a crack in the conservatory. Ian's concerned, though, that someone might be trying to give me a warning. He's warned me not to do any more investigating.'

'And he is completely right,' said Fran. 'And that goes for both of us. Does Ben know yet? He was away, wasn't he?'

'No, not yet. I'm not looking forward to telling him. But what do you think about my tunnel theory?'

'Fine as far as it goes, but listen, Lib, you aren't going to do anything to put it to the test, do you hear me?'

'Yes, I hear you,' sighed Libby. 'I was lying awake last night after Hal and Pete left realising that someone has been watching me – us, probably. It's a bit creepy.'

'I've hardly been involved,' said Fran, 'so I don't suppose anyone's been watching me.'

'I've been trying to work out who it could be.' Libby lodged the phone between shoulder and ear and went to fetch milk. 'It's obviously somebody in the village. I wish Rosie would get in touch.'

'That's a bit of a non-sequitur,' said Fran, surprise in her voice.

'Not really. I think she was on the trail of that Bruno51, who could also be the murderer, and I'm now even more worried for her safety, despite what Ian says.'

'Hmm,' said Fran. 'I think she's OK. For what it's worth.'

'Really?' said Libby, brightening. 'Like, properly all right?'

'I haven't any evil premonitions, and my brain tells me she's all right,' said Fran. 'Can't help any more than that. Listen, if you would feel better, you can always come and stay here. The bed's still made up from last time.'

'No, I'm fine, thanks,' said Libby. 'Hal and Pete offered to put me up, too, but Ben will be home today, so I shall be protected.'

'If nagged,' said Fran.

Libby giggled. 'Indeed.'

In fact, Ben arrived within ten minutes, having been called, much to Libby's annoyance, by Ian, who had his mobile number. After a flurry of reassurances and remonstrances, Libby poured more tea and they sat down at the table.

'Ian was worried about you,' said Ben.

'I was fine,' said Libby. 'He didn't think anyone would come back, did he?'

'No, he didn't want you feeling insecure on your own.'

'Hal and Pete and Fran have all said I can go there, but you're home now, so we'll be fine, and as I've been effectively warned off any more investigating, there will be no need to come after me again, will there? As I said to the others last night, I don't think it was meant to do much harm. If it had, they would have fired the house.' She shuddered.

'And this will mean you don't do any more poking your nose in.' Ben looked at her sternly.

'I know, I know.' Libby sighed. 'But I do so want to know how it all turns out.'

'Of course you'll know. Patti will tell you, and I've no doubt

Ian will come and do his Poirot-style round-up after it's all over. And I don't expect Ian will ban you from attending the Nativity service if you want to go.'

'If it's cleared up I'll go,' said Libby, 'but if not and the murderer's still at large, I shan't.' She stood up. 'I'm going to ring Hetty to tell her you'll be at lunch, then I'm going to have a shower.'

Ian sent the fresh-faced Sergeant Maiden to the Manor to take statements from Peter and Libby, and had thoughtfully not bothered with Harry, who was run off his feet with Sunday lunches in The Pink Geranium.

Sitting at the kitchen table with a large mug of coffee and looking wistfully at the equally large glasses of red wine in front of Ben, Peter and Libby, Sergeant Maiden snapped his notebook shut.

'That all seems clear,' he said. 'Would you be able to come into the station to sign these sometime?'

'Of course,' said Peter. 'We'll come tomorrow – and we could bring Harry, too.'

'Thank you.' Maiden took a sip of coffee. 'If you don't mind me saying, Mrs Sarjeant, you do manage to get yourself mixed up in some nasty stuff.'

'I know.' Libby sighed. 'I'll try and do better.'

Sergeant Maiden grinned. 'I wouldn't worry. You and Mrs Castle have been really helpful over the past few years.'

'More help than hindrance?' asked Ben. 'I doubt it.'

'It's Mrs Wolfe, now, Sergeant,' said Libby. 'Although I still think of her as Fran Castle, too.'

'I don't suppose you can give our little ferreter here any news on how the investigation's going, can you?' said Peter.

'Sorry, sir, no.' Maiden grinned. 'I'm sure you'll hear all about it soon enough. Getting close now.'

'That wasn't fair!' exploded Libby after Ben had ushered the Sergeant out. 'Taunting us like that.'

'Too nosy fer yer own good,' said Hetty, setting dishes of vegetables on the table. 'Lucky you wasn't burnt to death.'

'Gee, thanks, Hetty.' Libby wriggled uncomfortably. 'I'm

trying not to think about it.'

Hetty shrugged. 'No point in that.'

After lunch, when Hetty went to put her feet up in her little sitting room, Libby and Ben put the kitchen to rights, and Peter invited them back to his house, as Harry would be finished at the restaurant.

'So did the fuzz put you in the picture?' he asked, almost as soon as he walked in the front door.

'No such luck,' said Libby.

'I was thinking,' he said, giving Peter's bottom a friendly squeeze as he passed him on the way to the kitchen, 'that the fire investigators will have been looking for an accelerant. Have they been back?'

'They were there when we left for the Manor,' said Ben.

'Would it have needed an accelerant?' asked Libby. 'It's a hedge. It would burn.'

'Not quickly enough, said Ben. 'It's been damp for weeks, without an accelerant it could easily have fizzled and gone out. Think how much difficulty people have lighting bonfires on Guy Fawkes' night.'

'Anyway, why did you ask?' said Libby.

'Won't they be able to trace it back to a particular person?' said Harry, putting his head round the kitchen door.

'Doubt it,' said Ben. 'It'll probably be petrol, and anyone could get hold of that.'

'Unless it's red diesel,' said Peter. 'And then *you* might be under suspicion.'

Chapter Thirty-one

'What?' gasped Libby.

'Bad taste, Pete,' said Ben.

'Sorry, cousin,' said Peter, with a grin. 'You know about red diesel, Libby?'

'Er – vaguely.' Libby looked from one to another. 'It's illegal, isn't it?'

'Only for use in ordinary road vehicles. It's legal for agricultural vehicles,' said Peter, 'and Ben has it up on the estate.'

'Oh. Well, I think that was in bad taste, too, Peter Parker.'

'Tea?' said Harry, smiling seraphically and pouring oil on troubled waters.

'The other thing I was thinking,' he went on, coming to perch on the arm of Peter's chair while the kettle boiled, 'was the witchcraft angle. They used to burn witches, didn't they?'

'So I'm a witch, now, am I?' said Libby. 'You're doing well this afternoon, Harry!'

'Calm down, petal,' said Peter. 'You know what he means. Is it a deliberate attempt to hook into that aspect of your murders?'

Libby shifted uncomfortably. 'Don't call them my murders. Anyway, it's nothing to do with me, now. I've been warned off.'

'And that's presumably what the murderer – or the arsonist – wants,' said Harry.

'I don't think the witchcraft angle has proved to be anything to with it, except obfuscation,' said Ben.

'Ob what?' said Harry.

'Muddy the waters,' explained Libby. 'Not a word in common use.'

'There, I've learnt something,' said Harry, getting up and

221

going to the kitchen.

'So will you really stay out of it now?' asked Peter.

'I don't have a choice,' said Libby. 'And to be honest, I don't see what else I could do.'

'Much as I would prefer you not to have anything more to with it, I have a feeling that this won't be the last we hear,' said Ben.

Harry brought in his beautiful decoupage tray with the usual collection of chipped mugs.

'Why don't you buy some new ones?' asked Libby.

'I like these,' said Harry. 'They make me feel comfortable.'

For a fleeting moment, Libby saw the hidden Harry, whose unknown background had left him vulnerable. She knew she wouldn't find out anything about this unless he chose to tell her, and had purposely never asked, realising that remembering it would upset him. The closest she'd ever come to learning anything was when, at his request, she'd become involved in an investigation into a homophobic attack on his friend Cy.

Harry sat on the sofa next to Ben and swivelled to put his feet up on Peter's lap. 'I think Ben's right,' he said. 'And I think that the old Rosie-bird will get you involved again. You see if she doesn't.'

'But she's vanished,' said Libby. 'The only way she could get me involved is if I went looking for her.'

'I seem to remember that happening before,' said Ben. 'In the middle of the night, too.'

'It wasn't the middle of the night,' protested Libby. 'And I remember Ian not being worried about her that time, too, so he hasn't got a good track record.'

Libby's basket began to ring.

'Talk about me buying new mugs,' said Harry, 'but shouldn't you replace that old hay-bag?'

Libby ignored him and took her mobile out of the basket.

'Libby, it's me, Rosie.'

Libby nearly upset her mug. 'Rosie? Good God, where are you?'

The three men suddenly sat upright, exchanging astonished

looks.

Rosie giggled. 'Aha! I've been doing some undercover detective work. I'm using a pay as you go mobile and I've been only using computers in the library. I knew your Ian and you would have a fit if you knew what I've been doing.'

'But where are you? Rosie, you must tell Ian.'

'I haven't got his number, only yours and Fran's – oh and Andrew's. I've been in touch with him so he knows I'm all right.'

'Yes, he said that, but we were still worried.'

'Well,' said Rosie, 'you can stop being worried. Why don't you come and meet me tonight and I'll tell you all about it.'

'Rosie, I wish you wouldn't ask me out on Sunday nights. I've always had a drink on Sundays. It will have to wait until tomorrow.'

'It'll be too late then,' said Rosie. 'Could I come over and pick you up? I think it's important.'

'Wait a minute,' said Libby. 'I'll ask the council.' She turned to her three listeners. 'Rosie wants to pick me up tonight and take me somewhere. She's been detecting on her own.'

'No!' said three voices, quite loudly.

'There,' said Libby into the phone. 'You heard that, didn't you?'

'Yes, I did.' Rosie sounded offended.

'Look, Rosie, it's tantamount to the heroine in the darkened house going blithely into the cellar when she hears a noise. As a matter of fact, we've just been talking about the case and you. As a result of the fire –'

'Fire? What fire?' Rosie echoed Fran.

'Oh, yes, sorry. Someone tried to burn down my house last night and Ian thinks it was a warning, so he's forbidden me to go anywhere near anything to do with the case.' Slight exaggeration, but forgivable in the circumstances, Libby thought.

'Oh.' Rosie was quiet for a moment. 'But what about the dating site?'

'Is that what you've been doing? Only Ian and his team have

been monitoring activity on there since you disappeared, so he'll know what you've been up to anyway.'

'No, he won't,' said Rosie, triumph in her voice. 'I told you – untraceable mobile and computers, new web-based emails. And both Bruno51 and I came off the site.'

'Well, you're quite mad,' said Libby. 'And I shall tell Ian *and* give him this number. Whatever you're planning, I beg you, don't do it.'

'I never thought you'd be such a coward,' said Rosie. 'No one would know who you are, after all.'

'Coward?' Libby was seething now. 'And what do you mean, no one would know who I was? Where?'

Rosie was silent again, obviously realising she'd slipped up.

'Well, go ahead,' said Libby. 'And I've told you, I shall tell Ian immediately.' She switched off the phone. 'Damn!'

'What?' said the three voices.

'She's got something planned for tonight and she's been communicating with that bloke from the dating site.'

'I told you so!' crowed Harry. 'I said she'd get you involved and she has.'

'I'm afraid he's right, Lib,' said Ben. 'She could be walking straight into danger. What exactly did she say?'

'Hang on a minute, I'm phoning Ian,' said Libby. Two minutes later, she swore again.

'Yes, we heard,' said Peter. 'You've left messages on both his phones. Now what?'

'Tell us what she said, Lib,' repeated Ben. 'See if we can work out what she's planning to do.'

Libby recounted as much of Rosie's conversation as she could verbatim.

'No one would know who you were,' said Ben slowly. 'That either means you would be somewhere you weren't known, or –'

'I would be in disguise of some sort,' said Libby, 'which sounds much more likely to me. No one would know sounds as though normally they *would* know me.'

'Something is making me think of our dear old moustachioed witch,' said Harry. 'The one you had tea with in the caff.'

'Oh, dear, back to the Black Mass again,' said Libby.

'Not necessarily a Black Mass,' said Peter. 'Just a coven meeting. A set-up to cover – as you've said yourself – a multitude of sins.'

'Do you think that's what Rosie's got herself involved in?' Libby turned to Ben.

'Could be.'

Libby picked up her mug and sipped while she thought.

'Do you suppose,' she said at length, 'that Bruno51, whoever he is, was in touch with Marion Longfellow and encouraged her to join this coven, or whatever it is? And that's why the feathers and pentagram were left with her body. She stepped out of line?'

'Possible,' said Peter, 'but what about the other woman? She wasn't on the dating site, was she?'

'Oh, yes. That's the stumbling block. Perhaps she found out about it?'

'The witchcraft or the dating site?' asked Harry. 'Which would she be most shocked about?'

'The witchcraft, I suppose,' said Libby. 'She was very churchy.'

'But so was the other one according to what you'd heard,' said Ben.

'That was why the first one was so shocked. The other one pretended to be churchy and was a secret witch,' said Harry. 'So, if this theory is true, where will Rosie be going tonight? S'obvious, innit?'

'The Willoughby Oak!' gasped Libby.

'Our Fran thinks it all goes off there, doesn't she. Bet that's it.'

The other three stared at him admiringly.

'You've been practising,' said Peter, patting his leg. 'For that, I shall make more tea. Unless anyone wants something stronger?'

Ben sighed. 'Better not. I have a feeling we might be going out tonight.'

'No,' said Libby firmly. 'We're not. You've already had your share of Hetty's lovely Shiraz, so have I, and we are not going to risk being breathalyzed. So yes, please, Pete. I'd like a glass of wine.'

Ben laughed. 'All right, so would I. Thanks, Pete.'

'So what will you do when the Rosie-bird calls you in a panic later on?' asked Harry. 'Call a taxi?'

'Dial 999, I expect,' said Libby. 'The police are slightly better able to deal with a possibly dangerous situation than we are.'

'You've changed your tune,' said Peter, coming in with a bottle and glasses.

'I'm just being a good girl,' beamed Libby. 'I'm not saying I won't get involved in things in the future, because I think life would be very boring if I didn't have something to do with my time, but in this case I think Rosie's put herself in a very dangerous situation, even if it isn't the whole witchy thing, and I think us going in would make it worse.'

Ben, Peter and Harry looked at each other in amazement.

'I never thought I'd see the day,' said Harry. 'Someone's taken our old trout away and put a ringer in her place.'

Between them, they finished Peter's bottle of wine, then Ben and Libby walked home along the dark high street. On Sunday evening, even the eight-til-late was closed, and only the yellow light from the small pub windows spilled out on to the pavement.

'Do you think Harry's right about Rosie?' Libby asked as they turned the corner into Allhallow's Lane. 'That she's going to some kind of Black Magic ritual?'

'It's a feasible theory, but it is all built on sand and speculation,' said Ben. 'I still think you might get a panic call later, as Harry does.'

Despite Libby's intention to keep out of the whole business, she found herself restless, her thoughts constantly turning to Rosie and the possible identity of Bruno51. If, of course, he was the murderer. Eventually, she left Ben in solitary charge of the sofa and the television, and took the laptop into the kitchen.

First, she tried to find significant dates for the celebration of Black Masses, or rituals, but nothing, not even the phases of the moon coincided with today's date. But then, she decided, if there was a coven meeting at the Willoughby Oak, it appeared to be simply for nefarious purposes, just as those she and Fran had learned about years ago, so the date didn't actually matter.

So, were they right in the assumption that the Willoughby Oak was somehow connected to the murders of Marion Longfellow and Joan Bidwell? Only, Libby realised, because of the very obvious pointers that seemed to draw attention to the involvement of Black Magic, or Satanism. And that argued someone seeking to divert attention towards it and away from someone else. Away from what? Drugs? But then drugs were likely to be involved with the coven. Libby scowled at the screen. It was all so confusing.

And what about Felling? Where did that come in? Just the knowledge that there was a police observation operation based on the quay? Then of course, there was the Rupert Bear theory, with drugs being landed at the inlet and smuggled up a tunnel to – oh, yes, to the Willoughby Oak.

And the possibility of Bruno51 being Marion Longfellow's killer. Now, why had they thought that? Libby frowned. Oh, yes, it had been Rosie's original suggestion. And now Rosie was presumably testing the theory. Libby sighed with frustration just as her phone rang.

Chapter Thirty-two

'Lib, something's happening.' Fran's voice was quavery, and Libby felt a rush of adrenalin.

'What? What did you see?'

'You remember those horrible suffocating feelings I used to get?'

'Oh, God. When you knew someone was dead.'

'Yes. All I could see was a face. I don't know whose it was. But it's to do with this.'

'Have you called Ian?'

'No. How can I say?'

'Call him,' said Libby. 'I've left two messages about Rosie today, and he'll need to know. If he's not answering, leave a message.'

'What about Rosie?' Fran's voice rose higher.

Libby explained. 'Now, go on, call him and come back to me.'

'What was that all about?' asked Ben, coming into the kitchen. Libby told him.

'What did I tell you?' said Ben. 'Panic phone call. You're not going to be able to get out of this one.'

'But it wasn't Rosie.'

'No, but how do you know it isn't *about* Rosie?'

The phone rang again.

'I've left messages on both his phones,' said Fran. 'What shall I *do*?'

'Oh, lord. I said if I heard from Rosie I'd call 999, but we can't phone with your sort of information.'

'Where did you say you thought Rosie might have gone/'

'Harry suggested the Willoughby Oak.'

'Then we must go there.'

'Hang on, Fran, Ben and I have both been drinking. We can't go out there.'

'I haven't. I'll come and get you. We've got to go.'

'That'll take ages,' said Libby. 'Much quicker if you go straight there and take Guy with you.'

'I can't!' Fran's voice was almost hysterical now, which was most unlike her. 'He's gone up to London for some exhibition.'

'Is Adam there?'

'No, he and Sophie are out somewhere.'

Libby looked helplessly at Ben, who was taking his own phone out of his pocket.

'Well, you're not going anywhere on your own,' she said. 'Hang on, Ben's thought of something.'

He was already talking. 'I know it's unconventional, but – yes, exactly. Will you? Thank you so much. You know? Yes, of course you do. Thank you.' He turned to Libby. 'Our fresh-faced Sergeant Maiden. He's going to come by and pick us up. Fran can meet us there. Tell her not to get out of her car.'

Libby repeated the instructions to Fran. 'And don't go right up to the tree, either. Maiden's going out on a limb for us here, we don't want to make things more difficult for him.'

Sergeant Maiden found Libby and Ben waiting for him on the corner of Allhallow's Lane.

'Not sure I should be doing this,' he said cheerfully, 'but I know DCI Connell trusts Mrs Wolfe's instincts, and as he's not here –'

'Yes, where is he?' asked Libby as she settled into the back of the car. 'I've left messages for him on both his mobiles today, and so has Fran. Mind you he probably thinks we're pestering him for the sake of it.'

'He's gone up to Scotland to see family,' said Maiden. 'A wedding or something. He went at lunchtime.'

'Oh, dear, no wonder he wasn't answering his phone,' said Libby.

'Oh, the wedding's tomorrow. He'll be back on Tuesday. He flew up.'

'Oh.' Libby felt an immediate let-down. No Ian as back-up.

'So Mrs Wolfe thinks someone's died?' continued Maiden swinging off down a high-sided lane that led into complete blackness.

'She's not sure, but she had the same feeling that she had before, when somebody actually had. If that makes sense.' Libby sighed. *None* of this was making any sense, really.

Suddenly, Libby realised they were slowing down just before the lane that led to the Willoughby Oak and the woods on the Dunton Estate. And there was Fran's car. Maiden switched off his lights. As they got out of his car, Fran got out of hers.

'Is there anybody there?' whispered Maiden, pulling up a hood to cover his bright hair.

'I've seen a few small lights, and I think there's a fire, but I can't hear anything.' Fran was shivering.

'Let me go first,' said Maiden. 'I don't want to use my torch if possible.' He looked at Ben, who nodded.

'Stay here, girls,' he said, and set off slowly behind the disappearing figure of the sergeant.

Fran and Libby stood huddled together in silence, peering into the darkness. Suddenly, Libby heard a sound behind her. Heart leaping into her mouth she turned, in time to see a shadowy figure slip into the trees.

'We'll have to go after the men and tell them,' whispered Fran, who'd also seen it. 'Come on.'

They began to pick their way along the rutted path, with nothing but a couple of pinpricks of light ahead of them. Not knowing what they might find, Libby felt as frightened as she ever had in her life. At last, she could make out the crouching shapes of Ben and Sergeant Maiden ahead.

'I told you to stay where you were,' whispered Ben.

'No, but Sergeant, someone was back there! They went into the woods,' Libby whispered urgently.

Maiden stood up. 'I don't think there's anyone here now,' he said, 'although there has been. Did you see just one person?'

'Think so,' said Libby, and Fran nodded.

'It looks as though they were all going then. However many

of them there were.' He turned to Fran. 'Do you think they heard or saw you?'

'They might have heard the car engine, but I'd turned off my lights.'

'Well, I'll never find whoever went into the woods, but I'd better go and check this site out. Stay here.' Libby saw him take something out of his pocket and realised it was a telescopic baton. He wasn't taking any chances.

He moved very slowly round the perimeter of the site, and now Libby could see the remains of a fire just the other side of the tree. Suddenly he straightened up and disappeared behind it. Reappearing a moment later, they all saw he had his phone to his ear.

He came back to them. 'Well, Mrs Wolfe,' he said in a normal voice, 'you've done it again. We've found a body.'

Ben and Libby caught Fran as she began to sag.

'Who is it?' asked Libby in a tight voice. 'Is it Rosie?'

'Is that Mrs George? I don't think so,' said Maiden. 'I haven't touched anything yet, and there's a cloak over the body. I'm waiting for back up-now.' He looked from one to the other of them. 'I don't know quite what to do with you all.'

'We'd go home if we could. I'm not sure how you're going to explain why you were here,' said Libby.

'Me neither.' Maiden heaved a deep sigh. 'Mr Connell would choose this weekend to go away. It'll have to be the super. Meanwhile, how are you going to get home?'

'Could we all squeeze into Fran's Smart car?' Ben asked dubiously. 'If she's fit to drive.'

'Of course I am,' said Fran from her place seated on the floor. 'I'm fine now.' And indeed, thought Libby, she sounded much stronger. She helped her friend to her feet.

'I think we can squeeze in, somehow.' Fran brushed herself down. 'And I don't think it's Rosie. Did you actually check that the – the -person was dead, Sergeant?'

Maiden jumped. 'Bollocks! No I didn't.' He turned and almost ran back behind the tree, and as he did, they heard vehicles approaching and saw blue lights sending their eerie intermittent warning through the night. Maiden appeared again.

'There's a faint pulse,' he said. 'Can you direct them to me?' He disappeared and Fran followed him.

'Fran!' said Libby.

'I can probably help,' said Fran, continuing towards the tree.

A police car followed by an ambulance arrived beside Libby and Ben. A uniformed officer got out.

'Sergeant Maiden's behind the tree with the casualty,' said Ben, forestalling questions.

'Casualty?' repeated the officer. 'He said –'

'Yes, but he checked again. He'll need the paramedics.'

The officer, giving them a suspicious look, went to check for himself, then came back and hailed the ambulance crew. Minutes later, Maiden escorted Fran back to Libby and Ben. She looked at Libby.

'We do know her,' she said. 'It's that nice flower lady we met in church.'

Libby gasped, her hand flying to her mouth.

'Sheila Johnson! Oh my God! It's her husband –' she broke off.

'Her husband what?' said Maiden sharply.

'I met him only on Friday.' Libby recovered herself. 'In the village shop. He was so nice.'

Fran gave her a keen look.

'Is that a positive identification, Mrs Wolfe?' asked Maiden back to being the formal police officer.

'Yes, unless I have to come and look,' said Libby.

Maiden looked from her to Fran. 'I think I'll trust you,' he said. 'Do you know where she lives?'

'In St Aldeberge, but you'll have the details, because her husband gave his DNA last week.' Libby frowned in concentration. 'Ken – that's it, Ken Johnson. But she'll probably have identification on her, won't she?'

Maiden and Fran looked at each other.

'No, Lib,' said Fran. 'She was naked under the cloak.'

Sergeant Maiden beckoned to one of the officers now standing guard by the newly strung police tape. 'Can you see

232

these people to their car?'

Libby held out her hand to him. 'Thank you so much for coming out on what must have seemed like a wild goose chase.'

He gave her a wry smile. 'I have to say it was worth it, but all the same, I wish Mr Connell had been here.'

They followed the officer's yellow jacket down the lane to Fran's car, where he stood and waited for them to drive off, with Libby jammed into the tiny space behind the two seats.

'Fran,' she said, as they turned onto the Steeple Martin road, 'why don't you stay with us tonight? Save you going back to an empty house. Balzac will be all right until the morning, won't he?'

'Thank you, Lib.' Fran met her eyes in the mirror. 'I didn't relish going back there on my own, I must admit. If it isn't any trouble.'

'Course it isn't.' Ben smiled at her. 'I believe the spare bed's even made up.'

'Yes it is,' said Libby. 'In case of a visiting child.'

Fran parked the car behind Libby's Renault opposite number 17, and Ben hauled Libby out of the back.

'Nightcap?' he asked, as he led the way into the sitting room. The fire had died down, but there was enough of a glow for Libby to poke it back to life again.

'Have you got any gin?' said Fran, subsiding into the armchair.

'We have. And tonic and ice,' said Libby. Fran gave her a grateful smile.

'So what do we think now?' asked Libby, when they were all settled with drinks. 'Thrown everything back into the melting pot, hasn't it?'

'You nearly let the cat out of the bag about the husband,' said Fran.

'I know, but it doesn't make any difference, does it? He'll be questioned anyway. Do you think she really was a member of this cult, or coven or whatever it is?

'It looks like it, but it could have been a set-up. You realise we still don't know what's happened to Rosie?'

'Oh, lord!' Libby put her head in her hands. 'I wish I'd bloody gone with her after all, now.'

'Do you think she was there tonight?' said Ben.

'No idea. It's possible, but whether we'll ever find out ...' Libby trailed off.

'Will we be able to convince the police to start a search for her?' said Libby.

'If it had been Ian, yes, but with Maiden in charge, I don't know.' Fran stared into the fire.

'They might make someone else take over,' said Libby. 'Someone who won't know us, or understand the situation.'

'Ian will be back on Tuesday,' said Ben.

'That may be too late for Rosie,' said Libby.

'They're sure to have started a search of the area, by now,' said Fran. 'After all, we told the sergeant about the figure we saw going into the wood.'

'Yes, but there was an awfully long gap between us seeing that and the back-up arriving,' said Libby. 'And there might have been any number of people disappearing into the night if it was a proper meeting of the witches, or whatever they are.'

'I did a bit more digging today,' said Fran. 'Modern witches seem to be either peaceful Wiccans, itself a modern religion, or organisations set up to hold Witches Sabbaths, or "esbats". Those are gatherings held purely for pleasure, apparently, like the ones we found out about at Tyne Chapel, or these at the Willoughby Oak. It's fascinating, actually,' Fran leant forward, warming to the story. 'All the descriptions of Satanic rituals that date back in history are from people, particularly the Church, trying to blame something other than God for all the disasters, and are by people who'd never taken part in one. The overwhelming evidence is that they were totally imaginary.'

'What about the so called witches, like the Pendle women? They were tried,' said Libby.

'And just read the evidence!' said Fran. 'They were uneducated women whose words could be twisted, if they were allowed to say anything. I'm sure they did concoct herbal remedies, and maybe they went wrong sometimes, but they weren't witches. The same thing happens in every civilisation; there's a section of the community that is either accused, or sets itself up as witches, or shamans.'

'I suppose so.' Libby looked doubtful. 'But whatever the situation is, this lot are holding meetings or Sabbaths or whatever just to indulge in orgies.'

'That's right, and drugs and hallucinogens have always been used. Most of the current stuff only dates from the early 20th century anyway, with people like Gerald Gardner and Aleister Crowley inventing it.'

'I've heard of Crowley, but not Gardner,' said Ben. 'It sounds as though you did a lot of research.'

'But it doesn't help us know what's happened to Rosie,' said Libby. 'If she went to the Sabbath or coven thing tonight, she could have been killed like Sheila Johnson.'

'Who isn't dead, remember,' said Fran. 'I thought she was. But she isn't. Hopefully she'll be able to tell the police what happened when she comes round.'

'If she comes round,' said Libby gloomily.

'And on that note,' said Ben, standing up, 'I'm going to bed. Come on Lib. There's nothing you can do right now.'

'And don't say, "stop worrying, it won't do any good." No one was ever able to stop worrying.' Libby stood up and picked up empty glasses. 'Go on up, Fran, you know where everything is.'

To her surprise, Libby woke in the morning and realised she must have fallen asleep almost as soon as she got into bed. But a big Rosie-shaped shadow rolled over her as she sat up and wondered who she could get hold of to see if there was any news.

Ben was already in the kitchen making tea for her and coffee for himself.

'Fran's up, too,' he said. 'She'll be down in a minute.'

Libby switched on the radio in the kitchen, the television in the sitting room, and the laptop.

'What's this? Information overload?' Ben put a mug of tea in front of her.

'Just seeing if there's any news about last night.' Libby scrolled through the news sites on the laptop. 'There doesn't seem to be, yet, but as soon as someone picks up the fact that Sheila Johnson was yet another flower lady at St Aldeberge the fat'll hit the fire.'

'Morning,' said Fran, appearing in the doorway. 'I've just thought. Do we know who owns the Dunton Estate?'

Libby swivelled to face her. 'No idea. We didn't bother to look when we were in the Felling Museum, did we?'

'Look now,' said Fran.

'Coffee or tea?' said Ben.

'Found it,' said Libby.

The Dunton Estate had been broken up not long after the second World War, like so many others. The house, not important enough to be taken over by the National Trust or English Heritage, had been sold and turned into apartments. Only a relatively small part of the grounds had been kept, the rest having been sold off.

'But it doesn't say who to,' said Libby.

'Well, it wouldn't. There was a fence round that wood, though, wasn't there? Someone owns it.'

'Or has appropriated it,' suggested Ben. 'If the people running this coven wanted privacy, probably easy enough to do that.'

'The same as they seem to have hung their dubious shenanigans on to the hanging of poor Cunning Mary,' said Libby.

'Always useful to have a focal point,' said Fran. 'Right, as soon as I've finished my coffee, I'm off. Thank you both for last night.'

'We didn't do anything,' protested Libby.

'You did. You organised Sergeant Maiden and then let me stay here.'

'And thanks to you, they found that poor woman,' said Ben. 'Go on, off with you, and if you hear anything before we do, let us know.'

'We will hear something, won't we?' said Libby, after Fran

had gone. 'The police will have to get statements.'

'We might have to go into the station,' said Ben.

'Oh, dear.' Libby stared gloomily at the television screen, which was showing her a map of where the sun would be shining later that day. Inevitably, it wouldn't be on Steeple Martin.

Chapter Thirty-three

Just before Ben left to go up to the Manor, his mobile rang. He answered, then raised his eyebrows at Libby and mouthed, "Ian".

'But you're at a wedding in Scotland,' he said. Libby perched on the edge of the kitchen table trying to work out what the conversation was about. Eventually, Ben switched off the phone.

'Sergeant Maiden decided Ian ought to know about last night. I can only suppose there's an official code that made him take notice of that phone call when he hadn't replied to yours and Fran's, but after he spoke to Maiden, he listened to your messages. He said someone will be round to take statements later today, and he'll be in touch tomorrow as soon as he gets back. Meanwhile, you're to do nothing, and they've put out an alert for Rosie.'

'Why did he call you instead of me?' Libby looked affronted.

'I couldn't say,' said Ben, his lips twitching. 'And now I must be off. Call me when the fuzz arrive.'

'I shan't wait in for them,' said Libby. 'I shall go shopping. And probably to see Pete and Harry to tell them about last night. Harry will be pleased he was proved right.'

'It's all right,' said Ben, opening the front door. 'They're here already.'

Libby wondered if her neighbours were getting used to seeing police vehicles parked outside. It seemed to happen with alarming frequency.

The two uniformed officers asked some very basic questions, wrote down all the answers and asked Libby and Ben to sign each page. They were gone in fifteen minutes.

'I think,' said Libby, closing the door behind them, 'that was an exercise in box ticking.'

'To keep to the rules while something else is going on in the background,' agreed Ben. 'Well, at least you can go off on your news round now. Don't stay in Harry's for too long if you happen to turn up there at lunchtime.'

Before Libby set off to do her shopping, she called Fran to see if she'd arrived home. There was no answer, so she assumed not.

The last day of November had suddenly turned bright. Ali and Ahmed in the eight-til-late both looked more cheerful, as did Nella in the farm shop. Peter didn't look any different.

'You're early,' he said disapprovingly.

'I thought you'd want to know what happened last night. I'll go to the caff and tell Harry instead.'

Peter looked resigned and held the door wide. 'No need. He hasn't left yet.'

Libby recounted the events of the previous night and finished up with the morning's visit from the police and Ian's phone call.

'See?' said Harry. 'I said Rosie would get you into trouble.'

'It wasn't Rosie, though. It was Fran thinking someone was dead.'

'And you both thought it was Rosie, so I rest my case.'

'That's rather unfeeling,' said Peter. 'Try for a little sympathy, pet.'

'All right, all right.' Harry shrugged himself into his chef's whites. 'So what are you going to do now, petal?'

'Nothing, as Ian has instructed. I don't know what I *could* do, to tell you the truth. Just hope they find Rosie.'

'What's happening about the fire? When will they let you start the clear-up?' asked Peter.

'No idea. I'll ask Ian when he calls tomorrow. I think I'm going to have to get in a digger and a skip.'

'I'm off, then,' said Harry. 'If you fancy it you can pop in for soup at lunchtime. I'm trying a new recipe.'

'Is that both of us?' asked Libby.

'Just guinea-pigs, now, are we?' said Peter.

'You get free soup, what are you complaining about?' Harry

grinned and left.

'One o'clock, then?' said Peter to Libby, holding the door for her.

'I'll tell Ben. He might want free soup, too.'

And now there was nothing to do. Libby contemplated visiting Flo Carpenter and Lenny, or Hetty up at the Manor, decided she was too restless to talk to any of them and made her way slowly home, where, with a great feeling of martyrdom, she started work on a new painting of Nethergate in winter for Guy's shop. When she succeeded in finishing a painting, Guy would have postcards and prints made, and would provide a nice little income that at least kept Sidney in cat food. Sometimes, in the summer, she painted several small pictures which sold almost immediately they appeared in the shop, bought by tourists who loved the old world feeling of the town and wanted a souvenir.

On being invited to partake of free soup at lunchtime, Ben declined, being deep in some sort of estate business, and having promised to have lunch with Hetty.

'So it's just us,' said Libby at one o'clock, as she joined Peter at the big pine table in the window where the daily papers were, as usual, spread out.

'So we can talk panto instead of murders and witchcraft, can we?' Peter laughed at her expression. 'Come on, you're worrying about Rosie, aren't you?'

'Don't you dare say "stop worrying",' said Libby.

'I know, I know, but you could at least take your mind off it.'

'The soup'll do that,' said Harry, arriving with two steaming bowls. 'Do you want a glass of something with it?'

'I'd better not,' said Libby. 'I might have to drive somewhere later.'

'Oh? Where?' Peter and Harry stared at her suspiciously.

'I don't know. Don't look at me like that. I might go down and see how Fran is after last night.'

Peter and Harry heaved simultaneous sighs.

'Just eat your soup,' said Harry.

Peter determinedly talked panto at her as they ate their soup, which was delicious, and Libby gradually relaxed.

'Now,' he said after Harry had removed their bowls and replaced them with coffee cups. 'Just remember that you've got a rehearsal tonight. Don't go haring off on another wild goose chase.'

'It wasn't a wild goose chase last night,' said Libby indignantly. 'We might have saved that poor woman's life.' She looked thoughtful. 'We don't know that we did, though. Perhaps I ought to pop down to St Aldeberge and find out what's been going on.'

'If there's anything you need to know, Lib, surely your new friend Patti will tell you,' said Peter. 'Drink your coffee.'

Libby waited until she arrived home before calling Patti. She had to leave a message on the answerphone, but Patti answered her mobile on the first ring.

'Oh, Libby,' she said, 'I've been meaning to call you all day, ever since we heard about Sheila, but things have been going mad round here.'

'I can imagine,' said Libby. 'Anything I can do?'

'Not really, unless you can calm Alice down. We had to get Bob home from work, and Tracey's none too pleased because Alice won't be able to pick the boy up.'

'I don't suppose I'd be much use there,' said Libby. 'Alice seems to blame everything that's happened since Joan Bidwell's death on me, despite her being the one to ask me in. What exactly is the problem?'

'She's certain now that she's going to be next. The fact that a reporter rang up and said "Is it true another of your flower ladies has been killed". She was with me and heard it, and that set her off. Complete hysterics.'

'But Sheila Johnson was alive when we found her,' said Libby, a cold feeling settling in her stomach.

'Yes, she still is, apparently,' said Patti, 'but still unconscious. I don't really know much, except that the police have taken Ken to the station.'

'Under arrest, or simply to – er – help with their enquiries?'

'I don't know that, either. The police told me last night, as they didn't have any identification. Well, they did,' she corrected herself, 'because you told them who she was, but I gave them Ken's address and phone number. Alice came round here this morning to tell me Ken had gone off in a police car and to find out what had happened, then the reporter rang, and – whoosh! Up like a rocket. And somehow, the news has spread right round the village and I've had people on the doorstep, ringing me – God knows what. Well, he probably does.' Patti managed a weak laugh.

'You need a break,' said Libby. 'Can't you come up here to Anne for the evening?'

'It's tempting, but Bob keeps ringing me asking me what to do with Alice. I've told him to get the doctor.'

'That reminds me – you said you had to get Bob home from work. I thought he'd retired?'

'Oh, he does a part-time job in Nethergate. Just a couple of mornings a week, I think, and of course today had to be one of his mornings.'

'Well, he has no right to keep phoning you. It's his job to look after his wife.'

'That's actually why I'm out of the house,' said Patti, with another small giggle. 'He hasn't got my mobile number!'

'What's being said in the village about it all? Do they know any details?'

'I don't think so, unless they've made some up, which wouldn't surprise me. All I know is Mrs Johnson had been found by you and Fran, was unconscious and in hospital and they needed to get hold of her husband.'

There was a faint question in Patti's voice.

'I don't know if I'm supposed to tell you anything,' said Libby.

'Then don't. I'll no doubt hear about it eventually, and I fully expect there to be more questions from the police. Look if I hear anything else, I'll ring you, shall I?'

'Yes, and I'll see you on Wednesday? In the pub?'

Now it was relief in Patti's voice. 'Look forward to it.'

Almost as soon as she ended the call the phone rang again.

'Libby, I've got to be quick, but I thought you'd like to know we think we've found Rosie.'

'Ian! You're at a wedding!'

'Just going in. But I've kept in touch with Maiden.'

'But how? Where is she? Is she all right?'

'Her credit card details turned up at a hotel in London. If she's there, Maiden will let you know. Got to go.'

Libby was left staring at the phone. Credit card? Showed up? She shook her head. The wonders of technology.

After calling both Ben and Fran to let them know, she returned to her sorely neglected painting and tried to concentrate on that, but her mind wasn't on it.

Her next phone calls were, predictably, from Campbell McLean at Kent and Coast Television and from Jane Baker in her professional capacity as *Nethergate Mercury* reporter.

'I don't know anything, Campbell,' she said. 'All I'm doing is helping the St Aldeberge vicar with her Nativity pageant.'

'You must do, Libby. I know you. You wouldn't have backed away from this.'

'I'm not backing away from anything, I just don't know anything,' insisted Libby. 'I'm sure the police will let you know what you need to know.'

'That's it, they won't,' complained Campbell. 'We picked it up last night, but nothing since. It's already been dubbed –'

'The Flower Lady Murders, I know,' interrupted Libby.

'And a little bird tells me you had a fire the other night.'

'Really? Which little bird was that?'

'Could have been a fireman,' said Campbell. 'Not saying.'

'Please don't do anything with that, Campbell,' said Libby. 'It isn't relevant.'

'Of course not,' said Campbell, obviously a seething mass of professional curiosity.

'If there's anything I can tell you, you know I will,' Libby finished. 'And now I'm going.'

'It wasn't you,' she said to Jane five minutes later, 'who dubbed them The Flower Lady Murders?'

'Me? No,' said Jane with a laugh. 'I think you'll find that was a tabloid.'

'Oh, lawks. I hope they don't ferret out my connection.'

'Is it true you had a fire the other night?' said Jane.

'Oh, the same fireman told you, did he?'

'No we picked it up from the usual sources. I didn't call you about that because we don't work on Sundays and I thought this morning it would be insensitive. Are you all right?'

'Fine, thanks, and it was only a hedge. I'm afraid there's nothing I can tell you, Jane. When it's all sorted I'll tell you what I can, but at the moment I don't know anything. How's Imogen?'

'Lovely, thanks. Being very bright and appealing. We'll have to have a reciprocal dinner for you and the Wolfes. It's ridiculous to live so near and not see you more often.'

After ending the call, Libby sat in puzzled silence. Both Campbell and Jane had referred to the murders, as had Patti's caller. This meant the police hadn't released the knowledge that Sheila Johnson was still alive. This, Libby decided, was in order to lull the murderer into a false sense of security. She sighed and went to make tea.

Sergeant Maiden called just after five o'clock.

'You'll be pleased to know we've found Mrs George,' he said. 'Or rather, the Met did.'

'Alive?'

'Oh, very much. In a very nice, exclusive hotel in London. She was scared, but pleased it was us that found her.'

'So what has she been doing? And why was she there?'

'Actually, Mrs Sarjeant, she's staying there. For various reasons. But she's happy to see you or Mrs Wolfe if you feel like going to visit her. But if you don't mind, you'll have to report into the local police station and let them escort you. I can't give you any details.'

'Goodness! How dramatic,' said Libby.

'It's very serious, Mrs Sarjeant.' Maiden's usual cheerfulness had evaporated. 'I'm sure Mr Connell will explain things when he gets back.'

'Can we see Mrs George tomorrow?' asked Libby.

'I'm sure you can. If you ring me on this number when

you've decided when to go, I'll liaise with the Met.'

'Are we going, then?' she said to Fran five minutes later.

'Of course. I'll pick you up and we'll get the train from Canterbury. There's one that goes just after ten and gets in at about twenty to twelve.'

Libby then relayed this information to Sergeant Maiden, and ten minutes later to Ben when he arrived from the Manor.

'It's been an interesting day,' she said finally. 'And I still don't know what's going on. Perhaps I'll find out from Rosie tomorrow.'

'I'm pleased the police are being so careful,' said Ben. 'I'll feel better about you going off hot on the trail again.'

'Yes, but the police are organising it, so it must be all right,' said Libby. 'Now, do you want a drink before dinner?'

Chapter Thirty-four

The train the following morning was full of shopping-trip passengers, being the first of the day to benefit from Cheap Day Return prices. This meant Fran and Libby couldn't discuss the reason for their trip and had to content themselves with listening to the conversations of others, the most intriguing of which were those one-sided ones held with a mobile phone. Libby couldn't help laughing after a particularly explicit description of someone else's affair.

'Was she there, do you think?' she whispered to Fran. 'That's how gossip spreads, isn't it? I don't suppose any of those details were true, but they'll get passed on.'

'Which is what happened to Patti. We still don't know who started the witchcraft rumour.'

'Ssh!' Libby looked nervously round, but no one appeared to be taking the slightest notice of them.

'Now we know that Sheila was connected with –' Fran paused, 'with the *group*, perhaps it was her?'

'But that would draw attention to it, as would the – ah – *accoutrements* of Marion's …'

'Yes.' Fran shook her head. 'I just can't imagine what Rosie's going to have to tell us.'

In a fit of generosity, Fran paid for a taxi to take them to the police station, where a very young DC was deputed to escort them to Rosie's hotel. He took them straight up to the first floor and along the deeply carpeted, wood-panelled corridor. The silence was so deep it felt solid.

He knocked at the door of number 7, and was answered by a female voice that wasn't Rosie. Libby and Fran frowned at each other.

'DC Millard,' said the young officer, and the door was opened by a young woman with a blonde ponytail and a determined expression.

'Mrs Sarjeant and Mrs Wolfe?' she said. They nodded and were handed over. DC Millard and the blonde stayed by the door while Libby and Fran went forward into what looked like the sitting room in an Edwardian country house.

'Oh, Libby! Fran!' Rosie flew across the carpet and enveloped them both in a hug.

'My God!' said Libby, pulling back. 'What have you done to yourself?'

For Rosie had purple hair.

'Oh, this? I'll explain everything in a minute. Do you want lunch? A drink?'

'A sandwich?' suggested Fran.

'Glass of wine?' suggested Libby.

'I'll fetch it,' said DC Millard. 'Tell them when you order.'

'I only have to order the sandwiches,' said a very dignified Rosie. 'I have wine here, thank you.'

She ordered sandwiches from room service and DC Millard departed on his mission, while the blonde officer took a chair in the lobby of what now they saw was a suite, and Rosie poured wine for them all.

'The hair,' said Libby.

'Start at the beginning,' said Fran.

'Right,' said Rosie. 'Well, I suppose that would be when I left Steeple Farm. The renovations I was having done were nearly finished, and I'd realised I was on a hiding to nothing with the dating site, until Libby and I worked out that Marion had been using it and been in touch with this Bruno51.'

'And we told you to keep out of his way,' said Libby.

'I know.' Rosie gave a deep sigh. 'And I wish I had, now.'

'But you didn't,' said Fran. 'And it all went wrong.'

'You'd better tell us how you kept in touch. Ian was tracking you on the website and you weren't there, either of you.'

'It was after I mentioned Marion Longfellow by her screen name. He suddenly got interested. I have to say, I was quite excited –' Rosie broke off and looked down into her wine glass. 'I'd realised that a woman over sixty on those sites is virtually invisible.' She looked up at Libby. 'I didn't tell you, did I, that I actually registered on three different sites? Each ad was different, and each picture was different, and I didn't think anyone would recognise me.' She laughed. 'Recognise me? I don't think anyone even looked.'

'But you said this Bruno51 had been in touch before,' said Libby.

'I might have bent the truth a little there,' said Rosie, colouring a little. 'I sent him a message and he acknowledged it. That was all.'

'So how did you keep in touch?'

'I sent a last message telling him who I was. You'd told me your Ian would track us, so I did that just before I closed the computer. You didn't see.'

Libby let out an impatient sigh. 'So then what?'

'I got an email via my website. I sent him a web email address and then we used my smart phone to email back and forth.'

'And so you met him?' said Fran, leaning forward.

'Not until the other night,' said Rosie. 'You see, the emails started getting a bit – odd. He started saying Marion and he had a very – er – *particular* relationship, and had she ever mentioned him. Of course, by that time I'd forgotten I'd pretended to know her, but I said no, anyway. So then he went on to ask if we'd shared any of the same interests, so I said flower arranging, as that was the only interest I knew.'

'Why was that odd?' asked Libby.

'It wasn't that. It was when he started asking about the other interests.' Rosie's colour was getting high again. 'That was when I moved up here.'

'You were going into hiding?' said Fran. 'From us? Ian? Or Bruno?'

'Everybody. I knew you and Ian would be angry with me, and I didn't really want Bruno finding me, which I decided he probably would if I stayed in the area.'

'So what were these other interests?' asked Libby.

'Well, it took quite a long instant messaging conversation to find out, as he was dribbling information in piecemeal, but eventually it turned out to be Black Magic.' Rosie took a deep breath and looked Libby straight in the eye. 'And that's when I decided I simply had to find out.'

'And what happened next?' asked Fran after a moment.

'I'm afraid I pretended to be quite excited about that. I was remembering what you'd told me about the dead cockerels and how Marion's body had been found, so I could see it was relevant. I let some of that slip, so he would think I really was a friend of hers, and it all came out. The coven was a bit of fun, he said. They all dressed up and got a kick out of the freedom it gave them. I asked if the rituals didn't mean something, and he immediately went on the defensive and said yes, of course. Then a bit further into our conversation he said that of course, they often had to take a little something to heighten the experience.'

'I knew it,' said Fran.

'And all this time you hadn't actually spoken to him?' said Libby.

'No.' Rosie shook her head. 'I spent most of my time in here with the smart phone. Eventually, I did go out and buy a cheap laptop, just to do some work in between messages. In the end, he sent me an email telling me about the next meeting, which was–'

'Sunday night,' said Libby. 'And you called me to go with you. I wish I had.'

'No, you don't.' Rosie shook her head again, quite violently. 'It was horrible.'

'So why did you go?' asked Fran.

'I thought if I had concrete evidence of what was going on I could give it to the police.' She looked up and took a deep breath. 'Anyway. He said to meet him at the gate of the old Dunton Estate. He said would I wear something distinctive. So I said I had red hair these days.'

'So that's it!' said Libby. 'You went out and dyed it?'

'I bought a bottle from one of those lovely Goth shops,' said Rosie with a smile. 'I did it here, and it went purple. I expect it's because my hair is so –' she slid a look at Libby with a shamefaced little laugh, 'so faded. It took too well.'

'So you met him,' Fran prompted.

'Well, not exactly.'

Libby and Fran exchanged glances.

'I parked my car, and this person suddenly opened the passenger door and got in. I nearly jumped out of my skin, but it was a woman, and she seemed so normal and – well, motherly, almost.'

'Sheila Johnson,' said Libby and Fran together.

'I don't know, but she told me where to drive, saying I was the lady they were expecting, but not mentioning Bruno. We drove down a track to where there was this huge old tree, and there were lots of other people there, all wearing cloaks. And a man opened my door and said welcome, and that was when they blindfolded me.'

'Oh, my God,' said Libby. 'How terrifying.'

'I was scared stiff,' nodded Rosie. 'Then they led me forward and I was told to take off my clothes. That was when I got really scared. I refused, and this one man, whom I took to be Bruno, said very gently that I couldn't join in the fun properly unless I did, and he'd thought this was what I wanted. I had enough wit left to say that I'd never done anything like this before and couldn't I just watch for a bit.' She shook her head. 'Then they all laughed and led me a bit further and told me to stand there. After a minute my blindfold was taken off and there they all were, a dozen of them, all wearing cloaks with huge hoods so I couldn't see their faces. Then they turned away from me and began chanting. One of them was in the centre and he began passing something round. I don't know whether it was just an ordinary joint or if it had cocaine in it, but suddenly they all began to sway and the chanting got louder. I realised they were high and then one of the women threw back her cloak and I saw she was naked, and the one in the middle pulled her towards him. And he had the most enormous –' Rosie stopped, brick-red again.

'Erection,' said Libby and Fran together, and Libby saw the

policewoman look up.

'Yes. And then – well, it just developed into a free-for-all, so I turned and began to creep away, but someone caught me. It was a man and he started whispering vile things in my ear, and telling me I was turned on, wasn't I, and I wanted to be sick. Then there was a shout and they all went quiet. I was let go and when I turned, they were all bending over something on the floor, then one of them said something and they all began to melt away. I mean, it was so weird. They just all left, quite silently. Into the wood across the field, down the lane. And there was this one person, the man in the centre, I think, and he was looking at me. I just ran for my car and drove hell for leather out of there and straight back here.' Rosie leant back in her chair and took a sip of wine. 'It was ghastly.'

'I wonder what had happened to Sheila?' said Libby. 'Overdose of whatever they were using, perhaps?'

'Could be heart failure,' said Fran, 'but she was lucky.' She turned to Rosie. 'We thought it was you.'

'Did you?' How?' Rosie looked bewildered, and Fran explained.

'So you saved her life,' said Rosie. 'That's something, I suppose. Has she told the police anything?'

'Last I heard yesterday she was still alive in intensive care, so I don't suppose so,' said Libby. 'And you were right about the drugs at the Willoughby Oak, Fran.'

'Just a shame that Ian didn't keep it as a crime scene,' agreed Fran. 'Still at least they know now that Marion was part of the coven, or whatever they like to call themselves, and that Bruno would seem to be the leader. But who is he? He's good at covering his tracks.'

'But why were they chatting on the dating site?' asked Rosie. 'If they knew each other in real life. Very well, it seems.'

'To protect themselves?' suggested Libby. 'As you were, with your web-based email.'

'I suppose so. Weird, though,' said Fran. 'And the police obviously think he's likely to come after you, now?'

'It would seem so,' said Rosie, glancing towards the officer in the lobby. 'They won't let me go back home, anyway. They're keeping an eye on my place and Andrew's flat. The trouble is, I let him know who I really was.'

'So he could track you down. And what? He thinks you know who he is?'

'He certainly thinks I know as much as I do about the coven and the drugs. But then, he'll know the police do too, now, so I don't see why I'm in any danger. After all, the lady who's in hospital can tell them when she wakes up, can't she?'

'No, actually, Rosie. Because he thinks she's dead. You're the only one who might give him away,' said Libby.

'But I don't know who he is!' cried Rosie. 'How could I give him away?'

'Perhaps he thinks you do know. After all, you said you were a friend of Marion's. He'll think she talked to you about her life and other friends, and you may have put two and two together.'

Rosie looked aghast and Libby's phone rang.

'Are you with Rosie?' asked Ian.

'Yes, she's just told us all about Bruno and Sunday night.'

'I'm sending someone to fetch you all,' said Ian. 'Someone's tried to burn down Rosie's house.'

And DC Millard came in with the sandwiches.

Chapter Thirty-five

Rosie sat between Libby and Fran in the back of the unmarked police car, shivering occasionally.

'If I'd been there,' she said repeatedly.

'Look, you weren't. And what could you have done to prevent it? You probably would have given the alarm, too,' Libby said.

'Thank goodness Andrew went just at that time to feed Talbot,' said Fran.

'Just like Harry and Pete being with me when we found my fire,' said Libby.

'Yes, it's already happened to you, hasn't it?' Rosie turned her head slightly to face Libby. 'Do they think it's the same person?'

'I only know what Ian told us on the phone,' said Libby, 'but it's a fair bet, isn't it?'

'Excuse me,' said Fran, leaning forward to speak to the driver. 'Where exactly are we going? Only my car's in Canterbury.'

'That's all right, ma'am. We're going to the police station to meet DCI Connell.'

'He's back already?' Libby looked at Fran with raised eyebrows.

'On his way, apparently. Driving straight from Gatwick.'

'He'll be in a mood them' muttered Libby, settling back in her corner.

Ian had obviously arrived only minutes before them at the police station. As they were all shown into his office he was still snapping instructions into the phone and to a scared-looking female officer at the desk.

Dismissing her and their escort, he waved the three women to seats and stood leaning on the desk with his head down. They watched in silence. He raised his head.

'I want to say how sorry I am, Mrs George,' he said eventually. 'We should have been watching your house more closely. We unfortunately couldn't afford to have someone there permanently, so we were simply using regular patrols. It was very lucky that Professor Wylie happened to go along when he did.'

'Is Talbot all right?' asked Rosie.

'Professor Wylie took him back to his flat with him. Not that there's much damage to your property, it was mainly the building materials which had been left outside.'

Rosie nodded. 'Will I be allowed to go back there?'

'I'd rather you didn't, until we've apprehended the person who did this,' said Ian. 'At least, not on your own.'

'Is it the same person who burnt my hedge?' asked Libby.

'It looks like it. The same accelerant was used.'

'Was it red diesel?'

Ian looked startled. 'No! Why?'

'No reason,' said Libby.

Ian cast her a suspicious glance before continuing. 'However,' he said, 'had you not continued to make contact with this man, he wouldn't have felt the need either to silence you or warn you off.'

'On the other hand,' said Rosie, rallying, 'the fact that I did had the direct result of Fran worrying about me and therefore saving that poor woman's life.' She looked suddenly frightened. 'She *is* still alive, isn't she?'

'Yes, she is, and of course, you're quite right.

'Is she still in a coma? What caused it?' asked Fran.

'Massive dose of one of the so-called legal highs,' said Ian. 'Traces of which were also found in Marion Longfellow's system.'

There were exclamations from the three women.

'So the Black Magic thing was at the centre of it after all?' said Libby.

'Part of it, Lib. We think smuggling is the real heart of it. The reason for the first murder.'

'Because of the inlet?'

'In part.' Ian smiled at her eagerness. 'Now Mrs, George, I know you said in your statement –' his eyes flicked to a computer screen, 'that you couldn't see anyone clearly on Sunday night, but is there any chance you could recognise a voice?'

'I doubt it.' Rosie shook her head. 'Nobody spoke in a normal voice.'

'Ian, it's got to be someone Sheila knows.' Libby leant forward.

'And her husband is, in fact, with us now.' Ian smiled round at their shocked faces.

'What did you expect? He was the obvious candidate, but in fact he was at the pub in the village on Sunday night, not prancing around under a tree. However, he has told us a good deal. And of course, he couldn't be the person who tried to fire your house, Mrs George, because he was here.'

'What's he told you?' asked Fran.

'That the group of devotees, if you can call them that, is called the Temple of Astarte, a name which means nothing, just gives a spurious spirituality to their meetings. You've seen it before, Fran.'

'I know, at Tyne Chapel.' Fran shivered.

'Exactly. Apparently it was Marion Longfellow who introduced Sheila and her husband Ken. I must say, having met them both earlier in the enquiry I wouldn't have thought it of them. He is very tight-lipped on the subject of the other members, although he does admit that the most senior member appears to be the supplier of the drugs, which vary from time to time. Ken says he was getting fed up with it, especially since Marion died. I think, though he hasn't exactly admitted it, that he and Marion were having an affair.'

'Is that all?' said Libby when Ian appeared to have finished. 'No other suspects?'

'What do you expect us to do, Libby? Bring in every man

and woman in the surrounding area and accuse them of witchcraft?'

'People in the village. What about them?'

'We've spoken to Miss Pearson and your friend Alice and her husband Bob, as well as the two churchwardens Mr Brice and Mr Blanchard. As you would expect, all shocked and well-alibied. We asked them for the names of any other friends of the Johnsons but none of them seemed to move in similar social circles, other than the church.'

'So what do we do now?' asked Libby with a frown.

'You do nothing. Fran can collect her car and take you home, or we will, and we will take Mrs George to Professor Wylie's flat. I'm not forbidding you to go to St Aldeberge to see Miss Pearson and your friend Alice, but you must not start poking your nose into anything more. Understand?'

Libby stopped herself from looking at Fran and nodded.

'Right. Thanks for coming in, and once again, Mrs George, I'm sorry about the fire.'

Dismissed, the three women stood up and the female officer escorted them from Ian's office.

'Didn't even get a chance to ask him how the wedding was,' muttered Libby.

Rosie, was spirited off to be driven home in a police car, and Libby and Fran were driven back to where they'd left Fran's car earlier that day. By this time it was beginning to get dark, but Libby had something on her mind.

'Will you drive me to the inlet?' she asked Fran, when they were inside the car.

'The inlet? At this time of day? You wouldn't be able to see anything.'

'If you don't want to, drop me at home and I'll go on my own. Actually, you'd better do that, because otherwise you'd have to drive me all the way back to Steeple Martin.'

Fran sighed. 'I'll do that, but if you're determined to go, I'll follow you, if only to make sure you don't get into any trouble.'

Libby smiled. 'Good. I'm sure there's something to be seen there. And possibly in the dark.'

'Fluorescent parcels of drugs?'

'Don't be sarky. I just thought perhaps a gleam of metal …'

'Metal?' Fran risked a quick frowning glance at her friend.

'Just thinking,' said Libby.

It was completely dark when Fran dropped Libby by the side of her own battered Romeo the Renault.

'What exactly are we going to do there?'

'I just want to have a look. Have you got a torch in the car?'

'Yes.'

'Good. See you there.' Libby got into her car, started the engine and began her seven-point turn.

It was totally black when they left their cars at the end of the lane and began to walk along the path to the edge of the cliff, and both of them were pleased they had torches.

'I'm pretty sure Ian wouldn't like this,' said Fran.

'I know he wouldn't, but I've got a theory.'

'Oh?'

'Well, this unknown bloke who was seen with Marion Longfellow in The Red Lion by George, sounds like the same one who Mrs Dora was referring to and Bruno51. Why haven't we seen any trace of him?'

'Because we haven't met him?'

'But we must have done. He must be part of this circle of people.'

'But don't forget, I probably wouldn't know if I had met the murderer. I haven't in the past, have I? It would make Ian's life very simple if he could just parade suspects in front of me and I could say "That's him!".'

'So it could be Ken?'

'But he was at the pub Sunday night. He couldn't have had anything to do with Sheila's attack.'

'He's admitted he was part of the coven.'

'If he was there he'd never have got back home in time for the police to find him there. She was identified on the spot, and the police already had his details, so they would have been on to him really quickly.'

'So what's your theory?'

'I've got a couple,' said Libby. 'But one is, why are we assuming the murderer is a man?'

Fran stopped and turned to Libby.

'But Rosie –'

'Forget that,' said Libby. 'Yes, Rosie saw at least one man last night. But the leader of the coven or whatever they are doesn't have to be a man, and there's nothing easier than to pretend to be a man online to lure women in. Remember, Rosie didn't even talk to him on the phone.'

'But what about Mrs Dora's man? The one George saw with Marion Longfellow?'

'He might have nothing to do with it. Or be a member of this Astarte mob from outside the village. All the way through we've thought the murders have to have something to do with the village – or more specifically, the church – community. It might not have.'

'But the first murder was Mrs Bidwell, and she was actually killed *in* the church.'

'But we know now the church was full of people from outside the village. It could have been anyone. And it could have been a woman.'

'Not Patti.' Fran made it a statement.

'I would hope not,' said Libby, frowning down at where waves splashed against the side of the cliff. Glinting in the light from her torch she saw what she'd hoped to see. 'Look.'

Fran gingerly leant closer to the edge and peered over. 'What is it?'

'Metal.' Libby got down on the ground and lay on her stomach to try and look closer. 'I remembered seeing something down there when we first came. You can only see it from this side of the inlet, not the other where the two houses are. I'm surprised the police haven't found it.'

'Is it a shopping trolley?' Fran joined Libby on the ground and trained her torch on the same spot.

'No. It's a wheelchair.'

They looked at each other, and then stood up.

'When was it put there? Not straight after the service?' Fran brushed down her coat.

'No, I reckon it was in someone's boot.' Libby turned the torch back to the path and began to make her way back to the cars. 'I shall have to tell Ian.'

'Yes, you will, but why was it suddenly so important to look for it today?' asked Fran.

'Because things are hotting up. We've had two fires and the attempted murder of Sheila Johnson. The police need to find the murderer, and when I remembered I'd seen something in the inlet that first day, which I took no notice of, I wondered if it was the wheelchair and if it was, if it had any fingerprints or DNA evidence left.'

They reached the cars and Libby took out her phone.

'You said you had a couple of theories,' said Fran. 'One was that the killer might be a woman. What was the other?'

'I've already said, that the mystery man may have nothing to do with the case.'

'But Dora knew him, she said.'

'So she did.' Libby shrugged. 'Oh, well, I'll just report this to Ian and go home. I feel we're probably doing the "heroine going into the haunted cellar" routine out here in the dark.'

'We are.' Fran looked round the deserted cliff top and shivered.

'Go on, you go home,' said Libby. 'I'm just going to call Ian.'

'Send him a text,' said Fran. 'Then he won't bawl you out.'

Fran got into her car and drove off. Libby got into hers and sent a text to Ian. Then called Ben to tell him she was on her way. It was just as she put the phone in her pocket and switched on the engine that she became aware of a pinprick of light on the other side of the inlet. She squinted through the darkness and realised that it was a light in Marion Longfellow's cottage. As she watched, she saw a brighter light go on.

'Oh, God, not another fire,' she whispered to herself. Risking turning on her headlights, she began driving towards the road, where she could cross to the other side of the inlet. Once across, she turned off the lights and engine and freewheeled nearer to the cottage.

'OK, not a fire,' she muttered. 'Just someone inside.' She took out her phone and this time rang Ian's number.

'What?' His exasperated voice snapped at her.

'Ian, there's someone in Mrs Longfellow's cottage.'

'Where are you? I told you to go home and do NOTHING!'

'Did you get my text?'

'No. That's not an answer.'

'I'm at the inlet. Obviously.'

'Get out of there. Now. I mean it, Libby.'

'But – there's someone –'

'I heard you the first time. It's already being dealt with.'

'You mean you knew –?'

'No, of course not. We're sending someone out. Now GO.'

The phone went dead and Libby put it on the seat beside her. And realised she was going to have to reverse along a pitch-black track.

She opened the car door cautiously, to see if she had any room to turn the car round. She hadn't. Shutting it as quietly as she could, she started the engine and put the car into reverse. The reversing lights gave a faint glow behind her, but not enough to illuminate the track. With a sinking feeling, she realised she could easily reverse right over the cliff edge. Very carefully, twisted at an unnatural angle, she slowly released the clutch and the car crept backwards. After what could only have been a few feet, she braked and turned to the front to give her aching neck muscles a chance.

And someone was staring in at her

Chapter Thirty-six

Her foot jerked off the clutch pedal and the car jumped forward and stalled. As it did so, the car door was pulled open.

'Get out of the car.' Her arm was being pulled with such force she thought it might break. Then the figure threw itself across her and fumbled for the seat belt. Libby tried to scream, but found herself muffled by a strong hand, then dragged out of the car on to the ground.

'Made it bloody easy for me, haven't you, you interfering bitch?' Libby peered up into the darkness, sure she recognised the voice, but the hood and scarf covering the face defeated her.

Comforting herself with the thought that Ian was sending reinforcements, she tried to scramble to her feet, aware of every limb trembling violently, and a strange feeling of blood draining towards her feet. Her heart was beating so loudly she was certain it could be heard yards away. Perhaps I'll have a heart attack, she thought vaguely.

'Now, what will it be?' whispered the voice. 'Fire in the cottage? Or shall we send the car into the sea?'

'To join the wheelchair?' Libby croaked out.

'Oh, yes, I saw that you'd seen that. Really gave the game away, didn't it?'

And Libby realised who it was.

Gavin Brice pulled her to her feet and holding her arms, peered into her face.

'Might as well send you over the cliff in the car,' he said meditatively. 'Got to get rid of the car, anyway.'

'But it will be seen, as soon as the police arrive,' said Libby in a voice quite unlike her own.

'And I'll be long gone.' He shook her. 'See out there?' He

jerked his head towards the open sea, and, to her surprise, she managed to make out the shape of a small boat riding about two hundred metres offshore without lights. 'Couldn't go on for ever. I should have gone before you started poking your fucking nose in.' He peered at her again. 'Back to the house.' He swung her round so that she stumbled and began to push her towards the cottage.

Libby wondered why they were going there, if he meant to push her and the car off the cliff top, then realised he couldn't risk getting her into the car while she was conscious, as she'd fight and probably send them both over. So, what? He could have hit her over the head out in the open. But perhaps, said her confused brain, he didn't have anything suitable out there?

Inside the cottage and she could see his pleasant, open face now dark with anger and what? Confusion? Her own cleared as she realised he didn't actually know what to do. If he let go of her she could run. He had to find something to silence her without letting go of her. She followed his frantic eyes in their search of the room. And there, just out of reach, was a stone Buddha. Their eyes alighted on it simultaneously, and, as Libby twisted to get at it first, the blue lights appeared, flashing through the uncurtained window.

Gavin Brice fought hard. He tried biting, slapping, pushing, punching, anything without letting go of Libby's left arm, until a quiet voice said behind him: 'Enough, now, Mr Brice. I think you'd better come with us.'

Libby slumped to the floor and fell backwards onto a table leg. There was a flurry of activity above her, a good deal of swearing and then a gentle hand on her shoulder.

'Can't keep out of trouble, can you Lib?'

She shook her head and dissolved into tears on Ian's shoulder.

Peter cancelled the Wednesday night rehearsal. Patti was coming over to see Anne, and Harry was able leave Donna in charge after nine o'clock, so they were all able to gather to hear Libby's story. Number 17 being too small to accommodate so many people, Peter suggested the theatre bar, which had the advantage of easy access for Anne's wheelchair and on-tap alcohol.

'Tell us all, then, petal,' said Harry, once they were settled. Fran sat protectively on one side of Libby and Ben on the other. She smiled at them both before beginning.

'Well, both Fran and I said we were the stupid heroines going into the cellar last night –'

'Eh?' said Guy.

'You know, in the films where the woman hears a noise in the night and goes off to investigate where no right-minded individual would go,' his wife told him. He nodded.

'But I really intended to go home after I sent Ian a text. It was just that I saw this light, and I was worried that there was going to be another fire. So I went to investigate, and tried to back out, only he heard me.'

'Garbled, but instructive,' said Peter. 'Who heard you?'

'Gavin Brice,' said Patti, in a voice of doom. 'My churchwarden. I still can't believe it.'

'It was so obvious, really,' said Libby. 'I'm sure anyone else would have jumped to it straight away. It had to be Gavin who injected poor Mrs Bidwell with the succo – er – succ –'

'Succinylcholine,' said Ben. 'I looked it up.'

'Call it sux, dear. That's what the doctors say,' said Harry.

'OK, sux. He went with the old priest to give her communion, he was the nearest to her. And the old priest was very unsteady on his feet and couldn't see very well. And of course it was Gavin moving the wheelchair out of the church and into his boot, because he was always allowed to park close to the church when he brought Mrs Bidwell to church. He was also used to the wheelchair and how it folded.'

'But why did he kill her?' asked Patti. 'And why in the church, for goodness' sake?'

'It was exactly as I thought,' said Libby, 'he was involved in both drug and people smuggling. Border Protection boarded that boat just off shore last night.'

'What boat?' asked several voices. Libby explained.

'Anyway, the boats would run into the inlet and offload

whatever it was.'

'And how did they get from the bottom of the inlet up to the top?' asked Fran.

Libby gave a smug smile. 'My Rupert Bear theory was right. There is a tunnel which goes up to the field behind Marion Longfellow's cottage from a cleft in the rock. Gavin would go and collect the illegal immigrants or the drugs or both in his minibus – remember you told me he took people into Felling in his minibus? – and drop them near the marshes. Then they would be picked up by someone else after they'd made their way across. Gavin would hand over any drugs he had to a contact somewhere – don't know where. And Joan Bidwell saw him. Or at least, he thought she did.

'Ian said Gavin was raging against her being a snooping old –' she looked round, 'Well, a snooping old *person* who watched him at night from her window.' Libby paused for a sip of wine.

'We think he got hold of the sux through his drugs contacts,' she continued. 'That is, Ian does. They believe it was being used to get rid of any illegals who were no use to them any more, or were causing trouble.' She shivered. 'Then, of course, because Marion Longfellow was a member of his witches' coven, she "had a word" with him. As she'd mentioned to Sheila. Who, incidentally, didn't know Gavin was the head witch, or whatever he was. Marion had recruited her and her husband because she fancied Ken. And Gavin didn't like that, because he'd been having an affair with Marion and Ken rather took his place. Oh –' she turned to Patti and Fran. 'And Ken was the man Dora was talking about, and the man George at The Red Lion saw with Marion.'

'So she said what to Gavin? She'd seen him murder Mrs Bidwell?' asked Anne.

'We don't really know, but she knew enough about him to guess it was him, and she was going to try a spot of blackmail,' said Libby. 'So she had to go. And believe it or not, Sheila Johnson was an accident. An overdose of whatever they were taking.'

'But why did he make Marion's death look like the result of a Black Magic ritual? And you haven't answered the question of why he killed Joan Bidwell in my church. It must have been very risky – anyone could have seen him putting the wheelchair in his car and that would have given the game away, surely,' said Patti.

'Well, mostly because she told him earlier that morning that she wanted to talk to him after the service. He decided he couldn't risk killing her on the way to church, so it had to be in church. I suppose he thought old Mr Roberts wouldn't notice. He was sure she was going to tell the police about the smuggling.' Libby sighed. 'And do you know, I bet she wasn't. I bet she couldn't even see what was going on in that inlet. But also, Patti, he was motivated by a very deep dislike of you, personally. He hid it very well, but as well as a general hatred of women vicars he was worried that, with your background and your interest in alternative religions, you'd find out about his coven. He was trying to drive you out. The emails and letters to you and the police, and laying out Marion's body were all part of an attempt to turn opinion in the village further against you and to make you decide to leave. I don't think he ever thought the police would seriously think you were involved in the deaths.'

''And Marion was going to blackmail him about it,' said Patti. 'Lovely congregation I had. And what about your friend and the dating website?'

'I knew she was a pest from the start,' said Harry.

'It turns out that Gavin was Bruno51, and used the website to lure unsuspecting ladies of a certain age into the coven, and he and Marion used it to talk about meetings. And it's how he kept in touch with the Astarte members. Gavin was paranoid about using his email accounts. The police found he had several.'

'So Rosie was actually useful for that,' said Fran.

'Except that it very nearly got her house burnt down and her into trouble,' said Peter.

'Very nearly got mine burnt down, too,' said Libby, 'And OK, before you all say I get myself into these messes, I know.

All right?'

'You were asked in,' said Patti, 'and I'm sure the police wouldn't have cleared it up without you.'

'I'm sure they would,' said Fran. 'They usually get there as quickly as we do.' She turned to Libby. 'And why the fires?'

'Ian thinks he was panicking,' said Ben. 'Either warning Libby and Rosie not to say anything or actually to – harm them.'

'But we don't know the full story by any means,' said Libby. 'I had to make a statement last night, obviously, but a fuller one this morning, so Ian came with Sergeant Maiden. They'd both been up for a good part of the night, and Gavin, after not saying a word, decided to come clean and try and blame his paymasters in the drugs racket. Who, of course, are much higher up the chain than he is. He hasn't got a clue who they are.'

'Ian says they stop one hole and the rats immediately find another,' said Ben. 'Gavin's little racket's been stopped, but the organisations are so huge they'll just find another mug. There are always criminals who are willing to take the risk.'

'I still don't know one thing,' said Fran. 'Gavin was supposed to be "well-alibied" for Sunday night. How come?'

'He said he was at home with his son Joe. Turned out Joe was off in Canterbury with his girlfriend. Gavin never gave it a thought that the police would check up on him.'

'So that's that,' said Harry, standing up and going to the bar. 'Another successful case for Sarjeant and Castle.'

'Wolfe,' came the chorus.

'Sorry,' said Harry with a wink at Fran. 'Now, who'd like champagne?'

'Champagne?'

'Courtesy of your friendly local vicar,' said Harry.

They all turned and looked at Patti, who turned a fiery red. Anne took her hand.

'Very grateful,' she mumbled. 'For the support and the friendship. Thanks.'

Then they were crowding round her, patting her on the back and shaking her hand. Libby stepped back and found herself next to Anne.

'I can't thank you enough,' she said, her eyes on the back of Patti's head. 'She's back to normal.'

'Not sure I did much really,' said Libby, feeling awkward. 'And I did put myself in a couple of stupid situations.'

'Maybe, but now you've got something to be really proud of,' said Anne.

'I have?'

Patti turned and caught Anne's eye. They both grinned at Libby.

'The Nativity Pageant!' they said together.

'Oh, no,' said Libby.

First Chapter of *Murder at the Monastery*

'How's the self-catering business going?' The Reverend Patti Pearson kicked her way through last autumn's leaves, that still lay at the side of the path.

Libby Sarjeant frowned. 'Not brilliantly. Steeple Farm's got a six month let at the moment, but the Hoppers' Huts don't seem to have taken. I think they're too small for self-catering.'

'And still no thoughts of any more writing or painting weekends at the Manor?'

Libby shuddered. 'No. Put us right off, that last one did.'

'So you haven't got much on at the moment?'

Libby turned and looked at her friend suspiciously. 'Why?'

Patti laughed. 'I was just hoping to save you from being bored.'

'You're not going to rope me into another church thing, are you?' Libby had helped devise a Nativity Pageant for Patti's church, St Aldeberge's, the previous December.

'Not exactly.' Patti stopped by a stile and leant her elbows on the top. 'What a lovely view.'

Libby surveyed the wooded valley before her. 'Yes, it is. I forget how pretty our part of the world is, sometimes.'

'I wish Anne could get up here.' Anne Douglas, who lived in Steeple Martin, Libby's home village, was confined to a wheelchair.

'Aren't there any country walks suitable for her chair?' said Libby.

'A few, but they're all rather sanitised and landscaped.'

'Yes, I suppose they would be.' Libby turned to face Patti. 'Come on, then, what did you want me to do?'

'It isn't exactly important,' said Patti. 'It's out of interest, really. Have you heard of the Tredegar Relic?'

'No. Is it Cornish?'

'The name's Welsh,' said Patti, 'because that's where Saint Eldreda came from. Have you heard of her?'

'No.' Libby shook her head. 'You talk in riddles, woman. Let's get back to the car and head for a pub.'

It was a Wednesday afternoon, Patti's regular day off, when she joined Anne for dinner and stayed overnight. However, Anne, working for a library in Canterbury, didn't get home from work until later, so Patti had taken to coming and spending time with Libby first, after finishing her stint in the St Aldeberge community shop.

'St Eldreda,' Patti continued in the car, 'was an obscure saint who came from Mercia on what is now the Welsh borders. As far as anybody can tell. I don't suppose she was actually anywhere near Tredegar, but that's what it's become known as.'

'What has?'

'The relic. St Eldreda married a nobleman who brought her to Kent and after he was killed, Egbert, who was King of Kent, gave her some land and she set up a house of prayer. He did the same for Domneva of Minster.'

'Who?'

Patti sighed. 'Sorry, I'll keep it simple. Well, St Eldreda's monastery became quite famous after her death because miracle cures began occurring after pilgrims had visited her tomb. But then the first chapel was destroyed by fire, it being made of wood, we assume. So St Eldreda's relics were removed for safe keeping.'

'Ewww! Do you mean her skeleton?'

'Yes. Now this bit is where things get complicated. It appears her family wished her bones returned to Mercia, but somehow a compromise was reached and they were only given a finger. Which is now known as the Tredegar Relic.'

'Ah, got it. So what's the mystery?'

Patti shot her a quick look. 'Who said it was a mystery?'

'You wouldn't have mentioned it to me if it wasn't.' Libby beamed smugly and turned her gaze to the passenger window.

'Look there's a pub. Shall we stop?'

'Libby, I can't have a drink at four thirty in the afternoon! Let's go back and you can make me a nice cup of tea.'

'Oh, all right. But it looked a nice pub,' said Libby wistfully.

'You can get Ben to bring you here one evening. If you're not rehearsing anything, of course.'

'You know we're not at the moment,' said Libby. 'Go on then, about these bones.'

'The Tredegar Relic was housed in an abbey church in Mercia, but when dear old Henry tore everything down, it appears the Relic was lost.'

'Dissolute Henry's Dissolution. What about the remaining relics in Kent?'

'They're still here. Somehow, the Augustines, who were good at that sort of thing, got them moved to Canterbury Cathedral, and they were left intact. When, centuries later, the nuns returned to their site, which of course was practically ruined, they, or their mother house, managed to raise enough funds to build a small house. It's now St Eldreda's Abbey, and,' said Patti, pulling into the side of the road, 'it's over there.'

First, all Libby could see were rather typical stone ruins. Then she made out other buildings, including what looked like a modern church.

'They incorporated a farmhouse that had been built on the land by a previous owner, and subsequently they've built a marvellous new chapel.'

'So that's why you wanted to come out here today. To show me this. But I still don't know what the mystery is. And anyway, you're an Anglican, not a Catholic.'

'They are now Anglican Benedictines,' said Patti, 'and one of them is an old friend, Sister Catherine. And the mystery is that the Tredegar Relic has turned up.'

'Turned up? How?'

'In an auction catalogue. Bold as brass, apparently. And the girls want to find out what's going on. They've applied to the auction house who can't, or won't, tell them anything about the supposed seller.

'The *girls*?'

'The nuns,' giggled Patti. 'They're a jolly bunch.'

'I always thought,' said Libby, 'that nuns would be totally against female priests.'

'Well, Catherine isn't. Would you like to meet her?'

'Now?' Libby looked nervous.

'Actually no, not now. They have visiting hours which stop at four. We could make an appointment.'

'We'll see. Come on, I want that tea now. And you can tell me what delights you have in store for me.'

'The nuns want to find out more about the seller of this supposed relic,' said Patti, settled in front of Libby's fireplace later.

'I expect they would,' said Libby, busying herself with wood and firelighters. 'Still cold for April, isn't it?'

'Look, Libby, are you interested or not? It doesn't matter if you aren't.'

Libby sat back on her heels and grinned up at her friend. 'Of course I'm interested. You – and they – want me to find out who the seller is and what the provenance is for this relic. I haven't got a clue how I'll go about it, but it sounds just what I need at the moment.'

'Oh?'

'Yes, Patti. You were right. I'm bored.' She got up and made for the kitchen. 'Just going to make the tea.'

She came back with two mugs to find Sidney the silver tabby happily purring on Patti's lap.

'He is a tart, that cat,' she said, handing over one of the mugs. 'Come on, then, how do I start with this business? I know next to nothing about convents, nuns, relics or saints. Or auctions, come to that. And how come just a bone is in an auction?'

'It's in what's called a reliquary that was made for it when it went back to Mercia. It's a gold and jewelled box, very rare. They were usually pieces of jewellery, pendants and so on, that could be worn. They are also far more common, if that's the word, in the Eastern forms of Christianity, and more even than that in the Eastern religions. Anyway, presumably because it

272

was so precious, someone hid it away very carefully when it went back to Mercia and even the Cromwells didn't manage to get hold of it.'

'And now it's appeared?'

'Someone browsing the online site of a very respectable auction house spotted it and looked it up. The whole story was there, but not how it had come into the possession of the seller. This person now looked up our Abbey and sent them an email asking if they were the sellers.'

'And they weren't, of course,' said Libby.

'No, and the auction house won't tell them who the seller is.'

'Well, there's nothing to say it's illegal,' said Libby. 'Whoever hid it back whenever it was could have kept it in the family and it could have become an heirloom. The Abbey wouldn't necessarily have a claim on it, would they?'

Patti frowned. 'I suppose not. But they are interested in where it's been. After all, it could have been stolen all those years ago, not hidden by one of the nuns or monks.'

'So you just want me to look into its provenance? They don't want to get it back?'

'Well, of course, they'd like it back, but it is a bit idolatrous in my opinion. I think they just want to know.'

Libby stared into the fire. 'I don't see what I can do apart from ask the auction house, and maybe have a look back at the history of the old Abbey in Mercia. It might be interesting.'

'You haven't got the constraints of living as a nun,' said Patti. 'They've got computers, of course, but they are bound by the routines of their days and haven't got the freedom to travel.'

'Hmm. I don't see me travelling to Wales to find things out, you know.'

Patti put her head on one side and grinned. 'You're thinking it might not be what you want to do after all, aren't you?'

'I am, a bit,' said Libby with a shamefaced grin. 'But I'll do a bit of background research and see if I get anywhere.'

'Right.' Patti stood up. 'I'm off to Anne's. Coming for a drink later?'

'Of course. Are you eating at Harry's?'

'Of course. My weekly treat, The Pink Geranium.'

'See you later, then,' said Libby.

The Pink Geranium, the mainly vegetarian restaurant in Steeple Martin, was owned by Harry Price, who lived with Peter Parker, cousin to Ben Wilde, Libby's significant other. Libby's son Adam lived in the flat above the restaurant when he wasn't staying with Sophie Wolfe, step-daughter to Libby's best friend Fran, in the seaside resort of Nethergate. Peter, Ben and Libby had fallen into the habit of meeting Patti and Anne in the pub on Wednesday evenings, and Harry would join them if the restaurant permitted.

This evening, before Patti and Anne arrived, someone else appeared at their table.

'May I join you?' asked Dominic Butcher.

Libby allowed herself an inward sigh. Dominic Butcher had recently been cast in an Oast Theatre production, and as a former professional actor, thrown his weight around until stopped by the director. He also had the temerity to have the same name as Libby's eldest son.

'Of course.' Peter politely shuffled his chair closer to Ben's.

'Dominic.' Ben nodded and turned back to Libby. 'So what exactly do these nuns want you to do?'

'Find out the provenance of this relic – sorry, reliquary. I don't see how I'm to do it.'

'St Eldreda's Abbey,' said Peter dreamily. 'Lovely place. Very atmospheric.'

'Oh, you know it?' Libby said in surprise. 'I'd never heard of it.'

'They allow occasional drama performances there,' said Peter. 'Even Murder in the Cathedral. I wonder ...'

'What?' asked Ben and Libby together, somewhat nervously. Peter's projects had occasionally been known to lead to as much off-stage drama as on.

'Murder in the Cathedral,' said Dominic, obviously not liking to be left out of the conversation. 'I was in that myself, you know, a few years ago –'

'I could write a play about St Eldreda, couldn't I?' Peter turned bright blue eyes on his cousin. 'And if we could find anything out about this relic –'

'Reliquary. Who's this "we"?' asked Libby.

'If the nuns gave me permission, I'd naturally help you.' Peter gave her his most charming smile.

'I suppose we could ask Patti what she thinks,' said Libby.

'What do I think?' Patti pushed Anne's wheelchair up to the table. 'Evening all.'

'I was just telling them about St Eldreda and the reliquary,' said Libby.

'And I thought it would make a great play to put on in the Abbey ruins,' said Peter.

'Oh.' Patti looked surprised. 'I suppose it would. Tell me more.'

Ben pulled out a chair and introduced Dominic. 'And I'll go and get your drinks,' he said, 'while Peter persuades you to use your good offices in his cause.'

By the time Ben got back with a tray of drinks, Peter had finished.

'I think it's rather a nice idea,' said Anne. 'Can we talk to Catherine about it?'

'She's a friend of yours as well?' said Peter.

Anne and Patti looked at each other and smiled.

'Of course,' said Patti. 'I'll ring her tomorrow. She'll want to talk to Libby, anyway.'

Libby opened her mouth and shut it again.

'Well, I'm happy to offer my services if it comes off,' said Dominic. 'I've done a bit of directing you know, as well as the telly.'

Anne looked at him curiously. 'Were you on television?'

Dominic smiled deprecatingly. 'I was Alf in "Limehouse Blues".'

Anne looked blank.

'It's a TV soap,' Patti explained. 'Anne doesn't watch much television.'

'Ah. Well, I'm actually thinking of going back to my former profession now, anyway,' said Dominic, glad to be in the forefront of the conversation at last.

'Oh.' Patti gave it the downward tone to convey lack of interest, but Dominic carried on.

'I was an SHO, just about to qualify as a surgeon,' he said.

Libby shuddered to think of a patient under the alcoholically shaking knife of Dr Butcher.

'If it gets off the ground, Dominic, I shall direct it myself,' said Peter. 'And Libby's an ex-professional too, you know. She'll be on hand.'

'And we just hope,' said Ben, 'that the combination of you two doesn't lead to any more murders.'

More Libby Sarjeant Murder Mysteries

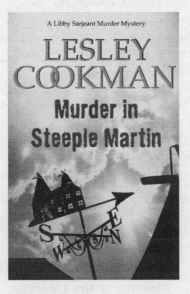

A Libby Sarjeant Murder Mystery

LESLEY COOKMAN

Murder in Steeple Martin

Murder in Steeple Martin

Artist and ex-actress Libby Sarjeant is busy directing a play for the opening of a new theatre in her village when one of her cast is found murdered. The play, written by her friend Peter, is based on real events in his family, disturbing and mysterious, which took place in the village during the last war.

As the investigation into the murder begins to uncover a tangled web of relationships in the village, it seems that the events dramatised in the play still cast a long shadow, dark enough to inspire murder.

Libby's natural nosiness soon leads her into the thick of the investigation, but is she too close to Peter's family, and in particular his cousin Ben, to be able to recognise the murderer?

ISBN 9781908262806   Price £7.99

Murder at the Laurels

Steeple Martin amateur detective Libby's friend, and sleuthing partner, psychic investigator Fran Castle, suspects that there is something suspicious about the death of her aunt in a nursing home. When Fran's long-lost relatives turn up and seem either unconcerned or obstructive, Libby and Fran are sure something is wrong, particularly as the will is missing.

As usual Libby needs little persuasion to start investigating, even if she doesn't see herself as Miss Marple. They discover surprising links to Fran's own past but, as the murders multiply and the police take over, can the amateur sleuths keep on the trail?

ISBN 9781908262813   Price £7.99

Murder in Midwinter

Kent village sleuth Libby and her psychic investigator friend Fran befriend Bella Morleigh, who has inherited a derelict theatre. When an unknown body is discovered inside the theatre, they feel duty bound to help with the investigation.

Although Libby is rather distracted by the preparations for her friends' Civil Partnership ceremony, she's getting the hang of using a computer to dig for information. However, when a second body is found it is one of Fran's psychic moments that makes the connection between the deaths; a connection with startling results.

ISBN 9781908262820   Price £7.99

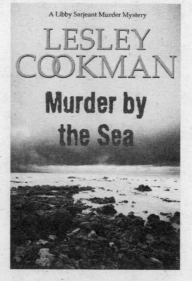

Murder by the Sea

Psychic investigator Fran Castle gets a request from the police to help when a body is discovered on a rocky island in the middle of Nethergate Bay. Libby Sarjeant is on the case too, as they delve into the shameful world of the exploitation of illegal immigrants.

Libby's partner Ben is concerned that her occasionally over-enthusiastic investigations might get her into trouble: his worries seem justified as Libby and Fran get on the trail of a war-time fascist spy and they become a nuisance to a killer.

ISBN 9781908262837   Price £7.99